SCYTHEMAN

By

Chris McMahon

Sytheman

Published 2013 by Lanedd Press, an imprint of Pop & Top Publishers.
www.popandtop.com.au
Please direct all enquiries to the publisher at:
publisher@popandtop.com.au

ISBN: 9780992299422

Cover Artist: Daryl Lindquist
Edited by: Tracy Seybold

National Library of Australia Cataloguing-in-Publication enty:

Author: McMahon, Chris, 1965-
Title: Scytheman / Chris McMahon
ISBN: 9780992299422 (paperback)
Series: McMahon, Chris, 1965- Jakirian Cycle ; bk. 2.
Dewey Number: A823.4

Chris McMahon's website: www.chrismcmahon.net

This novel is dedicated to my wife Sandra, for her love, support and unfailing faith in me.

Acknowledgements

Thanks to all the people who contributed over the years to the final work that the Jakirian Cycle became. Getting anything into print really is a team sport. Special thanks to my editor Tracy Seybold, cover artist Daryl Lindquist and critique partner Gary Kemble. Thanks to all the very patient readers of the first *Calvanni* edition in 2006, who have waited some time to see what happens in *Scytheman* and *Sorcerer*.

A Note on the World of Yos

Yos is a world where all metal is magical, and cannot be forged, appearing as *glowmetal*. The weapons and armour are either constructed of natural materials or a special class of composite ceramics developed for hardness or the ability to hold an edge while maintaining strength and flexibility.

Glossary

Bakta - A clear alcoholic spirit distilled from the baal cereal crop.

Calv - A long knife made of lanedd.

Druid - Magic user who relies on the Essence of Heaven, which varies according to movement of the suns and moons. Ability common.

Druidin - Class of Druid that gives no allegiance to the Temple of the Sisters.

Eathal - Natives of the vast cavern complexes of Kelas and evolutionary cousins to humans. Male and female known as thal and thel. Thickset and hairless, with sensitive eyesight.

Glowmetals - A naturally occurring blend of light, energy and metal. Arising in all sizes, shapes and combinations, they can neither be created nor destroyed, but can be manipulated to store and release their native energy.

Greatscythe - Staff-like weapon with twin concealed lanedd blades, one at either end, operated by a mechanism central to the haft.

Heat - Biological mechanism triggered by the extreme cold of Storm Season. Gives life-giving warmth, but releases inhibitions and makes self-control almost impossible.

Kelas – Continent formerly ruled by the Bulvuran Empire.

Lanedd - Specialised ceramic that can be cast into a blade, which holds a razor-sharp edge that can be sharpened.

Mought - Heavy cast ceramic used in armour, blunt weapons and fortifications.

Priestess - Wielder of Earth Essence, which flows only in certain locations. Ability to access Earth Essence rare in men (Priests).

Sarlord - Ruler of a Sardom by right of royal birth.

Scythe - A short pole weapon with a single lanedd blade.

Sisters - Yos' two suns, Larus and Uros, also worshipped as goddesses by the people of Yos. Larus, the Yellow Sister, and Uros, the Red Sister. Larus is the larger of the two.

Sorcerer - Wielder of magical Fire. Ability derived from hereditary and extremely rare. Practice currently outlawed by the Temple of the Sisters.

Storm Season - Sudden drop in surface temperature and subsequent violent storms that arise twice a year when Yos' two suns, Larus and Uros, eclipse.

Sundar - Supreme ruler of the Eathal of Yos.

Suul – Class of ruling nobility in Yos. Also Suulvey, senior peers and Suulqua, nobles of minor rank.

Temple of the Sisters – Dominant religious force in Kelas.

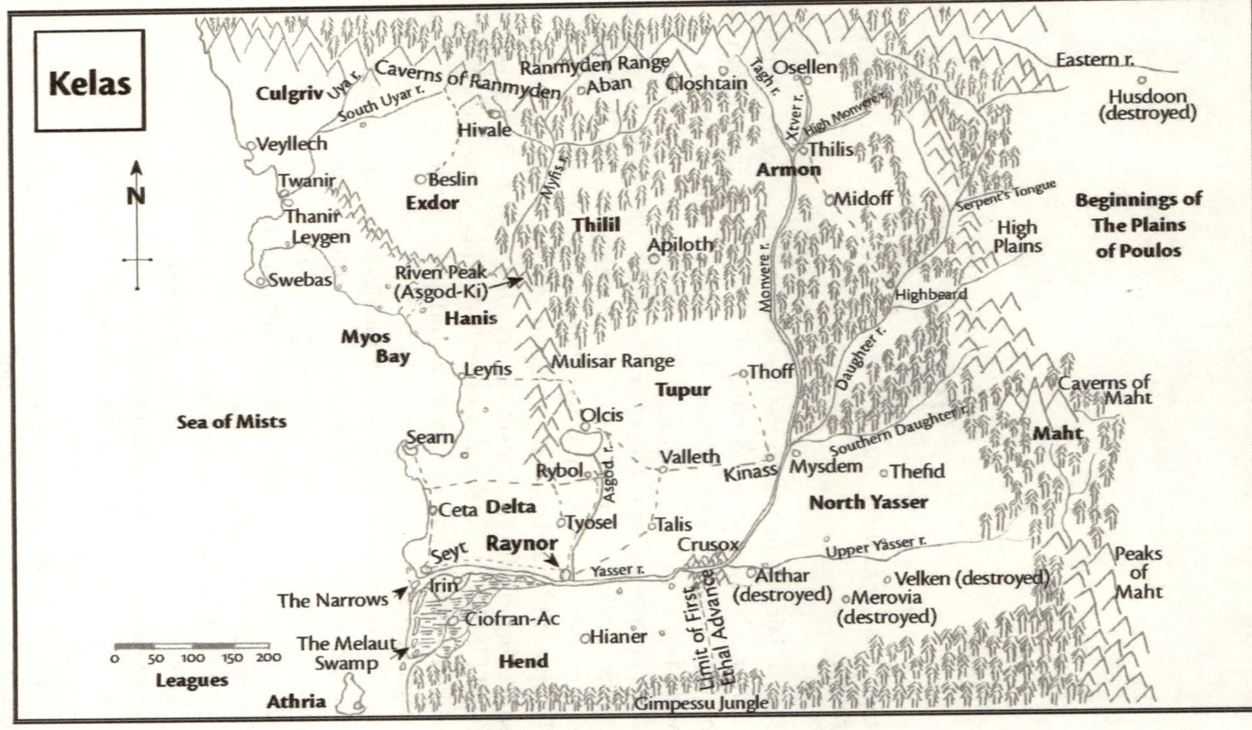

Kelas
N
Culgriv
Veyllech
Twanir
Thanir
Leygen
Swebas
Uyar r.
South Uyar r.
Caverns of Ranmyden
Ranmyden Range
Aban
Closhtain
Tagh r.
Osellen
Eastern r.
Husdoon
(destroyed)
Hivale
Beslin
Exdor
Myfis r.
Thilil
Armon
Thilis
Xtver r.
High Monvere r.
Midoff
Serpent's Tongue
High
Plains
Beginnings of
The Plains
of Poulos
Apiloth
Highbeard
Riven Peak
(Asgod-Ki)
Hanis
Monvere r.
Daughter r.
Myos
Bay
Leyfis
Mulisar Range
Tupur
Thoff
Caverns of
Maht
Sea of Mists
Olcis
Valleth
Kinass
Mysdem
Thefid
Maht
Searn
Rybol
Asgod r.
Southern Daughter r.
North Yasser
Ceta
Delta
Tyosel
Talis
Crusox
Upper Yasser r.
Peaks
of
Maht
Raynor
Seyt
Yasser r.
Althar
(destroyed)
Velken (destroyed)
Merovia
(destroyed)
The Narrows
Irin
Ciofran-Ac
Hianer
Limit of First
Ethal Advance
The Melaut
Swamp
Hend
0 50 100 150 200
Leagues
Athria
Gimpessu Jungle

Prologue

Eighth day of Storm Season. Torren Cintros sits on the Athrian throne.

Kalyth laid his hands on the cracked battlement of Blackthorne Tower. The furious wind numbed his face, bearing all the chill of the waning Storm Season. He blinked against it, his eyes watering.

'Damn you, Belin.' His voice was harsh. Raw from disuse.

He kept his gaze on the wide valley below the tower, determined to look anywhere but the stairs that led to the Temple of the Iris. His callused hands curled into fists, squeezing against the pain. Every day it was the same. He would fight the magical Compulsion that drew him to the ruined temple, and the pain would grow until he could no longer resist it. His legs and back were on fire with it, the muscles in his neck twisted with the desire to turn towards the stairs. He fixed his eyes on the overgrown graves of his wife Mari and his children on the slope below, fighting pain with pain. It would take only a single step, a single twitch and the Compulsion would have him.

At first he had been unable to resist it. The spell would take hold and he would run to the Iris like a crazed fool. After twenty-five years, he could fight it for almost an hour.

His legs began to tremble. His eyes drifted away from the view. He squeezed them shut.

Would Belin make an appearance today? The man who commanded him to leave his family to die to save the Emperor's squalling babe? *Damn them all.* The Empire had fallen. The Eathal were stronger than ever, and his wife and children were still cold and in the ground. If the Emperor's boy still lived, he would change nothing now.

'The Scion.' Bitter bile filled the back of his throat.

If he dared to move, he would spit on the Scion. Spit on all the Suul nobility. Traitors. *Self-serving bastards.*

His head jerked to the side, and his eyes opened. *Stairs.* A tiny particle of relief flowered in the muscles of his neck. The pain in his legs became unbearable. His right leg spasmed forward and before he knew it he was in motion, tears flooding down his face in relief as the pain vanished. There was no stopping it now.

He hissed air through his teeth in fury as he rushed down the stairs, past the small guardroom in the ruined tower that he had made his home, down and down into a maze of narrow tunnels. In this dank labyrinth, he knew every cracked tile, every fallen block of masonry, every sharp curve and jutting piece of head-cracking stone. He pushed against a concealed panel and raced up the stairs behind it, taking the stone flags two at a time until he reached the Temple rooms above. It was bright here. The roof had given way five years ago.

The corridor beyond emptied into a domed chamber, shafts of light stabbing down through cracks in the roof onto the wide floor mosaic. The design was comprised of five identical panels of flame and smoke, linked together by the great Iris at the centre.

As soon as his feet touched the coloured tiles, Kalyth staggered to a halt. He sucked in a lungful of the dusty air, the skin beneath his ragged beard prickling with sweat. He glared at the Iris.

Kalyth carefully circled the floor. After an hour or so, blue lights would flicker at the corners of his vision and he would be free to leave the tiles. Sometimes he would visit the Kaidell estate to teach the warriors, but his visits were becoming less frequent. The newer troops mocked him behind his back. The crazy hermit of Tower Blackthorne, they called him.

As if he had a choice.

Kalyth knelt at the small fireplace he had built at the edge of the tiles. He took a small lead glowmetal from his pocket and rubbed it briskly on the stone. It remained cool in his fist, but he kept a careful eye on the bands of greyish light in the glowmetal as they thinned. Just before the bands became fully metal, he tossed it into the fire pit. Immediately it released the stored heat. The tinder curled with smoke then popped into flame. He flicked the little glowmetal out of the fire with a stick and carefully nursed the small fire into life. Satisfied, he scooped up the glowmetal, already cool to the touch, and slipped it into his pouch.

If only he had never returned to the Kaidell estates. After the defeat of the Eathal, it had seemed natural to take work as weaponmaster to Belin's nephew and heir, Linnas Kaidell. The man was no warrior, and a far cry from Belin – or at least the Belin he had known – but Kalyth had been young and eager to start again. Then the whispering began, night after night. By day, he would find himself staring at the sight of the ruined tower on the horizon. He should have left then. Instead, he had searched through the ruins and found the Temple.

And the Iris had come alive.

Belin Kaidell – a man he had known as a simple warrior – had stepped from the Iris, his eyes alive with blue light, his face drawn into a mask he barely recognised, an archaic spear strapped to his back. Kalyth shivered at the memory. Two lines of glowing blue had lashed out from Belin like hungry snakes, holding him fast, biting deep, binding him with a magic that compelled him to return to the Iris each day. He had been forced to make his home amid the ruins of Blackthorne, as though standing vigil on the memory of his life, forced to endure the taunts of his men, and the ridicule of that worm Linnas.

He sat at the edge of the mosaic and watched the Iris.

He would never forget Belin's eyes. They had fixed on him as though considering a new mount. 'I may have a use for you.'

A use for you.

Belin had ignored his pleading questions.

'I trusted you, Belin. More than life,' muttered Kalyth, stabbing the fire with the stick.

He had given up trying to understand the change in Belin, or his old general's inexplicable command of magic. No. After a time, it was not Belin that he feared. He quickly learned that Belin was not alone in the Iris.

The other mind within the Iris took the form of a horned beast in his dreams, bringing with it a madness of bloodlust and desire. Kalyth would wake in fear, heart hammering, his clothes damp with sour sweat.

Since that first time, the Iris had only come to life twice. Each time, Belin had sent the snakes into his mind and left in silence. Inspecting him without a hint of acknowledgement.

Light flickered off the tile near his feet.

His head snapped up.

'No.'

Sweat rolled off his forehead, chilling immediately in the cold air beneath the dome.

The Iris was stirring.

Kalyth dropped the burning brand back into the fire, his gaze fixed to the Iris as the glowing light rose and expanded. A distant song grew at the edge of his hearing. He covered his ears against it and became aware of his breath, coming now in ragged gasps. Soon the whole Temple was swathed in light, a turning whirlpool that scattered his tiny fire and flung the burning brands at the wall.

Belin stepped from the Iris. Like the other times he had manifested, he seemed no older than the day he first appeared with the babe almost thirty years before.

'What do you want?' asked Kalyth, edging to the very limit of the mosaic.

Belin raised his hand and blue lightning leapt at Kalyth, who grunted in fear as the twin streamers struck his head. His vision was lost in glowing blue, but it was over quickly. He trembled as he watched the glowing lines flow back into Belin like ghastly appendages.

Belin turned to go, then suddenly paused. The passive, drawn expression fled and a new tension overtook the old general.

'Kalyth,' said Belin.

His heart leapt. This was not the high, thin voice he had come to dread. It was a voice of command and deep solidity, more like the Belin of old. The lights had also vanished from his eyes. For the first time since this nightmare had begun, Kalyth looked into the familiar grey eyes of his old commander.

Kalyth stepped towards him, drawn by instinct.

'Kalyth. I have only a moment before the Ward takes me again. The boy is in danger. You must protect him. The Ward seeks him. It has breached the Athrian Iris ...'

Belin jerked. The grey eyes filled once more with blue light, the face becoming slack and cold. As though nothing had happened, Belin turned back to the Iris.

A heartbeat later the Temple was cold and empty.

Released, Kalyth fled the Iris. He paused on the slopes outside to look down at the tiny shapes of the Kaidell estate buildings in the distance. Belin had broken through some sort of forced control.

The hairs at the base of Kalyth's neck stood on end. All these years ... had Belin been as bound as he was? Overtaken by this *Ward* he had spoken of? Could it be that Belin had not betrayed him? Not abandoned him as he thought?

Kalyth's eyes fell on the graves of Mari and his children.

He gritted his teeth and started the climb back to his small room in the tower above. What difference did it make? He was still trapped.

And his family was still dead.

Chapter One

Eighth day of Storm Season

Cedrin tensed as the clerk examined his tattoos.

'I don't recognise those chest marks. What are they?' The clerk scratched the stubble on his chin with a dirty fingernail.

Cedrin shifted his grip on his greatscythe and pulled his robe closed. He turned to his friend Marken, meeting his golden eyes briefly. Marken's face was drawn, as pale as he had ever seen the golden-skinned Cioan. His long golden hair was tied back roughly, his fine silk shirt crushed and stained from their night on the streets. Cedrin looked no better.

'They're Athrian,' said Cedrin.

The clerk's eyes narrowed. He leant back on his chair and tapped the stylus on the table.

'I know them,' said a warrior behind the clerk, leaning on a spear. 'They are Brotherhood tattoos.'

The clerk shrugged, squinting back at the list. 'Makes no difference to us.'

Cedrin could hardly believe it. Since first light, he and Marken had been walking the Merchants' Quarter, approaching mercenary companies to see if there were places for them as scythemen. They had tried seven companies, starting with the biggest, most well-equipped outfits. One look at their Brotherhood tattoos and they had been turned away every time.

'Right. You have your own weapons so ... buy-in is ten rubies each,' said the clerk.

'Ten rubies? Aren't you supposed to be paying us?' said

Marken.

The man looked back at them, eyes calculating above dark circles, cheeks sunken. 'Ten rubies buy-in. And lucky to be offered it.'

The blood pounded through Cedrin's temples, a wave of anger flooding through him. He immediately suppressed it. It was the ghost of the Heat racing through his emotions. The Heat, a survival mechanism triggered by the cold, never made for a clear head. He looked back past the clerk at the crowd of men standing listlessly around the training yard behind him. Most looked like refugees, traders or workers fallen on hard times. Hardly any of them looked like warriors. He scanned the chests of the men, then the clerk and the spearman beside him. None were marked with the Way of the Scytheman – a tattoo of the Larus sun-symbol nestled into the Y-shaped symbol of the Underworld god Kallor.

All at once, Cedrin understood. These two were fleecing desperate men. No doubt they had already made a small fortune taking this fee then arranging quick assignments for their 'clients' – the more dangerous the better. Dead men need no pay. No wonder they were not fussy.

'Come on, Marken,' said Cedrin.

'You're making a mistake,' said the clerk.

'No one will take you with marks like that,' called out the spearman as they walked away.

'Now can we go to Kranor's company?' Marken slung his finely-crafted mought staff across his back.

Cedrin nodded. His step-father Tarral had given him a contact in the city – Kranor, a man he had known in the legion. They had learned that Kranor ran his own mercenary company, his operations centred in a tavern called *The Scytheman*. It would have been an easy matter to go there first, but Cedrin was never one to take hand-outs. He walked his own path. He wanted to know what his options were before he faced an unwelcome reception at Kranor's headquarters.

Cedrin stopped a young boy hurrying past carrying a basket. 'Can you tell me where *The Scytheman* tavern is?'

The young boy rattled off a quick series of directions. He was jumpy and as thin as a rake. Cedrin pulled a few bits from his pouch, pressing the small cream-coloured mought coins into the boy's palm.

'I thought we were out of money,' said Marken.

'We are. But a few bits will make no difference,' said Cedrin.

They trudged down through the Merchants' Quarter, then through the deserted market. Storm Season – the time when the eclipse of Yos' red and yellow suns plunged the planet into bitter cold – had turned. The suns were well out of eclipse, but it would be days yet before the effects of Storm Season passed. Anyone with a roof over their heads would remain indoors until the return of the summer temperatures.

'Why don't you sling that thing across your back?' Marken pointed at Cedrin's greatscythe.

Cedrin tightened his grip on the solid mought haft of his greatscythe, running his eyes over the elaborately-worked phoenix crest and the central mechanism that released the twin lanedd blades. 'I like the feel of it.'

Marken shrugged.

They had arrived in the old capital Raynor two days ago. The first night they had managed to rent a small room, but the flood of refugees over the last few weeks from the destruction of the southern Sardom of Hend at the hands of advancing Eathal had sent prices soaring. Last night they did not have enough money to buy a place by the fire. They had tramped the streets until well after midnight, battling the madness of the Heat, finding every doorstop and lee brimming. They had eventually found a fire, but Cedrin refused to think about that, or the Sorcery he had used to ignite it. His Old Blood had already cost him enough. Skye, his oldest friend, who had escaped to Raynor with them, had parted ways with him rather than be close to his … curse. That had been hard.

'There it is.' Marken pulled his cloak tight around him and pointed up the street.

There was no turning back. They had barely escaped Athria with their lives. Both he and Marken had sworn to leave the Brotherhood of the Night behind and seek a new life as scythemen.

They stopped under the dirty wooden sign. Most of the paint had flaked and the picture was nondescript, but enough remained to show the name of the tavern. *The Scytheman.*

'Lucky if we're not poisoned.' Marken shivered.

'Lucky if we can afford it,' said Cedrin.

'Let's hope the day-price is a little more reasonable than the rates we were getting last night,' said Marken.

They both turned towards the door.

'You know our contacts here in Raynor still owe us from the last job,' said Marken.

Cedrin frowned. It was true. Their contacts in Raynor did owe them money. But it was risky. Too risky. He and Marken had made a good living smuggling for the Athrian Brotherhood, but any sway he had with the black market in Raynor relied on his Brotherhood contacts – most of whom had tried to kill him and his friends in Athria.

Cedrin reached up to his lucky ring, feeling the familiar weight between his thumb and forefinger. It hung on a leather cord around his neck. It was the signet ring of his real father, the Suul lord Belin Kaidell. A man he had never known.

Thunder rolled across the grey sky. A heartbeat later hail pelted down on them, followed by heavy droplets of chill rain.

'That's it!' Cedrin pulled the hood of his robe up as he ran to the door. He rapped smartly on the thick planks.

A plate slid across, and a bearded face stared out at them. 'One sapphire. Each. Can you pay?'

'Aye. Aye!' The sleet had soaked Cedrin and was seeping down through his robe. The price would leave them with only two opals and a few bits, hardly enough for a meal.

The man looked past them left and right. Begrudgingly, he closed the wooden plate. They could hear a series of bolts being drawn inside.

'What were they expecting?' said Marken from the side of his mouth. 'A battering ram?'

Cedrin smiled as the door opened, a warm draft of tobacco-filled air rushing outwards like the breath of paradise.

The man's meaty hand held them back from the step. 'One sapphire. Each.'

Cedrin's hand shook with the cold as he fished two of the big blue coins from his pouch and handed them over. In Athria, it would have bought them a room for the night and a meal. Here it was a place by the fire and breakfast if they were lucky. But warmth was priceless, especially after the night they'd had. The man jingled the coins expertly, then stepped aside, letting them past into the tavern room.

'You're to be out at dusk, otherwise you have to pay the night-rate.'

Cedrin nodded. 'Aye.' If they could not convince Kranor to take them, they would be back on the streets again, facing the Heat.

The doorman slid the bolts home, and they pushed through the crowd. The room was packed to overflowing. Cedrin sighed with relief as the warmth soaked into him.

'There.' Marken pointed to a corner table with two empty seats. *Odd to have seats to spare with this crowd.* As they approached, the three men sitting at the table regarded them with wariness and contempt. Cedrin scanned them for tattoos, but each had a cloak drawn close about them.

'Do you lads mind if we share the table?' asked Cedrin, poised to sit in any case.

One of the men, with a powerful set to his shoulders, hefted a greatscythe and slammed it across the table. The conversation in the tavern stilled as people turned towards them, whispering and watching.

'The Scion or the Warlord?' The warrior's words resounded in the silence, his eyes set hard.

Cedrin narrowed his eyes. This madness had taken the city like a disease. Yesterday Osterac, a Suul from the city of Olcis, had marched into the Warlord's court and declared himself the Scion, the long-lost heir to the Emperor's throne. A major riot had broken out as thousands of refugees supporting the Scion had clashed with the Warlord's men. Hundreds had been taken as slaves and many killed. As if the Warlord would give up the Emerald Throne after thirty years! The whole thing was ridiculous.

Cedrin stared back at the big man. His cloak had fallen open as he leant across the table, revealing a uniform. Cedrin smiled. They were city guards.

'The Warlord,' said Cedrin, his voice level.

The big warrior laughed, a sound like a grunt, and lifted his greatscythe.

'Well, sit with us then. Too many of the Scion-scum around here for my liking.'

Cedrin sat, casting a wary gaze at the crowd. There were whole families here, looking fraught and nervous as they gathered around the fire. Refugees, most likely. But most of the crowd were scythemen, their short pole weapons leaning against tables and walls close to hand, their scythes' razor-sharp lanedd blades covered with leather sheaths. A few others had greatscythes like Cedrin, staff-like weapons with twin concealed blades. None of the warriors were uniformed. They watched Cedrin and Marken, talking in low tones. Those whose chests were bare were all marked with phoenix tattoos, the crest of the old Bulvuran Empire – and the mark of the Scion. *Great.* What the hell had they walked into? At least the place was warm. That had to be an improvement.

'Most of those buggers were at the riot yesterday.' The warrior jerked his thumb at the refugees. 'No way to prove it now though. All their mates are in chains. They'll be joinin' em' soon.'

The refugees stared back at Cedrin and Marken, their eyes hostile. Supporters of the Scion – the nostalgic dreamers and the desperate, longing for a return to a golden past.

'I'm sure they can hardly wait,' said Marken, a mocking smile on his drawn face.

The guardsman frowned. Cedrin studied the guardsmen at the table. All were well within the grip of the ale. He caught Marken's eyes and shook his head slightly, cautioning him to silence.

'The Warlord should have hung Osterac straight after,' said the big guard.

'And the Sisters' Druids with him,' added a thin guardsman at his side.

'Straight after?' asked Cedrin.

The big guard looked at him as though he were a simpleton. 'Straight after the declaration. The so-called *Scion's* declaration in the public court. The Warlord should have hanged that damn Osterac then and there.'

'That's right,' said the thin guardsman. 'Who was it that saved Raynor from the Eathal after the fall of the Empire? The Warlord, that's who.'

'Who wants to go back to the Empire now? At least under Warlord Daran a man has the right to carry any weapon he wants through the streets,' said the big guard.

Cedrin found himself sympathising with them. He had no love for the privileged. 'In Athria, the Suul nobles still have weapon rights. It's rarely enforced these days, but if they catch you with a scythe, they can make you regret it.'

The big guard looked at them with a knowing eye. 'Thought I recognised that accent.' He leaned closer. 'If you ask me, I would go back to Athria. It could well be the safest place in Kelas in a few months.'

That would be good advice if so many people in Athria did not want him dead.

'Look at the state of Kelas, though,' said Marken. 'You can't tell me the Eathal would be breathing down our necks now if the Empire was still intact.'

The big guard's frown deepened.

'Hend is in ashes beneath the advancing legions of the Eathal Sorcerer-Lords, the capital Hianer destroyed, and the Yasser States did not lift a finger. If the Empire was in control, they would have met the Eathal in the field to defend their province, and these poor unfortunates would still be in their own homes.' Marken waved at the refugees.

'Hend is no damn province of the Yasser States,' said the big guard. 'It was them that sided with the Eathal in the first war. We owed em' no favours.'

'I thought you said you was for the Warlord,' said the thin guardsman to the bigger man's left. The third guard glowered at them in silence.

'We are, of course,' said Marken, untying his golden hair and letting it fall across his shoulders. 'But you can't say the Suul did nothing for the people. Someone has to rule. Look at the chaos in Kelas since the fall of the Bulvuran Empire.'

The three guards leant in towards Marken, knuckles white on their tankards.

'Marken. Why don't you see if you can get us some breakfast?' said Cedrin.

Marken gave him a flashing smile and left the table for the kitchens. The guards relaxed. Marken's courtly ways had been an asset selling contraband to the Athrian Suul, but men like these did not appreciate the finer points of debate.

'Now, where you lads off to?' asked the burly guardsman.

'North. We hope to join a caravan and hire ourselves as scythemen,' said Cedrin.

The man nodded knowingly, taking a draught of his beer. 'Tough game. Yeah, a tough game. Although you're here at the right time. The Inner City is full of merchants chaffing at the bit to get out of Raynor, all just waiting for the end of Storm Season.' He leant closer to impart another bit of confidential advice, his breath stinking of stale ale. 'If you take my advice, I would try to get on a caravan well before the end of Storm Season. Once the merchants have left, I wouldn't be surprised if Daran seals the city.'

The thin guard nodded in mute approval.

The big guard took another draught. 'And another thing. You would be best to stay off the streets. With the Eathal coming, the press gangs are looking for young, able-bodied men, just like you.'

'Best off the streets,' agreed the thin guard.

Marken arrived back from the kitchens with a loaf of bread. 'They are going to get us some real food. Meanwhile, I thought this might help.'

Marken broke off a section of the bread and handed some to Cedrin. It was stale and as solid as rock, but he savoured it just the same. His stomach rumbled, uncoiling like a hungry snake.

The five sat in silence for a time until, with a heavy sigh, the big guard stood and reached for his greatscythe. 'Time to start my shift. You watch these Scion-suckers, lads. They will cut your throat and drink your blood soon as look at ya'.'

'We'll be careful.' Cedrin tried to look grateful for the advice. Watching some of the faces in the crowded room, Cedrin could almost believe him.

A serving man arrived, laying two small platters on the table. The meat was poor and tough, the vegetables old and tasteless, but they soaked up every drop of the watery gravy with relish.

Cedrin's fingers played over the familiar shape of the Kaidell signet ring as he tried to think of his next move. He saw the serving man returning and sat straighter, fixing a smile on his face. 'We need to speak with Kranor. Is he here?'

The short, pot-bellied man looked at Cedrin as though he were an idiot.

Cedrin asked again, this time louder. 'Is Kranor here?'

'I heard you the first time. I'm not deaf, by Uros. Kranor owns the place. He's upstairs.'

Cedrin pulled his last opals from his pouch and offered them to the man, trying to seem nonchalant. 'Tell him Tarral sends his greetings.'

The man unwillingly pocketed the coins and left the table, weaving through the crowd to the kitchen. Cedrin marked his reluctance as strange.

Alone at their table, the cool stares of the warriors seated around the room were even harder to ignore. As well as the phoenix, he could see the distinctive tattoo of the Way of the Scytheman on many of them, the mark of the professional warrior. If he was successful with Kranor, these men might be his new brothers, his new competitors. His shoulders tensed. Here, he was the outsider. A beginner. After more than a decade working his way up through the ranks of the Brotherhood of the Night, it was a daunting prospect.

He laid Tarral's old greatscythe across the table and stared back at them, giving nothing away. They had no way of knowing how good he was with the weapon. He flicked back his robe, showing the six degrees of the calvanni across his chest, the tattoos that marked him not only as an expert with a long knife, but also as a senior member of the Brotherhood of the Night. He slipped a calv out of his chest-harness and started trimming his fingernails with the long knife's razor edge.

A thin man came out of the kitchen and made for their table with an air of annoyance. He wore bright clothes of orange and red, crafted from a fine, soft fabric that shimmered as he moved. Even though mostly bald, he was only just past middle years. His eyes were hard as gemstones as he took in their calvs and Brotherhood tattoos.

'I thought so. Neither of you would be old enough.' He threw a pair of coins onto the table like a challenge.

Cedrin's eyes flicked to the coins as they rolled to a stop. *The two opals he had given the servant.* He quickly sheathed his calv. Clearly, he had miscalculated.

'Who are you?' The man stabbed at them with an ink-stained finger. 'And don't try my patience.'

'I am Cedrin, Tarral's son,' he said. 'Tarral told me to find Kranor. That he would help me find work.'

'Do you have any proof of this?'

Cedrin lifted the greatscythe from the bench and passed it to the man. 'This was Tarral's.'

The man took the weapon in his long, bony hands and appraised it like a buyer. His eyebrows shot up and his eyes flicked back to Cedrin. 'Stay here.'

He disappeared through the crowd, carrying the greatscythe.

'Do you think it was wise to let him take it?' Marken asked.

'What choice do we have?'

The man soon reappeared. 'Follow me.'

He led them through the kitchen and up a wooden stairway to the first floor.

Cedrin walked slowly, trying to look casual. Inside, his guts were churning. He forced himself to unclench his fists, but could not stop his eyes from sweeping around him, alert for anything. They needed this. He would have only one chance to win over Kranor – one chance to get him and Marken off the streets and start a new life.

The upper landing led to a short corridor with three joining doors, all wooden and smelling of wax and polish. A big man leant against one of the door frames, a heavy club dangling from his belt, a friendly smile on his face as though he were an old drinking partner.

'Wait here until Kranor calls for you,' said their thin guide, as though he had just washed his hands of something unpleasant. He disappeared through one of the doors.

'Don't mind Indon. He hates to be dragged away from his tallies. Not a bit out of place, that's Indon,' said the big guard.

Cedrin smiled. 'You worked for Kranor long?'

'Yep, years. Ever since I scored a wooden one.' The guard tapped his left leg, the hollow sound of wood answering from beneath the leather trousers. 'Used to be a harena handler in the legion 'til I got mauled.'

Cedrin winced. The big, horned war-harena were notoriously ill-tempered.

'Looking for work, eh?' asked the guard, eyeing them sharply.

They nodded.

'Athrian too. Accent's a give-away. Listen,' he said, leaning closer. 'Be straight with old Kranor. He's a good judge of men and if he gets a whiff you're hiding anything, he'll just as likely call the Guard on you.'

A man called out from one of the adjacent rooms in a gruff voice and the guard walked to the door, opening it a fraction to peer inside.

'Send them in.' The voice was hard and uncompromising.

'Yes, sir.' The guard turned to them. 'Well, come on lads. He won't stay in a good mood forever.'

Cedrin straightened his harness and pulled his robe tight to cover the Brotherhood tattoos, then walked into the room followed by Marken.

Kranor was a big man, his tightly-curling hair more grey than black, the fringe coming down low across his forehead. He was dressed in a light shirt, patterned in grey and white. He had only one arm, his left sleeve pinned neatly at the shoulder. His face was fine and angular, with dark eyes beneath heavy brows. Despite his late middle-age, he was in the peak of fitness with a look of sharp alertness.

'Well, Tarral. You are looking good these days.'

Cedrin felt a jolt of apprehension. He had never tried to deceive Kranor, just gain his attention.

'I am not Tarral,' said Cedrin quickly, apologetically. 'I'm his son, Cedrin. I'd have hoped the scribe had explained ...'

'Yes, I know,' said Kranor, abruptly, almost with irritation. It was obvious he was to ask the questions.

He picked up Tarral's greatscythe and looked at it fondly. In fact, he almost smiled as his eyes followed the contours. Almost.

'How is Tarral,' asked Kranor, looking up from the greatscythe, his eyes impassive.

'He is well ... sir.'

'And is he still in the silk trade?'

Cedrin tensed. Kranor was testing them and something in his posture said if they failed, they may not leave the building free men, if at all.

'He never dealt in silks as far as I know, sir. He is a master glass smith and makes the best lanedd blades in Athria.'

Kranor nodded, placing the greatscythe between them on the desk.

'Of course. My memory is not what it used to be,' he said casually. 'So what of his wife Isabo? Are they still childless?'

'I had no idea he was ever married to an Isabo. He has been with Emily for as long as I know. They are far from childless with three sons and a daughter.' The words seemed to ring falsely, and Cedrin felt a strange mixture of regret and longing as he included himself in Tarral's family, as though he had invented himself and his past again. A different past in which he was more than just a step-son.

Suddenly Kranor burst out with a hearty laugh. Cedrin smiled uncertainly, looking back at the guard who was watching them impassively from the doorway.

'Sit, Cedrin. Why don't you introduce us to your friend?'

Cedrin sat as Marken come forward.

'Marken, son of Macil.' Marken smiled as he introduced himself. Kranor took Marken's arm in a fierce grip, and Cedrin saw his friend wince. There was prodigious strength in that arm.

'Sit, Marken.' Kranor came around from behind the desk to sit on the edge in front of Cedrin and Marken.

Cedrin felt himself lean back from Kranor, on edge.

'My apologies for the interrogation but I had to be certain.

There are a lot of bad types around,' said Kranor with a wide smile. 'Let me take your robes, I have these rooms heated during the Storm Season. Would you like some wine or bakta?'

'Bakta please,' said Marken.

'Aye and me too, please,' said Cedrin, as Kranor took their robes.

'Of course. Something to get the chill off.' Kranor hung their robes on a wooden stand, his eyes growing hard just for an instant as he looked back at their tattoos.

Cedrin searched Kranor's face, but whatever he had seen was gone. Kranor poured two shot glasses of the clear bakta spirit, and handed them across, smiling. What was there to worry about? Both of them were armed, facing a single guard and a one-armed man.

'So. How is Tarral? The old war-harena,' said Kranor.

Cedrin took the good-quality bakta in one gulp, savouring the delicious warmth as it spread through his chest.

'He is well, his business has thrived. He has four kilns and a contract with Regent's Hill.'

Kranor casually reached behind him. He swung Tarral's heavy greatscythe from the table. At first Cedrin thought he was simply picking it up, but then his arm was moving fast. *Too fast.* Cedrin and Marken leapt to their feet, glasses flying as they reached for their calvs.

Kranor spun the heavy greatscythe like a toy.

Before Marken could reach his weapon, the heavy cast haft slammed into his solar plexus. He dropped without a sound. The greatscythe was a spinning blur.

Cedrin heard a click.

'Ugh,' gasped Cedrin. The lanedd point of one of the greatscythe's blades was at his throat. Cedrin's right calv was poised only halfway to a blocking position, his left barely out of its sheath.

Shit.

* * *

Hukum, supreme Sorcerer-Lord of the Eathal examined his

reflection. His green eyes glittered back at him from under his heavy brow ridges, slit irises narrow in the light of the glowplants. He snarled, showing his sharp teeth. *Yes. Still a fine looking thal.*

He looked up as a military messenger, dressed in standard-issue hide armour, shuffled into the room. Hukum suppressed his irritation. The demands of rule were never-ending. It was impossible for the Sundar of the Eathal to even select a new outfit without a full entourage. The room was uncomfortably crowded. His bodyguards stood alert and impassive across the walls, while a small army of scribes and no less than three Sorcerer-Lords from the Junta, the ruling council of twelve, hovered about. The ever-present purist Verst, never passing up an opportunity to advocate the death of all humans. The scholar Eith, a representative of the last faction to oppose the continuing conquests, always waiting to pass judgement on Hukum's failures like his master Venan. And the Sorcerer Zekon, an expert on supply and logistics, senior commander on his General Yeffrij's staff and Hukum's military liaison.

The messenger hovered uncertainly, awed – of course – by his presence.

Hukum eyed the fall of his new robes critically. He swept them back off his shoulders, admiring the raised muscles of his upper torso, the grey skin peppered with colourings of yellow and tan.

'Dispatches from Tupur, my Lord Sundar,' said the messenger, his voice hoarse with tension.

'Commander Zekon will deal with it,' said Hukum.

The messenger bowed and handed the message capsule to Zekon. The old Eathal's hairless skin was grey and wrinkled, but he flicked off the lid of the capsule with a deft movement, swiftly scanning the lines.

'Excellent news from Tupur, my Lord. The city of Talis has fallen. Yeffrij has taken more than twenty thousand able-bodied slaves. Still no sign of any forces capable of slowing our advance.' Zekon bowed. 'My congratulations, Sundar.'

'Twenty thousand! That is excellent news. We will have need of them,' said Hukum. It had irked him that so many of the humans had fled their advance into Hend. The slave count had been low until now. The Vengeance – the long-awaited revenge of the Eathal on the humans who had enslaved and slaughtered them thousands of years ago – proceeded according to plan.

'There are six thousand more captives; those too young, too old or infirm to work. Yeffrij asks what is to be done with these.'

'Such a slave force will be an enormous drain on our resources.' Eith shifted in his chair. 'They will need to be fed. Clothed.'

Not even his scholar's robes could hide Eith's sagging belly. Hukum's lip curled in disgust. He glared at Eith and the tirade ceased. At least Eith was easily intimidated. His master Venan, who had the support of the scholars' guild, was a different matter. In fact, it was rarely possible to shut him up.

'They should all be killed. Outright. As a matter of policy,' said Verst, the thin Eathal's face drawn back in snarl. 'We need no human slaves. There is no work that our own people cannot undertake.'

Verst, at least, was predictable.

'More salve,' snapped Hukum. *Why can these idiots never celebrate my successes?* Always, they bickered over details.

A serving thel, a young female Eathal, stepped up onto a stool and rubbed cream into his bald, dome-like head until the skin gleamed. Hukum watched the swing of her paps beneath her robe and made a mental note to have her brought to him later.

'What should I tell General Yeffrij?' asked Zekon.

Hukum sighed. 'Kill all the slaves unable to work. Send my congratulations on his victory.'

Father. Hukum smiled. It was his son Staraz, touching his mind across the Sorcerous link of the Bridge.

'Out. All of you,' said Hukum. The three Junta lords bowed and withdrew, followed by his staff. Only his bodyguards remained, as silent and rigid as statues.

'Yes, my son,' pulsed Hukum across the link.

I have reached the Shattered Temple with my warriors.

'Excellent. Soon you will have your revenge, Staraz. The human Raziin has served us well, and now your patience will be rewarded by his death.'

Thank you, father. I have not forgotten what you asked for. I will bring his head back to Maht as a trophy. I have the lungii spike already sharpened.

Hukum laughed. 'I will look forward to it, my son.'

I will return soon. With that, the Bridge was severed.

Hukum clapped his hands in delight. Soon Raziin would be dead – led to his death by the magical Compulsion Hukum had woven – and his son Staraz could take his place at his right hand. Staraz would inherit the new Eathal empire. The former glory of the Eathal at last restored after all these thousands of years under the heel of the human Cinanac Emperors.

Staraz. A fit successor. As vicious and ambitious as he was himself – and a powerful Sorcerer. Unlike his second son Faivel. Whereas Staraz had always pleased him, Faivel had never ceased to displease. Soft and weak like his mother, he had the strength but not the will to use it. Now that the Eathal were about to take their rightful place as a power in Kelas, it was time Faivel showed himself to be worthy of his family's blood.

Hukum would need new leaders in Kelas. Governors loyal to him to rule the new dome cities they were building in the ruins of the human settlements. It was time to use all the tools at his disposal, even the defective ones. Perhaps two years banished from formal court – banned from holding any position of worth – would be enough to teach Faivel, his weak, second son, the meaning of duty.

Hukum turned to one of bodyguards. 'Find Faivel and bring him here.' The big guard bowed, leaving silently.

Faivel spent his time consorting with his enemies, studying so-called *ancient texts* with the traitor Venan, reading the human tongues, professing to be seeking truth. Did he not know the only true knowledge was that which loaned strength? Hukum grunted in acknowledgement at the depth of his own wisdom.

He would heat Faivel like a twisted piece of glass in the fires of the Vengeance and shape him into a blade worthy of his House. That, or shatter him utterly.

Some time later, Faivel entered. Tall and thin, his scholarly robes hung loose around his frame. A large manuscript was tucked beneath one arm. 'You summoned me, Father?'

Hukum looked up from his map of Kelas. Faivel's eyes were distant, bored, as though he found his father beneath him. The mere sight of Faivel's face usually made Hukum angry. Now it sent him into a rage. While his peers were shedding blood, Faivel was wearing soft robes and reading. Reading!

Hukum stepped across the room and struck Faivel across the face. He seized the book and tore it to pieces.

He looked back at Faivel, waiting for that same sulky, wounded expression he always wore when Hukum spoke to him, but his eyes remained cool.

Hukum hesitated, sensing some change in the boy. He could not pin it down. 'When I last sent you from my sight, I told you to dress as a warrior.'

Just for a moment Faivel's eyes flashed with defiance, but it was quickly gone, replaced by contempt, as though Hukum were the one to be pitied. *He!* Supreme leader of the Eathal.

'My patience with you is at an end. For years your weakling of a mother has defended you, allowing you to shirk your duties. No more. You will report to my bodyguards each day for training. When you are ready, you will be sent into Tupur to command a unit on the front line.'

Faivel's mouth opened in shock, and Hukum felt a surge of triumph. That had certainly wiped away Faivel's smugness. He leered forward, staring into Faivel's eyes, but once more Faivel's eyes were cold and hard. Perhaps there was some hope for the boy.

'I will make you a son I can be proud of, Faivel.' Hukum reached up to lay his hand on Faivel's bony shoulder. He could not help comparing him to Staraz, who at even twelve years was brimming with muscle.

'A great time for the Eathal is upon us. We need leaders, not scholars. Understand? I need my sons strong enough to rule.'

'Yes, Father.' Faivel stared back without a flicker of emotion.

Hukum took away his hand. 'Go.'

Faivel bowed and withdrew.

A servant came forward to pick up the shards of the torn manuscript. Hukum's jaw clenched as he recognised Cioan glyphs on the parchment. *A human manuscript.*

Hukum waved the leader of his bodyguards over to him.

'I want him to bleed,' said Hukum, his lip curling in disgust. 'Bleed.'

'As you wish, my lord.'

Hukum turned back to his reflection, pushing Faivel from his thoughts. Instead he thought of Raziin – drawn by his Compulsion, unable to stop himself from travelling to the site of his impending death, all the while knowing his hours were numbered.

Hukum chuckled.

Vengeance was indeed sweet.

Chapter Two

Ellen Cintros stared at the tray of delicacies. Of all the things she had expected in Raynor, being forced to wait on the pleasure of others was not one of them. Now, when she needed to complete the last of her preparations to leave the city, she was being thwarted at every turn. She was the rightful ruler of the wealthy island-Sardom of Athria, yet she had been forced to flee, leaving her brother Torren to sit on the throne in her stead. As if things were not dangerous enough, her use of forbidden Sorcery to save Athria had made her an enemy of the Temple, whose Druids had a virtual monopoly on magic in Kelas. The Temple had tried to take her under edict of Purge and, when that failed, had tried to assassinate her.

Ellen took a small pastry then changed her mind, waving the slave-girl back towards her. She dropped the pastry back onto the finely-coloured porcelain tray and swept through her ante-chamber in a swirl of blue silk. A set of fine vases from the Cioan empire were set on a table by the wall, filled with fresh-cut flowers from the Warlord's greenhouses.

Ellen leant forward, sampling the delicate bouquet of an exotic flower. She was tired of waiting.

The two guards who flanked the doorway from her apartments to the main consulate rooms bowed as she approached, opening the doors for her.

One of her brother Estle's aides was hurrying past on some errand, and she stopped him with a gesture.

The man bowed low.

'Where are Valdas and Mendor? I sent for them hours ago,'

she demanded.

The aide smiled pleasantly, but his forehead creased with tension. 'The two Suulqua have been sent on an assignment by Lord Cintros. They should return within the month.'

'Sent—' Ellen growled, her sudden fury robbing her of words. As Suulqua – the most junior of Suul ranks – Valdas and Mendor would have had no choice but to obey Estle. 'Tell my brother I wish to see him immediately.'

'Lord Cintros has a full schedule today, my lady. The business of the Athrian consulate here in Raynor grows more pressing every day—'

'Immediately!' snapped Ellen.

The aide bowed, rushing back the way he had come.

Damn Estle!

What did he think he was doing, commandeering her men without consulting her?

Ellen stormed back into her rooms, hardly acknowledging the two guards as they stepped aside and opened the ornately carved and painted doors.

She walked through into her private chambers and looked over her equipment for the hundredth time: her scythe, riding boots, cloak and backpack. She opened the backpack and looked critically at the contents. She lifted it and frowned. It was too heavy … perhaps if she left some of the glowmetals behind? She frowned at the two outfits and the bundle of smallclothes she had managed to squeeze into it.

I can always buy more.

She dropped the pack and paced back and forward in front of her desk, her eyes flicking across to the sphere of glass that lay there, the glowmetal within rippling and shifting. *The Seeker.* There was no point looking into it again. Cedrin was still in Raynor – she had checked barely half an hour ago.

She walked through into her maid's small adjoining chamber. Ellen had chosen dark-haired Serel for the task of preparing her travelling clothes. Ellen judged her as the most level-headed of her ladies, and so far she had proven resourceful and discrete.

'How are you going with that, Serel?' she asked.

Serel looked up at her, needle and thread scattered around her small work table beside a small sack of gemstones. 'It takes time, my lady. If not sewn in properly, they will be too easily found – or simply fall out.'

Ellen sighed, looking at the poor girl's harassed face. She had been busy sewing the valuable gems into one of Ellen's riding outfits since dawn.

'Not a word, remember?'

'No, my lady.'

Ellen walked back through her private chambers and into the ante-chamber, sitting on a couch. She hit the golden cushions with her fist in frustration. Forcing herself to relax, she ran her hand along the silk. The calluses on her palms caught on the soft fabric.

A month was too long to wait. Cedrin's trail would be cold by then. She had to follow him now. Yet how was she supposed to get out of Raynor and follow Cedrin along the roads of Kelas without support? In the dead of night, it had all seemed so simple. Complete her father's quest. Follow Cedrin and somehow win him as an ally, working together to find the Scion. The true Scion. But she had counted on having at least two loyal Suulqua on the road. How could she – a senior Suulvey of Athria – tramp across the highways alone?

She sighed.

A slave girl approached tentatively, tray held precisely level. Ellen frowned at her, annoyed at her brother Estle's taste in slaves. Without exception they were all young, nubile – and hardly dressed. Ellen scanned the tray of food. She had done little but pick away at sweetmeats all morning, waiting for her two Suulqua to attend her so she could plan her pursuit of Cedrin.

'Bring me a selection of juices.' Ellen rubbed her temples in frustration as the slave backed away. 'Make them watered.'

'Yes, Lady Cintros.'

The doors opened and Estle walked through, a pleasant smile on his face as though they were on some social engagement. His bright orange and purple shirt was open across his chest, the collar stiff around his neck. His blond hair was loose across his shoulders.

'I hope you slept well, sister. I'm sure Uran is disappointed you did not come back for a second night.'

Ellen drew her head up, her hands trembling with anger. Her brother Estle had all but thrown her into a match with his ally Uran Cinnel, a Sorcerer eager for the power their union would bring.

'Where are my men?' Her voice was sharp like a whip crack.

Another slave-girl appeared and Estle waved her over, frowning as he looked over the tray of pastries. 'Your men?'

'Don't play the fool. *My* Suulquas, Valdas and Mendor. Where are they?'

'I sent them up the Yasser to the eastern border. Uran and I felt it was time we had first-hand reports of the Eathal strength in the region. We need to know if we can rely on this summer's baal crop.'

Ellen slapped her hand down into the billowing folds of her silk dress. 'You have no right! I want them ordered back.'

Estle's smile slipped a notch. He carefully nibbled a corner of the pastry. 'Why?'

'Because I am a Suulvey – a senior peer. They were part of my own entourage!'

Estle's smile grew thin. 'You are a Suulvey of the Athrian court. Here in Raynor your rank is more … honorary.'

'Torren sent me here on a diplomatic mission under his authority as Sarlord of Athria. *With* a full entourage.'

'Yes. To work with me, Ellen. I am the head of the Athrian consulate. All your staff are subject to my ultimate control. Not even our dear brother Torren would question that.'

Ellen fell back heavily onto the cushioned couch. Less than a week ago she had been the ruler of Athria. A sick feeling settled in her gut. She stared up at the shining marble walls, feeling trapped.

'So I have no position here?' she said, her voice thin.

'Uran has offered you marriage – that is not something to be taken lightly.'

Ellen shuddered as she remembered her dinner with Uran two nights ago. The feeling of his hands on her waist and the sense of violation as she realised he wanted her only for her Sorcerous blood, like some royal breeding stock.

The slave-girl arrived with her selection of juices. Ellen looked over them quickly and chose one. The crystal was cool beneath her fingers. She drained it in two gulps and dropped it back onto the tray.

'Hmmm. Of course, should you choose to refuse his offer, I see a great future for you here in the Athrian consulate,' said Estle. 'Of course, all *position* must be earned.'

Ellen looked up sharply.

'Which brings me to another topic,' said Estle. 'I was going to wait until things died down, but it is obvious you need to be more occupied here. I have arranged for you and your scribes to take over the tariffs and trade between Raynor and Athria.'

Ellen surged to her feet. 'Tallies? Is that what you want me to do? *You want me to count grains of baal!*'

Estle raised his hands in a conciliatory gesture. 'There is much more to it than that. With the siege inevitable, this summer's trade will be vital. Your scribes will be doing the clerical work, you will be a negotiator, an intermed —'

'If you think I am going to count bales, you're wrong.'

Estle grew grave. 'I am in charge of the consulate here.'

'Then hire a bloody merchant!'

Estle's smile was gone now; he levelled his finger at her. 'You are no longer Father's favoured little girl. This is the real world. Where real power has to be paid for.'

'Damn you, Estle. Why are you doing this?'

'Doing this? Listen to yourself. There is work to be done here, Ellen. You either start playing the game, or start doing what needs to be done.'

'Playing the game? So that's it. You are trying to force me into Uran's arms. What has he promised you? What is my brother selling me for? Tell me that!'

'*Uros.* I'm trying to gain you position! Fine. Forget Uran. In Athria, you managed the court scribes. I can't see what's so bad about. . .' Estle's eyes narrowed. 'What is this really about?'

Ellen pursed her lips and looked back at her brother defiantly. The door to her apartments cracked open. She had a brief glimpse of Serel's shrewd eyes before her maid surreptitiously shut the door once more. Her outfits were finished.

Estle gave a short, incredulous laugh. 'Are still following father's ridiculous quest?'

Ellen's face flushed with heat. 'Ridiculous? The dying words of Myan Cintros a foolish nonsense to be discarded?'

'That's why you wanted Valdas and Mendor.' Estle tossed the pastry away in annoyance. One of the slave-girls bent to pick it up. 'That's it, isn't it?'

'What I do is my business.'

Estle growled, advancing on her. 'You actually intend to leave Raynor – and all your responsibilities here – to follow this damned calvanni Cedrin? All for what? To fulfil some fool's dream of the Scion? Of the restoration of the Cinanac?'

'It was father's last wish!' she shouted, stamping her foot. Her eyes misted, tears of anger and frustration trickling down her cheeks.

Estle sighed and shook his head, casting a gaze around the room before turning to Ellen. 'It is a fool's quest.'

'Who are you to call it a fool's quest? You who stalk around Raynor like a dandified clown!' She wiped away the tears with the back of her hand. 'Father believed in the Scion. He believed the calvanni Cedrin, Belin's son, was the key to finding the Scion. The *true* Scion.' Ellen paused to take a breath. 'We both know what Osterac is.'

Estle's hands tightened spasmodically as he glared at her. Suddenly he struck out with his fist, shattering one of the Cioan vases.

'Ahh!' screamed Ellen in surprise, stepping back to avoid the cascade of water, ceramic shards and flowers.

'*Forget Father!*'

Ellen gaped in shock. She had forgotten Estle's temper. They had been close growing up, but only now did she really understand how many years separated them.

'Myan was living in the past,' he shouted at her. 'You think I strut around like a clown, eh? *How little you know* – and how much you have to learn! Here the fool is the best mask. There are so many factions, knives concealed in sleeves and words alike. You don't know anything, little sister, not about the realities of this age or the powers that move it.'

Estle took a shuddering breath, looked at the scattered mess of jagged porcelain and sobered. 'Let him go, Ellen. Let Myan and his dreams go, do your duty to Athria here in Raynor. Find a new dream. Your own dream.'

'I promised him, Estle. As he lay dying, I swore to him I would find Cedrin, protect him. Find the Scion ...' Blue lights flickered in the corner of her vision.

The Scion must stand in the Temple of the Iris.

The world swayed for a moment and she steadied herself on the arm of the couch. Estle did not appear to notice the lapse.

'Myan made you swear, but it was only *his* dream. You were not old enough, but Torren and I remember. *The Scion. The Scion.* What were his own two sons beside this Uros-cursed phantom of the Cinanac line?' Estle's voice dropped to a whisper. 'We both hated him, whoever he was, for taking our father away from us.'

Ellen took a step towards Estle, reaching to touch his arm. 'Do you really think the Warlord will save Kelas? Can he even protect Raynor?'

Estle looked at Ellen sharply and shook away her hand. 'How can you say that when Uran has shown you so much? We are rebuilding here, changing the order of the world, prying magic away from the Temple and reinstating it in the secular realm. The old Empire was decadent, rife with privilege, badly run, choked by failing rulers and the ever-present stranglehold of the Temple. It was ready to fall. The people were ready for change.'

A cautious knock sounded at the consulate doors.

'What is it?' they said together, in matching tones of pique.

A formally-dressed court messenger entered the room, studiously ignoring the shattered vase. He carried a jewelled tray, bearing a large envelope.

'A formal invitation, Lord and Lady Cintros,' said the young messenger, swallowing.

Estle snatched up the parchment, ripping it open. His eyes

moved quickly across the immaculately-scribed glyphs. 'Daran Kelath, Warlord of the Yasser States, invites Estle Cintros, Suul Lord of Athria and Raynor, and Ellen Cintros, Suulvey Lady of Athria, to a feast in celebration of the return of the Cinanac line.'

The messenger bowed and withdrew.

Estle broke into a hearty laugh. 'What is Daran up to?' He tapped the parchment against his chin in thought.

Ellen fell back onto the couch. *Now this.* Once more her plan to follow Cedrin had been derailed. She would have to attend this feast, if only to find out the Warlord's next move. Could Osterac be the real Scion? No. It was impossible, surely.

* * *

'Drop 'em,' said Kranor, his voice as cold as stone.

Cedrin let his blades fall. Marken was down, gasping for breath.

The suddenness of the attack had been devastating.

'Calvanni. *Brotherhood men.*' Kranor's lips curled back in disgust. 'They prepared you well. Even I almost believed that story. Did Tarral have to die to provide the details, eh? Or this greatscythe!' Kranor pressed the blade deeper. 'Do you even know what this is? It's a greatscythe of the One Hundred. Made for the bodyguard of the Imperial family. Scum like you aren't even worthy to touch it!'

Cedrin sucked in a breath, hardly daring to move.

'I suppose I should be flattered. This time they sent a sixth degree.' Kranor kicked away their calvs.

'Please—' started Cedrin.

'Shut your mouth!' said Kranor. 'On the floor.'

Cedrin knelt. Behind him, he heard the guard enter the room and imagined the heavy club, poised to crush.

'Who are you?' asked Kranor, his tone low but menacing.

The guard pushed Marken face-forward to the floor 'and planted his right boot on the back of his neck. 'I told you to be straight with him. I guess you don't take advice.' The guard's voice remained friendly, as though it was nothing personal.

Cedrin felt the lanedd bite deep.

'I'll ask you only once more. Who are you? Who sent you? The Warlord?' asked Kranor.

Cedrin swallowed from reflex and winced at the pain. 'I am Cedrin.'

Kranor's face was unyielding. There was no mercy there. None. 'But you are not Tarral's son, are you? I have known Tarral for half my life and no son of his would be a calvanni – certainly not a Brotherhood man.'

Cedrin realised it was true. Tarral had worshipped the Empire and the law that held it together.

'I'm Belin's son. Belin Kaidell's bastard,' said Cedrin, gasping.

Kranor frowned, then he laughed in amazement. 'Your sheer audacity is astounding – then again, assassins are not paid to be squeamish. Belin's children died at Blackthorne. Victims of the same assassins who killed the Emperor and his family.' He hesitated. 'Maybe I should just end this now.' Yet Cedrin could tell he was unsure, perhaps he had sensed the truth of what he said.

'I don't know how, but I was given to Tarral for safe keeping after the Last Days. I lived with him. I did not know the truth until I came of age.'

'You lie.' The blade dug deeper.

'No. *No*. The ring. Look at the ring.'

Kranor's eyes flicked to the emerald ring around Cedrin's neck. Cedrin saw his eyes widen as he took in the detail of the crest. For a moment the blade wavered.

'Any smart assassin could have found it, intending to use it just as you are, as a token to gain trust,' said Kranor, pushing the point. Cedrin felt a warm trickle of blood down his neck.

'No. I swear it's the truth,' said Cedrin.

Abruptly the point was gone. Cedrin fell forward, drawing in ragged gasps and holding his throat. *I'm still alive.*

'Give me the ring,' demanded Kranor, laying the greatscythe on the desk. Cedrin slipped the leather cord and ring over his head and held it out to him.

Kranor snatched it out of his hand. He examined it carefully, then sank back into the chair.

'There is no doubt this is Belin's ring. I thought it lost ... vanished with him the night the Emperor's family were killed.' Kranor's eyes lost their focus. He gripped the ring in his fist, squeezing it until his knuckles were white. Then the moment was gone, and he handed back the ring, passing it to Cedrin with reverence.

Cedrin slipped the leather cord back over his head. One thing was certain. The signet ring had saved his life. Kranor obviously held Belin in high esteem. Perhaps Belin's gift to Cedrin extended beyond the curse of Sorcerous blood.

'Hard to believe a young cut-throat like you could actually be Belin's blood.' Kranor motioned for them to get up.

They returned to the chairs, watching Kranor warily.

Kranor searched Cedrin's face. 'There is some resemblance to Belin's relatives. You are much taller than Belin, but many of his Suul cousins were tall.'

Kranor rubbed at his temples and swept back his hair. Only now did Cedrin see the faded Suul mark beneath the fringe. Cedrin's stomach churned. *Tarral never told me Kranor was a noble.*

'You do remind me of someone I knew.' Kranor studied him for a moment, then shook his head. 'If you are Belin's bastard as you say, then you could have the look of any of the Kaidells I've known over the years.'

Kranor hefted the greatscythe, spinning it casually, one-handed, to withdraw the blades. He handed it back to Cedrin.

Cedrin accepted the greatscythe warily. If this old warrior could do that much one-handed, what would he have been capable of in his youth?

The guard returned their calvs. Cedrin sheathed them slowly, his hands shaking with fatigue and adrenalin.

'Alvis. Have a dinner prepared in my private rooms,' snapped Kranor. 'And send for my wife.'

The big man bowed and left, the rhythmic sound of the wooden leg receding along the corridor.

'I'm not saying I believe you yet, but at least I can offer you a meal while I decide,' said Kranor smoothly.

The old warrior led them from the room and down another

set of stairs. Marken smiled at Cedrin, his hand rubbing the bruise on his solar plexus. 'Nice friends Tarral has. Forgive me if I don't want to meet any more.'

They passed four guards, all standing in military fashion, scythes held at the ready, and walked through a small ante-chamber into a formal dining room set with low tables. A slave waited impassively at the far end.

It was furnished like no other room Cedrin had ever seen. Sweeping across an entire wall was a single tapestry that by its sheer size looked as though it had once hung in a throne room. The phoenix crest of Bulvuran – the crest of the Empire – woven in stunning colours. The phoenix was wreathed in flame, head tilted up to the right, talons clutching a spear. Imperial standards and small tapestries hung from the walls. Legionary uniforms, crests, rings and human and Eathal weapons were set around the walls in cabinets.

Kranor walked over to one of the legionary standards. Its colours were faded, and part of the lower section had been cut roughly away. It also showed a phoenix crest, but subtly different. Here the phoenix was looking straight out, its countenance fierce as it gripped a greatscythe with both blades extended. Kranor touched the cloth and bowed low. Sensing them watching him, he looked back at them sharply, his eyes narrowed. 'The standard of the One Hundred. And the symbol of my company.'

Kranor seated himself at one of the low tables and signalled to a slave, who helped him remove his light shirt. He wore no harness beneath, his powerfully-muscled chest covered with finely-crafted military tattoos, including the phoenix crest of the One Hundred. Cedrin's step-father Tarral also had this tattoo, faded and lost amid scores of other military honours. Not until now had Cedrin truly understood its significance.

They sat in silence while the slave poured wine from a pitcher.

'So why have you come here?' asked Kranor.

Cedrin took a breath. This was it. 'We want to become scythemen. To join your company.'

'It's no light thing you ask,' said Kranor. 'I make no secret of my allegiance with the old ways, or to the Empire. Are you prepared to be marked with the phoenix? To be part of that?'

Cedrin swallowed. There was no backing out now. Everything that had happened had led him here to this choice. Besides – the phoenix mark was simply that of Kranor's company. He had no intention of becoming either a supporter of the Scion's lost cause, or a servant of the Suul. What he could see was a man of impeccable honour. A strong man who would run a tight and disciplined outfit. *That* he could be part of.

There was something else. The name of Belin meant something to Kranor. He could use that – to establish himself in Kranor's company he would need every advantage.

'Yes. I can accept that.'

Kranor nodded and turned to Marken. 'And you?'

Marken seemed relaxed as he sipped his wine, but Cedrin had known him long enough to know his emotions were churning under the surface.

'Of course,' said Marken.

Kranor nodded.

A door opened at the far end of the room and a stately woman walked through, her Suul mark freshly inked. Cedrin held his breath. She was well into middle-age but the years had not dulled her beauty, only given her a look of earthly sensuality. Her white skin glowed, her blonde hair was touched with silver and her pale grey eyes were soft, enticing.

'Who are these young men, my warrior?' she asked, smiling.

Kranor looked across at them, his eyes hard once more. 'Tell her.'

The woman's face was serene, her eyes filled with warmth. Cedrin felt the numbing sense of her power and carefully put down his wine cup. *Earth Essence.* The power of the Priestesses. He had been Tested like this before. It meant this place was holy ground. Only at certain places on Yos could the Priestesses access this power.

'I am Cedrin, bastard son of Belin Kaidell. I was brought up in Athria by the glassmith Tarral,' he said.

Kranor looked up at the woman. She closed her eyes for a moment then nodded.

Kranor leant forward in his chair, his body tense. 'You were part of the Athrian Brotherhood of the Night?'

'Yes. A smuggler. But I am finished with the Brotherhood,' said Cedrin.

When the woman nodded, Kranor let out a breath and sat back, more relaxed.

'Why would a sixth-degree calvanni walk away from the Brotherhood?' asked Kranor.

'The Brotherhood allied themselves with Raziin Cinnor to overthrow the Sarlord. My enemies in the Brotherhood planned to use us in the rebellion, then have us killed.'

'Hence your flight from Athria,' said Kranor.

'It is true, my love,' said the woman. 'Or … at least the truth as they know it.'

Kranor nodded. 'Belin's son.' He lifted his wine cup and drained it in one swallow, looking back at Cedrin in disbelief.

Kranor turned to Marken. 'And what of you?'

'As I said. I am Marken, son of Macil.'

The woman hissed. 'Lies.'

Kranor immediately tensed. 'Speak quickly if you value your life.'

Marken's smile vanished and he slammed his cup down onto the table, sloshing wine onto the polished surface. 'Very well. My name is Marken Kye, youngest son of Sanil Kye, Suulvey lord of Althar. Killed by the Eathal. My family fled to Athria by galley, and we were attacked by pirates. I and my sister hid among the dead and were rescued from the burning galley by the trader Macil, who raised me as his own.' Marken glared at Kranor, then looked up at the woman. 'Satisfied?'

'Truth,' she said. Her eyes refocussed once more and she leant against Kranor.

Kranor grunted. 'Yet another disinherited Suul, eh?'

Marken scowled.

'My apologies for the Testing. But I had to be sure.' Kranor reached up to touch the woman's arm. 'This is my wife, Salis Cintor. Suulqua of the court of Raynor.'

'As are you, my love,' she said, brushing his hair back from the Suul mark on his forehead.

Kranor growled. 'I was Suulqua to Emperor Riin.'

'A rank Daran still recognises,' said Salis.

Kranor snorted as he reached for his wine, fixing his eyes on Cedrin.

'So, young Cedrin,' began Kranor, as though talking amiably to an old acquaintance. 'How did you end up a Brotherhood calvanni? A knife fighter?' He eyed the razor-sharp blades of Cedrin's calvs, or long knives. 'If I know Tarral, he would have rather skinned you alive.'

Cedrin was getting tired of Kranor's questions, and this one hit just a little too close.

'Tarral didn't like it, not at all. He threw me out onto the streets.' Cedrin tried to keep the bitterness from his voice.

'He must have been fond of you. If you were my son, I would have shipped you off to the frontier,' said Kranor.

'What can you tell me of Belin?' asked Cedrin. 'When he sent me to Athria, it was with the message that he would come for me, but he never did.'

'Don't sound so sorry for yourself. You were brought up free and fed. That is more than most ever have, boy.' Kranor looked back at the standard of the One Hundred, his eyes sad. 'The last time I saw Belin was just before the fall of the Empire. He was retired then, but still weaponmaster at the Cinanac court. Tarral and I were in the One Hundred – the personal bodyguard of the Emperor and his family. We were ordered to join Riin on the battlefield. Riin was missing long before we reached his forces. It was only after we fought our way back to Raynor through the Eathal lines that we realised we had been tricked. Empress Evylin – and the whole Imperial family – were dead. Not one of us had died to save them. I have heard nothing from Belin since that time. He most likely died in the flames of Blackthorne's fall.'

Salis laid a hand on Kranor's shoulder.

'Who delivered you to Tarral?' asked Kranor.

Cedrin grimaced. The question had often gnawed at him. Tarral had never told him, and after the bad blood began between them, Cedrin's pride had prevented him from approaching his step-father to ask. He had seen Tarral on the day he left Athria, but staying alive seemed more important than family history at the time.

'I never knew his name,' said Cedrin.

Kranor sighed. 'It would have been one of Belin's lieutenants. Many died at his fortress Blackthorne in the Last Days. Others fought in the legions against the Eathal after Belin vanished. That was almost thirty years ago.'

Kranor looked down at the empty sleeve hanging from his left shoulder. 'It was a terrible time. Many ... many were lost.'

Kranor cleared his throat. 'So what sort of work are you looking for?'

'Something heading north,' said Cedrin. *And away from the coming war with the Eathal.*

'As far north as we can get,' said Marken, draining his cup.

'You think anywhere is safe anymore? The roads outside the Yasser States are not patrolled. You will find nothing but robbers on those roads. Brigands and bands of runaways who will cut your throat for the price of a meal,' said Kranor.

'Is there work?'

Kranor laughed. 'There is no shortage of work. The merchants can't flee from the Eathal fast enough. I can get you work on a caravan bound for Searn. There is one leaving straight after Storm Season. Can either one of you use a bow?'

They shook their heads.

'Pity. There are a lot of hungry predators roaming around after Storm Season, a bowman or two can be very useful. A few good bowmen can stop a palgur dead in its tracks.' He looked at them with a glint of malevolence. 'Of course, it won't stop a drakon. They get hungry too.'

Cedrin shivered. 'Surely all the drakon were slain during the Empire's height.'

Kranor grinned. 'Were they?' It was the first time Cedrin had seen genuine mirth reach his eyes.

Cedrin was sure Kranor was playing with him.

The rear doors opened and servants entered with generous plates of food. As the aroma of the cooked food reached him, Cedrin's stomach clenched in hunger. The Heat had taken a lot from him.

Salis took a seat beside her husband. She loosened the top of her gown, exposing the skin of her chest down to the top of her ample cleavage. As was the custom in Kelas, breasts were only bared in the intimate company of family and friends, where the uncovered chest was regarded as a symbol of the uncovered heart. Kranor poured her a cup of wine.

'You can stay here until the end of Storm Season,' said Kranor as they devoured their meals. 'You have your own weapons, that's good, but you will need to supply your own armour.'

'Armour?' asked Marken, raising his eyebrow.

'Yes. Mostly our men fight without it, but you never know when we need to go toe to toe with a well-equipped foe. I have a tattooist that will give you my mark, but if you want anything special you will need to pay extra. You might consider having a sigil inked in beside those Brotherhood marks to let everyone know that path is ended.'

Kranor watched them carefully as he started on his meal. 'Do you have money for the armour and the tattoos?'

'Of course,' said Cedrin. 'Funds are no problem.'

Marken almost choked on his meal.

'Excellent. I like a man who pays his own debts.'

Cedrin nodded; he had guessed as much. Where he was going to get the money ... now there was a thorny problem.

'Belin would have been proud to see you sworn to the phoenix, Cedrin. You will not regret it. We have new blood joining the cause all the time. Fellows just like you who have noble origins and firmly believe in the rightness of the Empire's restoration. I wouldn't have any other sort of man on my caravans.'

Cedrin concentrated on his food, uncomfortable with talk of the Empire's resurrection. The desperate dreams of rioting refugees clinging to the Scion's banner were one thing – the determination of a man like Kranor was something else entirely.

'Anything new at Court?' Kranor asked Salis.

'Daran has declared a feast to hand power over to this so-called Scion, but no-one believes him.'

Kranor laughed. 'Daran would never give up the throne. If

Riin himself walked into the public court he would have a fight on his hands. Nothing short of five legions will make that opportunist give way.'

Salis took a small sip of her wine.

'Any confirmation from Olcis on this latest Scion claimant, Osterac?' asked Kranor.

'Nothing,' said Salis.

'Another pretender,' said Kranor, stabbing at his steak with a knife.

'So you believe the Scion is out there? That Emperor Riin's child was rescued in the Last Days?' asked Marken.

Kranor stared back at Marken, his eyes cold.

Cedrin gritted his teeth. If only Marken could learn to keep his damn mouth shut!

'We had first-hand accounts from survivors,' said Kranor. 'We know the child was rescued. Who do you think started the Scion legend?'

By Uros, thought Cedrin. What had he got himself into?

* * *

'*Funds are no problem?*' hissed Marken as a servant led them down a corridor to their room.

Cedrin held up his finger to his lips, smiling as the servant opened the door.

With the door shut, Cedrin sank down onto the bed, utterly exhausted.

'Where are we supposed to get money for armour and new tattoos?' asked Marken.

'There is only one place,' said Cedrin.

'You have got to be kidding.' Marken paced the room. 'Why couldn't you have just asked Kranor for a loan?'

'We need to earn his respect, Marken. I am not starting my new life as a beggar.' Cedrin reached up to touch the familiar shape of the Kaidell ring, his fingers finding the notch in the gemstone where it had stopped a calv blade. 'One last bluff, and we can start this new life with enough cash to make a good show.'

Marken sank onto the bed, shaking his head. 'Ok. Ok. So it's back to the Brotherhood.'

'Yes.'

The same Brotherhood that had tried to kill them in Athria.

'As if escaping that madman Raziin wasn't enough,' said Marken.

* * *

'Anything?' asked Raziin.

'No, my Lord. The swamp is shallow in all directions,' said Merceth.

Raziin considered his faithful general. His scarred face was impassive, implacable. Merceth was always ready to follow his commands, always ready to cut when Raziin needed men bleeding.

Raziin looked out across the Melaut, a vast landscape of treacherous, stinking swamp. Longboats were just visible through the dark, lamps glowing at bow and stern through the swirling vapours of the bog. His men were using weighted ropes and poles to try and find a channel deep enough for their galley to pass. The maze of sand-banks and channels had defeated even his magically-enhanced sight.

'Send out the rest of the longboats,' commanded Raziin.

'Yes, my Lord.'

He looked down at the Athrian Brotherhood men chained to the oars, miserable in the cold. Dresil, once their leader, looked up at Raziin, his eyes dull with exhaustion and the effort of fighting the Heat.

The Athrians had told him it was impossible to navigate the Melaut; impossible to find the ancient, ruined city of Ciofran-Ac. Yet he had proved them wrong.

He had found the city, and been taken by the Seer of Ciofran-Ac. She had tormented him, tested him – yet had let him walk free with gifts. The first, a vision of an ancient power – a spear with a blade of forged metal that harnessed the realm of Fire. She had told him how the blade could be his. The second was a golden glowmetal, worn like a pendant around his neck. The glowmetal's special properties allowed it to absorb Hukum's Compulsion, the violet light within it writhing as it converted the subtle magic to groans and squeals. The last gift was the Final Matrix. His former master, Hukum, had feared to pass the knowledge of it to him – and rightly so. The magical construct allowed him to weave powerful magic. With it, he could dominate the minds of men, and combat another Sorcerer. No longer did he have to run from bitches like Ellen Cintros. He smiled. He would look forward to meeting her again.

A longboat appeared from the mist.

'Report,' commanded Merceth.

'Still nothing,' called Kyal, another of Raziin's lieutenants.

'Keep searching,' commanded Merceth.

Light flickered through the mist.

At first Raziin thought it was some sort of marsh-light, but it grew in intensity, brightening the mist like a rising dawn. Raziin tensed. He opened the Window and channelled the Fire, forming the Barrier matrix in his mind.

The light within the mist grew, the vapours of the Melaut shifting and swirling. Then all at once they fell away, revealing a ship. It was ancient in design, narrow and sharp-prowed, and glowed with lights of green, gold and white. Raziin ran to the rail. He scanned the decks, the Fire filling him, ready at his command. The craft had a single row of oars on either side. Closer now, he could see it was manned by skeletal spectres, flesh hanging off them in strips, clothes rotted to nothing around them. There was powerful magic here, and Raziin knew of only one power in the Melaut. The Seer of Ciofran-Ac had sent this craft to speed him to his destiny.

'What is it?' asked Merceth.

Raziin grinned savagely. 'Another gift from the Seer. Bring in the longboats!'

Raziin swept his gaze along the decks of the ancient vessel. There! At the tiller he saw the familiar face of the minitil – a human-Eathal half-breed – one of the servants of the Seer. He was the only living being on those radiant decks.

The men chained to the oars looked across at the glowing vessel in horror, many making the circle sign of the sun goddess

Larus for protection. Raziin grunted in annoyance. Larus was a god for weaklings – peasants.

'Bend to the oars! Follow the ghost-galley,' commanded Merceth.

Their galley lurched into motion. Above, the sky rumbled with the distant thunder of an approaching storm.

'Push them to the limit, Merceth,' said Raziin.

Merceth unslung the whip from his belt. 'Faster! *Faster!!*' he yelled. One man sat limply at the oars, fouling the stroke. The lash swept down across his back with a sharp crack, the tip cutting savagely across his exposed arm, ripping the flesh. He howled, throwing himself into the task. Another took the lash across the face; a cut opened across his right cheek. A curtain of blood immediately darkened his face. Unlike the first, he remained silent. Yet he too surged into the task. *And so pain becomes motion.* Twice more the lash fell. Soon they were racing through the darkness, running faster than they would have dared in daylight. Their tiller-man followed every twist and turn of the ghost-galley as it wove its path through the swamp.

Raziin walked back to his cabin and stretched himself out on the narrow cot, dropping immediately into sleep. In his dreams, the incoherent sounds of the glowmetal became the voices of tortured men and women, bleeding beneath his blade. He woke in the pre-dawn, refreshed.

Heavy cloud piled up across the sky, lit with the coming dawn. With a crack of thunder, the rain broke over them, savage and cold. The ghost-galley became insubstantial amid the grey torrent. Raziin welcomed the cool rain, and its freshness.

'Draw up closer to it, Merceth. We cannot afford to lose them now,' said Raziin.

'Yes, my Lord.'

Raziin revelled in the power within him, rekindled after the long dark hours of exhausted sleep. The stunted growth of the Melaut slowly gave way to small, densely-vegetated islands separated by open water. At last they were leaving the swamp behind.

Finally, as the unseen suns rose into the overcast sky, they reached the low islands that sealed the Melaut swamp from the

Yasser. In the distance, they could see the tall spires and bridges of Raynor.

The stroke faltered as the chained men glimpsed the great city in the distance, sensing the nearness of freedom. Let them have their moment of hope, thought Raziin. It will only heighten their despair when they realise the truth.

The ghost-galley slowed, turning to become a single line of brilliant white before disappearing entirely. Of the minitil, there was no sign.

The path was clear now. Raziin pulled the heavy sea-cloak tighter around him, warding off the chill as he watched the islands draw closer. He had banished the Heat. He had banished his Eathal master Hukum. He was compelled to travel to the Shattered Temple but, thanks to the golden glowmetal, the second half of Hukum's Compulsion would never reach his mind. Once at the Shattered Temple, he would be free to act. The Seer of Ciofran-Ac had opened the way for him as the dark goddess Uros had promised.

'Beach it, Merceth.'

The golden-skinned giant nodded. 'Yes, my Lord.'

The artefact the Seer had shown him could be none other than the Spear of Carris. The weapon the Cinanac had used to build their Empire. A weapon of immense power, it had been so rarely used most historians doubted its existence, thinking it a legend created by the Cinanac. The Eathal lived in fear of it, linking it to the Great Destruction of their ancient civilization. Now Raziin knew it existed. He grinned as he considered how he would taunt Hukum with its discovery. His breath came faster as he imagined that power at his command. A new Cioan Empire would dawn, one that placed the blood-goddess Uros in her proper place. And he – her chosen one – would have dominion over all.

Heavy squalls lashed down at the galley, beating at the exhausted men, but the lure of their freedom and the chance to leave the Melaut drove them on.

A jolt shook the galley as it beached on a low bank.

Here the craft would stay until the floods, when the low passage would open and it could be taken to Raynor. For now he and his men would strike out across the river in longboats, through the rain and the dangerous traffic that plied the Yasser river. First he had a price to pay: in blood.

Merceth approached him. 'Shall we release the men, Lord?'

'Leave them in chains.' Raziin's mouth was dry, his breath ragged with rising excitement. 'Kill them, Merceth, all except Dresil and his lackeys. We will need his Brotherhood contacts in Raynor.'

Merceth nodded and strode towards Raziin's black-clad warriors, giving curt orders.

Raziin's men bared their weapons, the grey-white lengths of lanedd ready to extinguish life with a cut or thrust. As though performing practice, they began the slaughter. Exhausted men screamed and pleaded, struggled pathetically in chains as their executioners worked their way through the ranks, leaving bloody death in their wake.

'Here is your salvation!' shouted Raziin. Blood covered the deck in a slick tide, washed away swiftly by the chill rain. He laughed with glee, walking close behind his men so he could watch the death of hope in each man's eyes.

As the last died, Raziin swept back his arms and raised his eyes to the unseen red sun. He alone knew the true heart of Uros. She was a savage goddess, a being of unparalleled lust and savagery.

'Take this gift, Uros. Give me strength, for there is more to follow.'

So much more.

Chapter Three

'Here we are, my lady. The seating reserved for the Suulvey.'

Ellen smiled at the page and sat at the empty table. She had been placed, to her relief, not far from the guests of honour. It was the position that would have been occupied by Uran's wife. The Sorcerer was trying to tempt her with hints of the privilege she would gain if they were married; and Ellen had to admit, it was a persuasive tactic. The self-proclaimed Scion, Osterac, and the Druids from Olcis would be only tables away. Uran himself, as the Warlord's closest adviser, would sit with him at the main table below the Emerald Throne. She hoped to get the chance to talk to Osterac and get some sense of the truth.

The Great Hall hummed with conversation. Sweat prickled beneath her heavy gown, and she fanned herself. The scents of spiced meats and perfume mingled in the heated air.

A servant filled her glass and she sipped tentatively on the wine, remembering her last adventure with the heavy red in Uran's apartments. Drinking too much, too quickly, had given her a heady sense of intoxication. She had become too intimate with the Sorcerer, allowing herself to see an ally and partner where there was only a Suul who wanted her as a brood mare to sire a line of Old Blood Sorcerers. She contented herself with watching the last of the Suulqua and the Suul take their seats further back from the dais. It was a feast for thousands, and the long tables sagged under the weight of food. Fine, delicately-tinted porcelains adorned every table, and the glasses were of the finest crystal, filled to the brim by willing servants.

A troupe of performers, clad in bright orange silks, ran into the room. Two took position, while the others ran towards them. Each was hurled high into the air, twirling with impressive skill. A collective 'Ooo!' went up from the crowd as each landed. Assistants raced in with a selection of blades and balls, which they began to juggle.

There was scattered applause.

The buzz of conversation rose a notch as the wine flowed and new arrivals packed the space between tables. Ellen tensed and instinctively reached for the fire as she saw flames gout into the air across the room. Realising it was another entertainer, a fire-eater this time, she laughed to herself. Still, it was important never to be too relaxed. The Athrian Temple still wanted her dead. She checked the position of the hidden throwing knife strapped to her thigh. *Good.* It was within easy reach.

The atmosphere was festive. What would it have been like, she mused, to have been here at the Empire's height, awaiting the arrival of the Emperor himself? She drained her glass and waved for more. She looked across at the Emerald Throne, which had been carved from a single gem for the first Emperor Carris more than two thousand years ago. The blocky base and thick arms conveyed a sense of solidity and strength, while the headrest, carved into the shape of a phoenix, gave a sense of menace; as though at any moment the phoenix would come to life and turn its head towards her. Once, the whole of Yos had bowed to the Bulvuran Empire, tribute flowing from every sardom and minor city-state.

A sharp dip in the conversation broke into her fantasy. Ellen looked across eagerly at the entrance to the Great Hall. A bodyguard of greatscythemen came first, surrounding the Warlord Daran. Although only of middle height, his presence radiated strength and command. His dark eyes swept across the court with focussed intelligence. Following the Warlord came the Suulvey, senior peers of the court, with Uran foremost amongst them, his silver eyes alert as he moved forward. Uran was striking in loose white linen trousers and a fine silver shirt that shimmered as he moved, contrasting his golden hair and skin. The cunningly-crafted shirt was open enough to show tattoos, but hid the lack of tone in his chest and stomach. The muscles between her shoulder blades bunched with tension as she remembered sitting next to him in his apartments, his chest bare, her own shirt open in the intimate custom, revealing her breasts.

Immediately following the Suulvey were Osterac and the Druids from Olcis led by the High Druid Ranlan. Two of the three High Druids, including Ranlan, were Templemen, Uros-Druids distinctive in their red robes. The third High Druid wore the dark robes of a Moon Druid and walked beside a yellow-robed Larus Druid. Six Temple Guardians flanked the Olcis delegation, their broad shields gleaming with lacquer, their long spears held at a precise angle. Ellen's friend Raphal trailed at the rear of the group, his brown scholar's robes flapping around his thin frame. A Larus Priest and Druid, Raphal had been confessor and spiritual guide to the Cintros family all through her childhood. He had been a second father to her, there for Ellen when her father Myan had been consumed with affairs of state. The kindly old man was not the least bit interested in politics, but he was an expert in the prophecies of the Scion, which was why Ranlan had insisted he join the Olcis delegation.

Osterac towered above the procession. As he drew closer, a jolt of excitement sent her heart racing. His features were perfectly proportioned, almost beautiful with dark curls and pale blue eyes. His shirt was open in the style of a warrior, revealing a lean, toned chest inscribed with finely-coloured tattoos. His skin glistened with oils. Warmth flooded her groin and her hand trembled slightly as she set down her glass. Her fingers lingered on the stem. *If he was the true Scion everything would be so much easier.*

How was she supposed to travel the roads of Kelas alone, chasing Cedrin? If there was any chance Osterac's claim was real, she had to stay and find out. A small voice inside her head berated her for taking the easy option, for staying amid luxury rather than risking the danger and uncertainty of the road, but she repressed it. She *would* follow Cedrin – she had promised her father that she would protect him – but first she needed to know if Osterac was the Cinanac heir. Ellen took another drink. The dry, almost bitter wine settled on her tongue. There was no doubting he was magnificent. Osterac *looked* like an Emperor.

Uran gave her a smile as he passed and Ellen returned it with as much warmth as she could muster. He moved on with the Suulvey, taking his place at the head table with Daran, Osterac and the Druids. She tried to catch Raphal's gaze, but he was too preoccupied.

Her table now rapidly filled with Suulvey from the procession, strangers who gave her appraising stares and made small talk with her while pointedly looking the other way. *Suul games*. Ellen was the newcomer here, her Athrian rank of Suulvey honorary at best. These high status Raynorians set out to demonstrate their social superiority almost as a reflex action. If she married Uran, their hostility would turn to obsequiousness in a moment. She did her best to ignore their barbed comments and was signalling a servant for more wine when the steward's staff rang out.

The Warlord stood, his dark eyes sweeping the room. Silence fell in an instant. There was no doubting who ruled in Raynor.

'This is the beginning of a new age.' Daran's voice boomed out across the open space. 'A new age of greatness for Raynor. Heralded by the arrival of one man.'

Daran let his words hang in the air. There could be no doubt who he was talking about.

'One man, supported by the ancient Temple of the Sisters. The Scion!' A cheer rose from the crowd, but he raised his hands for silence.

'And how do we know he is the true Scion? We know because the Temple of the Sisters, the Seat of Olcis, has given him its blessing. *We* believe because *Olcis* can be believed.' The Sisters' Druids flanking Osterac shifted uncomfortably.

'Impossible,' said Ellen under her breath. From what Estle had told her, there was simply no way Daran would give away control of Raynor. He was playing some game, he had to be. Yet how could he possibly prevent Osterac from taking power after a declaration like that?

For the first time, Ellen noticed the Yosini Druids that Daran usually surrounded himself with were absent. Followers of the earth-mother Yosini, also known as the Hidden Sun, they were sworn enemies of the Temple of the Sisters. Could they have fallen out of favour, perhaps?

'I have said enough,' said Daran. 'Let me say only one thing more. Raynor has always been ready to accept the true Scion, and now that the Sisters have given him to us, let us give him what he deserves!'

The people cheered, but uncertainly. Osterac raised himself as if to speak, but at a quick gesture from the High Druid Ranlan, he reseated himself and the moment passed. That one silent command cut through Ellen's fancies. She could hear Uran's voice. *He is nothing but an Olcis puppet.* With an angry growl, she pushed away her glass. The wines in Raynor were simply too good, and Osterac too perfect. She found herself watching him again, as Suulvey women flitted around him, fans darting in some birdlike mating code. What chance would she have to get him in conversation?

If Osterac did get control of Raynor, then it would be the Temple of the Sisters who would rule it, even if he was the Scion. A flame of anger lit within Ellen at the thought. The Temple of the Sisters had worked for centuries to create a stranglehold on magic. As soon as she had used her Sorcery to defeat Raziin, the Athrian Temple had issued a decree to take her under edict of Purge – a death sentence. She had barely escaped with her life.

A small army of servants entered the room, carrying the main course, roasted harena. Ellen had eaten nothing so far, and the succulent meat melted on her tongue.

'So how are you enjoying Raynor? Must be quite something coming from the provinces,' said the Suulvey lady sitting across from Ellen.

Ellen looked across at her. 'Provinces? Strange. I ruled Athria for a short time, and I was sure it was an independent sardom at the time.'

The woman snorted and turned away.

After the meal, the tables and settings were spirited away and a stringed ensemble began a dance tune. Daran and the High Druids moved through the crowd, the Larus Druid joining them.

Osterac was the first onto the floor, gliding across the marble faultlessly with a jewelled beauty in his hands. The wine soured in Ellen's belly, and she had a sudden urge to smash her glass.

'A dance, my Lady?' Ellen looked up to see a middle-aged Raynor Suul looking at her expectantly.

'Err … I must decline. Too much wine, I'm afraid.'

He scowled at her and stalked away, not even bothering to hide his annoyance. More Suul and Suulvey suitors asked her onto the floor, but she was in no mood for dancing and they soon stopped asking. Somehow she needed to get to Osterac.

Who could she ask for an introduction? Uran was at the Warlord's side, unreachable. She could see Estle on the floor, a stunning red-haired Suul in his hands. Ellen had no intention of going anywhere near Ranlan or the other High Druids – she had no love for the Temple – but she noticed Raphal standing alone at the edge of the dais. Ellen walked over to him.

'Ellen, good to see you.' Raphal's hands closed warmly around hers.

'And you, Raphal,' said Ellen, feeling part of the tension inside her unwind. It was good to see a familiar face. Raphal had been one of the key figures in her early life. She had missed him keenly after he left Athria to further his studies in Olcis. When she first arrived in Raynor, he had visited the Athrian consulate, using his gifts of healing to help ease her grief at the death of her father.

'Are you enjoying Raynor?' asked Ellen.

'Hmmm? Oh, yes. A fine library,' said Raphal.

Ellen smiled. It was typical of the scholar to see the world through the pages of some dusty codex.

'Any interesting books?' she asked.

Raphal cleared his throat with determination. 'Oh, yes. There is a fine volume on the foundation of the Empire written in the old style of Cioan. Interesting that the account differs from …' Raphal talked on in his soft voice, lost in his thoughts, while Ellen wondered how she could turn the conversation to the Scion. She could see no easy way. As part of the delegation, Raphal would answer no direct questions regarding Osterac.

'Raphal, how would I pass alone in the world?' asked Ellen.

He stopped mid-sentence and raised one of his bushy white eyebrows.

'How could I travel the roads without a cumbersome entourage?'

Raphal swept his hand back across his bald dome as he considered the problem, a gesture she remembered well from her youth. 'Well, let's see now. For someone like you, a Suul, to travel alone is strange. A Suul lord – or lady – on the roads is always bound to cause a stir.' He thought briefly then smiled. 'So you would not travel as a Suul. You would dress as a free woman of some appropriate trade or station and cover your Suul mark with something like a warrior's temple bracer ... or a leather band. And you must braid your hair well back.

'As to other problems. Hmm. You need a male escort. Someone who is tough and knows the streets. A woman alone makes too good a target, even if she can take care of herself.'

Ellen was sobered by that.

The music stopped and Osterac walked back towards the dais, women and men pressing him on all sides. He had already become a powerful political figure, even before his supposed installation as Emperor.

'Raphal, could you introduce me?' she said quickly.

'Of course.'

When Osterac passed by, Raphal caught his attention with a wave.

'I'm honoured to meet the Cinanac heir,' said Ellen, bowing slightly. She watched Osterac closely for his reaction.

Osterac returned her bow then gave her an appraising look. The same glance her former lover Palsus had given her when he stood revealed for what he was – a man who used her to get what he wanted. She tensed, sensing immediately that Osterac's charisma and his good looks were nothing but glitter, a smooth polish on the surface. She forced her smile wider, ensuring she presented a pleasant countenance. It was vital that none of her own thoughts or feelings showed.

'It must have been hard to grow up not being able to reveal yourself as the Cinanac heir,' said Ellen.

'Not at all. I always knew my destiny lay in Raynor,' said

Osterac smoothly. He leant in to her. His breath stank of wine. She forced herself to focus. Here was a chance to find out what his thoughts were on the major issues facing Kelas.

'So on the question of the Eathal ...,' she began. He turned away to smile at one of the young beauties from the dance floor and the words died in her throat.

'Eh?' he said, turning back.

'Well ... stand assured the Scion has my support,' said Ellen, harsher than she intended.

'Of course,' he said, then walked away.

Larus help us if he is the true Scion. The meeting had left her cold. It was hard now to imagine the sense of excitement she had felt only an hour ago.

Daran and Uran returned, followed by Osterac and the other Druids of the Olcis delegation. They gathered around the Warlord. Ellen, already standing with Raphal, hovered at the edge of the group. Osterac had taken one of the crystal wine decanters from a servant and was drinking from it like a flask.

'I think, noble Druids, it is high time the Scion received what is due to him,' said the Warlord.

Osterac leant forward eagerly.

Ranlan was wary. 'What, exactly, do you propose?'

Daran's face was unreadable. 'The people of Raynor have waited long enough. I have arranged a private ceremony to sign the formal documents installing Osterac as Emperor of the Yasser States.'

Osterac pushed through the Temple Guardians to Daran's side. 'Yes! Tonight!' he said, his face flushed with wine. 'Let it be tonight!'

Ranlan rounded on Osterac. 'Be silent! The signing and the coronation must *both* be public.'

Osterac turned pale. 'You forget with whom you speak,' he said to Ranlan, tapping his chest with the decanter. '*I* am the Scion and *I* say tonight.'

Ranlan and Osterac glared at each other. Ranlan darted a glance at Daran and Uran and Ellen saw a flash of fear in his eyes. The High Druid's face flushed red and he sagged.

'Please, my Lord Osterac,' said Ranlan, stepping towards

him. 'Don't you want every Suul in Raynor to see your investiture?'

Osterac straightened, looking down at Ranlan. His mouth twisted into a superior sneer. 'The Raynor Suul will see me as Emperor soon enough.' He turned to Daran. 'When will the coronation follow?'

'If we sign the documents tonight, you will sit on the Emerald Throne within two days.'

'Before the end of Storm Season! So be it,' said Osterac, magnanimously.

Ranlan stared silently at Osterac, his jaw clenched. He turned back to the Warlord. 'We must all be present. Including the Temple Guardians.'

Daran nodded. 'Of course.'

'And your own bodyguard is to remain here,' said Ranlan.

The Warlord hesitated. A smile teased at the corners of Ranlan's mouth.

'Very well,' said Daran, his tone subdued.

Ranlan straightened, recovering some of his poise.

Osterac pushed in front of the High Druid impatiently. 'Let's have done with this. There are many at the feast awaiting my attention.' He looked back over his shoulder, and Ellen followed his gaze to the young Suulvey woman.

Daran signalled his men and doors opened behind the throne, high on the dais.

'This way, my liege,' said Daran, bowing to Osterac.

Swaggering, Osterac walked up onto the dais, past the throne and into the chamber. The Olcis Druids and Temple Guardians followed.

'Farewell, Ellen,' said Raphal, joining them.

'Goodbye,' said Ellen.

Her view was abruptly cut by the solid torsos of Daran's bodyguard as they formed a line below the dais, blocking her access to the chamber. The small crowd of Suulvey who had gathered nearby surged forward, but they too were pushed back.

Ellen lifted herself onto her toes, catching a brief glimpse of an octagonal chamber with seven closed doors. The Temple

Guardians, spears and shields held ready, surrounded the Olcis delegation, eyes alert.

Then the doors closed.

The crowd of supplicants soon dispersed, leaving her alone by the dais with the silent bodyguards.

Only weeks ago, Ellen had been a lowly Suulqua, with no more responsibility than managing a score of scribes. She had been happy, keeping the secret of the Sorcery she and her father had shared. Then the unthinkable: her father assassinated, declaring her heir before his death; an awesome responsibility she had been ready to shoulder. She had only a brief taste of power before the attack on Regent's Hill. Now she was powerless once more, and without allies. Alone in her quest for truth.

She glanced up at the Emerald Throne, imagining Osterac seated there in fine clothes, a conceited expression on his face. Her fists clenched. Her head pounded as the last effects of the wine left her.

She pushed through the crowd towards her rooms, leaving the Great Hall and the strains of a new melody far behind her.

* * *

Two Suulqua pages shut the doors behind the Scion's entourage.

Daran fought to keep the triumph from showing on his face. Osterac was even more of a conceited fool than he had imagined. The idiot had fallen for his very first gambit. It made a mockery of all the late-night hours he and Uran had wasted planning.

Daran nodded to Uran and they flattened themselves against the walls, careful to avoid the holes installed only yesterday.

One instant later the room was filled with yellow-feathered darts. The tiny projectiles hit their targets with uncanny accuracy. Ranlan was the first to fall, peppered with four darts. The Druids and Guardians had time only to widen their eyes before the drug took effect.

Osterac was left standing alone in front of the tangle of bodies.

'What is this?' he demanded, his voice high-pitched with tension.

The doors opened, admitting a score of Daran's elite scythemen and seven *Druidin* – a new class of Druid he and Uran had created who gave allegiance only to Raynor. They carefully removed the darts and the Warlord advanced slowly towards Osterac. His stomach churned with fury. For this pretender, he had nothing but contempt.

Daran's hand lashed out, taking Osterac across the face. Osterac staggered back a pace, his eyes wide with shock.

'I'll tell you what this is, you stuffed popinjay. This is your undoing.'

Daran waved. Two burly scythemen advanced across the room. One carried a large cloth sack, the other a blowpipe. 'You know what to do,' he said to them.

One scytheman raised a blowpipe, sending a dart expertly into Osterac's cheek. The tall Suul swayed and collapsed onto the floor, unconscious. Casually they bundled Osterac into the sack and carried him away, flanked by half of the scythemen.

Daran waited, his heart racing. Uran had pleaded with him to leave before the High Druids roused – they were powerful magic users in their own right – but he had to be here. Had to see the look on Ranlan's face when he realised Osterac was gone.

He looked across at Uran. The Sorcerer was watching the Druids carefully.

'So far so good,' said the Warlord.

'So far,' said Uran, but his eyes never left the five Druids.

* * *

Ranlan gasped. The side of his jaw throbbed with pain. He was lying on his side on a marble floor, the members of his delegation and the Temple Guardians all prostrate on the floor beside him.

His awareness sharpened, memories rushing through him. The feast – Osterac demanding to proceed with the signing. Darts.

Ranlan pushed himself to his feet, still unsteady from the effects of the sedative.

The Warlord glared back at him, his dark eyes gleaming with amusement. He was flanked by ten scytheman and seven men in dark robes, three of whom wore the hollow-disk pendant of Yosini. His lip curled in disgust.

He looked around the room, his eyes searching feverishly for Osterac. Gone!

Ranlan rounded on Daran, shaking his fist in fury. 'You have overstepped yourself this time!'

Osterac had led them into a trap. The man's arrogance and conceit were boundless, and the fawning crowd had loosened Ranlan's control over him. He should have foreseen it. With so many witnesses, there was nothing Ranlan could do to bring Osterac to heel without destroying his credibility. He had thought when he demanded Daran's bodyguard remain behind he had ensured their own safety. With the support of many of the factions in Raynor, and the populace, Ranlan had never imagined Daran would be bold enough to attack them directly.

Ranlan gathered his power, tapping the strength of the red sun Uros – at its height now during Storm Season. He woke his fellow Druids and Guardians with skilful touches of magic. Now Daran would rue his boldness!

'Meet my Druidin, Ranlan,' said Daran.

The seven dark-robed figures now stepped forward. Ranlan immediately sensed their draw on the red sun's power. Ranlan watched incredulously. He had no idea the Druids Daran had gathered under his banner – the *Druidin* his spies told him of – were so advanced, or so numerous. Now, in the late afternoon, the Moon Druids with him would be useless. He and his fellow Templemen were masters of their art, but right here – faced with seven skilful practitioners – they were well matched. And there was Uran. The hated Sorcerer stared back at him, his silver eyes impassive, alert for any attack.

Daran had outwitted him. Considered his every move and countered it. Curse Osterac! Frustration churned within him, and he fought with the urge to attack Daran. It would achieve nothing, he knew, yet he longed to see the jumped-up legionary humbled.

The Guardians circled, ready to defend them, but Daran's scythemen made no move to attack. There was no need. The Warlord already had what he wanted. *Osterac.*

The High Druid advanced on Daran. 'Where is the Scion?' he demanded.

Daran smiled and examined his fingers as though bored, finally looking the Druid in the eye. 'Ranlan, you have no power here. You release your men to search *my* palace and I will have them quartered and fed to the harena. And you can take that as a prophecy.'

'You cannot hold the Scion. Raynor will destroy you if you so much as bruise him.'

'I'm not holding him,' said Daran with complete innocence. 'If he chooses to wander *his* palace, who am I to stop him? I'm sure he'll appear though. Perhaps in some slave boy's bed or lying in the Palardos in a drunken stupor. I'll have my servants keep an eye out for him.'

With that, Daran left, his Druidin and scythemen flanking him. The moment was gone and Ranlan had lost.

Suppressing his rage, the High Templeman stormed out of the room, stalking though the palace corridors in the direction of their Olcis apartments.

'I want Daran and his aides watched night and day. Alert our spies in the palace, all of them. Osterac must be found.' He looked around the corridor to ensure their privacy. 'Before the weak-minded fool says too much.'

Daran was taking a terrible risk with this abduction. There must be a way to turn this around on the Warlord. *By the Sisters and the holy Seat of Olcis, he will not get away with this!*

* * *

Osterac came to consciousness slowly, as though drifting into a bizarre nightmare. Soon he would awaken, he was sure, to a soft bed and soft flesh. Was the wine in Raynor so bad that he should dream like this? The room was dark, grey, and full of old gritty shadows like an endless predawn.

Eventually, pain broke the wishful spell. Osterac came to realise the throbbing ache in his head and the cruelly tightened ropes that held him to the wall by throat, wrists and ankles were real. With the shock of the rudely awakened, he remembered those terror-filled moments in the Warlord's throne chamber. The Druids falling, the Warlord turning to strike him …

'Uhh!' The realisation was like a blow to the stomach, and all at once he knew where he was: in a torture chamber. Osterac pulled at his bonds, struggling to free himself. He was a strong man and worked the ropes with manic determination, but they would not give. He studied the knots, puzzling out some way to untie them, but they were out of reach. His wrists had been covered by sleeves of rubber. He thought that strange at first, until he understood. The rubber was to keep the bonds from marking him. A surge of confidence flowed back into him. *They intend to release me.* He pulled at the bonds anyway.

'It won't do you any good, Anacian.'

Osterac ceased his struggles and peered into the gloom.

'Where am I?' He was shocked to hear the pathetic, pleading note in his voice. He swallowed, trying to put the force of command into it. 'You can't hold the Scion.' Yes, that was better.

His head turned left and right to catch a glimpse of his tormentor. 'Do you know who I am? I am Osterac Cinanac. Protected by the Hesguit of Olcis himself!'

The unseen man laughed contemptuously, walking out into the sparse torchlight. A snake of fear uncoiled in Osterac's stomach, and the urge to urinate was suddenly overpowering. He shivered.

'Who … who are you?'

The man did not answer. Osterac squinted in the gloom. He could see he was clothed like a Druid, a fact that confused him until he saw the hollow-disk sigil of the Hidden Sun. One of the Yosini Druids was to be his torturer. Osterac could see the faint golden tinge to his skin.

'Don't cry for Olcis, little man. The Cioan's were building Temples when the Anacians were grubbing in the dirt.'

Osterac's bladder throbbed, demanding release.

'You cannot mark me, Druid.' Osterac put as much force as he could muster into his voice. 'Not after the Warlord's declaration. If you so much as touch me, we will have all the proof we need. You, the Warlord and all your *Druidin* will sink in the same ship.'

The Yosini Druid laughed again. 'You really think you can threaten us, you primped up pretty boy? It is past the time for that sort of talk.' The Druid disappeared into the dark once more.

Osterac growled and pulled at his bonds in impotent fury. It was useless.

'If you set me free you will be rewarded.' Osterac raised his voice to fill the room. 'Set me free. Take me to the Olcis Druids and you shall be rewarded beyond your dreams. We can protect you, shield you.' Sweat prickled beneath his scalp and on his forehead, cooling immediately in the chill air.

The Yosini Druid not reply. He walked forward from the dark with a long polished box of dark wood. He laid it reverently onto a bench and opened the lid, drawing aside a soft purple cloth. Beneath was the distinctive glimmer of a glowmetal – a jagged crystal of gold metal and violet light.

The Druid's fingers rested lovingly on the glowmetal as he raised it from its case. The stunning purple shifted and strengthened at his touch. Osterac had seen many glowmetals used, and guessed this one must respond to the Essence the Druid fed it.

'To be used for such a purpose is sacrilege. Yet sacrifices must be made,' whispered the Druid. He closed his eyes in prayer. 'Forgive me.'

Cradling the glowmetal, the Druid closed on him.

'You are so arrogant,' said the Druid, his voice soft and low. 'Olcis has had its day. Do you think you are immune? Do you think the Warlord too stupid to understand the threat?'

The Yosini Druid came to a halt one pace away from Osterac. 'Do you think he would let you enter Raynor and take it away from him?'

The Druid shook his head and lifted the glowmetal before him as though giving reverence to a sacred chalice.

Osterac watched as the power within it built, the bright bands of violet light giving way to gold. He drew a shuddering breath. 'What are you going to do? *What do you want?*' he screamed.

'Who are you?' countered the Druid.

Osterac was sweating profusely now. Beads of it rolled down his forehead, into his eyebrows and down into his eyes. It stung. He tried to blink it away. He gave a nervous laugh.

'I am Osterac Cinanac, son of ... *Ahhh!*'

A blue-white arc of electricity lashed across the dividing space, forking like a living thing to enter his body through eyes and mouth, momentarily blinding him. But the blindness was nothing compared to the pain – every muscle clenched like a tight fist and the pain of release was excruciating.

'Please, please! Stop it! I can make you a rich man. A rich man! I have wealth. Coin, gems, all hoarded in Olcis. Please I beg you ...'

'You think I took this abhorrent duty for money?' hissed the Yosini Druid. 'Who are you!'

Osterac looked around wild-eyed, seeking for a way out.

With a vivid flash, the glowmetal struck once more.

Osterac was impaled on the arc, tossed like a harena's prey from the brilliant horn and thrown into a sea of pain and darkness. The agony was so intense he made no sound, just jerked and flapped in his bonds like a loose sail, his body out of control, his mouth open in a silent scream.

Then mercifully, the pain lessened. He was aware of a warmth in his groin and legs, and realised his bladder had opened. He hardly cared. All that mattered was release from that awful pain.

All at once his voice was returned to him, and he screamed, on and on until the last of the pain was gone. He sobbed in relief, his dignity gone.

He had been trained as a Suul warrior in Olcis. The training had been hard, punishing, but never had he felt pain like this. His body quivered. He could not endure it again. He knew that.

'Who are you?'

'Resius ... Osterac Resius. A Suulqua of Olcis.' He slumped in his bonds as the enormity of what he had just revealed dawned on him. All his life he had been prepared for the role of Scion, schooled in the history of the Cinanac Emperors and Raynor, their capital, until he believed he really *was* the Scion. After all, who deserved it more than he did? The Imperial line was ended. The Resius family could trace an unbroken line of ancestry all the way back to Carris himself. Raynor was still within his grasp. They knew his identity but what did it matter; the people thought he was the Scion.

'Where did you get this?'

Osterac struggled to stand, his body trembling with the effort. With difficulty he focussed on the ruby signet ring of the Cinanac, held between the Druid's fingers.

'It was found at the Serpent's Tongue, by divination,' said Osterac, gaining confidence once more. 'By the Moon Druids of Olcis. They found the spot where Emperor Riin died.'

The Druid nodded. He laid his glowmetal in the case and closed the lid, a grim smile on his face. Osterac had never felt such relief. A surge of confidence flowed through him.

'The knowledge will avail you nothing. The people still believe I am the Scion, nothing can change that.' *Nothing can stop Olcis from taking Raynor.*

The Yosini Druid met his eyes briefly. 'You are wrong, little mannequin, everything will change now.'

Seizing the box, the Druid walked into the darkness, slumped as though carrying a heavy weight. A door opened, and in the light of the corridor Osterac saw two big men framed in silhouette.

'Make sure he is clean, dressed and drunk before you deliver him to the Temple Druids. He must look very comfortable when you deliver him. Remember, you found him in the east wing with a serving girl, understand?'

Both men nodded, smiling. They were clearly enjoying themselves. Osterac struggled against his bonds. *Worms!* They would be the first to die when he took the Emerald Throne.

Nothing could keep him from his destiny.

* * *

Ranlan paced his room, his mind racing. With Daran's declaration at the feast, they should be in a stronger a position than ever. Yet with Osterac in the hands of the Warlord, nothing was certain. *Damn Osterac, that preening fool!*

One of his aides sat nearby, adding the customary closing flourishes to a letter to the Hesguit that he had just finished dictating. Like him, the aide was dressed in the red robes of a Templeman. His aides were all talented Uros Druids, but none yet wore the sigil of Uros, not having taken their final vows. He had deliberately delayed their advancement in anticipation of the delegation to Raynor – so that their real magical strength here lay hidden. Two Temple Guardians flanked the doors. Here in his apartments he was secure. Daran's spies, informants and assassins would never reach him. He shivered as he remembered the rain of darts flying through the throne chamber.

He paused at a window, looking down through the clearglass at the distant Yasser. Dawn already, with both suns in the sky. Dark clouds were building in the south. The view was partially distorted. He tapped the pane. Poor quality. The windows in his own luxurious apartments in the Citadel in Olcis were far superior. The docks, located at the junction of the Asog and Yasser rivers, were hidden by the mass of the sprawling palace. News reached him less than an hour ago that the men he had bribed to ensure a quick getaway on his battle-barge had mysteriously disappeared. There would be no quiet escape now. If things turned sour their only option would be an official exit. Ranlan ground his teeth, the muscles in his jaw bunching with tension. A retreat this soon after Daran's declaration would be tantamount to publicly admitting Osterac was a fake.

When he had planned the details months ago, he had been confident of the magical strength he could apply here in Raynor, but he had been forced to rapidly alter his assessment. No Druids from the Sisters' Temples in Raynor were allowed within the palace – he could barely get messages to them. And Daran was surrounded by these *Druidin* ... and that unholy Sorcerer Uran. What if the unthinkable happened? What if Osterac had been tortured into making a deal and he was stuck here? Trapped, and under the power of Daran and Uran? The support he had expected from factions within the Warlord's court was slow in coming, despite his generous bribes.

Ranlan growled and spun on his heel, resuming his pacing. It had been a long, anxious night, waiting for news of Osterac. He dare not report to his master, the Hesguit, with anything but success – and losing Osterac to the Warlord was a disaster. Osterac had been rigorously equipped for this assignment, schooled in the history of the Cinanac, given the best tutors and weapons training. They had spent months preparing him for every conversational scenario. Yet how do you prepare someone for torture? A muscle twitched in Ranlan's temple.

Surely he had covered everything. The Warlord dare not kill Osterac outright. The outcry would turn Raynor into a battleground and threaten to topple Daran from power. Ranlan's own agents would ensure the chaos tore the city apart. The wealth of Olcis would see another Warlord more sympathetic to the Temple of the Sisters on the throne of the Yasser States within months. More likely he would torture Osterac for information. If so, Ranlan was well prepared. He had drafted a damning speech he could deliver in the main court that would swing the Suul to his side. He could picture himself there – drawn up in the majesty of Olcis and righteous anger – as Osterac displayed the bruises and marks of his ordeal.

He smiled. He did not know what game Daran was playing, but he had played into their hands by making the public declaration. Nothing could stop them gaining control of Raynor.

The door to his apartment opened, and another of his aides entered. Catching sight of Ranlan, the man bowed. 'Your eminence. The *messenger* has arrived.'

'Send her in.'

'Yes, your grace.'

The *messenger* was an Olcis spy inside the Warlord's own household. One of a carefully placed network that he had been building here for years – some were even Suulqua. With the abduction of Osterac he had activated them all. His other High Druids had argued against it, fearing their exposure, but he had overruled them. Ranlan was convinced that if they did not put Osterac on the throne, the Temple was finished in Raynor. All was balanced on a point, with a steep slope to success on one side and a swift plunge to utter failure on the other. Unfortunately his brother Druids had been right – despite all his precautions, his spies were disappearing faster than ice in summer. But how was Daran finding out?

Ranlan poured himself a generous glass of wine. Usually he would abstain from strong drink, but he needed something to calm his nerves.

The spy was a serving woman of middle-age, holding a scrap of parchment. His aide stopped his writing and walked over to her, taking the dummy message from her hands. The aide checked her for weapons, looking carefully at her face as he did so.

'So, what do you have for me?' snapped Ranlan. He had not taken a moment of sleep, and it was beginning to tell.

The woman swallowed nervously. 'The Warlord and Uran have been in the Warlord's chambers all night, my Lord.'

'Don't call me Lord! It is *your eminence* or *your grace*. I am no Suul, I am an Olcis High Druid. A High Templeman. You understand?'

The woman cowered, bowing low. Ranlan's temper eased.

'What have they been doing? Their conversation. What have they been talking about?' he asked, convinced Osterac's whereabouts must have been betrayed.

The woman brightened. 'They have been drinking and singing songs all night long my ... your grace. Daran has been playing the lute and Uran singing. Warrior's songs,' she said. 'Bawdy tales. Uran has a fine singing voice ...'

'Is that all?' Ranlan's voice tightened with fury.

Startled, she nodded swiftly.

'Out! *Out of my sight!*' The woman fled.

Ranlan threw the glass at the wall. It shattered with a dull crack, splashing the plastered wall with red.

His aide patiently picked up the pieces of glass, then used a cloth to wipe down the wall. The young Templeman had been at his side all night, leaving only for brief periods of rest. It was gratifying to see such loyalty. This young aide was one of his most promising pupils, and Ranlan had been hard on him. The young Druid should have had his sigil years ago, but it suited Ranlan to have him as a servant. The fact that the young Druid had managed to swallow his resentment showed a fine character. The future of Olcis would be defined by young men such as this.

Ranlan tipped the flask of wine, pouring himself another glass. He was just about to drink when another of his Templemen aides rushed into the room in an excited flurry. 'He's back! Two palace men escorted him to the apartments. They said they found him with a serving girl.'

'Is he harmed?' asked Ranlan.

'No, your eminence. He is drunk, his clothes have been exchanged for finer ones, but there is not a mark on him. He is in good cheer.'

Ranlan winced as his heartburn flared. His stomach felt suddenly full, and he put down the wine, grimacing at the familiar discomfort. He would be unable to take food for hours now. 'Unharmed?'

'Yes, your eminence.'

'Send him in.'

Unharmed? Why would the Warlord abduct Osterac and release him again without torturing him?

The muscle in Ranlan's temple continued to twitch and he massaged it as he waited.

Osterac swayed as he entered. Ranlan studied him carefully, looking for the tell-tale signs of torture. He could see nothing but fatigue. He seemed, perhaps, a little less sure of himself.

'Quickly. Tell me what happened,' demanded Ranlan.

'They tortured me,' said Osterac, sinking into a chair near his table. Even from here Ranlan could smell the strong drink on him. Bakta, if he was not mistaken.

'Really,' said Ranlan, his anger growing. A sleepless night spent making and discarding plans, and here he was, drunk!

'Yes!' Osterac paled, and his hand flew to his mouth. He ran to the fireplace and vomited violently across the marble.

'Arghh! Save us.' Ranlan's own hand covered his nose

against the tell-tale reek of alcohol and vomit. Osterac continued to throw up until there was nothing left in his stomach.

Ranlan's aide helped Osterac back to a chair, giving him a cloth to wipe his mouth.

'Clean that up,' snapped Ranlan. It was a lowly task, but security was too vital to allow even a slave into his apartments.

His aide nodded, his expression one of blank servility. 'Yes, your eminence.'

Osterac lifted his head with difficulty. His eyes were bloodshot, his words heavily slurred.

'A Druid tortured me, a Yosini Druid. One of Daran's assistants. He used a glow ... a glow ... a glowmetal.'

'And then you went drinking afterwards?'

'They forced it into me!'

'Then where are the marks, you fool! Where is your skin broken? Bruised? Hmm?'

'The glowmetal ... was ...' Osterac's stomach convulsed, and he leant forward, dry-retching, making horrible sucking, choking sounds. He sank back into the chair, his chin glistening with bile.

Ranlan's lip curled in disgust. 'Let me guess. It was a magical torturing device, which caused you immeasurable pain, but left you completely untouched?'

Osterac's face flushed red. His glassy eyes pleaded for forgiveness. 'Yes. You have to understand. It was terrible ... terrible.'

'And it was a Druid of Yosini?' The discomfort in Ranlan's stomach blossomed into pain.

'Yes.'

'What did you tell them?'

Osterac's bloodshot eyes met Ranlan's for an instant, then darted away. 'Nothing.'

Nothing? Now Ranlan knew the man was lying. He seethed with anger. It was Osterac's belligerent insistence that he attend the 'signing' that had created this mess in the first place.

Osterac's story was absurd. A Druid of Yosini torturing him? It was against their creed. What a simpleton Osterac was. Any Druid could have told him: for a follower of Yosini to cause pain was to invite damnation. What stupid beliefs. A Yosini Druid as a torturer? Impossible.

Osterac rubbed his face with his hands. Ranlan's eyes swept across the fingers, unconsciously searching for something that was not there. His stomach convulsed, sending hot acid into his throat.

'Goddess have mercy! The ring. *Where is it?'* said Ranlan.

Osterac looked down at the table. 'They took it.'

'You fool!' Ranlan looked at Osterac with pure venom. 'Do you have the slightest idea what you have done? What we went through to get that ring? It was our one incontrovertible link to the Cinanac!'

Osterac's eyelids fluttered and he slumped forward. His head thudded onto the table and he began to snore loudly.

Ranlan could picture the Warlord in court, demanding to know where the ring was, intimating that it was a fake all along while he himself had possession of it.

'You damn fool!' Ranlan's contempt for Osterac flowered into hate. They had been so close. So close! If only Osterac had kept his monumental pride in check for one more week. He grimaced. One of the leading lights of a new generation of Olcis Suul in the court of the Hesguit, Osterac was always going to be hard to control.

As he watched the unconscious man, a chilling possibility occurred to him. What if Osterac had made a deal with the Warlord? Was it Osterac himself who had revealed the information about their spies? If so, he and his Temple Druids would be captured or destroyed by the Warlord before Ranlan could discover the truth. But what could the Warlord have possibly offered Osterac that could make him turn, with the whole of Raynor soon to be his? Doubt began to gnaw at Ranlan.

His aide was still busy trying to wipe up Osterac's mess. 'Leave that. Gather the delegation Druids and bring them here.'

He looked back to Osterac, snoring on the table. They had to be prepared for all possibilities.

Ranlan resumed his pacing. If Osterac had betrayed them, he would have to act quickly, before any plans he had formed with the Warlord could be brought to fruition.

The door opened, and his aide ushered in the four other Druids that had accompanied him from Olcis. The two other High Druids entered first, one a red-robed High Templeman like Ranlan, the other a tolerated representative of the Moon Druids. Following were the Larus Druid and their scholar Raphal, who was a Larus Druid and Priest.

The aide resumed his task of cleaning the mess near the fire. Ranlan ignored him.

'Thank you for coming, brothers.'

'So Osterac is back in our control, excellent. Where did our agents find him?' asked the High Templeman.

Ranlan grunted. 'He was returned by two palace servants, reeking of alcohol.'

'A ruse, surely. Was he tortured by the Warlord?' asked the Moon Druid.

Ranlan grunted. 'There is no mark on him. The only thing we know for sure is that the Warlord now has the Cinanac ring.'

'By the Sisters!' said the High Templeman.

'We could present the truth. Reveal to all how the Warlord abducted Osterac,' said the Moon Druid.

'He is unmarked. After the Warlord's performance in the court, who would believe us?' said Ranlan.

'We could have a copy of the ring made,' said the Larus Druid.

'And be accused of presenting a fake? I think not,' said Ranlan.

Ranlan took a slow breath to steady himself, then switched to the obscure dialect of ancient Anacian that the clergy of Olcis used as a secret language.

'Many of our spies have gone missing over the course of the night. The men we stationed at the docks have also disappeared. Someone provided that information.' Ranlan's eyes flicked over to Osterac.

'Why would Osterac do such a thing? He still has everything to gain,' said the Larus Druid.

'Bickering about this will solve nothing. We need him Tested,' said the Moon Druid.

'Easier said than done,' said Raphal. 'The only holy ground I know of in Raynor is the Temple of Mythar, well outside the palace. How do we get him there? The Warlord has sealed the doors against us.'

Ranlan looked across at Osterac, asleep on the table. The fool was in a drunken stupor while their plans fell around them. He turned back to his Druids.

'What if Osterac has made a deal? Can we risk a delay? If it was ever discovered Olcis had backed a false-Scion we would be finished in the Yasser States, our reputation in Kelas damaged beyond repair.'

'What exactly are you suggesting?' asked the Moon Druid.

Ralan lowered his voice. 'You all know what I am talking about. We have a plan in place for this very possibility.'

'Kill him? Are you mad? Now – after Daran has made the declaration?' said the Moon Druid.

'We need to be prepared,' said Ranlan stubbornly. He refused to be squeamish. 'We would arrange it as an unfortunate accident that reeks of assassination. The death of the true Scion would be a tragedy for all. We must be careful to place the blame squarely on the Warlord's shoulders. The resulting tensions will rip the city apart. Hopefully there is not too much damage done before our own factions take power.'

'Assassinating the Warlord – that is the tricky part,' said the High Templeman.

'Indeed,' said Ranlan. 'The timing will be crucial.' And they talked on.

Lying with his head on the table, Osterac tried desperately to still his heart and continue to snore. He had learnt the secret Anacian dialect in his youth, almost as a boy's prank. He had a gift for languages and it was useful to know what his masters said when they thought he could not hear. Never would he have dreamed the skill would one day save his life.

He could not believe the same Druids who had prepared him for the role of Scion over these past years were now talking calmly of his death. Now it was they, not the Warlord, who plotted against him. His head thumped with tension. Sheer frustration threatened to break his control. It was his destiny to have the Emerald Throne, and he could not let anything threaten that – including these Druids. He would have to get out of Raynor, raise his own base of support and return again – this time as his own man.

First he had to get to the Warlord and make a deal.

Chapter Four

'This is it,' said Cedrin.

The house was a three-storey wooden structure, squat and solidly built, well shuttered against the last of the Storm Season cold. The faded paint and sun-bleached timbers gave it a neglected aspect, and there was nothing to indicate that it was a major stronghold of the Brotherhood in Raynor. Cedrin thumped on the door and waited. There was no going back now.

The sound of the bolt being drawn was like a whip crack. The heavy wooden door opened a fraction, and a flood of warm air escaped through the doorway, carrying with it the enticing smell of se-tobacco. A man's broad face appeared in the gap, his thick jacket open to show five degrees of the calvanni. It was Galvis, a senior Brotherhood man in Raynor, who had been Cedrin's primary Smuggling contact for more than five years. Cedrin could see his pupils were dilated by the effects of the se-tobacco.

'Good to see you, Galvis. Keeping well?'

Galvis winced out at the daylight, unable to focus on Cedrin for a moment. The fifth degree's eyes widened when he recognised him.

'Cedrin, by the … You should not be here,' said Galvis.

Thunder rumbled in the distance, and a chill wind swept through the streets ahead of the rain.

'I'm not surprised you would say that, considering all the money you owe me,' said Cedrin, keeping his tone light.

Galvis looked up and down the street. The cracked

pavements were deserted. He leant closer to Cedrin and spoke in a harsh whisper. 'You don't understand —'

'Who is it?' It was a man's voice, low and cold. The speaker was still in the shadows of the corridor.

Galvis' face set hard, and he opened the door wider. 'Cedrin and Marken. Brothers from Athria.'

A tall, thin man stepped into the light. He was smiling, but his eyes were sharp, predatory. Cedrin immediately tensed. The tall man wore a tight-fitting leather coat that concealed his chest tattoos.

'Invite them in. After all – we don't want to let all the warm air out do we?' The man's face was lined and hard, his accent Raynorian.

'Come in,' said Galvis gruffly. He did not meet Cedrin's eyes as he and Marken squeezed through. A bolt of adrenalin sent Cedrin's heart racing. Galvis' reaction confirmed his worst fears. The Athrian Mask of Smuggling had reached Raynor – and the word was out. He and Marken were marked men. Outwardly he remained calm, but his skin was crawling. *They had to get what they came for and out of here. Fast.*

Galvis bolted the door behind them. Cedrin smelled a trap, but it was too late to do anything but play things through.

Cedrin had been in this house many times and knew the layout well. He, Galvis and his connections from the Raynor Brotherhood had shared many good times here. For years he had made the trip across from Athria with Skye, and then later Marken, to organise shipments. It had come to feel almost as familiar as his old Athrian haunts, yet now it felt like he was walking into it for the first time.

The tall man led them down a dim corridor into a low-ceilinged room lit by three oil lamps. Inside there was a table spread with bowls of se-tobacco and discarded pipes. Eight chairs were drawn up around the table, but the room was empty. Three of the pipes sat in ashtrays, their bowls still smoking. Whoever had been in the room had left quickly. The far doorway was covered with a bead curtain that still swayed with someone's passage.

'Sit,' said the tall man. He did not offer his name, and Cedrin knew better than to ask.

Galvis sat across from them, which Cedrin thought was odd until three women pushed their way through the curtain. They had long flowing skirts, their shirts open to reveal their chests. Each had a flower-tattoo beneath their left breast – the sign of the courtesan. They smiled as they came forward, but their eyes were hard and watchful.

'Well, never let it be said you stinted on a welcome,' said Cedrin, watching the women. They were small-busted for whores. Still, that may only reflect their host's taste in women, he thought.

The three courtesans moved in, one pushing Marken aside so she could sit between them. She leant in close to Cedrin and rubbed her hand across his thigh, smiling suggestively. Another stood behind him and began to massage his neck. Her fingers were strong, kneading into his muscles with swift, sure movements. He couldn't remember the last time he got a massage like that from a courtesan – they were usually skilled enough, but lacked the strength. The third courtesan was massaging Marken's neck, also standing behind him. At any other time Cedrin would have been pleased with the attention, but he remained on edge. He could feel the muscles of his neck resisting the woman's attempts to relax them.

'So, what business brings you to our humble house?' said the tall man. He sat beside Galvis, on the other side of the table.

Cedrin had planned to make small talk, leading up to asking for the money, but he had to move quickly.

'I won't take up much of your time. We are just here to pick up the profits from our last shipment,' said Cedrin.

'And take them back to the Brotherhood in Athria?' asked the tall man, his face impassive.

'Of course,' said Cedrin.

The man nodded. 'So. Nothing else then?'

Cedrin shook his head. 'Like I said. If you will give us the coin, we'll be on our way.' His shoulders tensed, and he was acutely aware of the woman's hands on his neck.

'Nonsense. We can't throw you out into the cold on a day like today. There's a big storm rolling in from across the river.

Best to stay,' said the tall man. 'Besides, there is someone who would like to meet you.'

'Who?' asked Cedrin.

The tall man smiled. This time he was genuinely amused – something that was less than comforting. 'Now, I can't tell you that, can I? It would spoil the surprise. Galvis, you may as well get the coin. Bring some bakta for our guests as well.'

Cedrin winced as a rough spot on the courtesan's palm scratched his skin. *Rough spot?* When was the last time he met a courtesan with rough hands?

'Now. While we wait, why not take a pipe, eh?' said the tall man, reaching across and lifting one of the smoking se-pipes.

Marken looked across to him. Cedrin shook his head slightly.

'No, thank you. I'm trying to cut down,' said Cedrin.

'Me too,' said Marken.

'Suit yourselves,' said the tall man, drawing back on the se-tobacco and exhaling a cloud of the pungent smoke.

Cedrin looked across at the courtesan beside him and smiled. She smiled back automatically. He could feel the lean muscle in her arms as she leant against him, muscle a courtesan would have no cause to build. He reached down and took hold of the hand massaging his thigh, his thumb absently brushing across her palm. Just as he thought. *Calluses.* Yet the skin on the back of her hand was smooth. That meant weapons training. He looked down at the woman's breast, forcing an appreciative smile onto his face, but it was just a pretext to examine her tattoo more closely. It was difficult to be certain in the lamplight, but the skin on her chest was a little too white; as though covered with powder. If so, that meant the flower tattoo was a fake.

Marken's courtesan was sitting on his lap now, laughing at his murmured small talk. Her hands were resting on his chest – a mere thumb's width from the handle of his calv.

'So does the Raynor Brotherhood support the Scion?' asked Cedrin.

The tall man gave a short laugh. 'That fool? He'll be dead in less than a day. Daran will not give up the throne.'

'No? Not a big supporter of a return to Imperial power then?' asked Cedrin.

The tall man looked back at Cedrin, trying to read him. Meanwhile Cedrin forced himself to shift his mental framework. Right now there were four potential attackers in the room – six if Galvis returned with this surprise visitor. He had no doubt each of the women had concealed weapons. He ran his eye across their clothing. The sleeves of their open shirts and their flowing skirts could easily conceal knives. Something puzzled him though. As far as he knew, the Raynor Brotherhood admitted no women to their ranks. So where did these three 'courtesans' come from?

'The Empire is finished,' said the tall man, his voice heavy with contempt. 'The best thing that ever happened in my opinion. Business has never been better.'

'True. Very true,' said Cedrin.

The curtain parted and Galvis returned carrying a tray, set with a bottle of bakta and five glasses. He set down the tray and unhooked a small bag from his belt, holding it up.

'Fifty-six rubies – mostly in Sealed gemstones. As agreed,' said Galvis, holding the bag out to Cedrin. To carry real wealth, you needed Sealed gemstones. They were marked with a magical imprint showing their value in coin. The Seal was recognised throughout Kelas.

As Cedrin reached for it, the tall man leant across and snatched it from Galvis' fingers. He set it on the table just in front of him and gave Cedrin a tight smile, as if to say: *It's not going to be that easy.*

'Here – allow me,' said the tall man. He could hardly keep the amusement from his voice. He poured them all glasses of bakta from the same bottle and slid the tray across to them so they could choose their own glasses.

'Marken.' His voice was harder than he intended, but Cedrin knew they were in danger. 'Take a drink.'

Cedrin pushed aside the courtesan and leant forward at the same time as Marken chose from the tray. 'Good times. Just like that time on the Spire,' said Cedrin. He saw Marken's eyes flick towards him as he registered the comment. *Good.* When they had attacked the Spire in Athria it had been far from a good time. They had been with Raziin and his killers – men who were waiting for the right moment to open their throats.

'No doubt, ami. No doubt,' replied Marken, his voice light and easy as he took a glass.

'That's enough for now,' said Cedrin to his two courtesans. 'Maybe later, eh?'

Taking his lead, Marken also separated himself from his courtesan.

'Here,' said Cedrin, reaching across to pick up the two smoking pipes of se-tobacco. 'Enjoy yourselves.' He passed one to Marken's courtesan and another to the one who had been massaging his neck. Both looked immediately to the tall man for orders. He nodded, slowly.

Each sat back and drew on the pipes. Their smiles never faltered, but Cedrin could tell they were not drawing the smoke into their lungs, merely making clouds of it by sucking it into their mouths. If he had needed proof, that was it. He had never met a courtesan yet who turned down drink or se-tobacco. It was one of the perks of the job.

'To the Scion,' said Cedrin, lifting his glass.

The tall man frowned at him, and Cedrin smiled back. At least he had succeeded in wiping the smug smile off the bastard's face.

'To his swift death, more like it,' said the tall man, downing his glass in one gulp. Cedrin sipped his more carefully.

He heard voices in other parts of the house. Doors opened and closed. He knew for a fact that there were at least six ways in and out of the building – and they were just the ones he knew of. His fingers tightened on the glass as he heard footsteps in the corridor.

A thickset man entered the room. He had a round, hard face and his eyes were dark and deep-set beneath heavy brows.

'Ahh. At last we can finish this business,' said the tall man, rising from his seat. The women put down the pipes, freeing their hands. They moved in closer. Marken's courtesan had her hand on his shoulders once more. They were not moving.

The thickset man was dressed in a cloak, as though he had just walked in from the street.

'You made good time, Morec,' said the tall man.

Morec smiled. 'I did not want to miss this.' His accent was Raynorian, but beneath it Cedrin could also detect an older Athrian one.

The tall man turned and smiled at Cedrin. 'Cedrin, I would like you to meet, Morec. The new Athrian Mouthpiece of Smuggling.'

Morec threw off his cloak. Across his chest were the six degrees of the calvanni. The Mask had selected a new Mouthpiece! The man had assumed the rank Cedrin himself had earned in the Circle of Blades only hours before he fled Athria.

'And before I return to Athria to set things to rights for my master, the Mask wants to see you two dead,' said Morec.

The women surged into action. The one massaging Marken's shoulders snatched his calv from his harness in one deft motion and lunged at him. Marken blocked the thrust, deflecting her arm with his forearm and kicked his chair between them.

Two of the women came at Cedrin, both armed with knives. Cedrin twisted to avoid a thrust, stepping in to head-butt the first attacker. She grunted in pain, staggering back with a broken nose. He threw his glass of bakta at the second woman. The glass struck her in the face, making her gasp as the spirit drenched her. In that split second he drew both calvs. Marken had reached to his boot and drawn out his throwing knife. Instinctively they drew together, protecting each other's backs.

The tall man clapped slowly. 'Bravo. Nice reactions. But it's not going to help you much. Ladies?'

The three women retreated to the corners of the room and drew blowpipes out from beneath their skirts, lifting them expertly to their mouths. Two were pointed at Cedrin, one at Marken.

Poison.

Cedrin swallowed, trying to rid himself of the lump that had suddenly grown in his throat. He looked at the woman he had hit with his glass. The spirit had drenched her face, dripping down her chest. It had stripped away the heavy body paint, sending a streak through the fake flower to reveal the real tattoo beneath. A *teremb* – the night-hunter. *The women were assanni.* Of all the branches of the Brotherhood, only the secretive assassins recruited women. He knew now that if the tall man opened his tight vest, he would see the tattoos of an assassin beneath.

Cedrin turned to Morec. 'You gutless scum! If you had any balls at all, you would face me calv to calv and earn those tattoos you are wearing.'

Morec chuckled. 'Are you kidding? And make the same mistake as Mat? No. I think not. Times are changing in the Brotherhood, and you and Marken are part of the past.'

'Galvis?' said Cedrin, appealing to his old friend.

The fifth-degree looked at Cedrin apologetically. 'Sorry, old friend. My hands are tied.'

Cedrin thought desperately. If he could rouse the powers of Sorcery that had saved him in Athria, perhaps there was a chance. He tried to still his mind, to find the Window that gave access to the power. There! He could see it. He reached for it, eager for a way out, but it slipped from his grasp. He tried again, and again, but the more desperately he tried, the faster it slipped away. The Window – and the power of the Fire – remained out of reach. It was hopeless. He was no skilled Sorcerer – merely cursed with the Old Blood.

Cedrin readied himself for one last desperate attack. He eyed the distances and noted the expert way the blowpipes were held by the three women. The chances were slim. Very slim. Marken was holding his knife lightly in his fingers, waiting for Cedrin's move.

A heavy pounding echoed down the corridor. Someone was at the front door.

'Stinking Uros!' said Morec. 'What now?'

'Galvis, see who it is,' said the tall man.

'*Now!*' said Cedrin.

Cedrin threw his right calv at the closest of the three female assassins and dived over the chairs. He felt a dart pluck at the hairs on his head and another brush past his right shoulder. He heard a woman shout in pain, the sound of a body hitting the floor, then the bead curtain swinging.

Shielded from the last blowpipe by the backs of the chairs, Cedrin swept his gaze across the floor. He could see one of the women on the floor, Marken's knife in her throat. She struggled as blood pumped from the wound, her eyes wide with terror. A second woman had backed to the rear wall, as though to lean on it for support. He could see blood on her skirt. Marken had escaped through the bead curtain.

'Get them!' thundered the tall man. He heard the sound of Morec's booted feet as he circled the table. The last of the female assassins was also closing in. Soon she would have a clear shot over the backs of the chairs. He had to follow Marken, but if he showed himself too soon, his back would be exposed to the blowpipe.

The woman was almost on him.

Just as she reached him, Cedrin shoved the chair at her, hard. She grunted as it struck her chest. The dart shot out of the pipe, hitting the wooden table with a resounding thud.

Cedrin leapt to his feet. Morec had a calv drawn and was closing fast. He could not leave him at his back.

Cedrin feinted forward. Morec blocked swiftly, but Cedrin's calv was not there. Instead he stabbed forward, trying for an eye. Morec ducked away and Cedrin's calv sliced across his right cheek, opening a deep cut. Morec yelped and backed away, sweeping his calv out in front of him to ward Cedrin off.

Cedrin turned to see the tall man had unbuttoned his jacket to remove a blowpipe. Beneath, Cedrin could see six degrees of the assanni. The tall man was the Assassin's Mouthpiece of Raynor, Kiff. A man Cedrin had heard rumours of, but never met. No wonder he commanded Galvis with such authority.

'Now for you, assassin!' shouted Cedrin, leaping up onto the table and making for the Mouthpiece.

As he hoped, Kiff backed away, delayed for the moment in loading his blowpipe.

Instead of leaping off the table at Kiff, Cedrin leant down and scooped up the sack of gems and coin. He turned and raced across the length of the table. To his left he saw one of the female assassins against the wall, her left arm hanging useless, her right hand trying to stop the bleeding in her left shoulder where his long knife had struck. The other female assassin had reloaded her blowpipe. She lifted it to her lips and swivelled it towards him.

Cedrin dived headlong through the bead curtains. A dart thudded into the wall behind him. He hit the wooden floor and rolled, coming up in a crouch. He saw Marken in the gloom, holding a small stool. A man lay prostrate at his feet, a bloody wound on the side of his head. The man's calv had fallen to the floor.

'This way!' said Cedrin, running past Marken to the closest exit. Marken snatched up the calv and followed. Cedrin sheathed his remaining calv and tied the sack swiftly to his belt as he ran. He turned left, then right, then left again, racing through the gloom, thankful he had memorised the layout long ago.

'Now are we done with the Brotherhood?' said Marken, his voice shaking.

Cedrin heard voices behind them. Shouting. Only two more turns, past the stairs and they would be out into the rear alley.

The sound of running feet thudded through the floorboards above his head – more than dozen men. Then he heard them on the stairs ahead.

'Damn it!' Cedrin stopped.

'What is it?' asked Marken, breathless with fear and exertion.

'We've been cut off.' Cedrin could hear voices behind them, coming closer. Three men. He drew his remaining calv. 'Come on!'

Cedrin turned and raced back the way they had come. There was another way, but first they would have to get past their pursuers.

He could hear the voices coming closer and recognised none of them. Galvis and Kiff – and the remaining female assassin – had stayed behind.

He stopped Marken at a corner and caught his eye. *Ready?* Marken nodded.

The three men rounded the corner at a run, calvs drawn. Cedrin felt a surge of relief as he saw none had blowpipes. At last, his kind of fight! The tightness of the corridor meant than two led, while the third waited behind. Cedrin and Marken leapt forward, each engaging one man.

His man stabbed forward. Cedrin reacted instinctively,

swaying aside and stabbing for the heart. The long knife sank to the hilt. The man stiffened, his momentum sending him past Cedrin. Cedrin swept on. The eyes of the third man widened in shock, flicking between Cedrin's face and the six degrees of the calvanni. He dropped his calv and ran. Cedrin picked up his fallen weapon and turned. Marken and the last man were circling each other, playing a cautious game. Cedrin heard more running feet. *There was no time!* Cedrin brought the heel of his right calv down on the temple of the last attacker. The man staggered, then collapsed to his knees.

'Let's go!' Cedrin ducked through a low doorway, one he had gone straight past before. A short corridor led to a narrow wooden stair.

'I thought we were supposed to be getting out of here,' whispered Marken sharply.

'Really?' replied Cedrin.

He led them up the stairs, then on to the central corridor of the upper floor. There were women and children here – families of some of the senior Brotherhood men. They backed away, the women watching them with narrowed eyes as they ran past. Three of the children raced away – no doubt to give warning to those below.

Cedrin turned into another corridor. 'Yes!' The way was clear. He ran to the window at the end of the passage. It was raining heavily outside, but he knew there was an easy, one-storey climb to the street down the side of the building. He reached for the catch, then froze. The sill had been sealed shut with wooden pegs. The window was clearglass, but reinforced with strips of mought. They could break the clearglass easily enough, but nothing short of a battering ram would get them through the mought.

'Stinking Uros!'

Cedrin set to the window sill with his calv, trying to prise out the wooden pegs.

'Ah, Cedrin? You might want to see this,' said Marken.

Cedrin turned. Kiff was standing in the corridor with the female assassin to his left. Behind them, Morec led six men armed with heavy clubs, each studded with sharp mought spikes.

'Nowhere to turn now, Athrian scum,' said Kiff. 'I was going to let you die swiftly, but now I think I will let Morec have his fun.'

An icy calm settled on Cedrin. He smiled.

'Hey, sweetheart. You give a great neck massage,' said Cedrin. The eyes of the female assassin glittered with malice. 'If you ever get tired of working for Kiff, come and see me and you can earn that flower tattoo, eh?'

Her jaw clenched and she swept out her blowpipe, but Kiff caught her arm. He shook his head.

Cedrin considered the odds. Then all at once, the Window came into focus.

'Make them die hard, Morec,' said Kiff. The Assassin's Mouthpiece and the other assassin stepped aside, letting Morec through with his men.

'Hold!' A deep, commanding voice filled the corridor. A thick Cioan accent. *He knew that voice.*

Morec and his men stopped.

From the shadows of the corridor came three warriors, dressed in black leather armour. One towered above the rest. Cedrin's heart raced as he saw it was Merceth, Raziin's lieutenant.

Kiff turned to face the golden-skinned Merceth. The giant looked down at him in contempt, speaking slowly in Cioan.

'Cedrin. If you have any ideas, now is the time!' said Marken.

'Just one.'

Cedrin turned to the window. He raised his arms and released the Fire. It raced through him in a short burst. The corridor flashed with golden light and the glass exploded outward.

The light vanished. The window – and most of the frame around it – was gone. The air was filled with the tinkling sound of glass hitting the cobbled street below, and the rain lashed in.

Marken was already through the gap, scrambling down the wet wall. Cedrin was close behind him. Heartbeats later they were running up the alley through the rain.

Cedrin looked back once to see Kiff and the woman aiming

blowpipes. Then he heard Merceth's voice, speaking gruffly in Cioan. The blowpipes were lowered.

He turned left and right at random, racing away from the Docks District – and the Brotherhood.

Eventually they found shelter in a doorway and stopped to catch their breath.

'By Uros! That was close.' Cedrin sank back against the stone wall and looked out through the rain. The grey light of the day seemed to brighten as the sheer elation of survival filled him. Then he saw again the shocked face of the calvanni he had killed in the corridor; and the assassin choking on Marken's blade, her hands to her throat as her life-blood pumped out. The death of enemies, he reminded himself. Killed in combat. It did not help to quieten his growing feeling of regret. He touched the bag of gemstones at his belt. *Still there*. They had won free with their prize, but the risk – and the price – had proved too high.

Marken's face was pale with shock. 'You know who that was?'

Cedrin nodded. 'Merceth.'

'That means Raziin is in the city,' said Marken.

'Why should we care?' Cedrin lifted up the bag. 'Have you forgotten this?' Cedrin opened it, showing him the gemstones.

'Well, I'm glad we didn't come that close to death for nothing. I just don't understand why Merceth would want us alive,' said Marken, still breathless.

'What do you mean? Surely Merceth just wanted to kill us himself?' responded Cedrin.

Marken looked at Cedrin for a long moment before comprehension dawned on his face. 'Ahh. I keeping forgetting that you don't speak Cioan.' He took a deep breath. 'Merceth ordered them to let us go – right there at the end. Actually he ordered them to let *you* go.'

Cedrin re-tied the bag to his belt. 'It doesn't matter. I don't care why Merceth wants me alive.'

Marken smiled. 'It's not Merceth. He would have been acting under Raziin's orders. The real question is why does *Raziin* want you alive?'

Cedrin pushed away from the wall. 'You think too much,

ami. Let's go get some tattoos.'

Marken straightened. 'Ah, yes. I forgot. Kranor's mark.'

'Yes. And I have something special in mind.' Cedrin pulled the leather thong holding Belin's ring from his neck, snapping the chord. For the first time in a long while he really looked at the emerald ring. *The Kaidell signet ring, once worn by the most powerful Suul in the Empire.* The Kaidell crest had been cunningly depicted using tiny pieces of gemstone set into a mought backing. It showed a black tower on a field of yellow. Looking closer, he could see a thorny vine curling around the tower's base, sprouting tiny blood-red flowers. The work was exquisite.

'It's time to be my father's son.' Cedrin slipped the ring onto the first finger of his right hand. It felt heavy and cool against his skin. 'It's time to be scythemen.'

He looked up to see Marken watching him. His face was still pale.

'Are you all right, ami?' asked Cedrin.

'I … I have never killed a woman.' Marken's voice was thick with emotion, his eyes glistening. Cedrin recognised the classic signs of shock. It was common with fighters once the blood cooled. He was feeling it himself.

He reached across and put his arm around Marken's shoulders, drawing him into a rough embrace.

'Don't think of it, my friend. They were enemies – nothing more. Better them laying cool and still than us, eh?'

Marken nodded, drawing a shuddering breath.

Cedrin pushed him out to arm's length. 'Come. Let's at least enjoy this coin.'

'Now that is something I can understand,' said Marken, with a thin smile.

* * *

Cedrin woke with a start, his heart racing.

As his awareness sharpened, he listened intently. He could hear nothing but Marken's slow breathing from across the room. Silently, he slid one of the calvs out of his harness and reached across to the lamp, turning the tiny wheel to lengthen the wick.

The lamplight pushed back the shadows.

Nothing.

The room was empty. He turned the lamp back down and lay back, absently touching the new tattoo on his chest. It was still tender. His thumb played over the Kaidell signet ring. He was still unused to wearing it, but that would soon change. As he settled back to sleep, his mind drifted into memories.

It was the day he was accepted to manhood. He had been twelve summers and almost as tall as Tarral, but that did not diminish the respect or awe he had for his father. The eldest boy of Tarral's family, he towered over his two brothers and his little sister, and now he was a man. Thirty-six boys had been accepted into the Raptor totem that day, and Tarral had stood proudly beside him as the Priests of the Temple had inscribed the sacred inks.

He had been awed by the splendour of the Temple, the rich and shimmering fabrics of the Priests and Druids. A Suul lord had been present, dressed in court finery, ensuring each man's name was listed on the census. Cedrin had written his in the large bold Anacian script Tarral had taught him. *Cedrin, son of Tarral.*

Cedrin had run home from the temple, his mind buzzing with new ideas. He was going to cast a new clearglass se-jar for his father, with a delicate tint of amber, complete with a lid. He had pictured his father's smile as he handed it to him, how proud he would be.

He had waited until the glass on the coals was almost ready to pour, then carefully mixed in the tints, just as Tarral had taught him. Then he poured the glass and settled to wait.

The jar would be perfect. Perfect. He could not wait to show Tarral. Tentatively he touched the bright ink on his chest. The punctures were still painful, but that was nothing. He was a man. The long weeks of preparation were finally over.

Today, Tarral would confirm him as heir to the glassworks and at last he would become a full apprentice. For as long as he could remember, that was all he ever wanted, to follow in Tarral's trade and to excel in the making of milkglass. One day he would be given the age-old secret of the lanedd and he would make the finest blades Athria had ever seen. Tarral's mark, *his mark*, displayed proudly on each perfect haft.

A sound interrupted his daydreaming. His heart fell as he saw Tarral enter the kiln-room, a garrison officer with him. He ran to the doorway, almost as though he could stop them from entering and discovering his secret project. But it was too late.

His father strode into the room and smelled the air. 'What's this, a bit of glass in the making, eh, boy?'

Cedrin nodded, crestfallen, his dishevelled hair falling around his face. He had worn it long then. 'A jar in tinted clearglass.'

Tarral walked over and inspected the cast with a critical eye. He was a large man, not tall, but thickset with solid muscle bulging from his frame. His skin was so dark his brown eyes were almost lost in his stern face. A faded Raptor stretched across his torso, obscured by scores of other military tattoos and honours. Cedrin always thought they made his chest look like a patchy mural.

Tarral rounded on Cedrin. 'How many times have I told you? No pours unless I am here.'

Cedrin nodded, desperately fighting back tears. He had never been so conscious of his new manhood as under the scrutiny of Tarral and the officer, and he struggled to act as he should.

Tarral rubbed his jaw as he looked at Cedrin. He had rarely seen his father uncertain, but he was now.

'Cedrin,' he began, placing his hand on his shoulder. 'I have arranged a commission for you in the garrison.'

Tarral turned his head to indicate the captain. 'This is Halath, one of the Outer Garrison captains. He has consented to take you into his division. You should get your things and go with him now.'

Cedrin was stunned. He could not accept that all his hopes would be so easily shattered. 'But I am the eldest,' he pleaded. 'I should work with you, Father.'

Tarral removed his hand. 'It is not your place, son.'

Cedrin could not understand. 'But I am the eldest ...' He looked from the stern-faced Halath to his father.

'I have decided – and you will obey,' growled Tarral.

Angry, Cedrin shouted back at Tarral, 'I don't want to go into the garrison. I want to stay and apprentice with you as a son should!'

'You cannot,' said Tarral.

'Why?'

'Because you are not my son!' thundered Tarral.

Cedrin stepped back, eyes wide in disbelief. Tarral must be joking, he thought, this was just some manhood jest, any minute they would laugh and it would be forgotten. But when he looked at Tarral, he knew he spoke the truth. Cedrin ran to the corner of the room and turned his back to them. There was no stopping the tears now.

Behind him, Tarral and Halath talked in low, grave tones. He wiped away his tears and looked back. They cast depreciative glances back at him. The old soldier shook his head and sighed, leaving the room after gripping forearms with Tarral.

Tarral walked towards him. Cedrin turned away. Tarral come up close behind him. He could feel his powerful presence there. He wanted to hug his father, for everything to be forgotten, but only a child did that – and now he was a man.

'Come with me, Cedrin.'

Without another word, Tarral led him into one of the storerooms, hefting a large mought-bound chest onto the floor and unlocking the fine, dusty mechanism with a mought key. Lined with fine cloth, the interior was littered with maps, papers, and a score of mysterious items of milkglass, clearglass and glittering fragments of strange crystal.

Tarral gave a grunt as he squatted on one knee, his right hand moving through the strange jumble. He withdrew something glittering and green from the chest and closed the lid with reluctance.

He turned to Cedrin and patted the chest. 'Sit here, Cedrin.' His voice was softer now, touched with rare compassion.

Cedrin sat on the chest, facing Tarral. The previous weeks had been the highlight of his life, becoming full of possibilities. When he had rushed back from the temple, the world had seemed to take on a special lustre. The sun was brighter, everything more mysterious, magic waiting around the next corner. Now the only things Cedrin felt were fear and sadness.

'Is it true?' asked Cedrin, his voice high and thin with suppressed emotion.

Tarral nodded. 'I had hoped ... things would work out differently.' He was silent for a time, and even at twelve, Cedrin could tell there was a struggle going on inside him.

'There is no easy way to tell you, Cedrin. I'm not your father. You are illegitimate. Your father was a general in the old Empire. When things began to fall apart in the Last Days, he sent you here, knowing you would be safe. He was to have come for you, but he did not. That's the way of it.'

Cedrin looked away from Tarral, anguished.

Tarral took hold of Cedrin's chin and turned him back to face him. 'Don't think ill of your father; he was a good man. He fell during the Last Days. A dead man cannot pay debts.'

Cedrin was crying freely as Tarral opened his hand to reveal a green signet ring, carved from a single gemstone. The elaborate crest was worked with minute pieces of gemstone.

Tarral took a deep breath and held out the ring. 'Your father was Belin Kaidell, Suul Lord of the Bulvuran court, ruler of the Delta province, former First General of the Bulvuran Legions,' said Tarral formally. 'This was his crest, Cedrin. Your crest.'

Cedrin's hand shook as he took the ring, as though that glittering circle embodied the curse that had been placed on him.

'He was a great man, Cedrin, a great warrior. You should follow in his footsteps.'

Tarral gripped Cedrin's shoulders, his huge hands dwarfing them. 'Accept the commission, Cedrin, I know you have ability. You could rise to Captain, even higher. One day, with your ancestry, you could become a Suulqua of the court and I would have been proud to have reared you.'

Cedrin pushed Tarral's hands away. The shame and sadness had ignited an inner defiance, now rising as a violent anger. For him, this was the deepest of betrayals.

'I don't know who Belin Kaidell was and I don't care. I don't want to be a soldier and I don't want to leave Lookout Hill. I want to work the forges with you, to learn the secrets of glass!'

Tarral grew grim. 'You are not my son, Cedrin. I cannot take you as an apprentice. With Erin and Yeris coming to manhood next summer, there is no room. You must choose another trade.'

'Then I choose nothing!' Cedrin shouted in defiance. He ran from the room, through the forge and out into the street, his mind ablaze.

He was not a real son – just some *bastard* to a dead general. Now he must stand aside for the real sons. He knew what Tarral wanted – he wanted him out of his house. Well, he *would* leave. He was man, he could go anywhere, be anything. He would show him.

Cedrin ran through the thronging streets to the crowded harbour. Finally he stopped, climbing to sit on top of one of the massive wooden pylons where it jutted above the wharf timbers. He opened his hand and looked at the ring. 'A curse on you,' he shouted as fresh tears coursed down his cheeks.

A desperate sadness ate into his heart. The tears slowed, but in his adolescent mind he vowed never to forgive Tarral. He wanted to throw the ring into the harbour, but something stopped him. What had been before was gone. The ring was a part of him now, a part of what he was going to be.

A shadow fell across him. Clearing the tears from his eyes, he looked up to see an old sailor. He had lost a leg and supported himself on a stout wooden cane, his clothes filthy and sun-bleached. His beard was short and shot with grey, but his smile was kindly.

'You can't cry, son. Life's too short for tears.' The sailor waved out across the hundreds of ships that crammed the harbour, his mind far away out to sea. 'Look at it. Open your eyes and see the world. Why, there's a piece of luck waiting around every corner.'

The sailor saw the gem-ring glittering in Cedrin's palm and let out a gasp of feigned surprise, pointing at the ring. 'Look. What did I tell you! That's a lucky ring.' He nodded to himself. 'Aye, I'm sure of it. I'd recognise it anywhere. A lucky ring.'

Cedrin looked at the ring with new eyes, wiping the tears from his cheeks. Maybe the old sailor was right, he thought, maybe it was. He watched it in his palm as it caught the sun and smiled. It would be his lucky ring.

Chapter Five

The Warlord held the ruby signet ring to the light, examining the crest and fine inscriptions. He shifted the ring in his fingers, trying to catch the wan illumination that filtered through the patterned blue panes. Rain beat at the glass in a muffled staccato as the deluges of Storm Season continued.

'So. It's real,' said the Warlord, squinting to examine the cut.

Daran was in his private court. He sat on a simple, carved wooden chair set one step above the floor on a small dais. His crest, the crossed spears and shield of the Yasser States, was painted high on its back. His close friend and adviser, the golden-skinned Sorcerer Uran, stood at his left. To his right stood three of his Druidin – one of whom, Analas, wore the hollow sun pendant of the followers of Yosini. Officially his Druidin were practitioners of Essence magic with no link to religion, but many followed the way of Yosini; a path to Enlightenment that allowed practitioners to worship any gods or goddesses as aspects of Yosini, the Hidden Sun. Rehvar, one of the first of his Druidin, wore no such adornment. Such a pendant would have been a farce around the neck of Daran's most accomplished assassin. Scythemen and spearmen flanked the base of the dais and the walls of the room.

'Yes. We've had it authenticated by three experts in Raynor and they agree without a doubt. It seems they actually discovered what happened to the Emperor's escort and the Emperor,' said Uran, his silver eyes intense.

Daran lowered the ring. It was one thing to pull down a false heir to the throne, it was another to touch on the fate of the

Emperor he had once sworn to serve.

Rehvar watched Daran expectantly. The Druidin's nondescript appearance made him perfect for his trade. Behind the bland, rounded face with its bronze Cioan hair lurked a sharp mind. Another of the refugees from the fall of Althar, Rehvar was adept with all Heaven Essences — Uros, Larus and Moon Essence. His power and skill approached that of a Sorcerer. He was a master of concealment, and with his skill in healing came a talent for poisons. Daran had sealed the fate of more than one false-Scion in this room with little more than a spoken command. The Warlord turned away from Rehvar.

His right shoulder ached around the old spear wound where the muscles had never knitted properly. He worked his arm absently.

Daran's plan had gone remarkably well; even so, they had a perilous path to tread. He looked across to Analas, who had undertaken Osterac's interrogation. The Yosini Druid looked drawn and haunted. Yet, as he turned to meet the Warlord's gaze, Daran saw resignation there. The Yosini Druids fought not just for power, but for the chance to resurrect their ancient religion – an order that had almost vanished with the founding of the Empire and had suffered another blow with the recent destruction of the former southern province of Hend. Daran gripped the ring in his fist. Sacrifices had to be made; by all of them.

When the delegation had first entered Raynor, it was obvious public opinion would force his hand – the support of Olcis had given the claim too much credibility. Rejecting Osterac at that point would have split Raynor in two from the Suul to the lowest beggar. No, he had to publicly accept the Scion – it was the only way to play for time. At first Daran had tried to trick Osterac, but the man had been faultlessly prepared and was always kept within sight of his handlers. Daran's agents worked day and night in Raynor and Olcis seeking evidence against him, while every passing hour the pretender became more accepted, diminishing the value of anything they might find.

Only yesterday it seemed as though the Hesguit would force him to desperate measures: a direct attack against Ranlan and

Osterac, killing them all. It would be impossible to achieve without leaving a score of witnesses, yet it seemed either that or watch all the carefully laid plans he and Uran had devised over years destroyed in a few months. No matter what the cost, Daran would never stand by and let Olcis play their games while the Eathal marched closer.

The fact was, he had been blindsided. His spies in Olcis had given them no warning of Osterac or the delegation's arrival. In prior cases, they had been forewarned and were able to produce convincing evidence against claimants long before they reached the main Court. Ranlan had chosen his timing brilliantly, with Raynor tense and overcrowded with the dispossessed and desperate.

Then came a stroke of luck. Carefully placed bribes within the Olcis delegation had led them to one of the younger Templemen – an aide to Ranlan himself. Dissatisfied with his success in the Temple and spurred by resentment, he agreed to defect to the Druidin in Raynor in return for a guaranteed position. He told them a great deal. The most startling revelation had been the secondary plan of the Olcis Druids. If Osterac was revealed prematurely or if he were compromised, Ranlan had planned from the outset to kill him and place the blame on Daran's head. In this scenario, Daran's own assassination would follow quickly, adding to the chaos and allowing the Hesguit to take control of Raynor by supporting factions sympathetic to his cause.

In this revelation, Daran had seen their only hope for avoiding outright chaos in Raynor. Somehow Osterac had to be maligned in the eyes of his keepers. It had been easy to apprehend Osterac and sow the seeds of doubt in the hearts of the Olcis Druids. Now, all he had to do was sit back and wait for the pretender's death. He would be careful to ensure there were plenty of witnesses to distance him from the deed. Then, his own security would have to be increased. He had three body doubles hidden in the palace, ready to go into action as soon as Osterac's death was reported. He himself would rule from hidden chambers in the East Tower until the Druids were sent packing back to Olcis.

Daran almost felt sorry for Osterac. Almost. The threat to him and to the future of Raynor was too great to allow pity.

The strategy had borne surprising fruit. Ranlan had gone frantic trying to find Osterac, activating agents all over Raynor. The young aide had been communicating regularly over the long night, revealing the identities of the Olcis spies – including a woman who had drawn Daran's own bath this morning – now *that* gave him pause for thought.

'Where did Osterac say they found the ring, Analas?' asked Daran.

'The Serpent's Tongue. It is the place where the Eastern Daughter meets the Serpent River. There is a defensible hill rising above the forking of the two rivers. They may have made camp on their way to Highbeard,' said Analas.

'And where were they betrayed?' asked Daran, with a degree of feeling that surprised him.

He had been a young general then, fighting in the eastern capital Husdoon against the Meadrel tribesmen. He and the other generals of the campaign had been the last to see Riin and his party alive as they left for Raynor under cover of night. He never would have believed, in that cold predawn, he would be the only commander to survive the fall of Husdoon; and the one to lead the remnants of the Legions to Raynor's rescue. He had become the Warlord, the saviour, raised by the people to rule them. How fickle they were. Thirty years ago they hated the Cinanac for abandoning them. Royalists were hung in the streets.

He examined the ring once more, remembering Riin wearing the ornate ruby when Daran had knelt fealty to him over thirty years ago. *To serve to death, to uphold.* He had kissed the ring and looked up into Riin's eyes. It had been the closest he had ever been to the Emperor. From a distance, the large man seemed dull, his wide face unremarkable. Yet up close, Daran was held by those grey-blue eyes, sensing the strength there and knowing he would give his loyalty to him utterly.

Daran shivered. It was as though a ghost had touched him.

Long ago, he and Uran had decided the Scion was a myth. The child had been killed in Raynor with the Empress and Riin's family all those years ago. There was certainly no evidence he had survived. Belin had fought his way to the Iris, activating the glowmetal that contained the Song of the Iris, but the Eathal Shapechanger had followed him. The Iris had exploded and nothing could have survived its destruction, of that Uran was sure.

Yet what if the real Scion had presented himself in the Great Hall, not a pretender, but Riin's flesh and blood? Someone who believed in the destiny of Raynor? Before Osterac's audacious claim, Daran would have dealt with him like the rest. But now – after being touched by the ghosts of his past — he was not so sure.

A young Suulqua messenger entered the room and bowed to Daran.

'What is it?' he asked, still weighing the unwelcome burden of the jewelled ring in his fist.

'Osterac is waiting in the outer chambers. He says he has to see you, urgently.'

Daran's eyes widened in surprise. Of all the people he had expected, Osterac and his keepers were the last.

'Tell him and his Druids I have no intention of giving them an audience this morning. I have better things to do,' he said, smiling at Uran beside him. 'Plenty of wine left, my friend?'

Uran lifted a decanter from a nearby table, weighing it with a disappointed expression. The dregs of the red wine swirled around the base. 'We can always call for more.'

'He is alone, Lord,' said the Suulqua.

'Alone?' said Daran. *So perhaps Osterac is not so stupid after all.* 'Send him in.'

Daran straightened on his throne, readying himself for the encounter.

Osterac looked tired and frightened, the whites around his pale blue eyes heavily bloodshot. He wore plain leather trousers and a full shirt that concealed his tattoos. *Not so eager to show off your phoenix tattoo now, are you?* Osterac flinched as he saw Analas, recognising his torturer, but recovered quickly. He tilted back his head and stood proudly. Even so, he was pale with tension.

'What do you want, Resius?' said Daran, playing with the Cinanac signet ring.

Osterac's eyes flicked to the ruby ring and anger momentarily crossed his handsome face. 'I want to make a deal.'

'What could you possibly gain when you have Raynor?'

'You know very well Raynor is lost to me!' stormed Osterac. He immediately lifted his hand to the side of his head, clearly in pain. His own outburst had worsened his headache.

One of the scythemen swung his scythe-butt at Osterac, but he dodged it with contempt. Daran was surprised by his agility. Apparently they had chosen a warrior to be false-Scion.

The scytheman advanced. 'On your knees to the Warlord!'

'Leave him,' commanded Daran.

With reluctance, the scytheman returned to his station.

'Why should I help you?' Daran feigned disinterest, yet his mind was rapidly exploring this incredible stroke of good fortune.

'If they succeed in killing me, it will mean massive insurrection. No-one will believe you didn't order it,' said Osterac.

Daran considered Osterac. Somehow the man had discovered the Olcis Druids' plan; or perhaps he had known all along.

'That is not enough,' said Daran.

'I barely escaped the apartments without being discovered. I *cannot* go back there.' Osterac stepped forward and knelt. 'I will do anything, *anything* if you get me out of Raynor alive.'

'Renounce the throne publicly.' Daran's heart raced with excitement.

They matched gazes for a long moment. Daran could sense the man had more strength and intelligence than he had given him credit for, but he was in an impossible position.

Osterac's head sagged forward. 'Very well.'

Daran could not suppress a smile. The Hesguit's plans would be ruined! All along he had contrived to discredit Olcis and to eliminate Osterac. Yet in the end, he knew the Druids would be inviolate – he would be lucky if he managed to coerce them into leaving Raynor at all. But now, new possibilities were opening up before him. A public declaration would give him a way to strike back directly against the Temple. If he could turn the outrage of the public against them …

Daran leant forward. 'Have no fear, Resius. You shall escape Raynor alive.'

The Warlord turned to Uran. 'Announce a public declaration by the Scion and the Warlord,' he said. 'And be sure to invite the Olcis Druids – and our Druidin.'

Daran rose from the throne. 'It's time for Raynor to show Olcis its claws.'

* * *

Ellen followed Estle as he roughly shouldered and elbowed his way through a crowd of Suul to the front of the balcony. He smiled pleasantly at those he displaced, always ready with a gracious apology. The crowd had built so rapidly they were lucky to gain entrance to the Great Hall at all, let alone reach a balcony that was not already thronged to a dangerous press.

News of the coming declaration had sped through Raynor. Since the feast, the Suul had been poised for the changeover of power, each wondering how the new regime would affect them. Outside, the Palardos was crammed with an excited mob that grew by the breath, crowding the palace walls despite the bitter deluge; ready to cheer their saviour Osterac.

Once at the rail, Ellen surveyed the crowd. The floor of the chamber had been filled by diligent Suulvey and opportunists eager to sell their places to the highest bidder. There were thousands here, covering the floor and rising balconies in a kaleidoscope of colour. The men dressed in immaculate trousers with jewelled harnesses across their chests, the women in fine skirts and stylish blouses open to reveal their breasts, or cut from gossamer material so thin they might as well be naked from the waist. The display had shocked her when she first entered Raynor, but now, only days later, it seemed passé.

There was no doubt what the assembled Suul expected. They were here to see Osterac declared Emperor and a new age of the Yasser States begin. Many hoped an Emperor could reunite

Kelas and raise an army against the Eathal. Others hoped for more wealth and power in the new regime. Ellen hoped for the rebirth of the Empire, yet was plagued by doubts. In her heart she knew Osterac was not Riin's son. If he was installed as Emperor, where then did that leave her quest for the Scion? Was she to pit herself against a reborn Empire?

The room erupted with a roar of voices. Ellen gripped the balcony rail and leant forward. A man pushed into her back, the jewels of his harness pressing into her skin painfully through the weave of her dress. A Suul woman pushed against her from the right, trying to reach the rail, her heavy breast squeezed against Ellen's shoulder.

Far below, Osterac and Daran entered the hall together, followed by a group of scythemen. Seeing the Scion, the roar of the crowd grew to an incoherent thunder.

Behind the scythemen walked the Olcis Druids, flanked by their Guardians. Behind them yet again were around twenty dark-robed men led by Uran and two Yosini Druids. These would have to be Daran's Druidin. Seeing them, Ellen knew instinctively something was wrong. The Warlord would never play his hand like this, not unless things were to fall in his favour. Alarmed, she gripped Estle's shoulder and searched the ranks of the Olcis Druids for Raphal. He stood at the rear of the Olcis delegation.

The crowd hushed. The Warlord climbed the dais and raised his hands to the assembled crowd for silence. The noise died, replaced by a tense expectation. Daran held more than just the eyes of those thousands as he began to talk, he held their hopes and dreams.

'Suul. Citizens of the Yasser States. Patriots. Friends,' he said, turning to sweep his gaze across the crowd, his face grave and tragic. 'Raynor has been betrayed!'

A sigh went through the crowd, a sound of frustration and confusion. This is not what they came to hear. What of the Scion?

'Ha! I knew it,' said Estle, his eyes bright.

'Betrayed in our very time of need and for no other motive than a desire for power!' said Daran.

Thousands cried out in angry denial. She felt an elbow in her ribs as the woman to her left fought forward, her lips drawn back in a snarl. The man behind her was shouting and shaking his fist. The vast crowd was turning, and the effect was frightening.

Daran pointed a finger at Osterac, standing pale and quiet beside him. For the first time she noticed his chest – and the fine tattoo of the Cinanac phoenix – were covered.

'We believed Olcis, but they have given us a false-Scion!'

The floor of the Great Hall churned as the Suul pressed forward. Throughout the room people shouted, trying to make themselves heard. The Olcis delegation were pushed towards the throne by a sheer weight of bodies, the Guardians striking with spear-butts to keep the crowd away, yet failing.

'It's over for them now,' said Estle, a fierce satisfaction in his voice.

She saw Raphal stumble and almost fall.

'Raphal!' called Ellen, her stomach lurching in fear as she watched the old Druid right himself and move behind a Guardian.

Ellen had both hands around Estle's arm, leaning in close to his body, although she could not recall moving there. She was shaking. The woman had pushed to the rail now, forcing her back. 'Kill them! Kill them all!' she was screaming.

Raphal!

* * *

Daran kept his face impassive as he looked out over the crowd. The fury of his Suul shocked even him. He expected hysteria like this from the mob, not his own court. In that moment he realised that the Suul needed a saviour as much as the lowest beggar. Even though they played their games and court life was much as it had always been, Daran now understood the fear that had been growing under the surface. He waited, letting the fury build. For now it served his purpose.

The Olcis delegation had now been pushed to within paces of the dais. Analas and his Druidin spread out to surround them, while Uran stepped up onto the dais at his side. The Sorcerer's concentration was total.

Daran turned to Ranlan. The time for deception was over and the High Druid's arrogance withered under the ferocity of his gaze. *Yes Ranlan, here is the time of your defeat.* He was the Warlord. The same man who had held the remnants of an Empire together against impossible odds. The man who *ruled* Raynor.

Eventually one cry was taken up over the others.

'Give us the Scion!'

Daran signalled for Osterac to take the dais. The Warlord stepped back onto the floor of the court and waved for Osterac to speak as Ranlan watched in horror.

Osterac looked up into the crowd. He looked ill, his skin a greyish colour. A look of disbelief crossed his face as the reality of what he was about to do confronted him.

Daran leant towards him. 'The exact wording we agreed upon,' he whispered harshly.

'No! Wait!' Ranlan tried to reach the dais. Daran's scythemen held him back with the hafts of their weapons, their faces cold. 'No, you fool. Stop it. Stop it now! There is another way. A better way!'

Osterac's face contorted with fury as he looked down at Ranlan. 'A better way, Druid? Like seizing the throne over my dead body!'

Ranlan went limp with shock, letting the scytheman push him back a step. The High Druid's determination soon returned, however, and Daran could see the look of calculation in his eyes. He had to get this over with quickly, before Ranlan found some way to silence Osterac.

'The declaration, Resius. Now!' commanded Daran.

'I, Osterac ...' he faltered, looking once more into the crowd.

Silence had fallen again, all faces turned to Osterac, waiting for him to speak.

'No, Osterac. Deny the Warlord! Take the power!' called Ranlan.

Osterac looked between the crowd and Daran.

'No, Ranlan. I will not rule Raynor with parasites like you

looking over my shoulder,' snapped Osterac.

Daran looked at Osterac sharply. The man still dreamed of ruling Raynor? He was deluded. After today he was finished.

Ranlan surged forward, pushing against the scythemen. 'No! I will keep you alive. I swear it on the Hesguit's seat!'

Osterac turned away and looked up into the crowd.

'I am Osterac Resius!' declared the false-Scion in a strong voice.

Daran's eyes settled on Ranlan in triumph as Osterac continued. He had won.

'I am a minor Suul of Olcis. I am not the son of Riin Cinanac. I was sent here by the Hesguit, with the full knowledge of the Council of High Druids, to take the throne and to bring Raynor under the heel of Olcis through a false claim to the throne ...'

Osterac continued to speak, but his words were lost. The crowd who had come to see him crowned now wanted him beheaded.

Daran took the dais again, ascending the steps swiftly, eager to capture the ugly mood of the crowd. As Osterac passed him, the false-Scion staggered, apparently overcome with the emotion of the moment and virtually falling into the Warlord's arms. Daran supported him then pushed him back to his feet at arm's length.

A dozen scythemen formed an escort around Osterac, leading him around behind the throne to the royal exit. Ranlan channelled a brief Essence spell, pushing through Daran's scytheman and racing to follow Osterac, but Uran barred his way. The High Druid glared at Uran, his eyes seething with hatred. A heartbeat later, Osterac was gone. He would be out of the palace within an hour with new clothes and a new identity.

Daran surveyed the crowd, struggling to hide his elation. He let the outrage build until the noise threatened to bring the vaulted roof down. In a vibrant voice, he yelled over the crowd. 'Who has betrayed us? *Who did we believe?*'

'*Olcis! Olcis! Down with Olcis!*'

'Yes! They care nothing for our peril!'

The Olcis delegation had been pushed behind the throne, the Guardians pinned between Daran's men. Ranlan stood only paces away from Daran, caught between Uran, the squad of scythemen and the tight ranks of the Druidin.

'I demand safe conduct,' yelled Ranlan over the rising outrage of the crowd. 'You cannot hold a Druid of Olcis. I demand safe conduct!'

'You will demand nothing!' said the Warlord, his voice powerful, commanding. He was once more the master of his own palace. It was time to let Olcis know who ruled in Raynor; time to give a clear signal to the angry masses outside the walls of the palace.

A great roar went up from the crowd.

'Down with Olcis!'

This was the moment.

'Take them, Uran!' commanded the Warlord, his deep voice filling the Great Hall.

Ranlan drew back, his face twisted with outrage. With a shout of rage, the High Druid sent a sleek, silvery bolt of Force at Daran. Whistling, it shot like a dart towards him. Daran leapt, but the arrow followed him. It was only a thumb's width away when it struck an insubstantial shield and disintegrated in a shower of sparks. Uran had saved him. Daran got to his feet and stood straight on the dais. It was important he was seen as a figure of strength in this moment.

The Guardians surged forward, attacking Daran's scythemen. In the close confines, spears and scythes alike were useless and the fight degenerated into close fighting with calvs and desperate grappling.

An expanding ball of red fire shot at Uran from Ranlan's fingers. The Sorcerer stood motionless, his silver eyes glittering with the force of his concentration. Like the silver dart, the fiery projectile exploded on an unseen barrier. Uran tilted his head slightly and Ranlan gasped. The High Druid's hands flew to his throat, his face turning red. He staggered, falling to his knees as Uran tightened an invisible vice around the High Druid's throat.

The Druidin closed in, surrounding the Olcis delegation. The other High Templeman and his four aides reacted instantly. Bolts of fire and Force shot between the Druidin and the Uros Druids of the delegation. The air shook with detonations as the missiles struck unseen shields. One of the Druidin collapsed, the silvery bolt that sliced through his side vanishing as he fell.

The High Moon-Druid and his attendants, Raphal and the Larus Druid threw themselves face-forward onto the floor. They clearly had no intention of battling the Druidin.

The air around the other High Templeman shimmered with Essence. He raised his hands, preparing to attack Uran and free Ranlan. Then one of Ranlan's own red-robed aides struck him a savage blow on the back of the head, sending him sprawling forward. Daran smiled. It was their defector. The other three red-robed aides faltered. Without the strength of the High Templeman, their combined shields fell apart, and they were driven back, two falling to bolts of Force. The last threw up his hands in surrender and let the Essence flow out of him, looking at the defector in shock and silent rage. The High Templeman remained motionless on the marble floor, while Ranlan remained on his knees, struggling ineffectually against Uran's magic. The defector tore off his red outer robe, throwing it to the floor and spitting on it. He walked to stand with the Druidin, glaring back at his former brethren in defiance.

The Guardians put up a heroic fight, but they were heavily outnumbered. Those who had not fallen were subdued.

The Druidin came forward swiftly, drawing torcs of mercury glowmetal from their robes. Each was a hollow glass circlet, the glittering silver metal and crimson light of the mercury glowmetals inside them shifting with each movement. Each of the liquid glowmetals had been carefully selected to neutralise the Druids' powers. They were incredibly rare, and Uran had spent years – and much of Daran's wealth – acquiring them.

They were powerless to resist as they were collared with the torcs. Once a mercury glowmetal was fitted around Ranlan's neck, Uran released him. Daran closed the distance between them, looking down at the High Templeman in contempt.

It was done.

Daran became aware of the shouting of the crowd.

'*Execute them!*'

'*Kill them!*'

'*Down with Olcis!*'

He had to get them out of here. He signalled to Uran.

The Sorcerer nodded and waved to Analas. Together they led the prisoners away, following the same route as Osterac through the doors at the rear of the dais; flanked by ranks of Druidin and scythemen.

Once the Olcis Druids were out of sight, the crowd began to calm.

Daran lifted his hands for silence. 'Have no fear. Justice shall be done.'

He turned swiftly, exiting the hall through the double doors and on to his own chambers, flanked by his elite guard.

He was elated by his victory, yet unnerved by the ferocity of the crowd, and how quickly they had turned on the Olcis Druids. He would need to offer them a victory against the Eathal, something to reassure them. One thing was for certain, Olcis would no longer bar their way.

He searched his pockets absently for the Cinanac signet ring, but found it missing. Strange, thought Daran, he was certain he took it with him to the Hall. Perhaps he had left it in his chambers. He pushed the thought aside and savoured the moment. Now the real task of defending Raynor could begin.

* * *

Ellen sagged into the plush cushions of the couch.

'My Lady?'

She slowly became aware of the offered tray of pastries the slave girl was holding out to her. She had no idea how long she had been staring at it without seeing it. Ellen shook her head and the slave girl backed away.

'What a day. What a day!' said Estle, beside her on the couch. He could barely contain his excitement and rubbed his hands together briskly. Ellen felt numb.

A low table had been set before the couch and laid out with teacups and a steaming pot of the aromatic tea Estle favoured. Ellen found the scent cloying.

Osterac was a false-Scion. It was a fact. All along she had known, yet part of her had hoped for an easy solution to her problems. She was relieved that Osterac had been unmasked as a pretender – she did not want a false-Scion on the throne – but with his downfall had vanished her last excuse for delaying her quest. But how could she leave the palace and pursue Cedrin without a single ally? All her life she had been sheltered within the privileged world of the Suul. Less than three weeks ago she had been the daughter of a powerful Sarlord, her life mapped out … safe. Now she had to leave that behind. It was not the physical danger – Ellen was confident in her martial skills – it was that she had always been surrounded by people, part of the court. The thought of being alone, completely alone, terrified her.

'Well, that is the end of it,' said Estle laughing. 'Daran is craftier than I thought.'

Her thoughts flew to Raphal. She had never met a more decent, loving man. How could she sneak out of Raynor, leaving him in the Warlord's dungeons? She would feel like a coward.

'What will he do with them?' asked Ellen, trying to sound casual, but she could not hide the concern in her voice.

Estle looked at her thoughtfully for a moment. 'Have no fear for Raphal. The Warlord will keep the Olcis Druids alive and well, they are worth too much in ransom money.'

Estle poured himself more of the tea. 'I never would have guessed they would be betrayed by one of their own number. A Templeman novice! Uran kept that one close to his chest, the wily old war hound.' Estle laughed once more, blowing over the steaming cup.

'To the Warlord!' said Estle, taking a sip.

Ellen gave Estle a hot look. How could he be so damned cheerful!

'What's the matter, Ellen, aren't you patriotic?' asked Estle. 'Raynor has been saved!'

'How can you sit there celebrating when one of our oldest friends is chained to the walls in the Eastern tower?'

Estle shrugged and his smile faltered. Ellen had hit the mark.

'He picked the wrong side. What can I say?' said Estle.

'We should ransom him ourselves. Give him sanctuary in the Athrian consulate.'

Estle grunted. 'Totally out of the question,' he said taking another sip of tea. The muscles in Ellen's neck bunched with tension. His casual dismissal infuriated her. Once more it brought home her lack of influence here. In Athria, she was a Suulvey, senior in rank to Estle, a member of the Council. Here in the Athrian consulate she was a minor diplomat, no better than a lowly Suulqua.

Ellen pushed herself to her feet. 'That's it, is it? Estle has spoken. That matter is closed?' She glared at him.

Estle put the teacup down on the low table. He had lost his good humour now.

'What's the matter? The tea's not refreshing enough?' snapped Ellen.

Estle's jaw clenched in anger, but he mastered himself. 'You are beginning to try my patience, sister.'

'Try your patience? Like some wayward child to be pacified?'

He signalled to one of his slaves. 'Bring me some wine,' he said with an edge of irritation.

Ellen took a deep breath and let it out slowly. There was nothing to be gained from provoking Estle. 'Surely there must be something we can do to help Raphal?'

Estle relaxed somewhat, facing Ellen squarely as though across a karass board in the final moves of the game.

'He is a prisoner of the Warlord. His release is purely a matter of negotiation between Raynor and Olcis. Athria has nothing to do with it.' His voice took on the tone of a reluctant teacher. 'You must learn to divorce yourself from personal ties. They can be a hindrance in diplomatic matters.'

'Yes. Of course. Thanks for the advice,' she said. 'I'll leave you to your wine. You will have to forgive me if I am in no mood for celebration.'

Ellen stormed out. She was sick of the impasse Raynor had forced on her.

She was so bound up in her thoughts, she almost ran into Uran. The Sorcerer was entering her brother's apartments as she was leaving, no doubt to celebrate a victory with Estle. As though by accident, his hands found her waist.

'Ah, my Lady!' His breath stank of wine and his eyes were shot with red.

Tactfully, she extricated herself from his grasp.

'Have you thought over my offer? It is a new era for Raynor. A new age,' he said, leaning over her.

Ellen side-stepped him into the corridor. She was still seething with anger and Uran was the last person she wanted to see. His victory filled him even more than the wine. He had been right about Osterac all along, and that in itself was like a raw wound.

'If you will excuse me,' she said, an automatic smile in place. 'I have business.'

'Of course,' he said, winking at her. 'Later then?'

Ellen smiled without replying, an ambiguous encouragement her court tutors had schooled her to use. Behind the mask, she wanted to strike out. In the whole of Raynor, Raphal was the one person she trusted; a Priest and Druid, a scholar who would do no harm to any man. Uran had put him in chains.

'I have to go,' said Ellen, turning to hurry towards her rooms, hating herself for the falseness she had been forced to assume.

Once within her rooms, she gave orders no-one was to disturb her. She stripped off the formal gown and put on loose trousers and a shirt, throwing herself into one of the solo training regimes her weaponmaster had taught her. The haft of the scythe was a familiar and welcome weight in her hands. She gloried in the movement, the tension easing from her neck and back.

Later, dripping with sweat, she set to thinking, absently swinging her scythe as she tossed everything around in her mind. She was determined to find the Scion and that meant following the only lead she had, the calvanni. But every time she tried to reason out the logistics of travelling on the roads, it defeated her. Never in her life had she travelled without a small army of attendants and retainers. Life on the roads, alone, mixing with the common people, was frightening and alien. It held a dark attraction for her, like the sweet taste of the forbidden fruit, yet still it seemed impossible.

She walked to her private balcony and opened the doors. The rain had stopped, but the air was icy, instantly chilling the sweat soaked into her hair and clothes.

She looked out over the city. The clouds had cleared in the west, and Yos' twin suns shone through the gap, still close together in the sky following the Storm Season eclipse. The rooftops and roads glittered in the sunlight. She inhaled deeply, taking the rain-scented air deep into her lungs. Storm Season would soon be over.

She leant her scythe up against the wall and stripped off her clothes, standing naked in the cold. Her nipples hardened and a wave of goose bumps raced across her flesh.

So much had happened since her father's death. Myan Cintros, like her, had been a Sorcerer and warrior. He had defended Raynor against the Eathal thirty years ago, leading Athria into a new age as an independent power after the Empire. He still lived in her heart.

She shivered.

'What would you do, Father? What would you do now?'

Ellen closed the doors and slipped on a silk gown, readying herself for a bath. She found herself drifting through memories of her father, sometimes laughing, sometimes touched by deep regret.

When she was fifteen, Myan had taken her out of her scythe class one afternoon to the southern cliffs near the Lighthouse tower. There they had fought for the first time, warrior to warrior. Ellen had given her utmost, determined to best Myan with her skill and please him with her progress. As she was about to land a blunt stroke to the neck, Myan ducked and stepped forward, sending her sprawling with a low spinning kick.

'That was an illegal move!' she had said, full of righteous anger, stung that Myan had tripped her so easily.

Myan laughed. 'Sometimes, Ellen, you have to break the rules to get what you want. Come, let's ride the cliffs.'

The day lived in her memory. *Sometimes you have to break the rules to get what you want.* Ellen picked up her scythe once more, and examined the lanedd blade with a determined eye. She had no idea how she would get out of Raynor, or follow the calvanni, but she knew she had to act.

It was time to break some rules.

Chapter Six

Marken lay back on the padded couch, relaxing for the first time since they had entered Raynor. The tattooist leant over his chest, making quick tapping movements as he worked. First had come the sigil that marked the first degree of the calvanni as an 'honoured former path'. Marken had paid extra to have the sigil stylised – it now swept around the bat-shaped Brotherhood tattoo, making it all but unrecognisable. Getting the first degree had been a necessary compromise to access the profits of the Brotherhood's smuggling operations. Another waste of time. Like Cedrin, he had been forced to flee and leave his hidden wealth in Athria. He had also taken the opportunity to get his sea-serpent totem touched up with fine new colours. The tattooist was now finishing off Kranor's mark, a small tattoo that showed the old standard of the One Hundred: a fierce phoenix clutching a greatscythe in its talons, both blades extended.

A fat woman dressed in Priestesses robes chanted rhythmically in the corner. Marken doubted that she was a real Priestess, but it was nice to have some ceremony to the event. Her voice was husky and quite pleasant in an earthy sort of way.

The interior of the Tattoo Temple was brightly lit. A series of fake columns had been set up to give a mystical air, but the low ceiling ruined the effect. Scores of small censers burnt around the room, scattered across the tables, benches and shelves. The incense was thick in the air, cloying against the back of his throat. It smelled cheap. At least the room was warm. Cedrin had changed one of the Sealed gemstones at a moneylender in the Merchants' Quarter and with real wealth in their pockets once more, doors were opening to them.

Marken patted the thick bulge in his pocket and flashed the tattooist a smile. 'Some watered wine would be nice.'

The tattooist jerked his head at a young girl sitting on a bench nearby and she padded from the room on bare feet.

'So kind,' said Marken. His tattooist grunted without looking up.

He looked across at Cedrin, who was on a couch across the room. The lanky former calvanni met his gaze, a small smile tugging at the edge of his lips.

'What have you done with your first-degree? The damn thing looks like a flower,' said Cedrin.

'Another critic! Well, a flower is better than a target,' he said.

Marken looked closer at Cedrin's own tattoos. He also had sigils showing the six degrees of the calvanni as an honoured former path, but in Cedrin's case the sigils were small and precisely intoned beside each degree. His tattooist was just finishing off the last of them. There would be no mistaking Cedrin's history. It looked as though Cedrin had chosen to highlight his past, rather than obscure it.

'So. You also want Kranor's mark?' asked Cedrin's tattooist. He was a big man, with hairy shoulders and a rough, weather-beaten face. He looked like a prize fighter.

Cedrin lifted up his hand and studied Belin's ring. It glittered in the bright light. Cedrin was hard enough to read at the best of times, but something in his expression gave Marken an uneasy feeling.

'Well?' prompted Cedrin's tattooist.

'Yes. But I want the best work you have ever done. I'll pay whatever it costs,' said Cedrin.

'Got it, rich boy. How big then?'

'I want it sweeping across my chest – like an avenging spirit. I want it fierce. I want people to see the phoenix and stop in their tracks. Understand?'

The tattooist smiled, revealing a cracked tooth. 'Yeah, mate. I know what you're lookin' for.'

The girl returned with the watered wine, but Marken

motioned her to put it on the table at his side. His stomach was churning. 'Cedrin. You can't be serious.'

Cedrin looked back at Marken, his grey-blue eyes lit with amusement. 'And why is that?'

'The mobs!' said Marken, tensing up. 'As if Kranor's mark was not bad enough. The city is a battleground and you want to walk around with one of the banners on your chest.'

Marken was furious. The one moment they were out of danger – with money in their pocket – and Cedrin puts them right back into it.

'Stay still, damn you,' grumbled Marken's tattooist.

'Been plenty of work that way,' said Cedrin's tattooist. 'Been doing at least twenty of the phoenix crests a day since the Scion turned up.'

'Relax, Marken. It's Kranor's mark – the mark of the One Hundred. The same bodyguard that Belin trained.'

'And who is going to know the difference? One look at that and people are going to see the phoenix crest – the mark of the Scion.'

Cedrin's eyes fell to the ring once more. 'You worry too much, Marken. In a few days, we will be out of Raynor and on the open roads. Then the only thing that will matter is what the warriors of Kranor's company think.'

Marken lapsed into silence.

'There. That one's done,' said his tattooist. Marken looked down to examine his small phoenix tattoo, which was about three fingers wide.

'That's good work,' said Marken, impressed.

'Thanks,' said the tattooist impatiently. 'Where do you want the mark o' the scytheman?'

'Just beside it,' said Marken. He and Cedrin had both agreed to also take the Way of the Scytheman as well. All Kranor's warriors had this mark, which showed their intention to follow the mental discipline and philosophies that encompassed the Way.

The tattooist started work, and Marken picked up the wine. He took small sips to try and settle his stomach.

He had said nothing about Cedrin's use of Sorcery to smash

the window. So far they had been lucky. No one suspected. Even so, discovery by the Temple was the least of his worries. The power in Cedrin was like a sleeping harena – and a bad tempered one at that. The fact that Cedrin could control the Fire at all was a miracle. Marken knew enough about magic from his studies as a novice Moon Druid in Athria to realise the power inside Cedrin would become harder to control the longer he went untrained. What he needed was a teacher, another Sorcerer who could show him how to use his gift. But where to look? Decades of persecution by the Temple of the Sisters had pushed the surviving practitioners underground.

Cedrin refused to talk about it, preferring instead to believe he could suppress his powers.

Marken shifted in his seat, venting his frustration. His tattooist glared at him. He smiled back, giving the man his famous, glowing grin.

Marken had never met anyone like Cedrin. His reserve hid a real compassion for those around him. Marken had seen it time and time again in Athria. Cedrin would look out for those under his command and challenge the decisions of the leaders of the Brotherhood when he considered them ill-conceived or if they placed his men in excessive risk. He guessed it was that courageous dissent that had put him on the blacklist of the Mask of Smuggling – that and the fierce loyalty he inspired.

It was Cedrin who had got him and Skye out of Athria alive, managing to lead them out of the clutches of the Brotherhood, past the revenge of the Athrian Suul and the reach of the renegade Sorcerer Raziin Cinnor. Yet despite the nobility in him, Cedrin had refused to have any part of the Suul. Perhaps acknowledging himself as Belin's son was the first step.

Marken watched the big phoenix tattoo take shape across Cedrin's chest. He put down the wine. Sooner or later Cedrin's power was going to explode from him. It could kill him – and everyone around him. It could get them all thrown into the dungeons of the Temple of the Sisters to await a terrible death by torture.

Marken felt nauseated – and it was nothing to do with the thick incense.

'Looking forward to the open road, my friend?' asked Cedrin.

Marken flashed him a grin. 'Of course. Nothing better for the constitution.'

'That's the spirit.'

* * *

A single bead of sweat ran slowly down Ellen's forehead, but she dare not move to wipe it away. She checked her Shadow Matrix. The Sorcery was still in place, rendering her invisible.

Four scythemen blocked the lower entrance to the Eastern Tower, their weapons casually tilted against the wall. Night had fallen and the corridors were quiet and cold. They shuffled about, trying to keep warm.

'Inspection tonight?' said one of the scythemen, picking his teeth. The sound of his voice startled her.

'I think we are fairly safe. Uran will be celebrating,' said the squad leader, Blade rank by his insignia.

One of the scytheman drew out a flask of bakta. He took a swig of the clear spirit. 'Ohhhh, that's it. This stuff was invented for Storm Season.' He handed the flask to the Blade.

'Yeah. It's good to get the chill out,' said one.

The Blade groaned in pleasure as the fiery spirit slid down his throat.

'Not worried about an attack by Olcis spies?' asked one scytheman, his face creased in a grin.

'What? With fifty warriors in the tower – and most of the Druidin upstairs guarding the Olcis scum?' said the Blade, looking down the corridor with a sly expression. 'I don't think so.'

Ellen was not in the habit of sneaking around corridors unseen. She could not help but wonder how many guards in the Athrian palace, seemingly alert and at attention, had only moments before been lounging around drinking bakta.

She moved forward, trying to ease past them, and felt one of the wooden boards move beneath her. A scythe, which had been propped up against the wall, shifted with the movement, sliding

122

to the floor with a loud thud.

The transformation was instantaneous. They snatched up their weapons and within a heartbeat the bottle was gone and they were in formation, their scythes crossed in front of the doorway.

Ellen froze. She was only feet away from them. She might be invisible, but that would do nothing to stop a lanedd point.

Desperately trying to control her breathing, she ducked under the crossed scythes, careful of her own weapon as she crept forward on her silk slippers. After what seemed like eternity, she stood on the other side of the doorway.

'Looks like it was nothing,' said the leader, giving a signal. The men relaxed, leaving the doorway open. Ellen stifled a groan, wiping the sweat from her brow with her sleeve. She paused long enough to catch her breath and then continued into the tower. She knew Raphal was inside, although she had no idea where.

She climbed the stairs, entering floors at random, following her instinct, passing scythemen and Druids – Daran's Druidin – busy on various errands. The Shadow Matrix belonged exclusively to the Realm of Fire. It was foreign to the Druids, detectable only by a gifted few if they were actively looking for it. As she passed deeper into the heart of Uran's power, Ellen felt an exhilaration fill her. It was exciting to defy him, to throw his talk of *siring* Sorcerers and his contempt for Myan's dream of Empire, *her dream*, back in his face.

Ellen guessed they would be keeping the prisoners close to the Temple of the Iris, on the upper floors of the tower. After almost an hour, she finally saw a corridor she recognised from her visit to the tower with Uran. The initial thrill of trespass had gone now. Her mind was growing unfocussed and her shoulders and neck ached from carrying her scythe. She knew she could hold the Shadow Matrix almost indefinitely in the comfort of her old study in the Cintros mansion, but the tension of this clandestine mission was a new challenge to her concentration. She saw increasing numbers of guards, most flanked by robed men bearing the sigil of Yosini, the Hidden Sun.

Turning a corner, she saw a guarded entrance: a set of wooden double-doors secured with a heavy locking mechanism. *This could be it.* She crept past a young Yosini Druid and through the ranks of guards towards it. She bent low to look through the large mought key-hole.

She saw movement. Darkness. Then, without warning, the doors swung open.

Ellen leapt back. She lost her footing and fell heavily onto the floor. Instinctively, she let go of her scythe and threw her hands back to break her fall, desperate to keep her hold on the Shadow Matrix. She succeeded, but the scythe flashed into existence three paces away, clattering wildly against the wall.

She looked back sharply at the guards. A team of men, led by a Yosini Druid, had pushed through the doors with an empty wooden trolley and the guard's attention was on them. Miraculously, the sound of the falling scythe had been covered by the thump of the trolley as it struck the door.

Through the doors, Ellen caught a glimpse of a vast room. Scores of craftsmen and Druids moved around some sort of massive platform. The doors closed again, cutting off her view. *What was Uran up to?*

Ellen recognised the Yosini Druid. Along with Analas, he had led Daran's Druidin against the Olcis delegation in the Great Hall. His golden skin and hair revealed Cioan ancestry. She guessed that like Uran himself, he would be a refugee from the destruction of Althar. He looked sharply at the men guarding the door. When his eyes fell to the scythe on the hallway floor, he stopped.

'Continue on,' said the Yosini Druid, waving the team of men with the trolley down the corridor. His face darkened as he turned to the young Yosini Druid stationed at the door.

'Is this what you call discipline?' said the Druid, picking up the scythe. 'Do you always leave weapons laying around?'

The young Yosini Druid stared dumbly at the scythe. 'It's … no weapon I recognise, master Calaphas.'

'Well, see it does not happen again. For now,' Calaphas looked at the weapon as though it were a strange species of fish, 'this is forfeit.'

After one last reproving glance, Calaphas turned sharply and made off down the corridor, away from the Iris and whatever was being constructed in the vast room behind the doors. Biting her lip, she followed. She cursed herself for bringing the weapon. She had never intended to fight, yet she could not bear to enter the tower without it. Now the finely made weapon with its proudly displayed Cintros crest could be the end of her – she might as well leave Uran a calling card.

Calaphas walked to a small storeroom where he placed the scythe. Carefully, Ellen entered the room after him and reclaimed the weapon, the scythe vanishing as she touched it. Calaphas headed back into the tower. Curious, Ellen followed him. It was easy progress as the guards and Druids made way for him, unknowingly letting Ellen through in his wake.

Sometime later, they arrived at a small, yet heavily guarded door of solid mought. Based on her knowledge of the tower, she was directly beneath the level containing the cracked Temple of the Iris.

'Greetings, brother Calaphas,' said the short Druid at the door. Golden skinned, he too wore the sigil of the Hidden Sun.

'Brother,' said Calaphas tersely. 'How are the prisoners? Have any decided to renounce allegiance to Olcis and join the Druidin?'

The little Druid shook his head. 'No. They are obstinate. Ranlan has not stopped threatening us with the righteous wrath of the Hesguit.'

'This is to be expected. We only have to keep them out of trouble and in chains until we can be rid of them.' Calaphas sighed. 'I wish Daran had let them go. They are bound to be more trouble than they are worth. With the *Raptor* nearing completion we need every man.' He paused, exhausted. 'Oh well, open up. I should check the torcs.'

The short Druid signalled for the door to be opened. Calaphas stepped through the low opening. Ellen – hardly believing her luck – followed through in his wake.

They entered a long corridor with many small alcoves branching from it. They were windowless and well-constructed, perhaps originally built to hold treasure. There were no doors, and Ellen could see some of the connecting walls had been removed to widen them into cells.

She saw the High Moon-Druid sitting on a narrow bed in the first alcove, his right leg secured to the wall with a thick mought chain. The length of chain allowed enough freedom of movement to walk between the bed and the chamber-pot in the corner. The cell was lit with a single oil lamp, but its dim corners also flickered with the lurid crimson light of the mercury glowmetal in the circlet around the prisoner's neck. The Moon Druid looked up at Calaphas without expression as the Yosini Druid checked the glass torc.

With business-like efficiency, Calaphas moved to each cell in turn to check the prisoners' torcs.

Ranlan was in the fourth cell.

'I demand to see the Warlord,' said Ranlan, his head held defiantly. 'You cannot think the Hesguit will sit by and let Yosini scum like you poison the minds of the innocent citizens of Raynor.'

Ranlan's tirade continued, but Calaphas studiously ignored him. Once he was done, he moved to the next prisoner.

The conditions were basic, but she was relieved to see none of them had been tortured. Her hands shook – but whether from fatigue or fear she was not sure. She swallowed, trying to suppress the feeling of sick anticipation that threatened her grip on the Shadow Matrix. Her determination to rescue Raphal was stronger than ever. She would certainly get him away from this!

Finally Calaphas reached Raphal's cell. A wave of relief swept through her when she saw he was unharmed.

'Ah, the prophet is awake,' said Calaphas.

Raphal gave him a warm smile. 'Men of learning rarely sleep, Calaphas. Especially in bondage.'

Calaphas gave a small laugh as he checked the clearglass mechanism that locked the torc in place.

'It is a pity you left Althar when you did, old friend. There was much we could have done together.'

Raphal straightened on his bed. 'Yes, but look what befell Althar.'

Calaphas laughed. 'You're not going to try and tell me you

saw that in a prophecy, are you?'

Raphal shook his head. 'No, you old rascal. Olcis had a better library.'

With a pleased grunt, Calaphas left and Raphal settled back into whatever thoughts he had been drawn out of. Silently, Ellen stepped to his side.

'Raphal,' she whispered.

The old man jerked upright. Ellen hardly recognised the hard, calculating look on his face as his gaze swept the room. 'Who's there?'

'It's me. Ellen.'

He reached out and touched Ellen's arm. His face softened then lit with concern. 'You should not be here. You are taking too much of a risk.'

'I have to get you out,' said Ellen.

They both froze as Calaphas walked back past the cells. The door to the corridor opened and closed, the sound of the locking mechanism loud in the quiet. Ellen's heart thudded as she realised she would not be able to get out of here without destroying the door – and raising the alarm.

'That's it then. I suppose the damage is done. You will never get out of here without me now,' said Raphal.

'How do I release the torc?' asked Ellen, her voice pitched low to avoid alerting the other prisoners. She needed no further complications.

'You won't be able to. It can only be opened with an Essence spell – and a complex one at that. You will have to melt the glass and let the mercury glowmetal flow out of the tubing. It is the only way. Then I can use my own powers.'

'But the heat...'

'It's the only way. If you shatter it with Force, the shards will kill me.'

Laying aside her scythe, she let the Shadow Matrix fall. Now she was at her most vulnerable and had to work quickly. With pin-point accuracy she let a hot probe of the Fire touch the outside of the torc. It was delicate work. The air above the clearglass shimmered, then the torc began to glow red-hot.

Raphal clenched his teeth, shaking with agony as the flesh of his neck began to char.

Ellen faltered. 'Raphal …'

'*Keep going,*' he whispered.

'What's that? Who's there?' called a prisoner from the next cell.

'It's nothing. Go to sleep,' said Ranlan.

Raphal's whole body shook with the intensity of the pain. Even so he did not utter a sound. Ellen's stomach churned with nausea, but she focussed on her task. Finally, the molten glass opened. The crimson and silver glowmetal oozed out of the gap, flopping onto the floor in one piece. Its crimson light danced across the walls and ceiling.

Ellen reached to heal Raphal, but he shook his head.

He closed his eyes in concentration and extended his right hand, his thumb and first finger raised in an arcane sign. With a sigh like ecstasy, he opened his eyes.

The clearglass torc sprang open and fell to the floor. Moments later the savage burn began to shrink, the darkened flesh sloughing away like a shed skin. Smiling, Raphal gestured. The chains melted from him, the molten mought hissing on the cold stone at his feet.

'Free – and whole,' he said.

Ellen was struck dumb with amazement. 'How?' she finally managed.

Raphal smiled. 'They should never have imprisoned a Larus Priest this close to a Temple.'

Realisation struck Ellen like a sudden wave. Of course! The Temple of the Iris lay right above them.

'Can you get us out without raising the alarm?' she asked.

'Yes,' he said. His eyes shone with a soft yellow glow – the bright power of the Iris.

'Who is that talking? There is someone here,' called the prisoner again.

'Who is it? Raphal! Answer me,' called Ranlan.

Raphal paused for a moment. Regret crossed his face. 'The others must take their chances.'

Raphal stretched out his hands towards the great rock slab above them. The ceiling – which was the floor of the Temple of the Iris – began to ripple and flow, peeling back like the petals of a flower. Through the gap, Ellen could see the dimly-lit dome that covered the Iris. Ellen had been well schooled in the forbidden arts of Sorcery, but she had never seen anything like this.

'How can Essence defeat stone?' she asked.

'Rock is of the Earth,' said Raphal.

Mysteries had to wait. She did not know how long they had before they were discovered; either from above or below.

Ellen gathered her power and concealed herself inside the Shadow Matrix. She propelled herself through the gap with a surge of Force. She landed lightly on the floor of the Iris, and circled. The Temple was empty, the vast space in virtual darkness. The great eye at the centre of the mural was dead and silent, the whole design riddled with cracks. She reached for the Window, using the Force Matrix to draw Raphal up through the gap after her. She put the old scholar down lightly on the floor of the Temple. Raphal raised his hands once more and the gap flowed closed, sealing itself. Where the opening had been the mural was fresh and new, the cracks healed.

Thanks to her prior visit to the Temple, Ellen knew how they could escape: through Uran's own apartments. She almost laughed at the audacity of the idea. She released the Shadow Matrix and took Raphal by the hand. 'This way!'

Ellen led them to the concealed staircase, casting one last glance around the gloom of the domed Temple before plunging into the darkness beyond. She reached for the Fire, thinking to channel light to guide their way, but Raphal tapped her lightly on the shoulder.

'Save your strength, Ellen. We will have need of your Fire if we meet Uran.'

Ellen's heart beat wildly. If they did meet Uran, he would try and take both her and Raphal prisoner – his duty to the Warlord would demand it. She had no intention of ending up in a cell next to Raphal and would have little choice but to fight him. She sent a quick prayer to Larus that he did not cross their path. He would be a skilled opponent – far more so than the renegade Raziin – and despite her disagreements with him, he was a good man and an important asset in the upcoming struggle against the Eathal. Any conflict between them could end with one – or both of them – dead or maimed.

The reality of her reckless rescue confronted her. She had been concerned for Raphal, but deep down she knew it was an act of defiance; a way of proving herself as resourceful or powerful in Raynor as Uran and her brother. For a sickening moment her mind played over the future she could have chosen. A Suul of Raynor, a wife to Uran, a power within the citadel of the mighty. Had she destroyed that future in one impulsive action? No, she would never accept that. Her path had always lain elsewhere.

Light blossomed in the stairwell, a full, warm light that cast back the stubborn shadows around the passage.

'There,' said Raphal, satisfied. The light issued from a ball hovering just above his head, and gave the old scholar a sublime radiance. The Raynor Iris may be shattered, but the Temple's power remained.

Ellen was surprised at the subtle elegance of the carved stair. The light also revealed the majestic frescos that had been hidden in the dark. Many Suul were depicted amid scenes of court life from the peak of Bulvuran's might. Only one man amid the multitude had been drawn looking back out at the observer; a striking man in the prime of his middle years, his eyes knowing, alive with power and vision.

'Asrellan. One of the most brilliant of the Emperors,' said Raphal, following her gaze. 'He found the sixth Iris.'

'Sixth? I thought there were only five?'

'Five faces, yet one point about which they turn – the centre.' Six Temples of the Iris and only two she knew of – Athria and Raynor.

Her vision flashed blue.

The Scion must stand in the Temple of the Iris.

Ellen leant back against the wall, screwing her eyes shut until the world stopped spinning. She opened them to see Raphal's concerned face.

'Have no fear, Ellen. I shall be out of Raynor tonight, and you will be far from blame.' He had mistaken her momentary faintness for fear.

Ellen led on without comment. The sooner they were out of the Eastern Tower the better.

At the end of the stair, Ellen activated the hidden release and they emerged from the secret passage into Uran's library.

Her head was thick with tension, but she forced herself to focus. Ellen re-established the Shadow Matrix, shielding them both from view, then slowly opened the doors to the main rooms. One of the mought hinges creaked ominously, seeming almost to scream into the quiet. Her stomach flipped. Blood pounded through her temples.

She heard a child call out and froze. Her hand gripped Raphal's wrist like a vice. She waited, but all was quiet again. Perhaps the child had a nightmare. Sweat had gathered between her shoulder blades. Then she remembered the guard's comment. Uran himself was not here, he was off somewhere celebrating, while his household – the First Consort and his children – were fast asleep.

She drew Raphal on through the apartment.

At the exit she paused. 'Uran keeps guards on the doors,' she whispered. 'I'll need to create a diversion so we can slip past.'

'No need, Ellen. I sensed they were both sleeping and used the Earth Essence to add a little depth to the slumber,' replied Raphal.

Ellen drew in a deep breath and let it out slowly, releasing her tension. She let go her grip on Raphal's arm and eased the doors open to see both guards slumped against the wall, snoring. Near a Temple, Earth Essence was a potent force, she realised.

Ellen and Raphal closed the doors carefully behind her. Then she led them past the remaining tower guards into the warm, empty corridors of the main palace. They ducked into an unused room and she released the Shadow Matrix.

She had done it! Her legs trembled as a wave of relief swept through her.

Raphal gripped Ellen's hands warmly. 'It was a grave risk, Ellen – but I am glad you took it. I owe you a debt.'

'Where to now?'

'With your help I will gather some things from my quarters and flee through the servant's entrance dressed as a pilgrim Priest. Then I will make my way to Olcis.'

Ellen smiled. She felt strong and independent for the first time since she had entered Raynor. She also had the sense that she had passed the point of no return. How could she possibly go back to her life in the consulate after this? Being subject to her brother's will, his political schemes, while her quest for the Scion went unfulfilled? With sudden clarity, she realised there would never be a better opportunity to leave Raynor. Raphal was clever, resourceful and streetwise. The perfect guide and companion.

'Raphal. I need your help.'

'Of course. What is it?' he asked.

'I am also leaving Raynor.' Ellen was surprised at the uncompromising strength in her voice.

Raphal lifted an eyebrow. 'Why, Ellen?'

'I must find the Scion, Raphal. Now that Osterac has been revealed as a fraud, I have to look elsewhere.'

Ellen hesitated. She knew that Raphal would never betray her. His loyalty to her family was beyond question. If not for the resources the Temple offered him as a scholar, he never would have left Athria. Yet he also owed allegiance to Olcis. How much could she ask of him? She bit her lip. In the end it was his decision. Ellen was too short of allies to second guess herself now. She took a deep breath then told Raphal everything. Her quest. The value her father Myan had placed in the calvanni Cedrin and how he was her only link to Riin's son.

'And you are sure you can find him again?' asked Raphal.

Ellen smiled. 'I can find him, Raphal, have no fear of that.'

'Very well. I am at your service, Ellen. My return to Olcis can wait – at least until I see you safely on your quest.'

'I will have to gather some things for travelling,' said Ellen. She shivered, both excited and scared by the challenges she would face. By dawn, her palace life would be a memory.

Chapter Seven

Cedrin's arms ached from the weight of the greatscythe, but he held it steady, waiting for Marken's attack. They were both stripped to the waist, lean muscles glistening with sweat. He focussed on Marken, trying to read his attack from the tension in the muscles of his chest, or a change in his stance. *Nothing.* His friend's lighter scythe swept down at his leg. Cedrin swivelled his weapon to block, but the attack had been a feint. The other end of Marken's scythe abruptly whipped towards his throat. He put his weight into the counter-swing, trying to stop the blow, but mistimed it. Marken laid the end of his scythe lightly on his exposed neck.

'Good thing we're not using blades,' said Marken.

'Aye,' he said.

Cedrin leant on his greatscythe and wiped the sweat off his brow, pausing to catch his breath. A group of five young warriors from Kranor's company stood nearby. One of them stepped up to Cedrin. 'Ahh … excuse me, Lord Kaidell?'

Marken lowered his scythe, his expression one of profound amusement. 'Lord already. You'll be Emperor by noon,' said Marken in a low voice.

'I'm no Suul, my friend,' said Cedrin to the young warrior. Although the young man was tall – only an inch shorter than he was – he must have been no more than fifteen. He was thin as a spear, but the breadth of his shoulders and his lean frame showed the promise of great strength.

One of the other young warriors was looking at his phoenix tattoo. 'I've never seen a finer tattoo,' he said, looking at Cedrin in admiration. None of them had failed to notice the six degrees, now marked as an 'honoured former path'.

Knowing how much Belin had been respected by Kranor, Cedrin had hoped to win respect in his company by declaring himself Belin's son. So far the plan had worked remarkably well – almost a little too well.

'But you wear Belin's ring. *The* Belin. And you are his son.'

Cedrin nodded. It was not the first time he had been approached today. The young warrior stepped forward, drawn by the glittering emerald ring on Cedrin's right hand.

'My name is Rastor. Can I… see it, sir?' The young warrior looked up hopefully.

Cedrin help up his hand as the young warrior leant forward. 'It's true! The crest of Kaidell, showing Tower Blackthorne,' said Rastor.

'Don't you have anything better to do?' snapped the training master, Kanis, walking towards their small group. Cedrin and Marken had only been in the training yard for four hours, but that rough, uncompromising voice was one they had come to know well.

Kanis was one of Kranor's senior men. He was powerfully built, his chest dotted with honours achieved in Kranor's service. His dark skin, red-streaked dark hair and wide face indicated a mix of both Cioan ancestry and the plains blood of the Meadrel tribesman.

'You've finished your drills, then?' barked Kanis at the young warriors. They withered as Kanis fixed them with his small, deep-set black eyes.

'No, sir,' they chorused.

'Then get to it,' snapped Kanis.

The young warriors turned to go. 'And Rastor!'

Rastor turned, swallowing as he met Kanis' gaze. 'Yes, sir.'

'Don't let me catch you calling this Athrian "sir",' said Kanis, jerking his thumb at Cedrin. 'He and Marken are new recruits, not honoured men. You and your mates would know ten times more about the greatscythe – or being a warrior – then they would.'

Rastor nodded, giving Cedrin a fleeting look of mortified

embarrassment before he hurried away.

Kanis stared at Cedrin and Marken, his face screwed up in distaste.

'You might have impressed a few boys, but it takes more than new ink to impress me. Watch yourself,' he said. Kanis turned his back on them and walked away.

'Charming,' said Marken.

'Very,' said Cedrin. So far Cedrin was pleased with how well they had been accepted by the men in Kranor's company. Kanis was the exception. Maybe it was just his way.

Kranor had kept the military structure of the Emperor's bodyguard intact. He had more than a thousand warriors scattered across Kelas – perhaps as many as two thousand – but his elite men were the One Hundred. Every one of Kranor's men bore his mark, and hoped one day to join this elite inner circle. Each of his mercenary companies was led by a handful of senior warriors from the One Hundred.

Their caravan would be leaving tomorrow for Searn, led by an old warrior called Xyanthius, who, like Kranor and Tarral, had been in Emperor Riin's bodyguard. The taciturn mercenary Captain had toured the yard earlier in the day, and had made a point of greeting him, enquiring briefly after Tarral. It boded well for their journey. Kanis and ten others from Kranor's One Hundred would form the core of their force, with ninety other warriors from Kranor's company joining them. His instinct about Kranor had proved correct. He ran a well-disciplined, well-organised company. They could not have made a better choice.

'Good time for a break,' said Marken.

'Aye,' said Cedrin.

They walked into one of the buildings to a water barrel and filled a cup each. Cedrin delighted in the cool water as it slid down his throat.

They had been hard at it since just after dawn. Marken working with Cedrin to teach him some of the basics of using a scythe. It was hard going. Cedrin found the long weapon unwieldy, and had yet to get a feel for it. The truth was he had always preferred the long knife.

A cool breeze swept through the doorway, making Cedrin shiver. They moved back into the sun, taking their cups with them. It was the last day of Storm Season, and at last the twin suns had true warmth. There was no rain today, and the biting cold was easing. The sleet that had fallen yesterday, which had been frozen overnight onto the flags and gutters, was now melting as the suns climbed higher.

Cedrin looked around the courtyard. From the street, the *Scytheman* looked like any other tavern, yet behind it was an extensive complex. More than a dozen buildings, some of stone, others of wood, had been joined together to form Kranor's headquarters. The rear yards of all of the buildings had been cleared to form a large open training area, roughly square and around two hundred paces a side. The area was flagged with stone, and a short roof had been constructed around the inside edge of the courtyard to protect the building entrances from the weather. Some of the buildings served as warehouses, others stables. Closer to the *Scytheman* were the armoury and barracks. Kranor had a small army housed here.

A group of warriors walked by. They had met a few of them at breakfast and Cedrin knew they had been in Kranor's company less than a year.

'Ho there, Cedrin,' said one of them, a short, dark-haired warrior called Lann.

'How are you, Lann?'

'Never better. I was telling the lads about that trick you did. Any chance to see it again?'

Cedrin smiled and pulled out his two calvs. The news that he was Belin's son had spread rapidly, and made him something of a celebrity. Since there was nothing impressive he could do with a greatscythe – yet – he had shown Lann a calv trick. Usually Cedrin was loath to perform like this, preferring to build his relationships slowly and steadily, but he needed to be seen as someone of note in Kranor's company, someone they would consider a leader. He did not intend to stay a new recruit any longer than necessary.

Cedrin flipped the first calv up into the air, sending the second after it. His hands shot forward, deftly catching each by the hilt and throwing them higher.

The men cheered and the crowd around him grew. Each of the calvs was razor-sharp, and one slip would see him cut badly, perhaps even losing a finger.

'Is that Cedrin?' he heard someone ask.

'Isn't that Belin Kaidell's son?'

The babble of voices grew, and he threw the calvs higher still, his concentration total.

Then the voices grew quiet.

'Let's see you juggle three of those.' Kanis' voice was cold and tense.

Cedrin looked across. A calv flipped through the air towards him from Kanis. *The angle was wrong!* He caught one of his calvs by the hilt, letting the other fall. Then he turned to block Kanis' long knife. He caught it less than a hand's breadth from his throat. The deflected weapon clattered back to the stone flags.

Cedrin's heart hammered as he looked back at Kanis. That had been a potentially lethal attack! With the calv in his hand he longed to advance on the bastard and teach him a lesson. Kanis stood relaxed, his greatscythe in his hands. Their eyes met. Kanis knew he wanted to attack. He was waiting for it. Cedrin remembered how quickly Kranor had moved with a greatscythe, and was acutely aware of the weapon's longer reach. Cedrin sheathed his blade.

Kanis grunted. 'Your time would be better spent learning the greatscythe. Belin's son or not, I have not seen anything worth harena shite from you so far.'

Cedrin kicked Kanis' calv back to him, keeping his face expressionless.

Kanis picked up his calv. 'Do you two have your armour yet?'

'No. We are picking it up later today,' said Marken.

'Pick it up now,' said Kanis, walking away. The crowd dispersed in silence.

Cedrin picked up his fallen calv. The tip had been chipped by the fall. 'Curse it,' he said, sheathing the weapon.

'With Kanis as Xyanthius' lieutenant, it's going to be an interesting trip,' said Marken.

'Aye.'

Cedrin watched Kanis as he walked away. For some reason the man had taken a set against him. As the new face in the company, Cedrin had expected to put a few noses out of joint, but he thought it would be new members of the company who saw him as a threat to their own advancement. Not only was Kanis a senior member of Kranor's force, he was dangerous. Cedrin could feel it in his gut.

* * *

By the time they left the training yard all the ice on the streets had melted, the air filled with freshness and warmth. People who had not stirred from the fireside throughout the long days of cold appeared in the streets, baring chests to the day. The last day of Storm Season was usually a time of carefree abandon, but from the outset, Cedrin had picked up an ugly mood.

'What's happened?' he had asked the armourer when they arrived to be fitted.

The armourer was a short rotund man, with large calloused hands and thick forearms traced with fine scars. A former warrior for sure.

'You haven't heard?' he said.

'Heard what?'

'Osterac was a fake. I don't know how Daran did it, but yesterday the Warlord got him to renounce his claim in front of a full public court. A mob has gathered on the Palardos. Daran will have his hands full. It will be more than a few hundred refugees this time – more like thousands. I'd want to watch out if I were you,' said the armourer, jabbing a finger at Cedrin's sweeping phoenix tattoo.

By the time they had tried to make their way to the *Scytheman*, the streets of the Inner City were uncomfortably crowded. The morning freshness had faded, giving way to rising humidity, and the mood of the city fermented in the steamy heat.

Cedrin shifted the pack on his back, adjusting the straps. He and Marken both carried their new leather armour. With the wealth they had recovered from the Brotherhood, they had been able to afford the best: stiffened leather reinforced with strips of dark mought.

As they squeezed through the crowd, both Cedrin and Marken kept their robes tightly closed. Twice they had turned corners into a mass of moving people, forced to backtrack and find other ways.

Cedrin led them around a corner, pushed on by the crowd. He was hoping to see one of the streets near the *Scytheman*. Instead they emerged onto the Palardos itself – the wide street that circled the Suul district and the palace of the Cinanac.

'I think we are a long way from the Merchants' Quarter,' said Marken. Cedrin suppressed his frustration. Somehow they had been completely turned around.

The armourer was right. There were thousands here, packed in tight. The edgy mood they had detected before had now turned to outright anger. The bright banners bearing the phoenix crest, which had been raised along the Palardos following Osterac's arrival, had been pulled down and trampled.

'Betrayers!' screamed a fat woman to Cedrin's left.

'We demand vengeance!' bellowed a man to his right, looking up at the sheer walls of the palace as though expecting an answer.

'Death to Osterac!'

'Death to the Olcis Druids! Down with the Temple of the Sisters!'

'Throw them into the harena pit!'

Only paces away a group of men were laying into a man on the cobbles with their boots. The man had curled into a ball, but Cedrin could see enough of his chest to see the freshly inked phoenix tattoo.

'*Let's get out of here,*' said Marken.

More people were arriving every moment and the street behind them was jammed. There was no way they could go back the way they had come. Cedrin pushed through the crowd, trying to find a street or alleyway that was not packed to bursting with people. Finally, after almost half an hour, he saw one. It was dark and dingy, and led into one of the poorer quarters of the Inner City, but right now he did not care. 'There,' he said, pointing it out to Marken.

People eyed them suspiciously as they passed. Cedrin returned their gazes with a hard stare. So far it had been enough to deter them. He realised then how much he had come to rely on the degrees of the calvanni to win respect. With their robes tightly closed they were no more than suspicious strangers.

'Down with the false-Scion!' called a huge warrior, a solid mought staff in his hands. He glared at them. The crossed spears and shield of the Warlord were inked on his chest.

'Down with Osterac!' called Marken. The warrior grunted and turned away.

They stepped over a beaten man. His face was an unrecognisable mass of blood and flesh. One of the mob was standing on the man's hand, his attention elsewhere, his boot heel grinding the fingers into the cobbles. The fallen man did not move.

They cut through the edge of the crowd into the alley.

'Finally,' said Marken as they saw empty space ahead. He broke into a run.

'No,' said Cedrin, waving him back. 'Just walk. We can't draw attention to ourselves.'

'Do you have any idea where we are heading?'

'Yes. Away from that mob!'

Behind them the noise of the crowd was like an angry roar, echoing through the stone-built canyons of the city.

Cedrin looked up at the suns, trying to navigate their way back to the *Scytheman*. The streets here were like a warren, and three times he found his way blocked by dead ends. Garbage was piled everywhere, beginning to stink as it thawed. Groups of men, dressed in ragged trousers and faded jackets, stood on the corners, watching them with predatory gazes.

'I think I've got it this time,' said Cedrin, weaving through a narrow alley and turning onto a wider street. A dozen men were milling about to their right. He turned left.

It was blocked by a wall.

'What you got under that robe, mate?' called a man from the

group.

Cedrin pulled the robe tighter around him before he turned. He watched the leader as he advanced. He was lean but well-muscled. He had seen enough street toughs in his time to recognise one. The sort who made a living from theft and extortion, surviving outside the Brotherhood in the gaps where they would not go. He had the crest of the Warlord tattooed on his left pectoral muscle. Cedrin's eyes flicked to each of the group. They all had it. *Diehard supporters of the Warlord.* No doubt they had been lying low the last few days – and now they were eager for payback.

'Nothing, friend,' answered Cedrin. A flush of sweat came out on his forehead.

Cedrin's mind raced. These were tough men, well versed in street ambush. They fanned out, blocking their escape. Some hefted crudely made clubs, others drew calvs. There was no way past them. If there had been three or four, maybe he would risk a fight, but a dozen?

'Then declare yourself,' said the leader, his lips drawn back in a death's head grin. 'Show us your tattoos.'

Cedrin eyed the alley. Tall tenements rose like giants on every side. Their only exit was an ancient chimney, rising like a blackened tree up the side of one of the buildings. Its big blocks would make an easy climb for former calvanni like them, even with the packs – *if* they could reach it in time.

Cedrin knew he had taken a risk with the phoenix tattoo, but he also knew the time for half-measures had passed. Determination filled him. After all they had come through – escaping the Brotherhood, Raziin Cinnor and the Athrian Suul – he refused to die in some Raynor back alley at the hands of scum like this. He reached for the Window, but it remained out of reach, as it had since he used his powers at the Brotherhood house. The Fire would not help him.

'Declare yourself I said!' snapped the tough.

'Be reasonable,' started Marken. 'We have nothing against the Warlord, we support him. We are just as happy to see the false-Scion fall as you.'

'Then prove it.'

Cedrin leant in close to Marken. 'Save your breath,' he whispered. 'Do you see the chimney?'

Looking over his shoulder, Marken eyed the chimney warily, then nodded.

'On my signal,' said Cedrin.

The leader's eyes narrowed. 'That's it. Take 'em, lads. Strip 'em down and let's see what sort of renegades we got.' He waved his men forward.

'Now!' yelled Cedrin.

He and Marken sprinted for the chimney. As they ran, their robes flew open. The gang leader's eyes widened as he caught a glimpse of the newly-inked phoenix tattoos. He whooped with delight.

'Get 'em! *Bloody royals.* We'll throw 'em to the mob!'

Cedrin reached the chimney first, vaulting up to grip the ancient structure, clambering upwards as the men came. Below he heard a crack and turned to see Marken fall, fragments of broken brick tumbling after him. *Rotten.* He hit the cobbles hard and lay unmoving. The toughs were on him, laying in with boots and fists.

'No!' Cedrin had lost Skye to the curse of his Sorcery, he would not lose another friend.

With a shout of rage, Cedrin released his hold on the chimney and leapt into the swirling mass below.

Chapter Eight

Uran bore the brunt of Daran's fury without comment. He was no less angry. He had been rudely snatched from a dream of soft delights and gentle curves to be told one of the Olcis Druids had simply walked out of his most heavily guarded prison.

'How could he have escaped? You told me the torcs were proof against the Druid's magic,' stormed the Warlord. He paced the coloured marble in front of his dais, fists clenched at his sides.

The pain in Uran's head, from alcohol and se, was so intense he could hardly think.

Calaphas stood below the dais, his face grim. Analas waited by his side. Both Yosini Druids knew enough to remain silent.

'They are. It *is* impossible for them to break free of the torcs,' said Uran.

'Then how did it happen?' snapped Daran. Uran was glad the Warlord did not have a weapon. The Sorcerer had not seen him this angry since his favourite concubine was discovered in bed with the Captain of the palace guard.

A servant leant over the low table in front of him, pouring tea into a delicate porcelain teacup patterned with diving raptors and sea beasts. Steam swirled above the cup, catching the morning light. Uran closed his eyes for a moment and inhaled the delicate aroma. The table, used for meetings of Daran's elite inner circle, was usually scattered with maps and documents, but had been cleared for last night's celebrations.

Uran reached forward and carefully cradled the cup. His hands shook badly, and he did not want to scald himself. He sat back in the chair and took a sip. It was a measure of his relationship with the Warlord that he was allowed to sit in his presence. As the hot tisane slipped down his throat, he forced his brain to work.

'It's obvious Raphal had outside help. There are signs his torc had been melted to release the mercury glowmetal – though his screams should have woken Raynor if that were the case.'

'How did they get in?'

'The outside doors were heavily guarded. They must have somehow entered from above, through the Iris. Then escaped the same way,' said Uran.

'I thought the cells were secure!'

'I thought so too. The floor of the Iris is constructed of huge slabs of solid granite, locked together and bearing the weight of the dome above. Not even I could shift them without bringing the whole structure down on top of my head.'

The Warlord stopped his pacing and waited intently for Uran to continue. From the look of Daran's eyes, the Warlord's head was little better than his own after last night's celebrations.

'Once the glowmetal was removed from the torc, Raphal could have used his own powers to release it. I still have no idea how they got into those cells. Not even a powerful Priest or Druid should have been able to get past our defences.'

Daran's dark eyes burned with intensity. 'What did you say?'

'I don't see how anyone could have gotten past our defences.'

The Warlord advanced, his voice low but menacing. 'No. *Not just anyone.* You said a Priest or Druid could not have done it. What of a Sorcerer?'

Uran laughed. He had thought of that, but he was the only trained Sorcerer in Raynor. His protégé Nacius was far from capable, and completely loyal.

'There is no-one in Raynor who could have done it. Unless they have concealed themselves from me with consummate skill. I have searched long and hard for anyone with the talent. The Blood is thin ...'

The Warlord pointed an accusing finger at Uran. 'You forget. There is another.'

It hit him like a cudgel to the back of head. *Ellen.* He himself had shown her the secret passage from the Iris.

'Of course,' he said, his voice hardly above a whisper.

'Could she have done it?' asked the Warlord, his face determined.

Uran nodded, remembering the elegant skill in Sorcery she had displayed on their night together. He rose, the pain in his head nothing to the sickening feeling of betrayal. He should have guessed, with all her talk of the Scion, of the *Empire.* And yet – the Temple of the Sisters was her own sworn enemy. Never would he have imagined her – a Sorcerer – coming to their rescue.

Uran put down his cup. It all snapped into place. 'She knew the way. She could have used the Shadow Matrix to pass through the doorway – slipping through unseen. Raphal must have used his own powers as Priest to breach the floor of the Iris. Clearly, I underestimated his skill.' He had been fooled by the man's humble manner and his lowly scholar's robes.

Daran beckoned one of his Suulqua. 'Summon Ellen Cintros at once.'

The Warlord turned to the Yosini Druids. 'Fetch me a torc.'

Analas hesitated and looked across at Uran. 'Do we have a torc capable of subduing a Sorcerer?'

'Yes. Only one. Find Nacius. He will fetch it for you,' said Uran. That was one glowmetal he kept carefully hidden.

The Yosini Druid bowed and left the room.

'Beware, my Lord,' said Uran. 'Ellen is powerful, and she is highly placed in Athria. We cannot serve her summary justice. Perhaps a banishment. She is Estle's sis—'

The Warlord cut off Uran with an enraged growl. 'That woman thinks she can defy me? I will make a slave of her!'

The Warlord slammed his fist into the table, the wood splintering at the impact. '*This is treason!*'

* * *

Estle put on his most charming smile, trying to appear relaxed. Usually he was pleased when invited to the Warlord's private court, but not today.

The Warlord sat stern and immobile on his carved wooden throne, flanked by Uran and three Druidin. Estle knew the two Yosini Druids, Analas and Calaphas, well. The third man Estle knew only from whispers. Of middle height, with a forgettable face, his hands and arms were marked by small scars gathered over a lifetime of working with messenger birds. One of Daran's field agents, but no ordinary one. This could only be Rehvar, Daran's deadliest assassin. A master of concealment who was only seen when he wanted to be — or was commaded to show himself. His very existence was a state secret. To see him here today, in a closed court, sent a poignant message.

The heat of the day had reached the upper chambers of the palace and although the wide panes behind the Warlord had been opened, the sultry breeze provided little relief from the humidity. Sweat stood out on Daran's brow.

Estle walked to the throne and bowed.

'Where is Ellen Cintros?' demanded Daran. 'She has serious charges to answer before this court.'

Estle bowed again. His eyes flickered to Uran, but he sensed no support from his sometime ally. Rehvar's gaze was steady. Emotionless. Estle swallowed, finding his lips inexplicably dry. *No matter. I must proceed as planned.*

'With regrets, my Lord, she has left Raynor on Athrian business,' said Estle lightly.

'Where was she last night, Cintros?' asked Uran, his face hard.

Estle coughed delicately to hide his discomfort, waving a slave towards him for some watered wine. He winced painfully and held his chest with one hand, the act so faultless they were held in check while he soothed his sudden malady. He had hoped Uran would support him.

His mind worked rapidly as he sipped the wine. When he had been roused to news of Raphal's escape, he needed no prompting to guess at Ellen's part in it. *Impulsive fool.* Surely enough, he had discovered her gone and had quickly bribed the servants and slaves, swearing the staff of the embassy to silence.

'My apologies, Lord,' he said, tapping his heart. 'My chest is weak. The apothecary holds some hope for me, but—'

'Enough,' said the Warlord, sitting forward on his chair and wiping his brow with a cloth.

'Get some fans in here,' commanded the Warlord. The servants waiting near the throne surged into action.

Estle suppressed a smile and waited patiently in the attitude of the perfect courtier, respectful, attentive.

'Enough of this acting. Answer the question. Where was she last night?' asked Uran. The Sorcerer knew him too well. That, however, was no reason to change his tactics.

Estle went for a slightly incredulous look, as though someone had asked him if the suns rose in the west. 'Well, she kept company with me, retiring early for her journey.'

'My patience is exhausted, Cintros. Where is the woman?' demanded Uran.

'Woman?' echoed Estle, struggling to look perplexed.

'*Ellen Cintros.*'

'Ah. I did not realise you were talking about a member of the ruling Council of Athria, a Suulvey and ambassador to Raynor,' said Estle. A vein throbbed in Uran's temple as he glared at him. Estle had never seen the man so dangerous. 'I'm afraid I can't tell you her whereabouts.'

'You will tell us,' said the Warlord, his voice low. 'We have reason to suspect her of treason. The crime is a grave one, Estle. You would do well to aid us. These accusations have a way of spreading.'

'I understand.'

Estle summoned a slave and picked a sweet pastry delicately off the tray.

They glared at him as he finished the pastry.

'I will have your answer, Estle. This is no morning to try me,' said the Warlord.

'My apologies, Lord,' Estle said, bowing slowly. 'As I said, she is on Athrian business and I will help you as much as I can.' He paused, then continued, his voice gaining strength. 'Let me assure you that Suul Ellen Cintros has no connection with these events. Surely there are a score of renegades who could have done as much, simply to discredit her. Such as the Traitor of

Armon, Raziin Cinnor, who – I may remind you – is still at large.

'When I tell you Suulvey Ellen Cintros is about the business of the Athrian court, it is no idle chatter. She was merely waiting here in Raynor for the easing of Storm Season to commence her commission and, by the rules of diplomacy, I am bound to tell you nothing.' His tone was uncompromising. Now was the time to go on the attack.

Estle raised a finger in accusation. 'These charges and innuendos give grave insult to a trusted ally. An ally, let me remind you, whose grain and supplies you will have dire need of, *if* you are to prepare for the coming advance of the Eathal swarm.'

The Warlord and Uran eyed each other in silence as Estle motioned for another pastry.

'Very well. You have made your choice.' The Warlord gave a signal, and a Suulqua came forward.

'The audience is at an end,' said the Suulqua in a reedy and pompous voice.

Estle bowed and withdrew, his expression solemn, yet still holding the pastry in a ridiculous attitude. He exited the room backwards, noting the murderous glance of warning he received from Uran. He shrugged mentally; it was not the first time they had been at odds. The simple fact was, Raynor needed Athria more than ever.

Once outside the room, Estle discarded the pastry with an expression of distaste. He was furious with Ellen, and yet his fury was coloured with respect. It was hard not to think of her as father's favourite – his coddled younger sister. He never dreamed she had the nerve to defy Uran and the Warlord and actually rescue Raphal. The fact that she had pulled it off was even more impressive. Very little got past Uran – Estle had learned that the hard way.

If Daran had any idea what she was really up to, Larus knew what he would do. There was little doubt in his mind. For good or ill, Ellen had set off on this quest to fulfil Myan's dream of the Empire's restoration. It was insane. He had done his best to thwart her, taking away all her men, trying to distract her with work and a chance to form an alliance by marriage with Uran. None of it had worked.

Myan's insanity had taken her.

He and his brother Torren, now Sarlord in Ellen's place, had done their best to survive their father's Imperial obsession and deal with the realities of the new world. Now Ellen had been snared into this quest for the Scion. He suspected that her idealistic nature was the crucial lever Father had applied to sway her into accepting this hopeless mission, yet he sensed there was more. There was something else driving her, something under the surface he had never been able to understand.

Still, there was nothing he could do now. Wherever she was, whatever she did, she was out of his control.

* * *

Ellen slid the wicker screen open a fraction and looked out across the wide lawns towards the Temple of Mythar. A breeze rushed through the gap, tossing back her hair. Here she was – a Suul – skulking in a narrow novice's chamber, with no entourage and no servants.

The small temple was built in the Cioan style, with great blocks supported on columns. It was surrounded by a sacred grove of ancient trees, tall and vibrant with health, each growing wild and unrestrained. The temple and its grove were bordered by lovingly-tended beds of flowers, precisely-clipped shrubs and neat hedges. She could see three yellow-robed Priestesses of Mythar in the garden even now, each bent to their tasks. Unlike the ornate structures of the Temple of the Sisters, this was a true Temple, built on sacred ground long before the walls of Raynor were raised. According to Raphal, it marked an ancient wellspring of Earth-Essence on the Yasser's bank.

It irked her to have to start her quest for the Scion like this. Still, she had to concede, right now their best strategy lay in concealment. Freeing Raphal had been the right thing to do, but the thought of the risk she had taken made her feel ill. Estle would be furious, guessing immediately what she had done.

There was no helping that now, or the reaction of Uran and the Warlord.

Ellen and Raphal had waited until the main palace gates were opened for a returning patrol then had slipped out into the night shielded by the Shadow Matrix. Raphal had led them to the Temple of Mythar, hidden in the southern quarter of the Inner City. From the street, the facade looked like any other three-storey stone dwelling, but the buildings opened into a wide open space. The Temple was concealed both by cunning design and the power of the Temple itself.

When they arrived last night, Raphal had taken her to see the flame kept alight within the Temple; the spirit of the goddess Mythar, ancient handmaiden of Larus. A dozen Priestesses had knelt around the simple oil-fed flame as it flickered in its apse. Ellen had been humbled by the deep serenity of the place, even so, that did not make her immune to impatience.

Ellen pulled the wicker screen closed. She had spent hours waiting for Raphal to return, bored and frustrated. She picked up her scythe. The narrow chamber did not even have enough room for her to swing the weapon. Two paces across, with a low bed and a single shelf, it was spartan at best. There was always the grove, but she doubted the Priestesses would appreciate her practising on the neatly-trimmed lawns outside the Temple. It would be something of an affront to the peaceful Mythar.

She was wearing her riding clothes; a light brown split-skirt of finely woven wool with a matching jacket. Her blouse was of fine white silk, and was already crushed where the straps of the pack had bitten into it. She longed for a bath and a change of clothes and suppressed her annoyance. The Temple had no servants – self-reliance was a virtue to the servants of Mythar – and the bathhouse was not heated.

She put down her scythe and unbraided her honey-gold hair, tying it back in a single tail. Without servants, the braids would be too difficult to handle.

She heard footsteps and tensed as the door to the room opened. It was Raphal. The old Larus Priest and Druid looked tired. Neither of them had slept.

'Any news?' she asked. Earlier they had sent one of the

Temple of Mythar's trusted servants to the *Scytheman* tavern to surreptitiously seek out news of Cedrin. Ellen's use of the Seeker showed her he had been there for two days now. Through the glowmetal, she had seen tantalising glimpses of faces and rooms, but nothing that could tell her what his plans were.

Raphal nodded. 'Yes. It seems Cedrin and his friend Marken have joined with Kranor's mercenary company as scythemen. They leave tomorrow on a caravan bound for Searn via the Delta province. Luckily a large group of refugees will be travelling with them. Two more pilgrims will surely go unnoticed. Two places have been purchased for us.'

Ellen felt a knot of tension in her chest dissolve. The sooner they were out of the city, the safer it would be for Raphal. It would also take her further from the Warlord.

'Pilgrims?' she asked.

'Yes. Why not travel as a Priest and Priestess of Mythar? The robes will conceal us well and do much to alleviate suspicion.'

Ellen nodded, struggling against a feeling of upset. This need for concealment ... she was used to being at the centre of court, at the forefront.

'A good idea, Raphal,' said Ellen, her throat tight.

The Priest rubbed his bald dome absently with his palm, as though to smooth down his absent hair. His bushy eyebrows came together. 'Are you all right, Ellen?' he asked, his kindly eyes as sharply perceptive as usual.

'Yes. Just tired.'

'We will need to be up before dawn tomorrow if we are to join the caravan. We will both need to get some rest,' he said.

'I would like to talk to you more about the prophecies of the Scion,' said Ellen.

'Strange. Most people can't wait to get away from me once I start talking about the prophecies,' he said with a gleam of amusement in his eye. 'But I must rest now. I will return at dusk.'

'Thank you,' she said as he quietly left the room.

She sat on the bed and stared at the faded plaster of the wall, picturing the serious face of the tall calvanni, his striking grey-blue eyes and dark brown hair. *Former calvanni.* It seemed he was serious about leaving the Brotherhood behind. Soon they would be travelling in the same caravan. The last time they had met, she was an Athrian Suulvey in command of a warship, with two Suulqua and scores of warriors at her command. Now she was a renegade without a single servant – not even a slave. He had rejected her offer of a life with the Suul, preferring his own independence. How would she possibly win him to the cause of the Scion? What sort of alliance, what sort of common goal, was possible between them? Her father had believed that Cedrin was the key to finding the Scion. 'You must find him and protect him,' he had said.

Her skin itched beneath the travelling clothes, chafed by the additional bulk of the Sealed gems sewn into the lining.

'That's it.' She could not just sit here.

She slipped out into the corridor and walked down the stairs to the ground floor. She had committed to this quest, to find Cedrin, to seek out the Scion. She needed to stay fixed to her course, for Myan's sake. So far her faith in her father had been rewarded. She had discovered that the Scion had been saved and that Belin was the Hero of the Last Days: the man who had battled to the side of the dying Empress to rescue the child. People like Estle and Uran could muster convincing arguments about the need to move into a modern era, but Raynor remained a fractured city of panicked mobs. How long could the Warlord retain control of even the Yasser States with the Eathal advancing? Only a united Kelas could turn back Hukum's legions.

The corridor on the ground floor was empty, so she walked out across the lawn and into the gardens surrounding the sacred grove. She approached a Mythar Priestess, distinctive in her dark yellow robes, who was trimming a shrub with a pair of shears. Her movements were slow and deliberate as she clipped at the stems.

'Excuse me?' Ellen waited for a long moment, unsure if the woman had heard her, but too conscious of interrupting her task to say anything further.

The Priestess looked up at Ellen, her eyes clear and touched with a hint of radiance, her soft round face calm.

'Can you tell me where the bathhouse is?'

The Priestess smiled and motioned her to follow. She led Ellen back to the paved walkway that ran around the perimeter of the garden, beneath the enclosing buildings. The Priestess' simple sandals whispered rhythmically on the stone as she walked, and Ellen kept pace in comfortable silence.

The suns were high in the sky now and their light was bright and clear. Golden shafts swept between the slender walkway columns, warm on the skin of her face and hands. There was a sense of peace to this place, a calm and quiet. The moment swelled, as though pausing. In that single heartbeat, everything became incredibly real, incredibly *present*: the green of the lawn, the life within the flowering shrubs and trees, the fine quality of the sunshine, the grain of the sandstone blocks that lined the walkway.

A sense of tremendous possibility filled her, excitement at the adventure to follow. What must it be like to be Cedrin? Free to walk across the world? Unfettered? His face swam into her mind again, as she had last seen it on the galley. She remembered the fierce determination and strength there. It was easy to believe he was Belin's son. She remembered the taut muscles of his chest when he swept back his cloak, and the six degrees of the calvanni and the raptor totem tattoo. There was greatness in him, she knew it. There must be a way to win him to her cause – there had to be – and she intended to find it.

Chapter Nine

Cedrin dived into the mob, scattering four of them with the impact. He was on his feet quickly, flinging off his pack and robe and drawing his weapons. He faced them with a calv in each hand, his back to the wall.

'Come on, you bloody cowards!'

They formed a tight ring around him and the unconscious Marken, snarling, tense, every one of them wired tight and ready to attack.

'Get him. He's only one man!' called the leader.

They came at Cedrin in a rush, but not all of them could close on him at once. His calvs flashed and blood sprayed across the stone. Three of them fell, fatal wounds opened across throat and heart, but they kept coming. He managed to stab one more in the shoulder before they pinned him up against the wall, forcing him back under a weight of bodies. They grabbed at his arms and hands, trying to prise the calvs out of his grip. He lashed out with a kick and heard a man gasp. The hold on his right arm loosened. He shook it violently, freeing his blade. He lashed out, slashing at throats, eyes. Two men screamed and fell back, savage gashes across their faces. One had lost an eye. Cedrin's left arm came free. He stabbed out, catching another in the belly. The attacker grunted and staggered back.

He warded the others back with quick motions of his two calvs. The man who had been stabbed in the belly was holding the wound with both hands. He looked down as blood gushed out from between his fingers. 'Ahhhh! Ahhhh!' His voice was panicked.

'My eye. My eye,' whimpered another.

'Sod your eyes! The bastard has ruined my face.'

The one he had stabbed in the shoulder was tapping his club into the palm of his left hand, his eyes dark with murder.

Cedrin squatted down, taking hold of his friend's robe. 'Marken!' He shook him roughly. '*Marken.*'

Half their attackers were down. If he had Marken at his side, they could send them running.

'Marken. Wake up!' He shook him again, but there was no response.

'He's killed three of us!' whimpered the man with the ruined eye.

'Four,' said the man with the wounded shoulder. 'Roti won't survive that belly cut.'

The leader watched Cedrin, his face twisted with anger and hate. Then he smiled. 'Stone him. He's a murderer. Stone him.'

Cedrin's heart missed a beat, his head spinning with adrenalin. If it was just him, he could make a break for it. But there was no way he could leave Marken. He watched helpless as they armed themselves with broken cobbles, shattered tiles, stones and sharp pieces of discarded mought.

They formed a loose ring around him, getting slowly closer. The man with the ruined eye roared and threw a piece of tile. Cedrin dodged it, but an instant later they were all pelting him with debris.

'Die, gutter scum!'

'Eathal spawn!'

'*Die!*'

A heavy blow to his temple sent his vision reeling. The deadly rain grew heavier, the projectiles finding their marks. He ran forward, lashing out with the calvs.

'Arghh!' One attacker fell, his throat slashed open.

A club flashed towards him, and he ducked. Then a stone slammed into his temple. Blood blossomed from a cut to his brow, filling his eyes. *I cannot see.* He flashed the calvs wildly, sensing they were closing on him. 'Ugh.' A sharp piece of mought sliced through the fabric of his trousers.

'Face me!' A new challenge rang out in the alley.

He heard his attackers laugh.

'Old bastard. Run on home!'

There was a whistling sound. *A greatscythe.* Two of his attackers cried out. Their jeers turned to cries of pain and fear. He wiped his eyes clear with the back of his robe. He regained his vision in time to see an old man, greatscythe whistling in a blur, send the remnants of the mob running out of the alley. He appeared at least eighty, thin and frail, yet his eyes were hard and clear, his face stern. As soon as they were out of sight, he locked the twin blades of the weapon away and doubled over, sucking in deep breaths.

He looked up at Cedrin and smiled. 'Not really up to it like I used to be,' said the old man, as though it were all a bit of fun. He pushed himself upright and knelt beside Marken. 'Quickly. We have to get you both out of here before they come back with more of their mates.'

They carried Marken to a concealed door in the wall of the alley. Once inside the small room, they lay him down and Cedrin sat against a wall. The man gave him a cloth and he held it to the wound on his brow to stem the bleeding. Marken had taken a nasty blow to the back of the head, and his golden hair was matted and stuck to his skull.

The old man disappeared through a doorway, returning a moment later with a bowl of steaming water and a pouch of herbs. He tapped some of the herbs into the water and the room was filled with a pungent scent. He dipped a cloth into the bowl and began to clean the wound.

'You two are lucky you picked my alley to get beat up in,' said the old man.

'I don't know how to thank you.' Cedrin was perplexed why the old warrior had come to their aid.

The man smiled and pointed to Cedrin's chest. 'That is all the thanks I need. When the phoenix calls, the Legion follows.'

He extended a hand and they gripped forearms in the warrior's clasp. There was surprising strength in the man's thin arm. 'My name is Lexus. I was once a Legion Captain, but that was a long time ago.'

'My name is Cedrin, this is Marken. We're ... working as

mercenaries.'

'I see you have the mark of the Way. Where are your weapons?' said Lexus.

'We decided not to bring them through the crowds,' said Cedrin.

Lexus clicked his tongue, touching the faded tattoo of the Way of the Scytheman on his chest with a nostalgic gleam in his eye.

'To never lie, cheat or steal. To devote yourself to the perfection of your martial skills. To empty yourself of emotion, become pure expression in the execution of your art. To conquer without cruelty, kill without hate and only when duty or necessity compels you. To have the power and determination to kill and yet the wisdom to choose when. To embrace duty — to your commander, to your nation — yet never surrender your own will, your own judgement of what is right,' recited Lexus. It was the code of the Way.

The old man turned to study Cedrin's tattoos with an appraising eye. 'There are not enough men these days who have the courage to stand up for a belief. That is why the Empire fell.' He paused, shaking his head. 'If Riin had lived, the Eathal would still be cowering under their rock.'

Cedrin started to protest, but the man stopped him.

'Don't deny it, you are a man of courage. I saw the way you faced those men. You could have fled and left your friend, but the thought did not even enter your head. It gladdens my old heart. If more young men like you had the courage to stand and fight for the phoenix, the Empire would live once more. Civilisation. Justice.' He swept his hands wide. 'All would return.' He sighed. 'No one believes, anymore. But those who still do, we have to keep the flame of hope alive.'

The old man began to sing an old legion song as he worked. Watching him tend Marken's wounds, Cedrin saw real belief and hope kindle in those old eyes. He wondered how many people waited in their houses, remembering a better age, secretly hoping for the Empire to return. Not whipped to a moment's frenzy in the fickle tides of the mob, but truly wishing in their hearts for a return to a more noble age; a time of solid virtue, of stability and growth.

'It's not too serious,' said Lexus. 'It looks worse than it is.'

Cedrin had always despised the privileged, especially the Suul of whom his mysterious father was a member. He had spent the years of his lonely manhood amid the desperation of the lower classes, a people who lived their lives balanced over the pit of slavery and starvation. Even so, he began to see the true power of the Scion, the real hope he represented to those same men and women. The life of the people was kept aflame in the image of their ruler.

Marken groaned, then his eyes opened.

'Ami. It all ended well then?' asked Marken, his voice rough.

'Well enough. I'm glad you roused. You're too much of a dead weight to carry all the way back to *The Scytheman* alone.'

Marken sat up on the bed. His face was pale but alert. He touched the back of his head gingerly.

Lexus took away the bowl and returned with three fine porcelain cups filled with a weak, aromatic tea. 'Here.'

Cedrin took a sip. It was hot and surprisingly refreshing.

'So, how do we get out of here?' asked Marken, taking a sip.

'We have no choice but to wait for the crowd to die down. If we get caught again, we're finished,' said Cedrin.

Marken looked grave. 'But Kranor wanted us to meet the merchant today. He'll have our hides.'

The old man nodded, his eyes shining. 'Ah! The mark of the One Hundred. I should have known you were Kranor's men.' He placed a callused hand on each of their shoulders. 'Have no fear about the mob, there is more than one path around this city. And for two of Kranor's men, I would gladly open the way.'

Soon after, Lexus led them deeper into the building. They saw it was less a single structure than a succession of them, each having grown alongside and on top of their predecessors. They climbed narrow stairs and squeezed through tight passageways. The place was a maze, but it was a path that Lexus knew well. At one point they scaled a ladder between two walls of dusty stone that had probably not seen the light of day in centuries.

'If most of the buildings in Raynor are like this, it heralds all sorts of possibilities,' said Marken as they reached the other side.

'Old habits die hard,' said Cedrin. Even though the Brotherhood had almost killed them, it was impossible not to take a professional interest in secret byways, which until recently had been their stock and trade.

At the top of a short stair, Lexus paused to shove aside a stout wooden door. The harsh glare of the suns stabbed into their eyes. They had reached the roof. As his eyes adjusted, Cedrin could see Raynor stretching out to the horizon.

The top of the building was like any other in Kelas, a steep, sloping roof of tile built against the heavy torrents of summer and storm years and the coming of the snow, leading down to decorated stone gutters. As Lexus led them across the treacherously slippery tile, they saw signs that others used the roof regularly. Ropes and planks had been set up across the most difficult parts, with ladders and make-shift stairs connecting the roof with neighbouring buildings.

'How many people know about this, Lexus?' asked Cedrin as they walked down a narrow plank, crossing towards the next roof.

The old man laughed. 'How many people look above their heads?'

Not many, he thought.

It was hard progress, with much climbing and scrabbling. When they had travelled for about an hour, they rested. Cedrin heard a large crowd and eased his way to the side of the roof. Hundreds thronged the street below them, hot and sweating under the suns. They had gathered at the gates of a big Temple complex.

Dominating the view was a mought statue of the Sisters' Dance that reached almost to the height of their roof. It was a classic depiction, with the two goddesses circling around each other, each turning to look out at the observer. Larus' face was serene, yet distant, her gaze implacable, sometimes filled with deep compassion and at other times hard. She was the source of fertility and growth and was coloured in yellow like the big sun of Yos. Uros' face was powerful, yet cold, focussed on some distant truth. Her gaze seemed to pass through you without seeing. It was chilling, as though to this goddess of destruction one human life was meaningless. She was depicted in vivid red, like the smaller of Yos' two suns; the goddess who shattered with a swift and sure hand.

The statue drew all their eyes. 'Locked forever in the rhythm of creation,' said Marken.

'That's the main Temple of the Sisters in Raynor,' said Lexus.

The crowd pounded at the ornate wooden gates, pressing in with the sheer weight of numbers. Their shouts and taunts were lost on the wind, but the angry buzz was unmistakable. If they were not sated here, where else would they turn?

'Why doesn't the Warlord disperse them?' This had been bothering Cedrin since the Palardos.

Lexus laughed bitterly. 'He was quick enough to scatter the supporters of the Scion – most of them ended up in chains. No. He will let this mob run. It's no secret how he feels about the Temple of the Sisters. And after the Sisters brought this false-Scion to the city, the mob will be out for blood.'

'It's a magnificent structure.' Marken seemed solemn as he looked down at the Temple below.

Three domes of white rose above high columns of marble, each twisted with coloured mought facing. Behind the walled courtyard, the long slender finger of a prayer tower rose skyward, the balcony a delicate lacework of sculpture. The Sister's Dance towered over the walls of the Temple, and those on the street would be held within the gaze of the goddesses.

Marken had spent almost two years as a novice Moon Druid in the Temple of the Sisters in Athria. It was always difficult to gauge what Marken was really thinking – he always presented a cheerful face to the world – but Cedrin suspected that he often regretted his decision to leave the Temple. Although talented, he had decided the life was too frugal for him.

'It's a bloody disgrace,' said Lexus. 'The Warlord lettin' the mob rule – running free to do his dirty work. It never would have happened in Riin's day. And his father, Emperor Cerrin, he were even tougher. Big Temple man he was. Would have broken them up and sent them home bruised and thinkin' better of it.'

'They will never open those gates with Druids behind them,' said Marken.

Lexus squinted down at the complex below. 'I don't see no Druids, mate.'

'They may be out of sight, but they will be there,' said Marken. 'Uros Druids will be holding the gates with spells of Force. If they fail, the Temple Guardians will be ready with javelins and spears.'

'Bloody Uros Druids – Templemen. They're the only ones you hear about. It might as well be called the Temple of Uros,' said Lexus.

'It does seem that way,' said Marken. 'Uros' power is inconsistent, but attuned to destruction. The Templemen use it well to dominate and rule. Larus is the more powerful of the two gods, but her Essence is a life-giving one. The Larus Druids can channel vast amounts of power, yet they can only use it to increase bounty, to bring fertility and growth and aid natural healing.'

'Aid in natural healing?' said Lexus. 'I saw an old legion mate of mine go to the Larus Druids for healing. One touch from them and his cancer ate him alive. He went in sick and came out dying.'

'Your friend should have gone to a Moon Druid. Larus Druids cannot discriminate. Their healing can sometimes speed the growth of contagion or a parasite – or in your friend's case – a cancer. They too are living things and grow faster under their touch. Larus is a goddess of growth, but she is blind.'

Lexus looked at Marken sharply. 'Hmmm. Never had it explained like that.'

There was flash of red from the crowd below, then a detonation. The gates shook.

'Someone is using Essence down there.' Marken's eyes narrowed as he studied the crowd. 'There!' he said, pointing. 'Do you see the two robed men in the crowd? They have the feel of Uros-Essence about them.'

Three red-robed Templemen emerged from the Temple building and stood inside the gates with their hands raised. A squad of Temple Guardians stood behind them, their spears levelled at the gates.

'Druids against Druids,' said Cedrin.

'The ones in the crowd are Warlord's men for sure. These *Druidin* I here tell about,' said Lexus.

There was a second detonation and an explosion of wood and splinters. The gates fell with a thunderous crash, and the Templemen fled across the courtyard to the Temple, leaving the Guardians to the crowd's fury.

With a roar of triumph, the mob swept in. The Guardians stood their ground, but there were only a dozen of them. They were soon pushed back, their spears and shields wrestled from them. One managed to fight his way clear and run for the Temple, the others disappeared from sight under the press. The mob surged on like an engulfing sea, swarming up the Temple steps. The sound of smashing glass reached them on the wind.

Lexus stood. 'Come on, lads. It will only get bloody now, and we have a while to go.'

They turned their backs on the drama below and followed Lexus across the roof. Cedrin could not wait to get back to the relative safety of Kranor's compound – and to get out of Raynor.

Chapter Ten

Skye carefully picked his way through the rubble, slipping between shadows, alert for any sign of movement. It was well past midnight and the last of the mob were gone. Most of the fires had died, but sporadic flames still danced across the darkened courtyard. The rich curtains and tapestries of the outer Temple chambers were nothing more than burnt tatters, the magnificent columns charred black. Oily smoke, thick and nauseating with the smell of burning human flesh, swirled in clouds. The Temple had been a place of worship for the rich, and the mob had vented their fury with a vengeance. The Sister's Dance had been toppled, unfortunate rioters now crushed beneath its massive mought sections. Only the four legs of the Sisters remained upright, firmly set into the cobbles.

Silently, Skye worked his way across the courtyard and into the Temple itself. The wooden seats and tables had been charred to soot, the beautifully-carved figurines that once lined the vast chamber shattered by the intense heat. After the flames had died, the more devoted of the mob had returned to cover the walls and altars with graffiti. Skye did not pause to examine anything. He had not come to poke through worthless trinkets. He climbed onto one of the altars and backed into the shadows of an apse. As his eyes adjusted, he could see into the Inner Temple – the sacrosanct chambers reserved only for the clergy. It, too, appeared gutted and destroyed, the path towards it blocked by a fall of heavy stone and mought facing from the heat-ravaged ceiling. He fixed his gaze and settled to wait.

He gagged at the burnt stench, struggling to breathe in the

stifling air. A muscle cramped in his thigh, and he stretched it. The hours crept on, and he wondered whether he had been sold a clever collection of lies. Sweat beaded his forehead and prickled across his skin, driven out of his body by the hot marble altar, which retained the heat of the conflagration.

He tensed as the image of the ruined Inner Temple and the debris before it began to shimmer. A moment later the illusion was swept aside. The Inner Temple lay untouched. Bright torchlight flooded into the main Temple, and Skye was glad he had chosen a vantage concealed from view. As his source had said, the Temple Druids would set the fire in the outer chambers themselves to cover the illusion, abandoning their Guardians to a grim death at the hands of the mob while they secured their survival.

Inside, he could see the black robes of Moon Druids and the yellow of the Larus Druids dispersed among the familiar red of the Templemen. There were at least twenty Guardians. He had been told they were fleeing Raynor tonight, running on the heels of Storm Season, taking their slaves and servants – and as much of their treasure as they could carry.

The entourage, almost sixty in all, began to move. In the centre, ten strong slaves carried a litter that housed a large iron glowmetal. They in turn were flanked by six Moon Druids. The red light of the iron glowmetal shifted, casting a bloody light around the ruin of the Temple as the Moon Druids stirred it to life. The power within it built to climax, then, with a *snap*, the Temple Druids and their servants vanished. Only a subtle shifting in the air revealed their passage as they made their way from the Temple, through the ruined courtyard and out onto the street.

Skye waited for another half hour, eager to enter the Inner Temple but cautious. At last, satisfied it lay abandoned, he made his way into the untouched wealth and luxury of the inner sanctum.

Rich tapestries lined the walls, running down to thick, woven carpets. Every niche was decorated with finely-tinted statues, figurines of lacquered wood, paintings or ancient vases. Very little of it had religious significance. The Temple Druids had lived in wealth to rival the Suul. Although valuable, these were not what Skye was after, most of them being too heavy to shift. He was seeking coin and gems. If the Druids had not stripped the place to the bone, he would become a rich man in one night's work.

After a quick and efficient search, conducted in the light of the torches the considerate Temple Druids had left burning, he found the treasure room. Inside the cunningly concealed side chamber, caskets and chests lay open everywhere. Most – those that had contained the higher denominations of coin – were empty, but whole chests of opals lay untouched. He ran his hand through the mought coins, laughing as the opals tumbled through his fingers. The floor was scattered with all manner of coin and precious gems, no doubt dropped in their haste to depart before the mob returned. Eagerly he opened his sack, filling it first with fallen gems and ruby, sapphire and emerald coins and then with opals. With the sack full, he tied it securely to his back, then stuffed opals into his pockets until they overflowed. He would live like a Suul!

He was reaching for more opals – wondering if he could use his shirt as a second make-shift sack – when he heard a noise. He fell instinctively into a crouch. There it was again, in the corridor outside. There was only one entrance! He extinguished the torches and climbed onto the top of the doorframe, hardly daring to breathe as he balanced on the open door.

A figure slid into the room. His moves were silent, skilful. He held a calv before him as he circled the room. This is no rioter, thought Skye. Satisfied, the intruder sheathed his weapon and knelt by the open chests. There was something familiar about him, but in the darkened room Skye could catch no more than a fleeting silhouette. The minutes passed as, like Skye, the man filled his sack and left.

Skye dropped silently. He followed the man to the brightly-lit chambers of the Inner Temple. He could not see his face, but his harness, the cut of the trousers and the boots – all were unmistakably Athrian. The thief stopped and Skye ducked behind a lacquer screen. An opal fell from Skye's pocket and clattered across the marble. The man turned, sweeping his gaze across the Inner Temple, his face framed in the light. *It was one of Dresil's bodyguards.*

Dresil. The bastard who had organised the rebellion in Athria. Skye's fist tightened on his calv. If the Mouthpiece's bodyguards were in Raynor, that could mean only one thing: the Uros-cursed cutthroat Dresil was here as well, and Raziin Cinnor was probably with him. Raziin had butchered Skye's partner Jaso like a side of meat. Jaso had been a brother to him, and now he lay cold and buried in the grave of a traitor. His heart grew hot with a desire for revenge.

The bodyguard stood there looking back into the Temple. It would be so easy to send a calv flying into his heart – easy and satisfying – but this man was just a henchman. No. He wanted Raziin. He wanted Dresil.

Memories of that night on the Spire rushed through his mind, along with a numbing fear. Few things could daunt Skye's heart, but one of them was magic. The night Raziin had killed Jaso, Skye had seen him pull Marken's knife from his throat and survive. Raziin had paralysed them with magic, freezing them in place like statues, taunting them. Skye would never forget the rage, and terror, he had experienced. All his life he had prided himself on his strength, his ability to defend himself and his family, and yet he had been forced to watch Raziin cruelly slay Jaso, his brother, while he was helpless, knowing he would be next.

The Temple of the Sisters preached that Sorcery was unclean – that the practitioners of the Fire derived their power from the demons of Kallor. That was why they had to be put to death. Even being near a Sorcerer could open people to the demon's mark, a soul-deep curse that would lead them on the path to possession and damnation. When Cedrin had glowed with the Fire on the ship from Athria, Skye had feared for his own soul. He could not even bring himself to come close to him, his oldest friend.

The bodyguard turned and fled into the night. Skye watched him as he disappeared out the doors of the Inner Temple. Every moment that passed, his chances of following him, of finding Dresil – and Raziin – slipped away. Skye surged into motion, fierce determination filling him as he gave chase, slipping between shadows, using every ounce of his skill.

Skye followed through the dark alleys and back ways of the city to a five-storey house in the Merchants' Quarter. Skye watched from the darkened shadows of a stairwell across the street as the man walked boldly to the front door and tapped out a rapid, complex pattern of knocks. The thick wooden door opened, briefly admitting a shaft of light into the street until it slammed shut again.

There was no doubt he had found one of the Brotherhood houses reserved for the elite. He had been to many of them on previous occasions, ramshackle dwellings within the Docks District, but never to one in the wealthy Merchants' Quarter. Tonight he would change that.

First he had to hide his loot. Skye scaled the walls of the building he had hidden against, finding easy purchase on the wooden structure. He levered himself over the gable onto the steep roof and walked up to the peak, careful not to slip on the slick tile. He lifted a tile with his calv and wedged his sack into the gap between two wooden beams. Taking the coin from his pockets, he stacked this neatly beside the sack. It would be safe here while he completed his business.

Once more on the street, he studied the Brotherhood house, searching for an entry point. Only a day before, he would have been hard pressed, but now the world was warming, and all the windows on the upper stories were wide open. He climbed to a window and silently slid through the gap, landing softly. He paused and listened.

The room was dark and as his eyes adjusted, Skye could see at least three sleeping figures. One shifted in his sleep. He waited for a few minutes until the man settled, then slipped through the door of the room into the lit corridor beyond. He heard laughter below and the hair on the back of his neck lifted. *Dresil's men.* Drawn by the sound of familiar Athrian voices, he crept down the inner stairwell to the hall, where they were drinking and playing dice. He paused in the shadows of the stair and watched them, his hand inching towards his calv. The loot from the Temple was spread on the table. Sitting amongst them, flanked by two bodyguards, was Dresil. The others he would have called friends only weeks ago. Now they were enemies.

The Mouthpiece looked thin and gaunt, yet he still possessed the same arrogance. It was this man who had conspired to kill Skye and his friends and nearly succeeded. Here he was, still commanding men like he deserved the privilege. When it was known he was finished as a power in Athria, that he had plotted the death of his own men, he would probably be given a swift and summary justice by the Raynor Brotherhood. But ... there was no way to be sure the slippery bastard would not escape.

Dresil rose from the table. Skye backed up the stairs, hiding in the shadows of the corridor. His heart thumped in his chest. The Pirate's Mouthpiece scooped up more than half of the coin – a leer of satisfaction on his face – and clomped up the stairs, humming a broken tune as he walked past Skye and along the corridor to his room. The Mouthpiece swayed on his feet as he fumbled with the key.

An image of Jaso raced through Skye's mind, his friend cut in two by Raziin's blade, his blood steaming in the night. His need for revenge burned hot. It was Dresil who brought Raziin to Athria. Skye's hand jerked to his harness. He felt the cool lanedd of his calv's handle before he even realised he had drawn the weapon.

Dresil pushed his way into the room, slamming the door behind him. Skye followed quickly, pressing his ear to the door. When he heard the sound of snoring, he picked the lock and crept across the floor to Dresil's bed. Now for the fun.

Skye pressed his calv into Dresil's throat, drawing blood with the edge. Dresil woke with a start and drew in a sharp breath.

'Shut your mouth or you're done for,' hissed Skye.

Dresil's hand reached slowly across the bed towards a tangle of sheets that could easily hide a weapon. Skye pushed his blade deeper. Dresil froze.

'Don't even think it,' said Skye.

'What do you want? Who are you?' rasped Dresil.

'I'm one of the calvanni you killed, Dresil. You and that

Cioan by-blow, Raziin. I'm back from the grave to claim you for Kallor,' said Skye.

Dresil was a tough man, but like most sailors, was superstitious. Skye could see him struggle with a moment's panic, his eyes flicking wildly as he searched the darkness. Skye knew his face was still in shadow. At best Dresil would only make out his outline.

'What do you want?' asked Dresil, more confident. 'Money? I can get you what you want, just ease up.'

Skye pressed the blade, causing Dresil to gasp as a thin trickle of blood began on his neck. 'I'll tell you what I want, Dresil. I want to know where Raziin is.'

'All right. I'll tell you,' said Dresil in a harsh whisper. Skye eased off and the former Mouthpiece took a shuddering breath. 'He is in Raynor, at the house of an Armon noble who is sympathetic to his cause.'

'How will I know the place?' demanded Skye.

'It's on the Palardos. Opposite the statue of the hero Melas.'

Skye's stomach tightened in fear at the thought of facing the Sorcerer. That memory – of being frozen and helpless, trapped by Raziin's power – flooded through his mind. His blade wavered, just for a moment.

Dresil's hand darted under the covers. Skye leapt aside just as Dresil released a poison dart from a miniature crossbow. It shot by him to lodge in the ceiling. The Mouthpiece drew a calv and rolled from the bed, roaring in defiance as he charged forward. Skye reacted instantly, slashing up through the old calvanni's guard then dancing back, ready for another attack. Dresil's calv dropped from his fingers and he swayed, his life-blood pumping from his severed throat.

Skye stepped into a shaft of light coming in through the window from a streetlamp. The Mouthpiece's eyes widened in recognition, then he fell forward and lay still.

Skye heard footsteps. Men coming fast. He raced for the window and was on the street moments later, racing to the Palardos.

Dawn was close when Skye reached the statue of Melas, standing dark and impassive in the empty Palardos. He looked across the wide street to the ornate seven-storey mansion. It was nestled against the wall of the palace itself. Raziin was highly placed, there was no doubting that.

Skye ran across the Palardos, a dark blur as he climbed the shadowed facade to the first floor windows. Finding them locked, he used a thin sliver of laminated wood from his kit to lift the catch and let himself inside. He padded through a banquet hall to the stairs and down to the ground floor. This was devoted to kitchens and servants' quarters. He continued on, swiftly searching the house. The first and second floors were designed for entertaining, their dusty, unused halls deserted. The apartments and sleeping chambers began on the third floor, where he found a sleeping Suul family. He left them undisturbed and crept up the stairs.

On the fourth floor was another hall, even bigger than those below. He softly pushed at the doors, smiling as they slid open without a sound. The floor was scattered with dark figures, sleeping on make-shift beds. Even in the gloom, he recognised their Armon armour and the golden skin and hair. The hall had been converted into a billet for Raziin's men.

His blood ran hot.

At the far end, he saw the silhouettes of two sentries flanking an arched doorway. *Raziin's chamber*. He picked his way through the warriors, choosing his footing with care. He drew as close to the guarded room as he dared and squatted down in the shadows. Then he waited. A man to his left muttered in his sleep and rolled over, his hand brushing Skye's boot. He slowly drew out his calv, prepared to silence him, but the man settled. Sometime later one of the sentries said something in Cioan to his companion and left, leaving the other man alone.

Skye took careful aim and threw his calv. The knife struck the man in his throat. He tried to call out, but only gurgled frantically as he fell. Skye leapt forward and caught the warrior's unbarred greatscythe with his left hand as it slipped from the warrior's fingers. The last thing he needed was a weapon like that clattering to the floor. He guided the dying man to the marble and laid aside his weapon.

Skye pushed through the wide wooden doors into the

chamber. Within, the room was dark except for the embers in the fireplace. He could make out the shape of a bed and hear a soft snore. He saw a single figure beneath the covers. He lifted his blade, stepping in. It was Raziin. Sleeping. Defenceless.

His blade hovered a finger's breadth from the Sorcerer's throat. Would a single thrust kill him? He had seen Marken's blade strike true and deep, yet Raziin had pulled the knife from his throat and sealed the wound with magic. Skye adjusted his grip on the calv. If he did kill him, would that release the unclean spirit? Would the demon's mark claim him? Skye had never feared to lose his life, but what of his soul? Would he be cursed with the taint, claimed for the darkness? A slave of Kallor, losing his mind as the demons came each night to eat his soul, eventually leaving him a mindless husk?

He took a step back. It was not too late to flee, to leave the way he had come and be content with the death of Dresil. It was a small revenge, yet he would be whole and untainted.

With a feeling of shame, Skye realised the truth. It was nothing more than fear. And to give into it, he was nothing more than a coward. He stepped in and raised the knife, gripping it with both shaking hands. *This bastard dies tonight.*

'Intruder!' It was the second sentry.

Raziin's eyes flickered open. Skye struck, but his blade cut nothing but pillow and sheet. Raziin had vanished.

Skye leapt back.

Now he had to face the Sorcerer.

He heard Raziin's chilling laughter. 'So, little man, you have come to meet your death?'

Skye marked the direction of the voice. Something rippled in the dark, like smoke, and the Sorcerer appeared, his hands extended, filled with gathering Fire. A bright crimson flare shot at Skye, expanding into a sheet of flame. Skye leapt high into the air, letting the Fire pass beneath him. As he landed, the bolt exploded into the wall. The house shook, dust billowing from the ceiling.

Men streamed into the room, all armed with greatscythes. Raziin released another bolt of Fire. Skye threw himself to the right, then gasped as the Fire caught his shoulder. A hulking shape was moving towards him. He heard the snick of a greatscythe mechanism and saw the blades shoot into position. As the man closed on him, Skye could see his face. Merceth, one of Raziin's chief lieutenants.

'Let me take him, Lord,' rumbled Merceth's voice in the dark.

There was only one way out. With a yell, Skye ran at the closed window, the force of his charge taking him through the clearglass panes with a shattering impact. Skye's left shoulder and arm became a sudden mass of pain. He twisted, throwing out his left hand to try and grab the sill. His hand came down on razor-sharp glass, which sliced deep into his palm and fingers. He gasped in pain and missed his grip. He reached out with his right hand for the ledge. For a moment he thought he had it, then his weight bore him down. Skye plummeted two floors, the fingers of his right hand growing bloody as they scraped the stone, seeking a handhold. By some miracle, he managed to hook his arm around a carving. Skye's left arm hung limply at his side, shards biting into skin and muscle.

He looked up and saw faces in the window. Skye leant into the wall, hiding his face. It was a dark night, and he would be virtually invisible to anyone above.

'It's four storeys straight down, Lord,' Merceth's deep voice said clearly. 'There is no way he could have survived.'

'There is no sign of a body below,' said Raziin.

'The streets are dark, Lord. And the view is blocked by the ledge,' said Merceth.

'I want the streets below thoroughly searched,' said Raziin, his voice full of low menace. 'Where are the sentries?'

'I was one of the sentries, my Lord. Veras is dead.' The sentry's voice was muffled.

'Come here,' said Raziin. 'I want you to be the first to examine the alley.'

He heard Raziin's yell of fury, then a moment later a warrior tumbled past Skye through the air, screaming. His cries stopped abruptly as he struck the stone with a dull, sickening thud.

'A shame,' said Merceth. 'I knew his mother.'

'I do not excuse failure, Merceth. You know that,' said Raziin.

'Yes, my Lord.'

'That calvanni came close. Too close,' said Raziin.

Skye squeezed his eyes shut, fury pumping through him. He knew it now – he could tell from Raziin's voice. If he had cut the bastard's throat in his sleep, he would be dead.

There was some low talking he could not make out, then Raziin's voice strengthened. 'Search around the sentry's body. If the calvanni fell to his death, that is where he will be found.'

'I'm sure he must be dead, Lord.'

'Find him,' said Raziin.

Skye's right arm was weakening. He scrabbled with his feet, trying to find purchase on the stone wall, but it was too far away. His fall had taken him out from the building. Only the jutting carving had saved him. The pain was intense, and his body trembled. Glass shards had lodged down his left shoulder, arm and chest, one long sliver dangerously near his heart. A slick flow of warm blood soaked into his leggings, and he could feel his strength failing.

He looked down to where the body of the guard lay sprawled on the stone cobbles and heard the noise of Raziin's men as they raced through the house. Soon they would be on the street, waiting for him to fall.

He had no choice. He released the grip, turning as he fell the remaining two stories to take the impact on his right side. His shoulder broke on impact. For a moment he was paralysed with pain, and darkness hovered. The shard near his heart had been driven deep, and the wound was bleeding heavily. He struggled to his feet. *Thank Larus my legs are not broken.* Skye fled into the darkness, fighting pain and gathering weakness with every step. Behind him he heard running feet, but he did not turn around. He crossed the Palardos and turned into the first dark alley he came to and kept on turning. Left, right, right, left, he lost track of the turns.

He ran until the dark around him seemed to take over the universe, until the steps behind him had faded to nothing. Then finally, exhausted, he sank to his knees. Both of his hands were useless, his chest and arms a mass of pain. With every breath, fresh blood pumped from the wound in his chest. His life drained from him.

He bowed his head. He had faced a Sorcerer. Where then was the demon's mark? Death drew near and the pain fled, and with it came clarity. There was no demon's mark. It was another Temple lie.

'Fool.' Skye's voice was slurred, like he was drunk. He scarcely recognised it.

As death approached, Skye felt his Meadrel blood rising.

He tilted his back his head. He could smell the wind, feel the gods of the four winds watching him. Yet he had never felt so alone. Where was his tribe? Where was his blood? His thoughts flew to Cedrin, the one man who had never treated him falsely, who had only ever given him loyalty. His brother. His blood. The man he had deserted.

Fear had cost him a friend. Fear had killed him.

His mind became restless, like a caged bird on the point of release. His eyes drifted shut, and he no longer felt the stone beneath him or saw the night. He saw his early childhood within the Wall of Sorrows, son of the famous weaponmaster Astor and his dark Meadrel bride, Ko-chan. Once more he saw his father's death, the proud warrior executed for killing a young Suul in a duel. The Suul had forced himself on Skye's mother, but the facts meant nothing to the Sarlord. Then the lean years in Lookout Hill as his mother worked the streets to put food in their mouths. Through it all was his mother's smiling face. Always accepting, never touched by regret.

'Never question fate,' she would say. 'The gods of the sky turn us this way and that, yet we are only Man and must return to the earth once more. Do you remember your prayer to the goddess of earth?'

'Yes, Mother,' young Skye would reply. 'I remember all the prayers. But what use are they?'

Ko-chan would smile. 'Do not question, my son. The heart of the Meadrel lays in the earth. When you are ready, you must return. You must say the prayers. Promise me.'

'I promise,' Skye would reply, eager to return to the streets to play.

Now, as the darkness pressed upon him, he knew it was

time. He must invoke the earth to accept his spirit; sink into Yos, become one with it. Slowly, his lips began to move, forming the words in the Meadrel old tongue. As he said the prayers, the rhythmic pattern came to life as never before. It spun like a whirlwind in his mind, spreading outwards through the city on white wings. It returned as a tongue of flame, warm and sustaining. Then it transformed into the form of a young woman. Her limbs flickered like morning sunlight on a pool of deep, cool water.

'Who are you?' he asked.

'The goddess of the Spring,' she answered, the words reaching his mind without sound. 'Do you wish to drink of its waters?'

Skye was suddenly possessed with a great thirst. A desire so strong he pushed himself to his feet despite his weakness.

'Yes. I must … reach the Spring,' he said.

'Then follow.'

Her presence lent Skye strength. He stayed close to her as she led him deeper into the ancient back-ways of Raynor. Finally, at a dead end, she turned to smile before walking straight through a wall of ancient brick. Barely conscious, half-convinced it was a dying dream, Skye followed.

The brick was an illusion. Within was a cave, lit by great braziers. The goddess was nowhere to be seen, but a young woman was there, laying out altar cloths. She screamed as he staggered towards her, leaving a bloody trail in his wake.

Women rushed into the chamber. They wore light shifts of white linen, and their hair was tousled from sleep. They formed a circle around him, yet none approached. He could see the younger ones looking across to an older Priestess with greying blonde hair, as though waiting for orders. She watched Skye calmly, her warm brown eyes noting his injuries.

An old Priestess entered the room, carrying a staff. Both her eye sockets were empty ruins, yet even so she walked with assurance. She stood in front of Skye, who swayed on his feet. The Priestess with the greying blonde hair came forward and stood at the blind Priestess' elbow, like some sort of aide, or lieutenant.

'Why have you come here?' asked the blind Priestess.

'The goddess,' said Skye in the ancient Meadrel tongue. 'I must drink of the Spring.'

* * *

'Watch out, Mother. The man is near collapse,' said Elleth, reaching out to guide the High Priestess out of the way.

The High Priestess raised her staff and a golden glow surrounded the man, easing him to the rough stone floor with a skilful manipulation of Earth-Essence. Elleth let her hand drop. After almost thirty years, she still underestimated her blind teacher.

'Take him to the Spring. Heal him,' commanded the High Priestess.

Elleth reached forward with her right hand, fingers extended. She drew on the Earth-Essence beneath, weaving it skilfully. She lightly laid the Testing spell on the prone man and immediately recoiled.

'He has the mark of murder on him, High Priestess. It is sacrilege,' said Elleth.

The High Priestess turned to face her, the empty eye sockets great hollows in her face. Elleth had never gotten used to them.

'That is the mark of death. Who can say if the slaying was for good or ill?' The High Priestess turned back to the man. 'The goddess has chosen.'

Elleth bowed her head in acquiescence. She would need three more adepts to lift the man. She gestured at two of the more experienced Priestesses, who came forward silently. The young novice who had first seen the injured man stagger into the cave trembled against one of the older women, her eyes still wide. Elleth waved her forward. It would do her good to face her fear. 'To the Spring.'

Two of the women positioned themselves at the man's legs. Elleth stood at his right shoulder and gestured for the novice to stand at his left. The young woman looked down at the ruined shoulder, still glistening with fragments of glass. 'There is so much blood,' she said. His chest, arms and leggings were

176

covered with red smears, and a spreading pool lay beneath him. Elleth was surprised he still lived.

'Quickly now,' she said.

The four women reached down to touch the body. A golden glimmer surrounded their arms, like glittering dust caught in the sun. The golden cloud ran from them to engulf the man until he was encased within it and floated free, hovering at waist height. Elleth nodded in satisfaction. The novice had mastered herself well.

They moved from the entrance chamber into the Temple's complex of interconnected caves. They guided the man's feather-light body with the tips of their fingers. Here and there, sturdy columns of discoloured marble or mought rose to support the ceiling. That a man such as this could find the Temple of the Spring worried Elleth. It was the most ancient and holy site in Raynor, and its location was a closely guarded secret. Some shrines and alcoves had been cut from the rough stone, but most of the cave lay unchanged since the first men, the Meadrel, had knelt here to worship. Their cave paintings, deceptively simple, and textured with the hidden rhythms of the Earth-Essence, covered every rough surface in an endless dance. Some of the drawings were faded, others were still bright with the tints of the earth. The closer they drew to the Spring, the more detailed and abstract they became.

The Spring chamber itself was like a womb within the earth, shaped long ago by life-giving waters. A small spring bubbled and steamed near one edge, running through an open channel in the rock to a large central pool. The true upwelling here was of the spirit, of the essential Essence. The water glowed with a pale-yellow luminescence. Every time Elleth saw the Spring, her heart soared. She revelled in the deep connection to life she felt here.

They laid the man on a natural altar near the pool's edge, releasing the spell. His eyes flickered open, and he looked up at the chamber's natural dome.

'They are swimming ...' he muttered.

Elleth followed his gaze. Painted above were depictions of the life of the plains people and the animals they hunted.

Intertwined with these were drawings of the gods the Meadrel heard on the wind, saw in the sky and felt in the earth. The scenes rippled and moved as though alive, animated by the power of the Spring.

'I will rest now … sink … to the heart … of Yos.' The man lost consciousness once more.

'Now, the Healing,' said Elleth.

The four women reached out, seeking the power of the Spring. As they filled themselves with the Earth Essence, its flow increased. The faint light in the pond grew until the waters glowed like molten gold.

Following Elleth's lead, they laid their hands on the man. Soon he was encased in a golden sheath, wrapped like a transforming insect in a chrysalis of power.

'The glass first,' whispered Elleth.

The shards of glass were moved slowly from his body. They fell bloody to the stone. Then they healed the cuts and superficial damage, leaving new skin. Elleth drew the shoulder back. She winced as it cracked into place. The bone knitted, spurred on by the Essence. The golden nimbus grew brighter until even the women squinted against the glare. Something was wrong. Elleth struggled to maintain her grip on him, but her power began to falter.

'Quickly,' said Elleth. 'Summon the High Priestess.'

The novice broke from the circle. Elleth and the two other women cried out with shock as the circuit was broken, but soon closed the gap. The young woman stood swaying, her long curling brown hair damp with sweat, her dark eyes terrified.

'Quickly, girl. If we let the power fade, his spirit will flee. We cannot hold him much longer. Only the High Priestess can save him now, if she wills it'

The young girl fled from the room. Above them the pictures were flickering in rapid movement, and the air above the Spring was crowded with half-seen figures.

'The doorway stands open,' cried one woman. 'It will claim us all!'

'Be silent. They cannot take the living,' said Elleth, suppressing her own fear. The atmosphere was heavy with power. The spirits of the Earth had come to claim one of their own. She kept her eyes lowered.

The High Priestess entered the room, her staff tapping ahead of her, the novice at her side. The young girl sought to take her arm as she moved across the rough floor. 'Don't be stupid, girl. I see better than you ever will,' said the High Priestess.

The High Priestess lifted her head and smiled, as though listening, then made her way to the altar. She laid aside her staff and walked to the man's side, her voice raising in a chant as she laid her hands on his chest. Immediately she gave a gasp and threw back her head. Then she screamed. The cry was so savage and primal that Elleth and the other women broke off at once and tried to drag her from the body.

'Stand back,' cried the Priestess, her voice full of the power of the Essence. Elleth stumbled back to the wall of the room, cowering with the others. Her limbs trembled. She had never felt such power before. 'I don't understand,' said Elleth. The young novice buried her head in between her breasts, sobbing. Strangely, this calmed Elleth.

The glow around the man's body now began to pulse and shift. Within it, they could see the form of his spirit, struggling against the bonds. It was powerful, suffused with the Essence. Elleth was stunned. *The man was an adept of the Earth-Essence.* Of course – he had spoken the ancient tongue of the Meadrel, a language handed down only through the line of Meadrel shamans.

Once more, the High Priestess laid back her head and screamed. This time her voice transformed, becoming a streaming well of power. The two woman beside her were tearing at their hair, lost in hysteria. Elleth blocked her ears and struggled to turn away, but she was mesmerised. The novice sank to the floor and curled into a ball, her head pressed against her knees, her eyes squeezed shut.

Like a kindling branch, the High Priestess' body burst into flame. The power of the Earth-Essence burnt within her, flaming like a sun's heart, but she was not consumed. As they watched, her breasts drew high, her old lank hair turned from grey to raven black and her eyes were restored. Then her hips grew slim and her face fair, until she appeared like an Empress. She was beautiful, with eyes of brilliant blue.

Her voice rang out through the chamber.

'I see thousands marching.
The Phoenix and the Drakon do battle.
The Old Races gather beneath the banners.
The power of Carris is raised by the evil one.'

She screamed again, a terrible sound; so full of the power that her breath glowed hot.

Elleth gathered the other women into her arms, calming them with spells of Essence, shielding them from the awesome power in the room. They must all bear witness.

'A prophecy,' cried Elleth. 'Through his spirit, she sees the future.'

The Priestess' body began to glow with a white heat. There was a blinding flash of red, then a tongue of flame surrounded her. Within it, she had grown insubstantial, like a ghost. They could see the wall beyond her, right through her body. Yet her voice was clear.

'He stands at the right hand of the Phoenix
I see.
I see!
No! It must not be!'

The High Priestess' face was creased with desperate concentration. The flame around her drew in on itself, consuming her. The flaming ball shot into the man's chest, vanishing from sight. The glow faded rapidly from the waters of the Spring, and the spirits fled the room. The pictures grew still. The novice opened her eyes, then slowly climbed to her feet, wiping away her tears.

Beneath the altar, the clothes of the High Priestess lay empty, untouched by fire, her staff beside them.

The man drew in a deep breath and sat up.

'Mother?' he said, in momentary confusion. Then seeing the walls and Spring, he leapt to his feet.

'Where am I?' he demanded in common tongue.

The three women looked at Elleth. She walked slowly down to the altar and took Skye's hands.

'You have been healed,' said Elleth. 'And now must sleep.'

She touched him with a potent Essence spell, and he sagged into her arms, deep in slumber. She staggered back a step under his weight and the others rushed to her side, helping to lay him back down on the altar stone.

'We must lead him far from here,' said Elleth, turning to her Sisters.

'Where has the High Priestess gone?' asked the novice.

'To the future,' replied Elleth.

Chapter Eleven

Cedrin could hardly make out Marken's face in the pre-dawn gloom. Around them the courtyard was packed with over one hundred of Kranor's men, outfitted with armour and standing beside their amelak mounts. The air was filled with excited talk and the bleating of the long-necked riding beasts, upset at being removed from their comfortable stables.

'Vanguard! Mount and follow me!' ordered Xyanthius, his powerful voice cutting through the talk.

The air filled with the creak of leather as the fifty warriors of the vanguard mounted and neatly followed the Captain out of the courtyard.

Cedrin licked his lips nervously. The men looked as though they had been born in the saddle.

'Ahh … excuse me, sir?'

Cedrin turned to see Rastor standing nearby. The young warrior also sounded nervous.

'Can I ride with you and Marken?' asked Rastor.

Cedrin looked over at Kanis. He was watching Xyanthius' column disappear out the gates, judging the moment when he gave the order for the rest of them to mount and follow.

'Of course, but the final disposition of the rearguard is going to be up to Kanis,' said Cedrin.

'Thank you, sir,' said Rastor. The young warrior turned back to his friends and waved them forward. They must have been waiting for the signal and moved their mounts up the line towards them.

'Just call me Cedrin.'

'Yes, s— Cedrin.' Closer now, Cedrin could see the relief on the young man's face. This was the young warrior's first assignment, and he was probably nervous at the thought of combat. Cedrin turned and eyed his mount. Right now he would rather face an armed warrior than a day in the saddle. He had never ridden before. Marken assured him it was easy, but Cedrin had noticed a twinkle in his eye at the time.

'Rearguard! Mount!' ordered Kanis.

Marken mounted his amelak smoothly. Cedrin levered himself up into the saddle, but the beast immediately turned, pushing into another warrior's mount. 'Whoa, there!' called Cedrin, trying to calm it.

'Relax, ami. Loosen the reins and ride easily,' said Marken.

Behind him Rastor and his friends broke into a chorus of laughter as the amelak continued to turn, letting out a long, tortured bleat.

Kanis rode down the line. 'What's going on back there!' he thundered.

Marken grabbed the bridle of Cedrin's mount, guiding it into position. Rastor and friends fell into formation behind them. By the time Kanis rode past them, the line had steadied.

Like the vanguard, the rearguard comprised fifty warriors. Five of them were from Kranor's One Hundred and would act as lieutenants under Kanis. Cedrin had come to know most of the fifty men, many of whom had served with Kranor for less than two or three years. Most had worked the trade routes out of Raynor before and were unconcerned with the dangers ahead. As they rode out the gates, they talked aimlessly and joked amongst themselves. Lann and his friends were at the front of the column. There was one latecomer to the company, the grim warrior Sindar, who rode in silence at the rear. His chest was covered with heavy armour, his shaven head crowded with fierce tattoos of the demons of Kallor. He was tall and moved well. Those riding nearby gave him a respectful distance.

They were barely out of the courtyard gates before the column slowed. Although first dawn was more than an hour away, the streets of the Merchants' Quarter were already packed.

Their column changed formation, and they rode two abreast as they wove through the crowd. Most were on foot, carrying bundles and pushing handcarts. There were thousands of them, all leaving Raynor.

An armoured escort pushed past them, the soldiers forming a square around three Suul on sleek long-limbed narsiit. They were magnificent creatures, built for speed. All three had their wings tightly furled. No one uttered a protest as they forced their way through.

The pace slowed even more as they approached the massive walls. Rastor was more relaxed now, swapping jokes with his friends, Cedrin and Marken forgotten. As first dawn broke, they were still in the queue. Ahead he could see Xyanthius and his men passing through the gate. Cedrin's inner thighs were already rubbed raw from the unfamiliar saddle, his buttocks bruised. He gritted his teeth against the pain and tried to distract himself by looking around the crowd.

'Quite a mix, eh?' said Cedrin.

'Yes. It's hard to tell the travellers from the refugees,' said Marken.

One family led a string of seven amelak, each piled high with bundles. Some distance behind him he could see an old man and young woman in robes of dark yellow. Something about them caught his interest. Each held a simple wooden staff topped with a cast mought figurine of a goddess. They had knotted cords of leather around their waists, simple sandals and carried bundles on their backs.

'Hey, Marken. Do you recognise that Temple order?' asked Cedrin, pointing behind him.

Marken studied the pair. The woman looked down, her face hidden by the hood of her robe.

'Hmm … Ah, yes. That's a staff of Mythar. They will be a Priest and Priestess on a pilgrimage to other holy sites.'

'Forward!' called Kanis.

The suns were above the horizon as they passed the western gate into the Outer City. Here they turned off the road, and the pace picked up. Cedrin was already exhausted when they reached the warehouses of Alechul the merchant. Xyanthius and

Kanis wasted no time, quickly organising their formation around the harena-drawn wagons. Cedrin was surprised to see they were mostly empty. Those few that were full carried the merchant's wealth – and his family. Alechul was leaving Raynor, fleeing before the Eathal like so many others to the promise of safety in the north. They were to guard him and his wagons as he travelled the sea road to Searn, stopping at the cities between to gather his stock. From Searn he would take ship for the independent port of Swebas, far to the north.

They were soon back at the main road, where the empty wagons were loaded with paying travellers. Alechul might be leaving Raynor, but he was not going to pass up an opportunity to make money. Cedrin noticed the Priest and Priestess of Mythar climbing into one of the wagons. One of Xyanthius' men offered the Priestess a hand, but she leapt up easily onto the high tray. As she landed, her robe flew back for a moment, revealing a fine woollen skirt lined with silk. *She must be a senior Priestess to have such a fine garment.*

By noon Cedrin was stiff with fatigue. His legs and back ached, and his thighs and buttocks were on fire. So far his first day as a mercenary had involved shoving people off the roads to make way for the wagons or being shoved off in turn by the well-armoured escorts of Suul.

By dusk they were barely three leagues past the western gate. They made camp at one of the many rural settlements nestled into the vast fields of baal around the city. Cedrin's arms ached from holding the heavy greatscythe, and he looked enviously at the warriors who used the lighter scythes or spears.

The dusk stop was not the end of the day. There were wagons to unhitch, harena to tether and feed, patrols and watches to be kept. When Cedrin finally stretched out in the small tent he shared with Marken, he fell instantly into a dreamless sleep of exhaustion.

* * *

Cedrin woke with a start.

'Up! Up! You lazy harena! You didn't join Kranor just to lie around. Or does that tattoo of the Way mean nothing?' Someone kicked his boot.

'But it's the middle of the night,' called back Cedrin, convinced he had just put his head down to sleep.

A face appeared inside the flap of the tent, one of Kanis' lieutenants. 'It's less than an hour to dawn, idiot.'

Beside him, Marken groaned.

Cedrin pushed himself to his feet. He was as exhausted as when he collapsed the previous night, and he felt cheated – as though the hours of sleep he did manage had been stolen somehow.

'They certainly keep different hours here,' said Marken, carefully combing his long golden hair.

'You're not wrong.' Life as a Brotherhood man had been a somewhat more nocturnal existence.

Outside, cook fires were already burning. Groups of warriors were training with their weapons, running through weapon drills or sitting cross-legged in meditation. The discipline of the Way of the Scytheman included perfection of martial skills as well as mental focus. They had both risen too late to join in. Tomorrow would be different, vowed Cedrin.

The air was beautifully fresh, sweeping in across the baal fields. He inhaled deeply, revelling in it. Cedrin had forgotten how good it felt to be outside the city. He and Marken rapidly stowed their tent and joined one of the campfires for breakfast. Thankfully they were not on sentry duty, otherwise they would have had to wait to break their fast until the caravan started moving. The warriors nodded greetings to them as they sat.

'How did you sleep?' asked Lann, who was eating with a group of warriors who had already trained.

'I'm not sure if I did,' said Cedrin.

Lann laughed. 'I know what you mean.'

Cedrin heard Rastor's voice and saw him and his friends push into the circle. The young warrior's face lit up when Cedrin nodded to him. Laughter and excited talk rose around the group.

Nearby, he heard Kanis giving orders in his gruff voice. He could just make him out in the pre-dawn gloom, walking down the line of fires, speaking briefly at each. An immediate tension ran through the group around the fire and the conversation faltered.

'Finish quickly. I want you all in formation before dawn,' snapped Kanis as he walked past them.

The bean stew and bread were basic, but it was hot and Cedrin was ravenous. It vanished from his plate, and both he and Marken went back for seconds.

As first dawn broke, they were all in formation beside their mounts: amelaks saddled, weapons at the ready. They surrounded the wagons, which were hitched but virtually empty of people. Alechul had not even roused from his tent, and most of the travellers were still trying to get cook fires lit. Xyanthius and Kanis walked down the line, checking the men and equipment.

Orders were quickly given for some of the men to go out on patrol, others to help organise the rest of the caravan. 'The rest of you – stay in your lines,' commanded Kanis.

Cedrin could see the more experienced warriors slinging their weapons and taking the opportunity to relax. A slow stream of travellers made their way up through their ranks and into the wagons. The Priest and Priestess of Mythar had roused early and were walking towards one of the wagons near him and Marken.

'Looks like we are in for a wait,' said Lann. 'You want to show me some calv moves?'

Cedrin smiled. 'Why not?'

He slung his greatscythe across the pommel of his amelak's saddle and drew a single calv from his harness. Like most of the warriors, Cedrin had not donned the heavy chest armour. Once the day warmed it would be way too hot, and it was unseemly to cover your honour marks if there was no possibility of combat. The exception was the new warrior, Sindar. The silent warrior remained in full gear at all times.

'I'll show you some basic blocks and attacks,' said Cedrin.

Lann drew a small knife from his belt – it was barely more than a skinning knife.

'No. You need a long knife.' Cedrin drew his second blade

and passed it across to Lann.

Lann's friends gathered to watch. They were soon joined by Rastor and his friends and other nearby warriors, all bored as they waited for the caravan to fill.

'Now. Start with a simple attack,' said Cedrin.

Lann stabbed in with exaggerated slowness. Cedrin batted his blade away in annoyance.

'Full speed, Grandma,' he taunted.

Lann's forehead creased in concentration, and he lunged in. Cedrin saw his shoulder flinch even before the blow began. He deflected the blade and stepped in, the edge of his calv at Lann's throat in a heartbeat.

Lann's eyes widened.

'By Uros, I didn't even see him move,' said one of Lann's friends.

He heard snatches of excited conversation. '… sixth degree… Belin's son…'

Cedrin stepped back, watching Lann carefully. He stayed frozen in position. 'Relax, Lann.'

He kept working with Lann, lost in the art of knife fighting. Gradually Lann's blocks grew faster, and better timed. As second dawn passed, Cedrin began to feel real heat in the suns. Sweat glistened on the taut muscles of his chest, running down across the tattoos. The group around them grew bigger, and they called encouragement as they continued to parry and lunge. Lann's blade slipped through his guard and Cedrin swayed to avoid it, hooking his leg underneath Lann's leading foot and sending him thudding onto this back. The crowd laughed and cheered.

'You should be practising the scythe,' came a cold, hard voice. Kanis. Cedrin's eyes swept up. The rearguard leader stood at the edge of the group.

'Harena-pokers like those calvs will do you no good if we are attacked by real warriors,' said Kanis, his voice pitched to carry across the crowd. He swept his dark eyes across the group, daring anyone to challenge him. 'Back in formation!'

The crowd melted away.

Lann handed back Cedrin's calv, which he sheathed along

with his other knife. He swept back his hair, standing tall as he turned into the cooling breeze. He sensed eyes on him and looked up suddenly. Just for a moment he met the gaze of the young Priestess. Her face was mostly hidden by her hood, but he saw the small, dark shape of her totem tattoo on her left cheek before she turned.

Kanis walked away, but Ruus, one of his lieutenants, remained to get them in order. He was a medium-built warrior of Anacian stock. Cedrin had always found him firm, but fair.

'Come on, Kaidell, you have caused enough excitement for one day,' snapped Ruus. 'Get your greatscythe and get in position.'

Cedrin went to correct him – after all he was no Kaidell – but then stopped himself. His thumb played over the emerald signet ring on the first finger of his right hand. He had Kaidell blood, there was no denying that. His whole plan had been to gain status in Kranor's ranks by declaring his link to Belin.

* * *

Their pace increased. The mounted travellers now left them far behind. They, in turn, had gradually outpaced those on foot. The great lumbering harena found their pace and pulled the wagons forward effortlessly. Cedrin soon grew accustomed to the amelak and its rhythms, and the pain in his thighs and rear receded, along with the exhaustion.

The oppressive humidity of the first days after Storm Season had eased, and insects rose from their sheltering boughs and hives to bring the world alive with movement. Twice Cedrin saw birds dig themselves from deep burrows near the road. The air was soon thick with them, taking flight to feast eagerly on the clouds of insects; while the great raptors of the Mulisar ranges circled far above them, looking for larger prey. Across the plains, herds of fast-footed narsell could be seen in the distance. According to Lann, these were sometimes pursued by palgur, the great hunting cats of the steppes. Kranor's talk about the need for bowmen was no idle chatter.

By the end of the second day, they were well on their way to

Seyt, capital of the Delta province. They camped in a broad meadow, cut by a fresh stream. The wagons of the merchant lay together in the centre, surrounded by the livestock and the camps of the warriors. Around these yet again were the fires of the refugees. Scores of them dotted the night. Whole families of freemen who were lucky enough to have the wealth to flee slavery at the hands of the Eathal. Minor Hend Suul who had lost their fortunes, now dispossessed and bitter, rubbing shoulders with the men and women who once supported their wealthy lifestyles. Slaves who had been freed by the unlikely tides of war and had been clever enough to profit by the change. All were here together, speaking mostly in the sharp dialect of Hend. At some fires, voices raised in hopeful song; at others, violent arguments broke the peace of the night, but mostly they spoke in subdued voices, sharing the horrors of the Eathal advance and their hopes for a future in the north.

Just after dusk, with the caravan work behind them and their bellies full from the cook fires, Cedrin and Marken sat on a low hill on the edge of the camp. Cedrin drew a breath of the warm night air, sweet with new blossom. Xyanthius may be driving them hard, but he did not stint on food. Cedrin had never eaten so well. He kicked their small fire with his boot and threw on another branch, watching the flames with the satisfaction of a weary man finally at rest. Marken sat beside him, his eyes glittering golden in the firelight as he drew deeply on his pipe. The sky was clear and scattered with the bright stars of Yos. Neither of the twin moons had yet risen.

'Pipe?' Marken held the pipe by the bowl and proffered the long carved stem.

'Aye,' replied Cedrin, taking the pipe and drawing deeply on the se-tobacco.

Cedrin had not felt this relaxed since before Storm Season – since the night Mat, the former Athrian Mouthpiece of Smuggling, had thumped in his door, throwing him and Marken into a failed rebellion that had forced them to flee to the mainland. Now Athria and Raynor were far behind, and they were in the company of men who shared their marks. Cedrin had been relieved to discover that the men of Kranor's company were not all dedicated to the cause of the Cinanac. Many saw the phoenix as a warrior's cult, led by the great warrior whom they served: Kranor of the One Hundred. They were the masters of their own destiny, proud in their skill and free on the roads, honest coin jangling in their purses. It felt good to be part of this new brotherhood.

They sat for hours, swapping stories and grandiose dreams as the stars turned. The new crescent of Asic raised itself above the crest of the world only to be overtaken by the fleet-footed moon Rea, which also showed only the merest crescent. Their easy talk and laughter was broken only by the soft hiss of the burning tobacco as they shared one bowl after another.

Marken tapped Cedrin on the shoulder. A figure moved purposefully up the hill towards them. As they neared, Cedrin could make out the dark skin and wide features of Kanis.

'Your watch is due,' said Kanis. He looked around the campsite with irritation. 'Your fire should be down in the middle of the camp with the other warriors.' He glared at Cedrin, waiting for him to respond. Cedrin remained silent, slowly tapping out the bowl of his pipe on a rock. 'Get your scythes and walk the perimeter,' snapped Kanis.

With a weary sigh, they climbed to their feet. Marken hefted his scythe, while Cedrin lifted Tarral's greatscythe with a grunt.

Kanis watched Cedrin carefully. A wicked smile appeared on his face. 'You shouldn't walk around with something you don't know how to use, boy.' He pointed to the greatscythe. 'Let me do you a favour. I'll take that off you and get you a little spear, something a beginner can use.'

'No, thank you, sir. I'd like to keep it, if you don't mind.'

'Oh really?' replied Kanis, casually slipping his own greatscythe from his back. 'Well, the least I can do is give you some lessons.'

Kanis' greatscythe leapt to life, seeming to spin around his head with a power and will of its own. He handled the heavy haft as though it was weightless. As he watched the warrior's display of skill, Tarral's greatscythe grew heavy in Cedrin's hands.

Kanis brought his greatscythe down into a guard position,

both blades locked away. He stepped in towards Cedrin. 'Now. Do you think you can defend yourself?'

Cedrin held his greatscythe in front of him, his tired muscles quivering with the strain. The blades of his own weapon were also locked away, turning it into a heavy staff. Kanis laughed as he advanced. A short, harsh sound. 'Now, see if you can block this strike to the head.' Kanis immediately swept his greatscythe at Cedrin's groin.

Desperately, Cedrin blocked, but realised too late the move had been a feint. The other end of the greatscythe slammed into his temple, knocking him from his feet. He hit the ground hard, still clutching Tarral's greatscythe. For a moment he was dazed. The stars spread out above him, blurring as he tried to focus on them. They were soon replaced by Kanis' leering face.

'You've got a lot to learn. I can still get you that little boy's spear.' Kanis laughed. 'You just let me know.'

Cedrin raised himself to his feet, his vision still reeling as Kanis disappeared, laughing, into the night.

'I swear I'm going to kill that whore-son. Just put a calv in his hand and I'll cut him into pieces,' said Cedrin.

'Are you all right?' asked Marken, concerned.

'Aye, just a bit bleary-eyed.'

Marken smiled, although Cedrin could see it was strained. 'I wish he would try it on me next time.'

Marken had been trained in the scythe by his step-father, Macil.

Cedrin touched the side of his head, wincing as he probed the wound. A lump had risen, but the skull beneath seemed intact. 'I know one thing for sure. If I'm going to lug this great lump of mought around, I'd better learn how to use it.'

'Well, I bet Kanis never tricks you with that move again,' said Marken.

They both laughed, recapturing some of the relaxed mood.

They set off at a steady pace around the perimeter of the camp. Their watch would last almost till dawn. His mind was alert, his body humming from the se-tobacco, but he knew that come tomorrow he would regret not catching some sleep when he could. Even so, the night was pleasant and the air sweet.

They soon forgot Kanis and fell into the rhythm of the watch, eyes alert, carefully listening for any sounds of treachery or the approach of mounted warriors. The caravan was probably at its safest this far inside the borders of the Yasser States, but Kranor had stressed that times were desperate and the wealth of Alechul was a worthy prize. They had to keep a close watch at all times.

They made one circuit, then another. With no external threats, they moved closer to the fires at the edge of camp, stealthily moving in to watch the faces around the circle and catch snatches of conversation. It was easy for an experienced Brotherhood man like Cedrin to weave close to fires unseen and, in his short time, Marken had picked up the skill remarkably fast. Cedrin often accused him of using the Moon-Essence, an accusation that Marken denied whole-heartedly, but with a twinkle in his eyes. It proved a dull exercise, since most people were asleep. At one point he heard the tell-tale sounds of lovemaking, but he gave that fire a wide berth. Cedrin was no voyeur.

They approached a fire on the edge of camp. Here, a Suul lord sat still and alert, listening to the night, his servant asleep at his feet. A small twig cracked under Marken's foot and the man looked directly at them, reaching for the greatscythe at his side. They froze and the man relaxed, returning to his thoughts and the night. As they retraced their steps, Cedrin began to wonder if he too was a refugee from the fall of Hianer, or simply an impoverished Suul, fleeing Raynor. He seemed a haunted man.

On the other side of the camp was a small fire concealed from view in a hollow. They worked their way closer. Although it was too dark to make out the yellow robes, Cedrin immediately recognised the Priest and Priestess of Mythar. They were deep in conversation.

'How's your head?' asked Marken.

'How do you think?'

Marken suppressed a laugh. 'Listen, why don't we ask the Priestess to heal you? I could try, but the Moon-Essence is not very strong tonight.'

The blow on his head had been a savage one and, although

the pain had receded, it would no doubt trouble him for many days. Why not ask the Priestess? She could only refuse.

'All right.'

Marken nodded and they worked their way back from the fire. They turned to approach once again, this time with enough noise to give them warning.

'Ho there,' yelled Cedrin, striding into the circle of light, Marken following close at his side. It was always polite — and safer — to give forewarning to a camp when approaching.

The two clergy ceased talking and watched them approach from beneath their concealing hoods. The woman gave a start, her slim white hand touching her heart.

'My name is Cedrin; this is Marken. We are two of Kranor's men.'

'We are humble servants of Mythar, travelling on pilgrimage,' said the Priest, throwing back his hood to reveal a thin face with cropped white hair on his temples and a bald dome. He raised his staff and the figurine as though as evidence.

Cedrin waited for the young Priestess to speak, but she said nothing. The Priest remained kindly, yet aloof. He knew those on pilgrimage from temple to temple often followed strange rules and he let it pass. Perhaps the Priestess was forbidden to speak. He knew little of the ways of the holy ones.

Cedrin bowed, tense and uncomfortable. 'Worthy Priest, Priestess. I have taken a bad blow to the head. I saw your fire and wondered if you had any skill in healing?'

'No,' said the old Priest, at the same time as the Priestess said, 'Yes.' Cedrin raised his eyebrows. The Priestess was under no vow of silence then.

The Priest smiled, but did not quite succeed in hiding his discomfort. 'What the Priestess means, my dear boy, is she has the means to heal you, but is under a solemn vow not to use her power until we reach the Temple of the Broken Peak, on Asgod-Ki.'

Cedrin looked across at the Mythar Priestess. She dropped her head even lower, hiding her face in the shadows of her hood. Her body was rigid with tension. Cedrin had met only a few Priestesses in his time, but they had all shared a deep sense of transcendent calm. Never once had they failed to meet his gaze – usually they were fearless. Then again, he had never seen one outside their Temple before. Perhaps they were more subdued outside their sphere of power.

His eyes lingered on her. There was something about her … Aware that he was staring, he turned away. It was not wise to provoke a woman of power, especially one who held the mysteries so close to her heart. Only the most revered of the Priestesses were chosen for pilgrimage and only the most powerful dared to move beyond the confines of their Temples.

'Sorry to trouble you. Ah … Larus be with you,' said Cedrin. He backed away from the fire.

The Priest raised his hand in blessing. 'The blessings of Larus and her handmaiden Mythar be with you.'

* * *

Ellen looked up, torn with frustration as she watched Cedrin walk away. She had a plan now – a new way to bring him closer to the Suul – but first she had to somehow win his trust. For days she had thought furiously, trying to come up with some way to approach him. When she spied him near the west gate in Raynor with the new phoenix tattoo, her heart had skipped a beat. Not only had he chosen Kranor – last of the true patriots in the city – he had taken to the phoenix with dedication. When she saw him wearing the emerald signet ring of Kaidell, the plan had come to her.

Yet when Cedrin walked into the camp, she felt completely unprepared. She had been wearing the same clothes for two days and felt miserable. Less like a woman than a tramp. Her hair hung lank against her head, full of dust and sweat. Cedrin would not think her much of a Suul if he saw her like that. Although it tore at her to do it, when he had looked her way she hid her face.

The need to conceal herself had gone against the grain from the beginning. She was the daughter of Myan Cintros, yet here she was setting after Cedrin like a thief! Following him around to Uros-knows where, cowled and concealed like a dramatic assassin in some bad comedy. She sighed. She and Raphal were still well within the boundaries of the Yasser States. It was agents of the Warlord she was truly hiding from, not Cedrin.

'The ways of the Goddess are strange,' said Raphal.

'What do you mean, Raphal?' asked Ellen.

'Oh, the young man with Cedrin. He was one of my brother Crephis' prodigies – the most talented Initiate of the Moon we had seen in a generation. Alas, he forsook the Temple life. I never thought to see him again.'

'He studied to be a Moon Druid?' asked Ellen, hardly believing what she had just heard.

'Yes. Marken Kye. We had high hopes for him, Crephis and I. He was a refugee from Althar. His father, Sanil Kye, was a Suul lord, one of Riin's most trusted allies in fact. Sanil fell with the Althar Legion and perished like the rest. I knew him personally,' Raphal shook his head. 'He has a fine mind, that lad, but a troubled heart. There is much bitterness in him, despite his cheerful demeanour.'

Her image of Cedrin and his calvanni friends had always been of dangerous and, she had to admit – low class – thieves. The more she discovered, the more she realised Cedrin was a man of singular determination and character, who was surrounded by remarkable men.

Ellen stretched her back. Her undergarments clung to her skin, clammy with old sweat. Longingly, she thought of the soft feather mattress and the fine fabrics of the gowns she had left behind. And servants! The flight from the palace and the Temple of Mythar had been exhilarating, and an opportunity to leave the constrictions of Raynor. Now she was tired and sore from long hours in the wagon, jolted by every rock and rut in the road. She shuddered as she recalled the press of unwashed bodies, knowing that tomorrow she must endure it again.

When the plan came to her, she had wanted to declare herself to Cedrin that night, but Raphal had urged patience, challenging her to find the best way to start their new alliance. So she had waited, her mind tearing constantly at the problem while the boredom became almost overwhelming. Still she had no answer. She carried enough wealth to buy the whole of

Alechul's caravan and hire Xyanthius' warriors for a year – yet she could find no easy way to start a conversation with a former calvanni.

Just picturing his face made her stomach flutter in strange ways. She had not forgotten the way he had rejected her on the galley. Raphal had been right. It *had* to be different this time. Everything depended on it.

'I could have healed him. It might have been a good way to break the wall between us,' she said, thinking of his grey-blue eyes.

'Use Sorcery on him?' said Raphal. 'He would not thank you for that. Believe me, we are much safer following him in secret for now. Until the right time presents itself.'

Raphal placed a hand on Ellen's shoulder. 'Patience, Sister. Try to get some sleep.' His eyes twinkled as he stood up with a groan and walked to the fire. Laying out a blanket, he settled down to sleep.

Ellen's stomach clenched. *More waiting.* She was not cut out for this. She slapped her thigh in frustration, her hand moving before she could control it. She looked sideways at Raphal, half-expecting him to stare at her in admonishment, but his eyes remained closed.

She swept the cowl back from her face, feeling the soft night air on her skin. She had never seen so many stars shine so brightly or smelled the night air so sweet and warm. She slipped off the headband that covered her Suul mark and swept her fingers through her hair. She was still getting used to wearing it unbraided.

Replacing the headband, she carefully reached inside her tent and slipped out her scythe. She looked back at Raphal. He was snoring softly now. Smiling, she walked out of the camp into the dark night, slowly at first, then faster, marking her way in her mind as she went. She came to a deserted strip of turf, concealed from the camp by a low ridge, and threw off her robes. She danced around the clearing like a madwoman, laughing as she imagined Cedrin discovering her in this insane frenzy.

Under the stars, alone with Yos, she was possessed with an intense feeling of freedom. In the distance, she heard the sound of bubbling water, and she ran through the night towards it. The air fled around her with a low roar, and her heart beat wildly. Her stiff body rejoiced in the movement.

She was breathing heavily when she reached the small pool, her clothes soaked with sweat. With an exhilarated laugh, she stripped them off and plunged into the water, which was still icy from Storm Season. The shock took her breath away, and she swam like a demon to warm her numbing limbs. The cold soon drove her from the pool, and she sat on the soft grass by the bank, her long hair falling wet around her shoulders. As the night warmed her, she felt more refreshed and alive than she had for years.

She took her scythe and began to practise, her limbs flashing in the silver moonlight, her hair swinging around her as she turned. Ellen pushed herself to her limit and beyond, until finally, exhaustion forced her to stop.

She stood naked under the stars, her skin glittering with sweat, her chest heaving. She dropped her scythe and ran to the pond, diving head-first into the pool to rinse off the sweat. She gasped at the cold and was out of the water almost as quickly. Reluctantly, she shook the dust out of her travelling clothes and dressed. Ellen lay back on the grass, the frustrations of the day behind her, content as she looked up at the stars. She was not Ellen Cintros, the daughter of the mighty Myan – or the disinherited heir to Athria's throne – she was simply Ellen.

Wait for the right moment, Raphal had said. She would win Cedrin to her side, and together they would find the Scion. Together. There was a strange feeling in her belly – something that set her heart racing. She wondered what his touch would feel like. Ellen laid her hand above her left breast. What would his hand feel like on her skin? Rough. Hard. Something swam, low in her belly, leaving warmth in its wake.

She pushed herself to her feet and gathered her scythe. She should get some sleep, but she knew that tonight it would not come easily.

Waiting was not something she was good at.

* * *

Raziin sat on a hill with his greatscythe across his knees, looking down at the wide plains and valleys of Tupur. They had left Raynor far behind, striking out east from the city towards the wild hills and forests of the Crusox and the Shattered Temple. Below him, mists hung like shrouds in the hollows, lit blood-red by Uros in first dawn. It was glorious. He had been granted a vision this night. The goddess craved not only blood, but grief; the agony of souls in torment. And what she hungered for, he would bring eagerly. He would open rivers of blood, oceans, yet upon those oceans would sit a new world of pain. A great cry of torment would rise up like a song of worship to the Red One above.

The Spear of Carris hovered in his mind, like a sweet promise of power. The Seer of Ciofran-Ac had shown him the way. She had seared it into his mind with her blazing, crimson eyes. He could still hear her voice.

The calvanni, Cedrin. He holds the key to the Power.

He will stand within the plaza of Cinanac in Olcis at the feast of Asic's Blessing… You must stand with him in the Temple. You must reach first for the Power. Do you understand?

He had once blamed the half-Blood Cedrin for his defeat in Athria and his fall from Hukum's favour – after all, if not for Cedrin's inept Sorcery, Raziin and his men would have succeeded in putting the puppet Jorrel on the Athrian throne. Yet now, since his time with the Seer, he knew this defeat had merely been one step on the road to his destiny. When he used the Sorcery of the Final Matrix to reduce Cedrin to a quivering wreck, it would no longer be for revenge, it would be for pleasure alone.

Larus cleared the horizon and the red light vanished, the mists glowing a brilliant white. It was always the same, the golden light banished the red. *Damn Larus. The yellow goddess is fit only for peace-loving fools.* If only Uros would swell and devour pathetic Larus for all time. Only one sun should rise on Yos, one goddess above all. And beneath her bloody light the people should kneel to him. Perhaps, with the power of the Spear, he could make it a reality. He would forge a new empire, wiping the Warlord and phoenix of the Cinanac from the face of history as Carris had once wiped away all that had come before him.

He would need a new sign for this reborn Empire. His own totem was the *keerhound*, the big war dog of Armon. They were fearsome beasts, originally bred for taking down harena, but he wanted something more. The Drakon was more to his liking. Yes, this would become his new banner. When the time came to build his new Empire, this would be his standard. And when he finally crushed Hukum … Raziin laughed out loud. His former Eathal master's chosen totem – his symbol of strength – was also the Drakon. For him to be defeated by it was a twist of irony that appealed to Raziin, something that would increase Hukum's shame and misery before the end.

As the mist thinned, Raziin peered ahead, trying to make out the cracked dome of the Shattered Temple. Nothing. It was behind the next rise. Inside him, the first part of Hukum's Compulsion throbbed and prodded, pushing him onward. Unable to defend himself against it, it had sunk into the depths of his mind, and now compelled him to enter the Shattered Temple. Not so the second part of his former Eathal master's Compulsion, which would have seen him kneel to receive a death-blow. This had been defeated by the golden glowmetal the Seer had gifted to him. It writhed like a living thing around his neck, the bands of purple light rippling as it absorbed the psychic energy. It also gave voice. The inhuman sounds were like the misery of the people of Kelas, kneeling to him, bowed with burdens great and many.

It was a sweet sound.

Chapter Twelve

A ring of bright fires lit the fighting circle. Almost all of Xyanthius' one hundred warriors – except for the six on watch – stood waiting for combat. Cedrin stretched his back and shoulders to loosen the muscles. He turned the greatscythe around in his hands, flipping it into an outside block, then reversing it into a strike. After a week of practising every morning and night with Marken and the other warriors, he was beginning to get a feel for it. Only yesterday he had mastered the release and withdrawal of the blades. Not that he would need them tonight.

They were camped just off the road in the hills above Seyt, the walled capital of the Delta province. He had sailed there twice for the Brotherhood. Cedrin could see the lights of the city, far below, and the black silhouette of the Seawatch tower near the harbour. The refugees would be making their own way from Seyt. At the provincial capital, the empty wagons would begin to fill with the Alechul's wares. It was on the unpatrolled roads north from Seyt, where the Legion patrol ended, where the caravan would come under threat. Neither Alechul nor Xyanthius wanted the presence of unarmed and unpredictable civilians to complicate the protection of the wagons.

Tension had been running high among the men, the warriors tired of policing the volatile mix of Hendian refugees. To help ease off some of the strain, Xyanthius and Kanis had organised a greatscythe tournament with a coin prize of ten rubies – more than two months' pay. The contest was to be held without blades. Xyanthius wanted no serious injuries. To ensure it, he had made a hefty donation to the local Temple of the Sisters to secure the services of a Moon Druid. The big moon Asic was nothing more than a thick crescent, yet Marken assured him even this would provide enough Essence for a trained Druid to work potent healing spells. Rea, just off full, had risen early and already fled the sky.

Beyond the fighting circle scores of travellers from the caravan watched in silence. The Moon Druid and his two brown-robed healers had just arrived and had set up a temporary infirmary in a covered wagon. Cedrin looked for the Priest and Priestess of Mythar, but they were gone. Strange, he thought, they were in the crowd only moments ago.

Rastor grinned at Cedrin across the circle, and he smiled back. The young man had quickly gained his confidence since they had been on the road, and Cedrin had rarely seen him without his five friends.

The first two warriors were called into the circle and Cedrin watched nervously as they squared off. He was anxious to make a good showing with the greatscythe, but keenly aware of his lack of skill with the big weapon.

'Begin!' called Xyanthius, the old warrior watching the two combatants keenly as they slowly closed on each other.

Their two greatscythes blurred into motion, the hafts tapping out a quick rhythm as strike met block in rapid succession. Beside him, his long hair tied back into a series of tight braids, Marken watched the combat carefully.

'Strike!' called Xyanthius, holding out his right arm to indicate the winner. Cedrin had not even seen the blow fall. In this contest, the first fighter to land a potentially lethal strike won the round. In real combat, the deadly lanedd blades gave no second chances.

Xyanthius looked at his list. 'Cedrin and Ruus.'

Cedrin walked into the circle, trying not to think about the fact that Xyanthius had paired him with one of Kranor's One Hundred.

Ruus advanced from the other side of the circle, the fires lighting his broad chest and reflecting from the polished mought of his greatscythe. His eyes were focussed, seeming to look through him.

'Begin!'

Ruus swayed from side to side, his eyes never leaving Cedrin. Cedrin changed his feet, readying to step in with a feint. Ruus' eyes flicked down, then the warrior shot forward. Cedrin swung his greatscythe up, ready to counter an attack, then grunted as something slammed into his solar plexus, winding him.

'Strike!'

Ruus smiled. 'Better luck next time, Kaidell.'

Cedrin nodded, gasping for air as he walked back to the circle.

'That was short,' said Marken.

'Very,' he croaked.

There were two more combats, the second going into a second round after both warriors landed a strike at the same time.

'Marken and Lann.'

Cedrin handed Marken his greatscythe. 'Good luck.' His friend flashed him a grin.

At the signal, Lann launched a furious series of attacks. Marken kept his head, moving back and blocking well, then he counter-attacked. Lann swayed to his left then jabbed the haft of his weapon at Marken. The golden-skinned warrior dropped his weapon to block, but it was a feint. Lann's face lit with the anticipation of victory as he swung his greatscythe into a powerful blow to Marken's head. At the last minute, Marken turned on his front foot. Lann's blow sailed past him without landing, and Marken's greatscythe swung around to land on Lann's neck.

'Strike!'

There were nods of approval from the onlookers as Marken walked back to the circle. Any calls or applause were forbidden, as these could distract the combatants. This was not so vital now, but in a match with blades, a distraction at the wrong time could make the difference between a blade touched lightly to an opponent's throat and a severed jugular.

Two rounds later, Marken was matched with Rastor. The

young warrior was fast and skilled. Cedrin could see the greatscythe, heavier than Marken's usual weapon, was slowing his blocks. Twice Marken almost had him, but then Rastor got Marken with a series of four attacks that ended in a jab through Marken's guard and into his unprotected ribs. His friend walked back to the circle, holding his side.

Rastor turned to Cedrin, flushed with victory. The young warrior nodded to him before walking back to the circle. It seemed Cedrin's poor performance had done nothing to dull the young warrior's respect for him. Kanis had not missed the exchange, and his dark eyes bored into Cedrin's, who looked away. He had no interest in provoking the bad-tempered warrior.

Marken was pale with pain.

'Is the rib broken?' asked Cedrin.

'No, just bruised. Your little friend is quite the fighter,' said Marken.

The bouts continued, even more furious than before as the level of skill increased. Never had Cedrin seen such displays of mastery. The phoenix was a warrior's cult, surviving intact from the days of the Empire. Like real combats, most were over in moments. Cedrin soon recovered his breath and was pleased Marken had escaped with only a bruise. Very few walked away unscathed. One warrior had two ribs broken and another suffered a fracture as Kanis' greatscythe slammed into his forearm. The Moon Druid healed both men. Sindar was very skilled and won his first two bouts with contemptuous ease. His footwork was excellent. He defeated Ruus in his third bout, landing a jabbing blow to the back of the warrior's neck that sent him staggering.

A generation ago, a skilled warrior could rise far in the ranks of the Legion, even to the rank of Suul – as Kranor had. Cedrin realised that gathered here were some of the best warriors in Kelas, easily rivals of Raziin's men or the Warlord's personal guards.

'Rastor and Kanis,' called Xyanthius.

Cedrin tensed as he watched Kanis move across the circle. Kanis had fought twice already and was a savage opponent.

Cedrin touched the wound at his temple. The skin had healed, but it was still tender to touch.

Rastor squared off. To the young warrior's credit, he stayed calm. He now faced one of Kranor's One Hundred, like Cedrin had less than an hour before. Kanis' dark eyes stayed focused on Rastor.

'Begin!'

Rastor swung in to the attack, landing a flurry of blows.

'Stay cool, Rastor,' whispered Cedrin. Even as he said it, he could see the young warrior's anxiety eroding his concentration.

Kanis fell back smoothly, turning each blow with ease. Then Rastor overextended. Kanis shot in, sweeping his greatscythe into the young warrior's groin.

Rastor gasped and froze.

'Strike!'

Kanis reversed his greatscythe and smashed it up into Rastor's chin, knocking him back off his feet. There was a shocked silence. Cheating was a blatant violation of the code of the Way. All eyes turned to Xyanthius to see if he would disqualify Kanis. The mercenary Captain's eyes narrowed, but he said nothing.

Cedrin and Marken ran into the circle and knelt at Rastor's side. Ruus joined them a moment later. The young warrior groaned, his eyes misting with pain. He reached out and gripped Cedrin's forearm. Ruus gently probed the chin. 'It's broken.'

Cedrin turned to face Kanis. The warrior's small, dark eyes were filled with triumph. A hot fury pumped through Cedrin, and the Window flashed past his vision. It was not what he wanted. He wanted a calv in his hand. Kanis was of the same breed as Mat, the Brotherhood Mouthpiece he had beaten in the Circle of Blades – a mean and vindictive *harena*. There was nothing to be done but stand up to men like that. Yet now was not the time.

'Cedrin, help me with him,' said Ruus.

He helped Rastor to the Moon Druid and his healers. The young man was sobbing, tears flooding down his cheeks. Rastor's hand gripped his arm tighter. Cedrin knew the real pain he felt was the humiliation of crying like that in front of the other warriors. He squeezed his shoulder. 'It's just the shock. It means nothing.' Rastor nodded and drew in a shuddering breath.

The Moon Druid touched Rastor lightly on the jaw. His eyes grew unfocused for a moment as he concentrated his power. 'A simple fracture. Take him to the wagon.'

They lifted Rastor up into the covered wagon they were using to treat the wounded.

'Leave him in our care, please,' said one of the healers tersely. Clearly, they were not invited to stay.

Cedrin met Ruus' eyes as they walked away. Ruus said nothing, but Cedrin could tell that he too, was furious.

Cedrin and Marken rejoined the circle. They had missed two combats.

'Final bout!' called Xyanthius. 'Sindar and Kanis.'

Kanis walked across the circle to meet the silent, grim warrior. Sindar's pale blue eyes met Kanis' gaze with contempt.

'Begin!'

The combat was furious from the outset. Cedrin's stomach clenched as he saw how fast they moved. Sindar turned all of Kanis' attacks with swift and beautifully-executed blocks, but the power of the bulky half-Cioan began to tell. The grim warrior was gradually driven back to the edge of the circle. If he went beyond the ring of watching men he would lose. Kanis' victory seemed inevitable when Sindar flipped onto the ground, tripping Kanis with a swift movement of his legs. He was on his feet just as quickly – with a greatscythe haft at Kanis' throat.

'Strike! Sindar wins.'

Just for a moment, something dark flashed through Kanis' eyes, then he forced a smile. He did not meet Sindar's gaze again, but bowed to Xyanthius and walked from the circle as the men cheered Sindar. In response, the silent warrior lifted his greatscythe, turning to acknowledge the crowd. Sindar was transformed, his whole face alive with passion as he drank in the adulation. Then the moment was gone, and the grim mask slipped back into place. He took the purse from Xyanthius with a nod of thanks and stalked back into the darkness without a word.

'Well, that's it then,' said Marken.

'Let's check on Rastor,' said Cedrin. He was worried about the lad.

As they approached the wagon, he saw Rastor's friends sitting nearby at a small fire. There was no sign of the Moon Druid or his healers.

'Where's the Druid?' he asked them.

They looked back at him nervously. 'The Druid and his healers left for Seyt straight after the last combat,' said one of them, a thickset lad with a small white scar in his chin. 'He set Rastor's jaw and put him in a healing sleep. He told us not to wake him.'

Cedrin nodded. 'Let me know when he rouses, will you?'

They walked back through the camp. Although they had eaten earlier, Cedrin was hungry again. All the training had doubled his appetite. They wove through the camp, looking for the campfire of a family from Raynor they had gotten to know after stepping in to break up a fight between one of their sons and a young refugee from Hend. They were free craftsmen, most of them carpenters, on their way to the northern sardom of Exdor to start again. The mother of the tribe was a skilled cook and worked miracles over the open fires of the camp. They had often returned to their fire at nights, trading tobacco for food and swapping stories over the campfire. The family had set their fire on the edge of the camp tonight. As Cedrin angled towards them, Marken tapped him on the shoulder and pointed. They were going to walk right past Sindar, who was sitting alone staring into his fire, his greatscythe cradled between his knees.

'Keeping good company, Sindar?' asked Cedrin, as he and Marken passed him.

The grim warrior broke off his brooding and looked up. The demon tattoos on his skull gave him a forbidding appearance. 'There is no other company I would prefer,' he said, his voice low.

Cedrin shrugged and turned away, feigning indifference. The truth was Cedrin was intrigued by Sindar. Other warriors in the company had long ago forsaken the heavy clothing and coverings of Storm Season, yet Sindar still covered his chest. This hinted at some dark past, something written in his tattoos that he wanted to conceal. Perhaps he too had been expelled from some brotherhood, but not a group like the Brotherhood of the Night, a more secret and dark elite that kept the rites of Kallor or Uros. For such a man, expulsion could be a death sentence. Or perhaps there was some deep dishonour marked there.

Cedrin touched the phoenix tattoo on his chest. In the last week with Kranor's men, the mark had earned him great respect. Knowing that he was the son of Belin, the warriors acknowledged him as one of their own. After his betrayal by the Brotherhood, it was a good feeling. He had become proud of the mark and proud of his blood for the first time. His thumb played over the emerald signet ring of Kaidell and he smiled.

They were almost at the family's campfire. One of the men raised his hand in greeting and Cedrin waved back. They were passing a pipe amongst them, standing at ease near the fire.

He heard angry shouts from the centre of the camp and turned to listen. Two men in a heated argument.

Trouble.

'I think that second meal is going to have to wait,' said Cedrin.

The voices were joined by the despairing cry of a woman.

Cedrin and Marken raced through the camp, running swiftly between the fires and small hillocks. It was important to head off any trouble before it escalated. The shouts become more violent, and Cedrin hoped they would reach them in time to halt any bloodshed. Ahead, he could see the two men, a woman trying to stand between them. A crowd had gathered to watch the fight. Cedrin and Marken lengthened their stride, but they were hampered by the growing press of bodies.

'You were born a slave, you will die a slave,' shouted one of the men. He was middle-aged, his face red, fists clenched by his sides, his once-fine merchant's clothes soiled by travel.

'I was never a slave in me heart, and I am no slave now.' The second man was big and heavily muscled from long days of physical toil. A white band of untanned skin showed where the slave collar had recently been broken free from his throat.

The merchant stepped forward, a pudgy white finger pointing in accusation. '*Now* you say you are not a slave. But you were happy enough for me to pay your way through Raynor and onto this caravan. Now you want to be free? Typical. I say you are my slave and will *stay* my slave.'

'Make way!' shouted Cedrin, trying to push through the crowd.

The big man, who had been speaking with his head bowed, raised his head, his eyes defiant. The woman took hold of one of his massive arms. 'No, husband. Don't,' she pleaded. He pulled out of her grip. Cedrin could see a white band at her throat also. Two slaves, husband and wife, freed by the fortunes of war.

Cedrin lifted his greatscythe, using the haft to roughly push through the crowd. Marken followed through behind him.

'What makes ya' better? Just 'cause ya' never done a day's work?' said the big man, his fists clenching.

'I was *born* above you,' said his former master in contempt, even as he craned his neck upwards to look the man in the eye. 'And don't think anything will ever change that.'

With a shout of rage, the big man lashed out, his powerful hands circling the other man's throat in a vice-like grip. The little merchant was lifted off his feet, his face transformed from arrogance to surprise – then terror. Judging by his reaction, he had never had a servant or slave touch him, let alone attack him. Cedrin shoved the last of the crowd out of the way.

'Put him down, big man,' said Cedrin, tilting his greatscythe into a combat position.

The woman looked back at Cedrin, her eyes wild with terror. 'Do as he says, please,' she pleaded with her husband.

The little man was choking.

'Release him! Last warning,' shouted Cedrin. He could see the big man was far gone into rage.

'Cedrin! *Knife*,' called Marken.

The merchant had drawn a slender dagger from his sleeve. Before either of them could move, the merchant plunged it deep into the chest of the big man. Blood pumped from the dagger-wound. Cedrin and Marken dropped their weapons and tried to separate the men. Despite the wound, it was no easy task to loosen the big man's grip. By the time they finally prised his fingers loose, he was beginning to weaken from blood loss. The merchant staggered back, taking painful mouthfuls of air as he clutched at his throat.

Four other warriors from the caravan pushed through the crowd. One of them was Lann.

The big man sank to his knees. He looked down at the dagger in his chest, aware of it for the first time. He gripped the hilt.

'Leave it!' said Marken.

The big man pulled it free with a gasp of pain. Blood spurted across the grass. The anger on his face seeped away, replaced by fear. He looked with silent desperation towards the woman, who rushed to his side.

'No. *No!*' screamed the woman. The blood was flowing freely now, soaking into her shawl as she knelt at his side, her arms around his broad shoulders.

His eyes fluttered, then rolled back.

'He's going,' said Cedrin. He and Marken helped her lower him to the ground as unconsciousness took him.

Lann and the other warriors closed in, looking to Cedrin. 'There was a scuffle,' Cedrin explained. 'The merchant pulled a knife and stabbed him. We better hold the merchant until Xyanthius can rule on it.' He looked at the fallen man. *If he dies, it's murder.*

Lann and one of the other men lifted the little merchant roughly to his feet.

'Take your hands off me!' said the merchant. 'Don't you know who I am?'

'No – and I don't care,' said Lann as he and the others led the man away. One of the warriors scooped up the bloody knife.

Marken gently probed the wound. It was steadily pumping blood. Cedrin had seen some knife wounds in his time, and this one looked bad. The blade had entered high in the chest, through the left lung, but the thrust had been angled so there was no telling how much damage had been caused internally. Their eyes met. Both of them knew the Moon Druid and his healers had already left the camp. 'It's deep. He has only moments,' whispered Marken.

The woman's hands desperately moved over her husband's face, as though to find and grasp some sign of life. 'Save him,' pleaded the woman, turning to Marken. 'Please save him. After everything we have been through... don't let him die here.'

'Can you do anything?' asked Cedrin.

Marken's face was grim as he looked at the wound. He looked up at Asic's crescent and closed his eyes for a moment. When he opened them, he shook his head. 'No. There is too little Essence.'

'Are you a Druid?' asked the woman, desperate.

'No... Yes ... I was only an Initiate ...' said Marken.

'Then you can save him. You know how to heal,' pleaded the woman.

'Yes, but the knitting of a wound like this – it's beyond my skill.'

The woman threw herself at Marken's feet. '*Save him.*'

Marken's face twisted with anguish. Cedrin had never seen his friend so torn. Even in the toughest situations, he seemed to be able to maintain his ironic humour, but not this time.

'You don't understand. There is internal damage. If I don't heal the wound properly, I will condemn him to a long and painful death. In a few more days, with Asic at quarter, I might have been able to risk it.'

Then it hit him.

'The Priestess,' said Cedrin. 'She is our only chance.' She may have refused to heal a bump on the side of his head, but surely no vow of pilgrimage was worth a man's life.

'Yes,' said Marken, his eyes alive with hope.

Together they carried the man through the camp. A crowd of refugees gathered behind them, led by the woman. The awful responsibility for the man's life gnawed away at Cedrin. He and Marken had been first on the scene. If only he had pushed through the crowd quicker, somehow gotten between them ... it was useless to speculate. Nothing could take away the reality of the dying man in their arms.

Finally they reached the fire of the Priest and Priestess of

Mythar. Both stood in alarm as they approached with the wounded man. The crowd swarmed around them, watching expectantly as they laid the unconscious man down by the fire. His wife knelt by his side, crying softly.

'What is this?' demanded the Priest, throwing back his hood. His face was stern, uncompromising.

'He is dying, Father,' said Cedrin.

Fresh blood was pumping from the wound, and the man's face was as pale as new snow. Marken pressed a cloth to the wound. 'It's deep.'

The Priestess rose, her head still bowed and covered by the deep hood of her robe. She seemed to swell somehow. The hairs on the back of Cedrin's neck stood up and he shivered. As she came forward, the crowd fell back.

Cedrin swallowed. 'You are his only chance, Priestess,' he said.

The dying man's wife ran to the Priestess and knelt at her feet. 'For the love of Larus, Great Lady, save him.' She took hold of the hem of her robe, her hands shaking. 'I beg you.'

The Mythar Priestess looked up to meet the woman's eyes. The firelight fell across her left cheek, lighting up the bird totem tattoo. It was a finely-etched piece ... and strangely familiar.

Chapter Thirteen

Ellen looked down at the woman. She knew what it was like to watch the life drain out of someone she loved. To have them fade from life, to become only a distant memory. If someone could have saved her father, would she not have begged them, just as this woman was begging her?

Raphal walked past her to stand over the unconscious man. He gave him a brief blessing to give him the protection of Larus on his journey to meet Kallor in his underworld realm of Llors.

'The Priestess in on a pilgrimage,' said Raphal. 'Those on a holy mission are not responsible for the folly of men.'

The crowd stood in silence. Despite what Raphal had said, they were waiting for her. In the realm of Earth magic, it was the Priestess who held the final authority.

Ellen had a sense that events were spiralling out of her control. For days she had tried to find the right way to introduce herself to Cedrin, and now here he stood with his friend Marken, only paces away. If she healed the man, he would know her instantly.

She looked down into the woman's desperate eyes and knew there was no choice. She had to save him.

Ellen straightened. She threw back her hood, careful not to dislodge the headband that covered her Suul mark. A wave of low, excited talk swept through the crowd, although they kept their distance.

'Cintros ...,' said Cedrin.

Ellen's heart raced as she looked across at Cedrin. He looked shocked. How else would he look? He would think her left far behind in Raynor. As their eyes met, she could feel his bewilderment turn to anger. She turned away quickly, not wanting to consider the implications. Marken, at least, seemed pleased to see her. His face was transformed with amazement, even hope. There was no time to think of that now.

'She is going to heal him,' cried one man from the back of the crowd.

'Larus be praised,' said another.

'And her handmaiden, Mythar,' said another.

'Praise to Mythar,' echoed a few of the others, anxious to please her.

Ellen knelt by the body. Silence fell, then she heard nothing but the whispering of cloth as the crowd fell to their knees around her. Some even lay forward on the ground rather than witness a mystery of Earth.

Ellen closed her eyes. She may not be a true Priestess, but her power was no sham. She opened the Window, letting the Fire fill her. Then she reached out with the Matrix of Form, seeking the Key. Without the essential pattern of the man's body, she could do nothing. Her first task was to find it. A real Priestess used the natural processes of the body to heal. She would recreate his tissue using the power of the Fire.

Time stretched out. Through the Matrix, Ellen could sense that the man was fading fast. The woman began to cry once more. It was a soft, forlorn sound.

There! She had it. She inserted the Key into the Matrix of Form.

Ellen opened her eyes and released the Fire, channelling it through the Matrix. For a brief instant the man was surrounded with a golden fire, then he was healed. The flesh around the wound had knit without a scar. The woman looked at him in amazement, touching the wound with her fingers as though she could not believe it. The man's eyes opened and he sat up, surprised to see himself inside a circle of onlookers.

'A miracle,' called one man.

'Praise Mythar!' echoed the others.

The woman threw herself at Ellen's feet, kissing her sandals and weeping with joy.

'Thank you for healing him,' said Cedrin.

Ellen's stomach flipped as she met his eyes. The tall warrior had recovered quickly, and now seemed calm, yet guarded.

'I see you are wearing your ring,' said Ellen. The crowd were still close, and it was impossible to say more. She was hoping that his link to the Kaidell blood would be the one thing that bridged the gap between them. Excitement built inside her. Now was the time. She would ask him to come back to see her, after the crowd had gone.

'Yes. And I thank you for returning it,' said Cedrin. 'I need to get this man to Xyanthius so he can pass judgement on the matter.'

Cedrin walked over to the former slave, helping him to his feet.

Just for a moment, Ellen almost called out to him, but then she saw the crowd watching her.

'You have been very lucky, my friend. You should thank the Priestess for healing you. You were at Kallor's doorstep,' said Cedrin.

The big man turned and nodded to her. 'Thank you, Priestess. I have nothing to offer you. No coin ...'

'You need offer nothing,' said Ellen. 'Go in peace.'

'Come on, friend,' said Cedrin, leading the man away.

So, after all her agonising, she had revealed herself to Cedrin, and he had simply walked away. Had it been a mistake to heal the man? As she watched the woman walking at his side, her face transformed with joy, she knew it had been no mistake.

Marken approached her. 'Suul Cintros?'

'Do not speak that name here,' whispered Raphal harshly.

'I understand. My apologies,' said Marken, bowing graciously. 'I do not know why Cedrin is so important to you, but have no fear. You have an ally in me.'

Ellen was impressed by Marken's refined speech and manner. This could be her only chance.

'It was Myan's dying wish that Belin's son be brought back to the Suul,' said Ellen, stretching the truth.

Marken shook his head. 'He is stubborn. I would have followed you to Raynor without a moment's thought – even if you were not promising the title of Suulqua.' So, she thought, Cedrin must have told Marken everything.

'Is there some way you can convince him to speak to me?'

'I will try. I believe your reasons run much deeper than you say … Priestess… yet I also believe he needs you – more than you need him.'

Ellen was relieved that Marken had offered his help, but was puzzled by what he had said.

'Good night,' he said to her, bowing like a courtier.

'*Almus carsicum*, brother,' said Raphal. *Peace surround you.*

Marken replied automatically in ancient Cioan, then gave Raphal a sharp look.

'That greeting is used by the Temple of the Sisters, not Priests of Mythar,' said Marken. 'Are you a Druid as well, Father?'

Raphal smiled. 'You have a short memory, my little Cioan. Don't you recognise the brother of Crephis?'

Astonishment crossed Marken's face. 'Raphal?'

Raphal smiled, reaching out to touch Marken's Brotherhood tattoo with his finger.

'You have wandered far, young Marken. To think that I would live to see the son of Sanil Kye in the Brotherhood of the Night,' he said, shaking his head. 'At least that path is ended for you now.' Raphal traced the glyphs declaring the Brotherhood a former path.

'We all do what we must,' said Marken, struggling to keep his demeanour.

'You once craved the knowledge of the Moon Druids, my son. The knowledge of healing. Is that no longer true?'

Marken and Raphal looked at each other for a long moment, a silent understanding passing between them that Ellen could not share. Even so, Marken seemed to shine brighter for a moment, as though Raphal had ignited some hidden flame inside him.

'Go. Find your friend,' said Raphal.

Marken bowed politely to Ellen, then left. In many ways, he reminded her of Estle, and she sensed she could grow to like him. He, like Cedrin, also had Suul blood.

'It seems the Goddess is working in our favour. We have an

unexpected ally,' said Raphal.

All she could think of was Cedrin's guarded faced as he walked away without another word. 'I need all the allies I can get,' she said, her voice harder than she intended.

Raphal placed a hand on her shoulder. 'Don't give up hope. Some of the best bonds are the hardest to forge.'

How, under the Suns and Moons, was all this to lead her to the Scion?

* * *

Marken found Cedrin on the perimeter, marching through the night, far from the fires.

'Cedrin. Wait.'

His friend stopped, waiting for him to catch up. As soon as he reached him, Cedrin started off again. For a time they marched side by side in silence.

'I thought all this was in the past,' said Cedrin.

Marken knew what he meant. Both of them had thought they had left their old life behind. Seeing Ellen Cintros was like seeing a ghost, a spectre following them from Athria.

'If it was revenge she was after, she would have acted long before now,' said Marken.

'Why follow us? Disguised like that? What could she possibly want?'

'Ask her,' said Marken. 'Talk to her. I'm sure she means you no harm, Cedrin. In fact, I think she is the only one who can help you.'

Cedrin stopped, turning to face him. 'She is a Sorcerer. I want no part of that world.'

As usual, Cedrin's face was guarded, his grey-blue eyes, dark in the night, giving nothing away. Even so, Marken could detect some note of tension in Cedrin's voice. There was something else here.

Marken gripped Cedrin's shoulder. 'I have said nothing to you about Sorcery, as I agreed, but I have been worried. You have a power inside you that is barely under control. You must confront it.'

'And I told you – I have denied that power. I don't need her and whatever designs she has for the bastard of a dead warrior.'

'This is a power you cannot deny.' He knew Cedrin feared the power, feared the stigma of using what the Temple of the Sisters called a curse. It was no easy burden. Yet it was a gift also.

'On the Spire in Athria, your power saved us. That time we were lucky. When will it be unleashed again?' said Marken.

'It won't be,' said Cedrin.

'Really? You have no true control over it.'

Cedrin was silent.

'Next time it could cripple you, kill you … or someone else,' said Marken. Cedrin stiffened. Marken knew he had him. 'Who will it be? Me? Any one of the warriors standing beside you, or another innocent?'

'Enough! Enough,' said Cedrin. 'This … power. It has already cost me one friend.'

Marken knew he was talking about Skye. The two had been as close as brothers and were partners long before Marken joined the Brotherhood.

'I don't understand why a Suul like Ellen Cintros should single me out,' said Cedrin. 'Maybe you're right. Maybe it is time I talked to her. Time I found out what else is driving her.' His voice hardened. 'Remember though, not a single word about the curse. I mean to leave that buried deep, and buried for good.'

Marken felt a wave of relief sweep through him. 'I won't say a thing,' he promised, trying to seem casual. The fact was, finding a Sorcerer to teach Cedrin was the main thing he was concerned about. For now, getting them talking was a good first step.

He still felt uneasy. Although the appearance of the Cintros woman was a blessing, Marken knew she would have her own purpose and would eventually exact her price. It did not matter. If Cedrin did not control his growing power, one way or another it would consume and destroy them all. It was only luck that had saved them this far.

The beast was close now, stalking him through the mist.

Cedrin struggled against fatigue as he pushed himself up another hill, his lungs burning as he sucked in the foul vapours. Dead yellow grass crackled beneath his boots, his feet slipping on the loose, cracked surface. The sky was a featureless grey, the mist shrouding everything. It was no normal mist either, nothing like the clean mists that swept across Athria on cool mornings. This was like the exhalation of some vast predator, its teeth black with rotten carrion.

He paused at the top of the hill, his stomach roiling at the stench. He could not see a single landmark … or place to hide.

A bellowing roar shook the ground. He ran down into a valley scattered with sharp, shattered fragments of flint, then up another hill. His thighs burned with pain, but he dare not stop.

The beast roared again. Closer.

His right foot twisted on a rock, and he slipped on the scree. He threw out his hands as he went down. Sharp rocks sliced at him as he tumbled, opening wounds on his forearms, chest and back. He slammed into a boulder at the bottom of the slope and felt a rib snap. For a long moment he lay frozen with pain, the cuts burning with the acidic dust. Then he pushed himself to his feet.

'What do you want!' he screamed out. The mist sucked the sound from his words.

The scree crunched under the beast's weight as it neared. He spun around, trying to face it, but he could see nothing. Then he felt its hot, rank breath on the back of his neck and heard the deep rumble of a growl through massive jaws. He turned swiftly, leaping back. It was like a huge hound with a skin of dark scales and a massive head like a harena. Its single horn was yellowed and cracked with disease, yet razor sharp. He reached up to his harness for a blade, but as he drew his calv it transformed into an orange rose. He watched, astonished, as the rose glowed, as though lit from within.

The beast snorted and withdrew behind a veil of mist. He could see its huge, dark shape lurking near.

'Why do you hesitate?' he shouted. Could it be the flower?

Cedrin brandished the rose like a weapon. The beast cowered, retreating further into the mist. The rose began to pulse and shimmer, sending orange streamers through the dead grey of the landscape. The beast struggled to turn, but Cedrin saw its body was far gone in disease, slowing it. A shaft of orange light touched its skin, and it bellowed in rage. As though unleashed, the light swelled rapidly, sheathing the beast in orange flame. The beast struggled, becoming indistinct; nothing more than a blurred shadow.

All around Cedrin the mists receded, driven back by the rose's light. Soon the suns appeared above, their light soaking the parched soil. Flowers shot skyward, climbing to bud and blossom in the passing of a breath. Trees pushed from the rocky ground like patient beasts-of-burden, the slopes thickening with lush grasses.

When the last sign of the beast had disappeared from the flame, it flickered and disappeared.

A woman walked towards him through the lush greenery.

Ellen.

Her honey-blonde hair was swept around her shoulders, her skin shone like moonlight and her eyes were deep green pools of mystery. The white silk of her dress whispered as she moved.

Cedrin was drawn forward. The cuts and bruises vanished, and his clothes transformed into those worn by the richest Suulvey. He reached up to touch the unfamiliar Suul mark on his forehead.

He presented the flower to her, and as she touched it, great trumpets blasted forth in the sky. A city of tall white towers and wide domes appeared in the distance. He could hear singing, the people of the city calling to stars and sky.

Their eyes met, and his stomach flipped. Her face became his world. Her lips were dark and red, and he bent down to give her a soft, passionate kiss. As they embraced, her body flushed with a rising heat.

Then over her shoulder, he glimpsed a spinning shape of blue.

Slender tendrils snaked from the blue thing into her mind,

grasping at her. A new tendril detached itself from the spinning shape and whipped at him.

He leapt back with a shout, drawing a calv.

Ellen screamed and dropped the rose. At once its light went out and the grey mist descended. The city was lost from sight. Where vapours touched the new growth, it faded and withered. He struck at the blue shape, to cut the parasite from her body, but even as he thrust towards it, it changed in shape. A great horn grew from it. Beneath, a head grew, teeth broken and bloodied. It struck the knife from his hands, and he was suddenly dressed in beggar's rags. Ellen vanished as the beast grew to its full size.

Its features swam. At first he saw two sets of eyes, then one, then two once more.

'What are you?'

'We ... are Behemoth.'

Then it opened its jaws and leapt ...

'Cedrin, wake up!'

He sat up with a gasp, shaking, his body covered with sweat. Beside him, Marken knelt in the dark of the predawn, his body sheathed in the strange milky glow of the Moon Essence.

Cedrin looked around the camp, the threads of the dream rapidly falling away. He blinked and the glow around Marken was gone.

'Was that Moon Essence, or did I imagine it?' asked Cedrin.

Marken sat heavily on the grass, his face drawn. 'You did not imagine it.'

So he was channelling the Fire again, the power rising out of him in his sleep. This was the third time since leaving Athria that Marken had woken him in the night when the nimbus of red had grown, his own hands protected by shields of Moon Essence. So far, the other warriors suspected nothing.

'Thank you, my friend,' said Cedrin.

Marken nodded and returned to his blankets.

Cedrin lay back. The Fire gave him strange dreams. This time there was the beast, then Ellen. He smiled at the memory of her, but his smile fled as he remembered the end of the dream when the beast returned. Both the terror of the beast – and the feeling of having Ellen in his arms – had seemed so real.

He left his blankets and stirred the fire to life. Light was touching the eastern sky, and the devotions of the Way would soon begin.

It had been hard enough to get Ellen out of his thoughts – and his dreams – since Raynor. Now here she was, following him, disguised as a Priestess. He had teased at the problem obsessively since she healed the dying man last night. Marken was right. If she had meant him harm, she would have acted long before now. For her to leave the protection of the Suul and follow him only served to support her claim that Myan had wanted him accepted by the Suul. She could have bided her time. Instead she revealed herself to heal a dying man. Why? He shook his head, stabbing at the fire. Compassion. 'Damn it,' he muttered.

'What was that, ami?' asked Marken, who had given up on sleep and was rolling up his blanket.

'Nothing, my friend. Something stuck in my throat,' said Cedrin.

He thought in time he would get her out of his thoughts. Her beautiful face, the way the sunlight caught her hair as it fell across her cheek. Those passionate green eyes. In part he had succeeded, but seeing her again had brought it all to the surface. He had convinced himself she was a manipulative Suul who cared for nothing but her own interests, and he had been able to muster some dislike to counter his … attraction. *Now she does this kind, selfless thing, and I am robbed of even that.*

He gritted his teeth, staring into the flames as they slowly rose over the burnt out embers of last night's fire. He could not let himself desire her. She obsessed him like no-one else ever had and it frightened him. That loss of control frightened him. Only a fool let himself desire what he can never have.

'Ready for the morning devotions, Kaidell?' asked Ruus, moving through the camp. 'Xyanthius wants to be inside Seyt before the gates get crowded, but I think we have time for at least one bout.'

'Still feeling confident, Ruus?' said Cedrin.

'Always,' said Ruus, with a wry smile as he moved past.

Around them men were already forming up the caravan, the breath of the amelak and harena steaming in the pre-dawn air.

Cedrin kicked dirt over the fire, smothering the flames. Some work with the greatscythe was just what he needed to clear his head.

Chapter Fourteen

Ellen revelled in the feel of silk on clean skin. The slender dress tapered as it fell to her feet, the tailored fit perfect. She smoothed down the soft blue fabric with her hands, thankful she had the foresight to bring a dress from Raynor she could put on herself. Her hired servants had done a fine job removing the wrinkles. She and Raphal had come into Seyt with first light and rented rooms near the Merchants' Quarter. Raphal had urged her to get basic accommodations, to stay in keeping with their role as Priest and Priestess, but she had insisted on large rooms with servants on call, and most importantly, a bath. She had luxuriated in the hot, scented water for hours while Raphal disappeared into Seyt on some private business, her maids appearing regularly with more heated water. The tub was small, the oil and soap of poor quality, but it was the best bath she had ever had.

Marken had taken her aside earlier that morning, just as the caravan was breaking camp. Cedrin wanted to meet. After she had settled herself in her new accommodations, she had sent a messenger to Kranor's Seyt compound to tell Cedrin and Marken to come to the tavern this afternoon. This time she would be prepared.

The dusty robe and the staff of Mythar, along with her filthy travelling clothes, were flung carelessly in the corner. As far as she was concerned they could stay there. She was through masquerading as a Priestess – and hiding her face like a leper.

She tied a slender black headband around her head, the finely worked leather covering her Suul mark. Ellen felt a thrill of rebellion to be dressed so casually. She would never have been able to appear in court in anything this simple. She had only ever worn this dress in her own apartments. Even the jewellery she had chosen was subdued: simple rings with small gemstones, a necklace with only a single small diamond and plain mought bracelets for her wrists. Her maids in the Cintros mansion would be furious with her for under-dressing, she knew.

Turning to leave her room, she saw her scythe laying across the bed. The blade could be concealed, yet the weapon would spoil the effect of her outfit. Raphal cautioned her at every turn, always lecturing her on the dangers. Yet here she was in a civilised city, one of the jewels of the Yasser States, a bastion of the old Empire. She *should* be safe. Even so, she had underestimated the Athrian Temple of the Sisters before. They had sent two assassins to kill her in Raynor. Perhaps not the scythe, but that was not her only weapon. She took a long slender dagger from her pack and tied the sheath to her left forearm. It would be concealed by the loose sleeve of her dress. She also had the throwing knife strapped to the inside of her thigh. It had been that weapon that had saved her in Raynor.

There was no way the Temple of the Sisters in Seyt could know she was here. It was likely they had ways of detecting the use of Sorcery, but that need not concern her. She would have no use for the Fire in Seyt – it was one of the safest cities in Kelas, everyone knew it.

Satisfied, she left the apartment. Once more the heady sense of excitement filled her. She had no retainers, no staff – no one to hold her back. Always before there were rules, commitments, schedules … demands. Here she was, on the road, her own time at her command. Never before in her life had she experienced freedom like this.

She walked swiftly down the stairs into the common rooms, heading for the exit. The rooms were packed with merchants and workers taking a midday break, the room loud with the buzz of conversation. At first only a few heads turned, then suddenly the whole room was looking at her. The talk faltered then ceased altogether. Even the servants, who had been busily weaving through the crowd with platters, had stopped in their tracks.

Ellen was startled by the reaction. Determined not to be thwarted before she left the building, she continued through the commons, feeling the eye of every man on her as she walked. She had almost reached the doorway when the inn-keeper intercepted her, bowing low.

'My Lady,' he said, looking up uncertainly as he straightened. 'I did not see you enter or I would have attended you immediately. You do us a great honour ...'

'I have rooms here,' said Ellen, a little taken aback. 'I came in last night.'

Ellen looked around the room. The silence seemed to press on her, and she was eager to be gone. She caught her reflection in the mirrors behind the bar and began to understand. She might be underdressed by Athrian court standards, but in a common man's eating house? Her blue silk dress shimmered in the dim light, the fabric dazzling against the plain homespun most of the men wore. She stood regally, as she had been trained from the earliest age, her honey-blonde hair swept back in a single braid. Her skin was fine and white, her eyes glittering green in a face unblemished by the diseases so common in the lower classes. Although she had considered the jewellery plain, in the lamplight it glittered around her throat and fingers, the finely-tinted mought bracelets accentuating her slim wrists.

'Last night?' said the innkeeper

She could see the man was at a complete loss. He could not reconcile her against the demure Priestess of Mythar in her tattered robe. In a way, that pleased her.

'I'd like to be on my way, if you don't mind,' said Ellen, moving around him.

The innkeeper's face fell, and he stepped in front of her again. His face flushed red, sweat forming on his brow. 'My Lady. Are you alone?' he stammered. 'We are far outside the Citadel here ...'

'I'm aware of that,' snapped Ellen, pushing past him into the street.

'Of course,' he said, bowing low as she left.

As Ellen left, the commons was filled with an uproar of speech. It was infuriating.

'Have they never seen a woman before?' she said.

On the street she allowed herself to wander. She tried to ignore the sighs and startled exclamations of passers-by and enjoy the sunshine, taking long breaths of the sea air. Like Athria, in Seyt there was a Suul district. The rulers of Seyt would rarely venture beyond the Citadel on the sea cliff wall. She was counting on it, for there were many there who knew her. This far inside the Yasser States she did not want to be recognised. People bowed before her as she walked, and Ellen felt her tension rise. In Athria, the Suul district was enclosed by the Wall of Sorrows. She herself had only ventured beyond it with a retinue. It would be the same here. No woman of the small provincial court of Seyt would ever walk the streets as she was.

'My Lady,' said one woman, bowing, her filthy robe torn on one side. Ellen smiled and nodded at her.

It was too late to turn back now, nor did she want to. This *was* freedom. She followed the run of traffic towards the sea wall and found a sprawling market, nestled below the battlements. The sea breeze was cool and fresh, and it swept back the stray wisps of hair from her face. Here she was, unchecked, without so much as a single keeper to bound her movements. Part of life, instead of a spectator.

She wandered through the markets, hawkers and beggars swarming around her. At first she politely turned them away, but they kept coming. Ellen tried to ignore them, but it was difficult when they pressed in so close. After a while she began to see the benefit of having guards on hand to push back the crowd.

There were others too. Men who did not come close, but merely watched. At one point she caught a glimpse of a man through the crowd, his clothes dirty, more than a week's growth of untidy beard on his chin. His eyes were as dark and hard as flint. She lost sight of him as the crowd pressed in, and the next time she looked for him he was gone.

Although she enjoyed the atmosphere, there was little there

to interest her. After about an hour, she was tired of the outing. Ellen purchased a jar of fruit preserved in honey and walked swiftly out of the market, turning left and right at random. Finally she lost the last of the hangers-on. She gave a sigh of relief and picked one of the fruit pieces from the jar. She sucked delicately on the fruit as she made her way back to the main streets of the Merchants' Quarter.

Today she would meet Cedrin. She had to make sure things went smoothly. She would need to build gradually towards her proposal. She would start with the history of Belin, then perhaps stress the great friendship between him and her father …

She heard the sound of a foot scraping across the cobbles and looked up. There were more than a dozen people in the alley, both men and women. These did not bow or greet. They stared. Some of them looked at her jewellery, their eyes gleaming and vicious, while others – men – looked at her body with unconcealed lust. Ellen felt a surge of anger, but suppressed it immediately. She looked behind her. Three men were following her, one of them the man with the unkempt beard. Instinctively she reached for the Fire. No. They were no threat yet, and she could not risk alerting the Temple of the Sisters.

Ellen quickened her step, now feeling foolish with a jar of preserved fruit in her hand. She wove through the maze of alleys, trying to get back to the main street that ran through the Merchants' Quarter. She checked behind her again. Two of the men still followed her, but she had lost sight of the bearded man. She turned left into a narrow alley, deeply shadowed by the tall buildings on either side. At the far end she could see the main street and hurried towards it. As she neared the exit, a man pushed himself out of the shadows. A man with an unkempt beard. Somehow he had got around her. He stood defiantly in her path.

'Move aside,' she demanded.

He laughed and drew an old calv. The blade was chipped and pitted, yet still deadly sharp along the remaining length.

'The jewels,' he said, passing a bloodshot eye over her body. 'Give us the jewels, then we'll give you a little party. Eh, lads!'

Ellen turned to see the other two men had closed in behind

her. *Trapped.* She threw the jar of fruit at one of the men, he dodged it easily and laughed as it shattered on the street behind him. The two other men also drew calvs. All their chests were covered. Not even a Brotherhood man would cover their tattoos like that.

'Av' to do better than that, lovely,' said the bearded man. 'Now come on! Hand over – or we'll cut you bad!'

All three were slowly closing on her, spread out on all sides. From the way they moved, she could tell they were used to this sort of ambush and used to working together. She could sweep them away in moments using the Fire, but she refused to risk revealing herself to the Temple just to battle scum like this. She was Ellen Cintros – taught by the finest weaponmasters in Kelas. She reached into her sleeve and drew the knife.

'Watch it, Beldor, she's got a dagger!'

The men grew nervous, and backed away, shuffling and brandishing their weapons. Ellen looked around at the men and the dirty alleyway. If she tried to take on either one of them, she would be exposed to attack from the others. She had to wait for them to make the first move. They circled, feinting in, trying to rattle her. She stayed light on her feet, focussed.

One of the men lunged and Ellen reacted automatically, side-stepping and slashing him deeply across the arm. He shouted out and dropped his calv.

'Bloody Uros, you she-demon!' said the man, nursing his arm.

Something moved to her left and she spun, expecting to block a knife thrust. A dark shape flew at her, too fast to see. It struck her in the side of the head. She felt sharp pain and her ears rang. A throwing knife clattered to the cobbles, along with her headband. The bearded man had thrown a knife, but it had struck her hilt-first. Her head swam, and she stumbled. One of them grabbed her right arm, trying to pin it. Another was rushing in from the side. The man with the wounded arm was hanging back. She ducked down, reaching under her dress with her left hand for the second knife. She drew it swiftly, stabbing it into the neck of the man who held her arm. Blood spurted across her face. He made a choking sound and staggered back. The bearded man growled and lunged in. She swayed aside and slid the long dagger through his heart.

The bearded man staggered back. His calv fell from his grip, and he fell face-forward to the cobbles. The man she had stabbed in the throat was already on the ground, although she had not seen him fall. She swivelled towards the third man, who turned and ran into the shadows.

Blood.

It was everywhere. On her face, her dress, on her hands, spreading out across the cobbles from the fallen men.

When she had fought the rebels in Regent's Hill, it had been night. All had been confusion and fury. Here the suns were high in a bright sky and all was quiet.

Using the dagger, she cut away some of the cloth from the bearded man's cloak and feverishly wiped the blood from her hands and face. She realised her carefully applied makeup would be smeared, and suddenly was crying. *'Damn it.'* Her hands shook, and it took all her concentration to sheath the blades without cutting herself. She was an idiot! Walking through the back alleys of the city, draped in jewellery. Now two men were dead.

Ellen wiped away the tears with the back of her hand and fixed a smile in place. When it came to faking it, there was no substitute for a lifetime at court. Once on the main way, she hurried back to her rooms, sometimes almost running. She looked behind her periodically. If the throwing knife had taken her blade first – she would be lying dead in a back alley, her body stripped and violated. Everyone was staring at her, some in shock, others bowing, which made no sense. Ellen wiped at her face, convinced it must be still smeared with blood. The stains on her dress had dried to a dull brown.

Reaching the tavern, she burst into the common room, almost colliding with the innkeeper who was just inside the door. The portly man took one look and blanched, dropping to his knees with his head bowed.

'My L ... Lady,' he stammered. 'I had no idea ...'

Ellen heard chairs hastily drawn aside and tables tumbling to the floor as they were knocked aside in haste. She looked up, still fearful, and saw the whole room was kneeling, heads bowed and still. She reached up and touched her forehead. The headband! The throwing knife had dislodged it. She stood revealed as Suul.

She fled across the room and up the stairs to her chamber, bolting the door behind her as she went. She stood for long moments, leaning against the door, cursing her own stupidity. It was vital that there was nothing concrete to connect her to Raphal's escape. She hoped to return to Raynor with Cedrin, once the inevitable furore over the Priest's escape had died down. Now she had endangered her own mission, perhaps even her life. Talk would spread of a Suul lady travelling with a Priest, in time reaching both the Temple and the Warlord's agents. The worst part was she had proven Raphal right.

A knock at the door startled her and she stood back, straightening her dress.

'Ellen!' The knock came again. 'Ellen, are you in there?' It was Raphal. She stepped forward and unbolted the door.

'Yes Raphal,' she said, trying to sound confident, but the quaver in her voice betrayed her.

The door swung open. Raphal eyes opened wide as he took in her outfit.

'You've been out?' he said, incredulous, his eyes fixed to the Suul mark. 'Dressed like *that!*'

Ellen turned her back so he would not see the tears brimming in her eyes. Gods!

'Yes!' she said defiantly, determined he would never know how close she had come to disaster.

'Dear, Ellen. You have more courage than sense. Oh, well. Once leaves have been seized by the wind they will never settle the same way again.' Raphal walked into the room and lifted the bag he was carrying onto the bed. 'These are more what I had in mind.'

She discreetly wiped the tears from her eyes and hid her feelings beneath a scowl. Raphal had brought her a set of leathers, simple but well made. She spread them on the bed.

'And this,' he said, passing her a mought head-bracer, patterned in gold and white triangles.

She took the bracer and tried it on. It was heavy and uncomfortable, but it covered the Suul mark well and – unlike the delicate leather headband – would provide some protection.

'What are these?' she asked, forcing a smile.

'They are riding leathers. Suitable for a travelling merchant's daughter with a touch of a wild streak.'

She ran a hand over them. The leather was soft and supple. 'I'm glad you weren't going to suggest I wear that robe again.'

Raphal smiled. 'Let's just say the life of Priestess doesn't seem to suit you.'

'These are excellent, Raphal. Ideal in fact, because we may have some travelling to do,' said Ellen.

Raphal raised an eyebrow.

'I am hoping I can convince Cedrin to take a little trip with me,' said Ellen.

* * *

Marken followed Cedrin through the crowd. They were working their way down to the sea wall markets to buy se-tobacco and bakta. The day was fine, the sea air fresh and clean, his belly full from their delicious lunch of grilled fish. Like Athria, Seyt had been settled by Myrians, and although Xyanthius never stinted on rations, it felt good to partake of something with a more delicate taste.

Marken was excited, and nervous, at the prospect of the upcoming meeting with Ellen. Much depended on it going well. Despite the trepidation Cedrin had expressed about Ellen Cintros and her motives, he had been talking about nothing else all morning. Cedrin kept glancing up to check the position of the suns in the sky and Marken knew he was just marking time. It made him wonder exactly what it was about Ellen Cintros that Cedrin really feared.

Their progress slowed as they reached the square above the markets. A mob had gathered and voices were being raised. Cedrin pushed through. People turned, ready with an angry word and thought better of it as they looked up at Cedrin. He was a rather intense fellow, and not a person anyone would usually choose to cross. Marken grinned at them as he followed Cedrin through.

In the centre of the square, a fat stall-keeper, his face flushed almost purple, had a young boy by the collar. The boy was no more than nine or ten years old, and the man was shaking him like a rag doll.

'I say we take him to the Temple!' screamed a woman, her red hair knotted, her skin touched with faint gold. Her blouse was open, showing both breasts and the flower-tattoo of a prostitute.

'He should be drowned!' said a man, his dark coat drawn tight. 'He's a Demon Spawn!'

The crowd shouted and the young boy looked around wide-eyed. In his hands, he clutched a cooked fish.

'An' you can give that back, you little thief,' said the fat stall-keeper, snatching the fish out of the boy's hands.

Cedrin turned to an old stall keeper, a man whose hair had long ago turned to silver, and who watched the scene with sad detachment.

'What's going on?' asked Cedrin.

The old man looked sharply at Cedrin, then sighed. 'They say he's got the cursed blood. You know, a Sorcerer. But all I see is a hungry thief.' The old man looked back at the fat stall-keeper who held the boy. 'He has stolen from Agnas before, but he's too fat to catch him. This time he took the boy by surprise, and I think he's out to make sure he doesn't steal from him again.' The old man glared at Agnas. 'The times are getting worse. I remember when we would do no more than give them a hiding or put them to work if we caught them. He means to drown the poor boy by whipping up the crowd and calling for the Templemen. Those red-cloaked bastards do whatever the crowd wants. Don't think they'd know what to do with a real Sorcerer if they ever found one.'

Marken saw Cedrin's brows draw together as he stared down at Agnas.

The fat stall-keeper's small eyes glittered. He knew exactly what he was doing, playing the mob like fools until they did murder for him. Looking around, Marken saw real fear in the crowd. The Temple of the Sisters had done a fine job of instilling the terror of the 'demonic' mark of Sorcery in the populace. Sometimes he detested the commoners. *Weak-minded fools*. This was why the Suul were so necessary.

'This can't pass,' said Cedrin, his voice low and dangerous.

Agnas shook the boy again. 'Well, what are we waiting for?'

Marken felt Cedrin tense, ready to launch into combat. His friend had always had a soft-spot for street-kids. In Athria, there was a whole flock of them who he would feed and pass coin to every other day. Many had proved useful as runners and information gatherers.

'It's just Uros-cursed superstition,' said Cedrin. 'It's not going to cost this boy his life.'

Men and women were crowding around the boy now. He looked back and forth between them, desperate.

Cedrin hefted his greatscythe.

Marken gripped his arm, trying to hold him back. 'Cedrin, don't get involved. Or they will drown you too.'

Cedrin shook off his arm. 'They must be stopped.'

The old man watched the exchange with interest. As he looked at Cedrin, hope grew in his eyes.

Cedrin waded in. Marken raised his scythe-staff and followed, protecting Cedrin's back. No one would surprise his friend with him at his side.

Cedrin struck one man on the arm and he leapt aside with a yelp. He pushed the prostitute aside firmly with the haft. Left. Right. His greatscythe rose and fell, and the crowd scattered. Moments later, they were standing in front of the fat vendor. The man paled as he met Cedrin's gaze.

'Be gone. It's none of your business!' said Agnas, his chest labouring to draw breath under his gross weight.

Cedrin swung the greatscythe into the man's belly. Agnas fell backwards, overbalanced, but otherwise unhurt. Released, the boy fled to Cedrin, burying his face in his leg. Marken watched the crowd. His hand itched to release the hidden blade of his scythe.

The crowd grew silent, their eyes fixed to Cedrin. Marken looked across at his friend, and the hairs stood up on the back of his neck. Cedrin stood tall, his face … regal. There had always been a mark of greatness about Cedrin, and Marken had known from the first moments he was destined for far greater things than the Brotherhood. That he was the son of Belin Kaidell did not surprise him at all.

'Look at you!' thundered Cedrin. 'You can smell the blood, like harenas screaming at a corpse.' Cedrin lifted the boy and showed him to the crowd. He had recovered from his initial fright and had tears on his face, streaking through grime and dirt.

'Is he a demon?' asked Cedrin. 'Does he look like a Sorcerer to you? And if he *is* a demon, then what does that make each of you?'

Cedrin seemed to grow taller as he faced the crowd. A light glowed in his face, a flame of compassion and purpose. Around them, the crowd was stunned into silence. Agnas regained his feet, but stood well away from Cedrin.

Cedrin had always been a man of little words. Yet here, in front of the crowd, he came alive. They were utterly at his mercy. On his chest the phoenix seemed to flex its wings as Cedrin drew breath. He let the boy down and pointed at him. 'Could there be any greater evil than calling for the drowning of a young boy?'

The men and women looked at each other, shocked as they realised what they had been about to do. One man turned and walked away, then another. Soon they all began to melt away. Agnas disappeared through the crowd, and moments later they were all gone. The shop-keepers resumed their trade, and it was as though nothing had happened. The light went out in Cedrin, and he became simply a tall, brooding man with a starving child at his feet.

'What's your name?' Cedrin asked the boy.

The lad looked up, still crying. 'Remis.'

'Where's your mother?' asked Cedrin.

The boy pointed back to the city then turned to Cedrin. 'It was cold, and she didn't wake up.'

He lifted the boy into his arms. It was clear his mother had perished in the long cold of Storm Season; consumed by fatigue and the Hunger.

'I'll take him.' They turned to see the old stall-keeper standing beside them, a piece of fruit in his hand. Cedrin set the boy down and the man gave Remis the piece of fruit. The boy sucked on it contentedly as they talked.

'That was a brave act,' said the man. 'And you held the crowd well. Are you an orator?'

Cedrin shook his head. 'No. I just couldn't let them murder a child.'

The old man nodded and took the boy's hand.

Cedrin dug some emerald coins out of his pocket. 'For the boy.'

The old man smiled as he took the coin. 'I'm going to need it.'

As they left, the boy was helping himself to another piece of fruit, sitting contentedly on the bench amid the man's wares. The suns had passed the zenith and they hurried down to the market.

'Almost time to see Ell … the Cintros woman,' said Cedrin.

That was a telling slip. Marken flashed Cedrin a grin.

'What?' said Cedrin.

'Hmmm? Oh, nothing.' This was going to be interesting.

Chapter Fifteen

Ellen checked herself in the mirror, adjusting the fall of her braid. Although the leathers lacked colour, they were very comfortable and, with the mought bracer, they would be excellent for fighting, allowing a wide range of movement. The close fit seemed a trifle provocative, but this made up for the lack of fashion. She wore only the golden gem-ring that her brother Torren had given her and a neck-chain set with a representation of Larus, also tinted gold.

'He is coming to talk to you, Ellen, not seduce you,' said Raphal, amused.

Ellen turned, giving Raphal a hard stare. 'I have entertained no such thoughts,' she said, indignant. Her cheeks flushed hot, and she turned away. It was important that this go well, nothing more. Even so, she could not resist one more sidelong glance into the mirror. What *would* he think of the outfit?

There was a polite knock at the door and a maid entered and bowed. 'The Athrian gentlemen have arrived, my Lady.'

News of a noble staying at the inn had spread more rapidly than Ellen would ever have imagined. She planned to be gone before first dawn tomorrow – long before the agents of the Warlord or the Temple's spies came looking for the Suul woman and the Priest she travelled with.

'Show them to the dining room,' said Ellen.

'Yes, my Lady,' said the maid, watching Ellen as though she expected her to perform some magic trick. She had obviously never served nobility before and was thrilled by it. The novelty would soon wear off, thought Ellen. 'That will be all,' she prompted. The young woman broke off staring, bowed again and left.

'Shall we, then?' said Raphal.

'Just a moment,' said Ellen.

Raphal looked at her quizzically.

'There is no point rushing in there,' said Ellen.

Raphal sighed and sat down. He reached for one of the books he had brought with him from Raynor and began to read, squinting as he scanned the tiny Cioan glyphs.

She began to pace, giving vent to nervous energy as she went through everything, one last time. This was it, the throw of the dice. She doubted she would get another chance with Cedrin. She could only hope her plan would work.

'Very well. Let's meet them,' she said.

Raphal put away the book with a sly smile. 'Lead on.'

Ellen wanted no eavesdroppers and had hired a private dining room. She led the way into the small, wood-lined chamber. At least she was prepared this time and meeting them on her own terms. Cedrin and Marken stood waiting for them. Both wore new shirts of plain weave, brightly coloured and open to the waist. Beneath, their chests were crossed with harnesses, sheathed with calvs. Cedrin's greatscythe and Marken's scythe were slung over their shoulders. She smiled at both of them, assuming an unruffled, pleasant demeanour, even though inside she felt anything but calm. Her eyes fell to the broad phoenix tattoo on Cedrin's chest, and her heart began to beat faster. Towering a head taller than Marken, he dominated the room.

Marken bowed formally, 'Suul Cintros.'

Cedrin tensed and Ellen realised immediately he was not the sort to bow to anyone. She stepped forward quickly. 'Please, no need for formality. Will you take a seat?' She indicated the lowset table, which was set with platters of cheese, fruit and succulent meats; as well as decanters of juice, water and strong red wine.

They unslung their weapons, laying them up against the wall, then sat. Raphal pulled up a chair across the table, discreetly out of the way.

'Wine?' asked Ellen. Cedrin and Marken both nodded.

'Just water for me, Ellen. My head can't take that heavy red anymore,' said Raphal.

Cedrin watched her steadily, his face guarded.

'Have you been enjoying Seyt?' asked Ellen as she passed him the wine.

'Yes. It's good to see it again,' he said.

'And you, Marken?'

'As thrilled as I am by caravan life, it is good to have a break once in a while,' said Marken, accepting the wine with thanks.

Ellen lifted the glass to her lips, but took no more than a sip. 'This is a little more pleasant than our last meeting, Cedrin?'

'Aye. After our first meeting on the galley, I never would have believed we would be sitting to a meal together,' he said, conscious of his thick dock accent.

Cedrin smiled at her and her belly flipped. He reached forward to take a piece of cheese off the platter and she watched the lean muscles of his chest ripple as he moved. She had not noticed it before, but he had taken the Way of the Scytheman. The small, distinctive tattoo was etched on his skin just below the phoenix of the One Hundred. Ellen knew Cedrin would be a dangerous man to cross, and yet she felt strangely safe and relaxed with him. Ellen fanned herself with her hand. *Warm in here.*

'Suul Cintros—' began Cedrin.

'Please, call me Ellen.'

'Ellen,' he said. Just for a moment his face softened, then it was gone. His grey-blue eyes met hers, and there was no compromise there. 'Here we sit in Seyt. For my part I have followed the new road I sought and am content to look further north. You are far from Athria and your proper place amongst the Suul. Far from Raynor where you could live as you would, despite the coming onslaught.'

Ellen watched him carefully. He had a rough background, but it would be a mistake to equate his heavy accent with a lack of intelligence.

'So it comes to this,' he said. 'I know my real father was highly placed in the old Empire, but what high purpose could I possibly serve that a Suul like you would follow me?'

'You were right to say Belin was highly placed in the old Empire,' said Ellen. 'The truth goes much further. He was part of Emperor Riin's inner circle. But even more than this, he was a close friend of both Riin and my father.

'Riin's father, Emperor Cerrin, was a cruel man, one driven by the Temple's power, obsessed by the Purge. As one of Cerrin's councillors, Belin came to be more of a father to Riin than Cerrin himself. Belin loved Riin as a son. When news of Riin's betrayal reached him, Belin fled to Raynor to save Riin's family from treachery.'

Ellen paused, there was so much she did not know. So much doubt. After all this time, uncertainties plagued her, yet this was no time to show them.

'Belin was a faithful general. A patriot who was ready to give his life for his Emperor and friend, and those they both held dear. What value would you place on acts such as these?'

Cedrin's eyes narrowed. 'You are talking about the Hero of the Last Days,' said Cedrin. 'That's a legend bound up with the Scion.'

Cedrin was being drawn into the power of the tale as she hoped.

'Belin *was* the Hero of the Last Days,' said Ellen. 'I discovered the truth of it in Raynor. He arrived too late to save the Empress, but escaped with the newborn Scion. Their fate is uncertain. Some believe they died.' She remembered Uran's cold eyes as he told her of the collapse of the Raynor Iris — with Belin and the child inside.

Cedrin leant forward. He took a long sip of his wine, his eyes unfocussed as he considered the implications. 'If Belin did die ... that would explain a lot,' he said. Ellen watched his thumb play over the emerald signet ring of Kaidell on his first finger. He looked back at her. 'If even this is true, why seek me out now?'

Ellen's stomach clenched, but her smile did not falter. The next moments would decide everything.

'The friendship between Myan and Belin was deep. When Belin vanished in the Last Days, Myan was bereft. The news that Belin's daughter and grandchildren died at Blackthorne only days after Emperor Riin and his family were slain, was a heavy blow. The grief weighed him down for many long years.'

She looked into Cedrin's piercing eyes. All his attention was focussed on her, his head tilted slightly. There was a fierce intelligence there, and a depth of feeling, yet there was also a coiled tension in him; a sense that he could explode into action at any moment. Perhaps Belin also had this quality.

'Then, only months before he died, Myan learned that Belin had a son,' continued Ellen. 'He was determined the remaining blood of Belin's line be brought back to the Suul. If he had found you, Cedrin, you would even now be a Suulqua of the Athrian court. Perhaps even a full Suul lord.'

Marken's face lit up at the mention of the Suul. Interesting. There were many disinherited nobles who dreamed of a return to court. If this drove Marken, it would give her a powerful lever to control him.

'But Myan is dead, I could never be received in Athria,' said Cedrin.

Ellen breathed a sigh of relief, but tried not to let the triumph show on her face. She had been right. When she saw him wearing the Kaidell ring, she had known he was ready to accept his heritage. So far so good.

'But you could be received at the court of the Warlord,' she said. 'If the head of the Kaidell family supported you, as he must. You are Belin's only son and you bear his ring.'

'What are you suggesting?' said Cedrin.

Her heart raced. Ellen slowly reached for her glass, taking a measured sip. She was pleased to see her hands were steady.

'I propose that we journey to the Kaidell estate. It lays only half-a-day's ride from Seyt. There we will meet with Linnas Kaidell, the nephew and heir of Belin, and petition him to accept you as a Kaidell.'

Cedrin shook his head. 'The Empire is gone. The deeds of Belin mean nothing to the Warlord. What place would I have at court? An Athrian from the docks with Brotherhood tattoos? Do I become a serving boy for the Suul, always living in the shadow of the full blood royals? Always feeling their contempt?'

Determination flashed in his eyes. She would defy anyone to

make Cedrin a servant. It truly was a pity he had not come to the Suul sooner.

'Linnas is your cousin, Cedrin. Your closest living blood. In fact – I am your blood.'

Cedrin leant back and barked out a laugh. 'We are related?'

'It's true,' said Ellen. 'We are cousins. Very distant cousins. My mother was distantly related to Belin. In fact, the Empress Evylin was a Kaidell.'

Cedrin reached across with his left hand, twisting the Kaidell signet ring around on his finger. 'I admit, being accepted by the Kaidell has a powerful appeal. But where would this lead?'

'Kranor himself is a Suulqua of the Warlord's court,' said Marken.

'True,' said Cedrin.

'You need not stay in Raynor, you could stay or leave as you wished. All Suulqua have an income from the court. Nothing would stop you from returning to life on the road after you were received,' said Ellen.

'We have another couple of days of leave from the caravan while Alechul gathers his goods,' said Marken. Ellen favoured him with a quick smile.

'Very well. When can we leave?' asked Cedrin.

'At first dawn,' said Ellen. She could hardly believe he had agreed.

Ellen was convinced Raynor was the key to the Scion and had thought long and hard over how to entice Cedrin back to the court. The first step was to make him a Suulqua. She had to gain the acceptance of Linnas, but surely that was a formality. After this she would need to find a compelling reason for Cedrin to come to Raynor with her – but she could deal with that once they had visited the Kaidell estates. She would need to check with Estle to ensure the Warlord's anger had eased and it was safe for her to return to Raynor with Cedrin.

Raphal could complete his journey to Olcis alone once she got him outside the Yasser States. Since the edge of the Warlord's domain was just beyond Seyt, that should not be too difficult.

Everything was falling into place.

'Very well,' said Cedrin. 'Let's see what Linnas has to say. It will certainly be strange to walk the lands of my father. The journey will be worth it, even just to see them.' He lifted his cup. 'To Kaidell.'

They lifted their cups. Now her hand *was* shaking.

'Kaidell,' she said, taking a large sip of the wine. It was poor quality, and green, but it tasted good just the same. She had done it!

Cedrin laughed and Ellen's heart melted as the hardness fell away from him. If Cedrin was received as a Suul, all things were possible. Once back at the Raynor court she would make peace with Uran and take Cedrin fully into her confidence. Her eyes fell to the phoenix tattoo that stretched across his chest. In time they could seek out the Cinanac heir together.

'Well, shall we eat?' said Ellen, suddenly hungry.

* * *

Cedrin watched Ellen as she rode ahead with Raphal. They were deep in conversation. The suns were high in the sky, and Ellen's honey-blonde hair swept around her shoulders, loosely tied. She certainly looked nothing like a Suul now, with the mought bracer and the scythe sheathed beside her. The travelling leathers fit her well, following every curve. As the heat of the day had risen, she had untied the buttons of her vest, revealing the gentle swell of her breasts. She looked back at him and smiled. He felt a strange knot of tension in his chest. He nodded back.

'Beautiful country, hey, ami?' said Marken.

'Hmmm. Oh, aye,' he replied. He wondered if Suul women revealed their breasts to friends and family, as was the custom in Kelas.

In life, Ellen was far above him – unreachable – yet she was the most desirable woman he had ever seen. She was beautiful, it was true, but beauty could be bought easily. What aroused him was her intensity, a power held in check, promising an even greater passion within. With effort he looked away, turning to watch the low hills that stretched away from the road. No. *I cannot afford to think of her like that.* She was an ally, nothing more.

Cedrin's amelak gave a mournful bellow.

'Don't ride with your knees so tight. You are suffocating the poor beast,' said Marken.

Cedrin realised Marken was right. His body was tense, his knees tightly clinched to the amelak's ribs. He relaxed them and the beast coughed once then breathed more easily.

He had to stay focussed. If Linnas accepted him as Belin's son, as part of the Kaidell line, he could build a mercenary company as respected as Kranor's. A group of elite warriors who followed the Way of the Scytheman. At last he could take pride in who he was, find his place in the world. Like Kranor, he could be a Suulqua, but not connected to court. There was something else though, something with a deep and powerful appeal. The simple acceptance of a family. To be acknowledged. It would be like finding a part of himself.

The party of four had set out from Seyt well before dawn. Cedrin and Marken had persuaded Xyanthius to loan them four amelak and they settled into a comfortable rhythm, striking out south from Seyt towards the Yasser. After the long days riding at the pace of harena, it was a pleasure to let the amelak stretch their legs.

Just before noon the road crested a hill and began to descend into a wide valley. Ellen stopped to let them catch up to her and Raphal. 'This is the beginning of the Kaidell estate,' she said, pointing at a marble marker stone by the road. The view from the hill was excellent.

'A fertile and wealthy valley,' said Raphal.

A wide swath of baal, golden and close to ripeness, was set along the winding course of a fast stream, flanked by long irrigation channels. Surrounding the crop were the smaller green knots of orchards and long rows of grapes. Beyond, Cedrin could see harena and amelak, and the thin cattle of the steppes, all grazing contentedly on the new growth that followed Storm Season.

In the centre of the valley floor lay the Kaidell mansion. It was broad and low, finely crafted, yet built without consideration for defence.

A single hill rose from the valley floor to their left. A tower of dark stone stood tall on the summit, dominating the valley. Its presence was stark, raw, like an untended wound. Around its base lay the tumbled stone of a shattered outer wall.

'That's Belin's Tower, Blackthorne. In its day it was joined to a fortified manor house and a small Temple. But that has all gone now,' said Raphal. 'Only the tower stands.'

'How was it destroyed?' asked Marken.

'It was destroyed in the Last Days,' said Ellen. 'By the designs of the same Eathal assassin who slew Emperor Riin's family.'

Cedrin's amelak tossed its head and snorted, impatient to be moving. The reins tightened as it strained forward with its long neck. All four of them sat for a long, silent moment, lost in private thoughts. There was some compelling quality to the tower. He turned away, but its image stayed in his vision like a bright flash of flame.

'The suns are already high,' said Cedrin.

'Yes. And the mansion awaits us,' said Ellen, urging her amelak down the steep road to the valley floor.

The new manor appeared to be positioned as far from the old tower as practical, and Cedrin found himself wondering why they had never simply rebuilt the original structure. The tower was intact and the hill was more defensible than any other position.

As they made their way into the valley, the tower loomed over them like some brooding guardian. Cedrin could not rid himself of the feeling he had seen it before. This puzzled him until he realised he had: thousands of times.

He lifted his right hand and looked at the Kaidell crest, a symbol so familiar to him he barely recognised it anymore. A black tower on a field of yellow, and growing about the tower a massive vine of thorns, sprouting red flowers like blood. *Blackthorne.* How many times had he looked dreamily at that crest, imagining, and now it lay before him, solid and real. The tower rarely left his gaze as they travelled down through the valley.

They soon left the Yasser road, turning onto a newly paved one that led directly to the mansion. Here they were met and escorted by lancers bearing the crest of Kaidell, a scythe also holstered before them in their saddles.

Linnas may have forsaken stone defences, but his valley was heavily patrolled. That spoke of a practical man and one not afraid to take risks. He had more chance of defending his valley against marauders with swift, mounted troops than men on some thick battlement who could do no more than shake their spears. Although – if the Eathal succeeded in vanquishing Raynor, he may wish he had rebuilt the tower.

* * *

Ellen watched the mounted warriors carefully as they escorted her and her companions to the manor. She had no reason to suspect treachery from Linnas, but it paid to be cautious.

On reaching the front of the estate house, the mounted warriors left them with a brief salute. She was dusty, hot and weary from the road and gratefully let a stable hand take charge of her mount. Riding an amelak was far superior to clanking along in a harena-drawn wagon, even so, she missed her narsiit. Her winged steed would have covered the distance from Seyt in little more than an hour.

A middle-aged manservant in the livery of Kaidell emerged from the house and led them into a small entrance chamber. Bowls of water and brightly-coloured towels had been set on a marble table-top, so that they could refresh themselves. There were no other decorations and little had been done to enhance the room's aspect since its construction.

Ellen briefly washed her face and hands, suddenly conscious of Cedrin. 'A pleasant journey?' she asked him.

'The view was magnificent,' he said, lapsing into an uncomfortable silence.

Marken looked from her to Cedrin, a pleasant smile on his golden face. 'Shall we have a pipe, ami?'

'Good idea.' They left the house to smoke a pipe in the courtyard.

Ellen motioned to the servant. 'Tell Lord Linnas that Ellen Cintros is here to see him.'

Much would now depend on the reaction of Linnas Kaidell. When she had conceived this plan, she had assumed that Linnas would be as honourable as his uncle Belin and would respect the bonds of friendship between Belin and her father. Now, as she stood in the stark entrance chamber, a worm of doubt began to gnaw at her. Even though they were unannounced guests, Ellen was used to grand entrances. Less than a week ago, she had entered the court of the Warlord with a full entourage.

Ellen removed the bracer and untied her hair, combing it carefully. She adjusted her leather garments, suddenly regretting not wearing something more formal. These leathers were hardly the attire of a Sarlord's daughter. She began to tie her hair into braids. Usually she would have maids to do this for her, but she had been getting more adept at it in the days since Raynor.

'Belin must have been a wealthy man.'

Ellen jumped, turning to see both Cedrin and Marken were back in the room. Her long blonde tresses slipped from her grasp and fell around her shoulders. She felt her face go red and hurriedly gathered the hair in her hands. *They had not made a sound.*

'He was one of the foremost Suul of the Empire,' she said, more abruptly than she intended. 'The issue of wealth was of no consequence.'

She quickly finished the braids, her hands moving deftly behind her head. She could sense Cedrin watching her and looked sideways. She saw his gaze drop from her raised arms to her waist and hips. Realising he was being watched, he looked up quickly and turned away, but not quick enough to hide the desire in his eyes.

The manservant emerged from the inner chambers of the house and bowed low. 'My Lady. Lord Linnas will receive you and your companions. If you will follow me.'

They were led through a maze of rooms to a central chamber. The room was dominated by a low dais. Here a large Suul of Anacian stock sat on an ornate throne. *Linnas.* He had dark hair and grey eyes. Stretched tattoos beneath his flowing silk robes showed he had once been in the peak of condition, but had long ago run to fat. Each side of the chamber was lined with warriors in full armour, equipped with greatscythes. Some were breathing heavily, and Ellen realised these had been summoned for the audience. *Was Linnas truly this wary of her, or was he trying to impress?*

The clear light of noon filtered through a roof constructed of alternating panes of clear and coloured glass, creating a chequer-board pattern on the richly-carpeted floor. Plants and painted screens were set around the borders of the room. A small crowd of perhaps a dozen councillors was gathered on the dais beside the throne. Just below the dais two richly dressed women, their breasts revealed by the cut of their gowns – in current Raynorian court fashion – watched Ellen with narrowed eyes. Slaves stood by them with feathered fans, their faces impassive as they worked in a steady rhythm to move the air.

Linnas watched them as they approached, his gaze cold and calculating.

One of the warriors came forward from the ranks across the left wall, a full Razor.

'Your guards are not permitted to carry weapons to the dais, my Lady,' he said to Ellen.

She looked back at her companions. Although Cedrin was the same height as Raphal, and only a head taller than Marken, he seemed to tower over them both, radiating strength. The warriors were all focussed on him. Cedrin swept his gaze across the guards and looked back at the Razor, his face impassive. Ellen saw the Razor tense, his left hand raised slightly, as though ready to signal to his men.

Cedrin walked up, the greatscythe loose in his hands. He paused a pace away. 'Here, friend,' he said, holding out the weapon. Marken followed his lead, handing over his mought scythe-staff. The calvs followed. She saw Cedrin and Marken exchange a quick glance.

Ellen led them across the carpets towards Linnas, conscious of the scrutiny of every person in the room. She could feel Cedrin's solid presence at her side. She noticed that Linnas was focussed on Cedrin as they came forward, studying his Brotherhood tattoos and the big phoenix crest.

She motioned for Raphal, Cedrin and Marken to hold back and advanced to the dais alone.

'Suul Cintros, this is indeed a surprise and a pleasure,' said Linnas, lifting a jewelled hand to his mouth to stifle a yawn. Ellen stifled her annoyance. In the subtle language of court, that was a direct insult. Ellen expected more respect for her name alone. Kaidell and Cintros had always been allies sheltered beneath the wing of the Cinanac phoenix.

'As it is for me, Suul Linnas,' she said, fixing a pleasant mask to her face. She had no need to be intimidated by Linnas Kaidell. He may be a rich man, but he was merely a Suulqua.

'And what brings you so far from Raynor? Is the court of the Warlord lacking in entertainment?' His expression was mocking.

'I have come about a matter that relates to the Kaidell family.'

The smile fled from Linnas' face. 'Really? I imagined your business to be somewhat different. Now – what matter do you bring before me that could possibly bear on me and my heirs?'

Ellen was outraged by his display of open hostility. What had she done to warrant this contempt?

'Belin's son,' she said simply and waited for the words to find the mark.

For a moment, Linnas appeared shaken, then his knowing smile returned. 'Very clever, Cintros, but we shall see how clever you are. We shall meet for a private dinner. It is obvious this discussion should be held in private. My servants will attend you.'

Linnas heaved himself up from his chair and left the room, followed by his councillors, leaving Ellen completely at a loss.

The Razor walked over to Cedrin and Marken. 'You two, come with me.'

Cedrin briefly met her gaze as they were led away, but she had no words for him.

The manservant reappeared and led Raphal and Ellen into one of the wings of the mansion.

Ellen leant in close to Raphal. 'Why did Linnas react like that?'

Raphal sighed. 'I think Linnas has been alone on his own estates too long. He sees plots and intrigues where there are none.'

'But why does he fear me? The Cintros have always been Kaidell allies.'

Raphal rubbed a hand along his bald dome. 'I don't know, but you would do well to remember he is not Belin. The name Kaidell does not guarantee loyalty and honour. Perhaps he sees you at a disadvantage and is merely concerned with profit. We shall see.'

Ellen put aside her disappointment as she approached her rooms. Raphal had adjoining chambers and they parted to refresh themselves for dinner. Ellen found her things had been brought to her room and three maids waited in attendance. She was grateful, at least, for the opportunity to have a bath and dress in private. She selected a green dress and draped it across the bed.

As she lay back in the wide bath, she realised how tired she was of the road and how much she longed for a return to familiar security. Here, at least, she had expected a welcome. That had made Linnas' treatment a hard blow. She had seen the affair as a formality, an easy stepping stone towards a return to Raynor with Cedrin; but where she had expected aid, she had found only fear and suspicion.

'Damn.' She hit the water and sent a cascade of soap and bubbles across the tiles. The maid eyed her warily before bending to soak up the suds with a towel.

Only a month ago she had been a Suulqua, living the carefree and comfortable life of privilege, impatient with life yet mostly content. She had a handsome lover, a father she worshipped and loved, the Fire a secret and special bond between them. Myan had been a great man. When he fell it seemed the world had fallen with him. Then the failed rebellion led by Raziin and rogue leaders of the Brotherhood: chaos and death.

She scooped up some of the scented water in a shell and let it trickle through her newly washed hair and down her back. The warmth was welcome.

She had to win Cedrin to her cause but could not move too quickly. First she had to befriend him. Taking him to Raynor as a Suulqua would provide an excellent pretext for getting to know him.

She rose from the bath and let the servants towel her dry and dress her, losing herself in the feel of soft fabric against washed skin, the smell of perfume and the flash and glitter of gems. She sighed, suddenly hopeful. Perhaps Linnas would be more reasonable when he saw her dressed as a Suul.

Soon after, Ellen was summoned to dinner.

She took her time completing her outfit. She was the senior Suul and her negotiations would be better from a position of strength. The insufferable man could wait.

Raphal tapped lightly on the adjoining doorway. 'Ellen. Are you ready?'

'A little while, Raphal.'

She dismissed the maids, carefully tying the throwing knife and sheath to her inner thigh. She waited half an hour then pushed open the door into Raphal's room, knocking first. He was praying in the corner and looked up as she entered.

'It's time,' she said.

Raphal groaned as he pushed himself up from his knees. A servant, who had been waiting in the corridor for about an hour now, led them to a small, informal dining room.

Chapter Sixteen

The dining room was a marked contrast to the main court, small and intimate, with a fireplace lit in one corner. Ellen was relieved to see no warriors. The room was hung with tapestries and lined with carpets, tastefully illuminated by candlelight. Linnas lounged at the small table, apparently unconcerned with her lateness. The table before him was scattered with an array of platters, the food half-eaten. *He has already indulged himself.* Ellen stifled her annoyance. No matter what, she would give the picture of calm serenity. As she seated herself at the low table, her jewels flashed on her white skin. Raphal sat unobtrusively to one side.

'I trust you are refreshed,' said Linnas, pausing between mouthfuls to ask after her.

In response Ellen only smiled, trying to look graceful, yet wishing he would choke on his food. The man had the manners of a harena.

'Now. What is this about Belin's son?' Linnas held his greasy hands in the air for a servant to wipe. 'My uncle's two sons died in battle, his daughter and two grandchildren when Blackthorne fell. There were no other heirs.'

Ellen smiled, realising what he feared. A rival heir. 'That is true. His legitimate sons and heirs were killed in the Last Days.'

Linnas' eyes became calculating, 'His *legitimate* sons?'

'You are very perceptive, Linnas, and you are correct. There was an illegitimate son. His name is Cedrin and, until recently, he had been cared for by a glassmith in Athria.'

Linnas snorted, reaching for another dish. 'And why does

this concern me, or Kaidell? For all I know Belin left a hundred by-blows from Athria to the eastern frontier.'

Ellen restrained her temper. *Arrogant, insolent man.* 'Yes, but they were not left the Kaidell signet ring.'

Linnas paused with a mouthful halfway to his lips. The news must be grave indeed to stop his appetite, thought Ellen scornfully.

Linnas' eyes seethed. 'So, it is as I thought – an Athrian plot to take my lands away from me.'

Ellen's face grew slack with astonishment. 'I care nothing about you or your estate. I came here merely to get your consent, so Cedrin can be received as a Kaidell Suulqua in Raynor.'

Linnas nodded, his eyes squinting with cold calculation. 'That is the first step. Then a few well-placed bribes and the favour of the Warlord will have this impostor in my place.'

She struggled for calm. 'I assure you – there is no plot. If a challenge to inheritance is what you fear, Cedrin will sign any documents you require to renounce the claim.'

'Will he?' said Linnas.

'Of course,' said Ellen.

'And when these documents are lost? Or disputed as forgeries? No, no, no. Don't think for an instant I will consider legitimising this bastard,' said Linnas.

She now understood why he had withdrawn from court and why he had never risen above the rank of Suulqua. Linnas' fears bordered on paranoia.

'There must be some way –' began Ellen.

'No.'

Linnas reached for a thick leg of roasted harena, lifting it by the bone. 'Still, you surprise me, Cintros. I had thought you came here with other business entirely.'

'What business could that be?' she said. How was she to turn this around? Would she have to start bartering like a merchant, offering coin for a Suulqua title?

He laughed, his mouth full of food. 'Yes, I know all about it. Yes. You and your refugee.'

Linnas waved at Raphal, and a chill ran down Ellen's spine.

'The Warlord has put a price on Raphal's head, you know.' Linnas leant closer to her, as though they had suddenly become confidants. 'And rumour has it, the Warlord is going to imprison you in a torc of mercury glowmetal.'

Ellen stiffened. *Linnas must have spies at court – and a well-stocked rookery of messenger birds.*

'Yes, you see. The Warlord and Uran knew it was you who freed Raphal – an old family friend as he was. Only the quick intervention of your brother stopped the Warlord from calling out the guard and sealing Raynor.'

Ellen sagged forward. *Raynor is closed to me.* Athria forbidden. She was lost – and now she would lose Cedrin as well.

'So,' said Linnas, tearing a piece of meat off the harena leg, panting with the effort of eating and talking at the same time. 'You see, you cannot force the issue. I knew you would come seeking sanctuary. I had intended to agree – at a hefty price – but now I see your true scheme, this is out of the question.'

'You insolent …' Ellen stood, tilting her head back in a regal pose. 'Do you know who you are talking to? I am Ellen Cintros, the daughter of Myan.' Only weeks ago she had the resources of an entire Sardom at her command.

'You seek to intimidate me with your talk of ancestry? Don't delude yourself, woman. I am the master here. With the simple wave of my hand, I could have my men imprison you both. Raphal would be a tidy prize, and I'm sure the Warlord and Uran would love to see you again.'

Linnas' threats sparked her defiance. 'When I try to intimidate you – you will know it!' With a surge of Force, she swept the leg of harena out of Linnas' hands and threw the table against the far wall.

Linnas was silent, but not fearful, his hand was poised to wave as if judging the moment. With sudden insight Ellen knew he had expected this. He had expected her to attack him. With effort she calmed herself and Raphal rose and stood beside her, placing a hand on her shoulder.

Ellen examined the walls. Concealed by the subdued lighting, she now saw the holes cut into the plaster.

Linnas' eyes lit up. 'Yes. You see now, don't you? Five men with blowpipes. A nerve poison even more powerful than the one that killed your father.'

Ellen's skin crawled. A memory of her father's face, pale in death after the poison took him, came unbidden.

'I came here seeking only kinship and welcome,' said Ellen, 'with no ill intent. I find you are so far gone into fear, you do not even know a friend.' She channelled the Fire into the Shield Matrix. She would now be safe from the darts.

Linnas watched her with a knowing expression, as though her entreaty were merely another tactic. She met his gaze once more and knew no words would reach him. He was locked within a tower of dark certainties. If not for the terrible sense of defeat she felt, she could have pitied him.

'We will leave at first light,' she said.

'You will,' said Linnas, his face flushed with victory. 'Leave knowing the Cintros will never, *never*, get my lands.'

Ellen swept from the room, her plans in ruins. She had never even considered that the nephew of Belin would be her enemy. Her enemy! And Raynor – closed to her! What now? She would need to continue north. She and Raphal had to leave the Yasser States as soon as possible. Raphal did need to return to Olcis. She would speak to Xyanthius and join his caravan. At least this gave her a pretext to stay close to Cedrin.

Doubts plagued her. What if, in the end, her pursuit of Cedrin led her nowhere? What if he finally rejected her and all the Suul stood for? What place would she have then, with Athria and Raynor closed to her? Would her old teacher, Erioth, shelter her in the far northern Domains of the Verial until the Athrian Temple rescinded its edict? Would Erioth's winged brethren even tolerate her in their secret enclaves?

She had to have faith. So far, everything that her father had told her in those dying moments had been borne out. There was a reason her father had valued Cedrin so highly. Somehow he held the key to the Scion. She was increasingly intrigued by Cedrin. Marken seemed always to defer to him, like his Lord. The other Scythemen, even Xyanthius' senior men treated him with respect, and it was not just the Kaidell ring or the link to

Belin.

Ellen sighed, forcing all the tumbling thoughts from her mind. She knew her next step. That was enough for now.

All she had to do was escape Linnas.

* * *

'Yes, my dear. It's true. I knew the Sarlord personally,' said Marken, flicking back his long hair.

The young serving woman sitting on Marken's lap was rapt, her mouth open in a silent 'Oh'. She was a petite little thing, with long brown hair and a fine face. Another woman, more thickset, sat with Cedrin.

Cedrin had seen Marken use this routine dozens of times. It certainly seemed that Linnas' mansion was a dull place for the serving staff. The two young women eagerly accepted their invitation to share a pipe of se-tobacco.

They sat together on an open balcony, watching the stars appear as the suns set, the clouds brilliant with touches of gold, orange and red. They had passed the afternoon amidst luxury, with fine food and wine theirs for the asking. Athria seemed a lifetime away, yet it was less than a month since they had sat, much as they were now, in the comfort of Lookout Hill, waiting for Storm Season to begin.

'Were you really in the Brotherhood?' asked the thickset women, running a hand across the degrees on Cedrin's chest. Her eyes were a dull brown and slightly protruding.

'Yes,' said Cedrin, forcing a smile. She was friendly enough, but he did not feel like discussing the Brotherhood – or its betrayal of him and Marken – with her. This close, he saw the skin on her cheeks was pockmarked. He could not help compare her to Ellen with her fine white skin and her intense green eyes, so alive with passion. Her lips ...

The girl leant in close and traced the line of a scar near his shoulder. She looked up and smiled. He could tell she was taken with him and would perhaps be willing if he wanted to pursue her.

He looked out into the valley. It was a peaceful scene, but it was hard to stay relaxed while others met behind closed doors to decide his fate.

Marken leant in to whisper something into the young serving woman's ear. She giggled, then flushed red. They both stood up, his hand resting easily on her hip. He led the girl back towards their rooms, and she went willingly, still rapt in attention at his continual stream of banter.

Cedrin tapped out the bowl of his pipe. The se usually suffused him with a feeling of wellbeing, but tonight it was only making him restless. He looked across at the girl and made up his mind. He had to find out what was happening.

'I might go for a walk to clear my head,' said Cedrin.

'I could come with you.'

'I need to walk alone,' said Cedrin, rising.

The woman's face fell, and she stepped back from him.

'Thank you for your company,' he said, leaning in to give her a kiss on the cheek. She brightened immediately and gave a short curtsey before rushing off into the building.

Cedrin walked down a short set of steps into the garden. Asic had risen, a crescent moon. Rea was still below the horizon. He could see warriors patrolling the courtyard in almost every direction. Linnas was certainly big on security. As he walked along the garden path, he passed two older warriors talking in low tones. They looked up as he approached. They exchanged a quick glance then one walked over to him. 'Cedrin, isn't it?'

Up close he saw the man was even older than he had thought, with sparse grey hair. In the dark, his movements were those of a much younger man.

'Yes,' said Cedrin, keeping his voice even.

The old warrior looked back around the garden, waiting for one of the nearby patrols to go around the side of the building.

The old man looked into his face for a long time, then he reached across and gripped his upper arm, checking the muscle in his bicep. 'Hmmm. Are you really Belin's son?'

'Yes,' said Cedrin.

The old warrior looked over his tattoos, then back at his face. He nodded, then turned back to his friend. 'What else did you hear from the dartmen?'

'The ring,' said the other warrior, stepping forward. His face was stern and heavily lined.

'You have the ring of Kaidell?' asked the old warrior.

Cedrin held up his right hand.

The old warrior took Cedrin's hand, squinting at the ring. 'Never thought to see that again.' The crunching tread of warriors announced another patrol returning around the corner of the house.

'The luck of Larus go with you, son,' said the old warrior, gripping his shoulder briefly.

'Don't linger here too long, friend,' said the other warrior. 'Linnas … well, he's nothing like Belin.'

The two men walked away. He saw them briefly once more as they entered one of the buildings beyond the mansion; perhaps a barracks. Why should two of Linnas' own warriors be so cautious? They had obviously believed he was Belin's son, yet had warned him away. It left him with an uneasy feeling.

The Blade leading the squad saw him. 'You there!'

Cedrin waited for them to reach him. The Blade recognised him as he approached. 'You should not be out of your room,' said the warrior.

'I apologise. I'll return immediately,' said Cedrin, walking back to the balcony. He sat and lit a pipe, watching calmly as the squad completed their circuit. He could hear soft talking and laughter from his room. It sounded like Marken was enjoying himself.

He could not shake the feeling of unease. When the squad disappeared around the side of the building, Cedrin extinguished the pipe. He vaulted the balcony railing, landing in the shadows. The walls of the mansion were made of stone blocks, with easy hand and footholds. He was on the roof in moments. The roof was tile, and he chose his footing carefully as he crept across it. He could see the big glass roof above the main court. It was dark, the hall below empty. To his left he could see a smaller section of glassed roof, a single smoking chimney nearby. He edged closer, looking down through the glass to an informal dining room.

Below he saw Linnas, platters set out before him, eagerly

cramming food into his mouth. There was no sign of Ellen. Perhaps they had already settled the matter. Curiosity gnawed at him. Perhaps he could ask her tonight? He smiled to himself as he imagined slipping into her rooms to surprise her. No. He would have to wait until tomorrow.

'Yes. But she dare not.' Linnas' voice rang out clear and strong, despite the intervening food.

Cedrin heard a low voice, catching snippets of words like 'heir' and 'legitimate'. He could not see the speaker. He put his ear to the glass.

Linnas laughed. 'To think she wanted me to recognise some half-blood Athrian, after all these years. If I had, we would have slaves and whores presenting sons all the way from here to Raynor.'

'Do you want him killed?'

'There is no need to risk our men against her. Besides there is no doubt he is a fake.'

'And the ring?'

'Surely a glass trinket. I care not. Just make sure they are gone tomorrow.'

Cedrin never asked to be a Suulqua. Yet to have Linnas dismiss him as some sort of charlatan … it made his blood boil. This whole journey had been a mistake. He stepped back across the roof, moving silently out of habit. He levered himself over the edge, landing lightly in the courtyard below. His heart churned with anger – and disappointment. Ellen had led him to this rich man's house to discover what he had always known: there was no place for him with the Suul. If there had been, wouldn't his father Belin have taken him straight to Myan, not to some glassmith?

Still, Ellen had done him a service in bringing him here. It had been a surprising gesture. For that at least she deserved his loyalty. Was it possible that people from two different worlds could be friends … companions. More?

'Don't be a fool,' he told himself. His heart felt suddenly hot.

He had no wish to disturb Marken and walked off into the dark, away from the mansion.

He was a follower of the Way of the Scytheman now, and

part of Kranor's phoenix cult: a warrior's cult. He need not bow to any man or woman, Suul or Sarlord. He could still carve out a destiny for himself. He *was* Belin's son, and no one could take that away from him. He vowed to honour the man's memory, to equal his deeds. Even knowing that he was the Hero of the Last Days, and that he had perished all those years ago had done much to heal the wounds inside him. He believed in his father now, believed in his honour. When he considered men like Tarral and Kranor, men of impeccable virtue and courage, then understood that they themselves had looked up to Belin: he knew that his father would have come for him if he could have. That was enough.

He had travelled far into the night, cutting across fields and roads, leaping fences, all the while climbing. As he walked, the night soothed him and the anger faded. He found an old, seldom used track and followed it up the hill. The path continued to steepen and he looked up. Blackthorne tower loomed above him like a silent sentinel.

He saw the faint flicker of a fire, then lost it. The brief glimpse of flame intrigued him and he set out to find its maker. When he reached the tower, Cedrin realised how massive it was. The walls, which had looked like tumbled ruins from the distance, stood many times the height of a man. He was fascinated by the place. Finding a gap in the stone, he forced his way through the rubble to stand in the space between the outer wall and the tower.

He lost track of time as he wandered through halls and ruined buildings, into darkened dungeons and up stone stairwells to the ruined battlements. He paused here, looking out across the darkened valley as the breeze caught his hair.

'Ahh.' He saw the fire again. It was below him, in what looked to be a dome, nestled into the western wall. He could see it through a gap in the roof. Curious, but cautious, he climbed back down and made his way towards it. He stomach growled as the aroma of roasting meat reached him. Circling the strange structure, he found the arched doorway and stepped inside, his eyes fixed forward on the fire. Three plump birds were roasting on a spit.

A mought haft slammed into his stomach. He fell gasping to the floor and struggled to spin away, his hand reaching to his harness. *Linnas' men did not return my weapons.* He froze as a blade touched his neck.

'Easy friend,' said Cedrin. 'I saw your fire and only thought to share it.'

The unseen figure grunted. 'It's well enough you call me friend when I have a blade at your throat. Ahh, you look harmless enough.'

Cedrin rubbed his neck as the blade was taken away. He never imagined he looked *harmless*. He watched the man in the light of the fire. His grey hair was wild and unkempt, his beard uncombed. His ancient cloak was stained, but had been carefully patched and repaired. Beneath, his clothes were faded, but clean. The haft of his greatscythe gleamed, and the smooth snick as he withdrew the blades revealed it was well maintained. A hermit with a greatscythe? Now that was strange indeed. Cedrin had thought to find some squatters who had sheltered from the Storm Season and were yet to move on, or perhaps some workers from the estate.

The dome concealed a temple. Despite the ruin, it had the air of an inner sanctum and he guessed it had never been a place of public worship. The old hermit had set his fire on the edge of a wide mosaic that covered the temple floor. The man walked along the inner edge of the design and sat down by the fire. Cedrin started to cross the mosaic towards the fire when the man hissed and leapt to his feet.

'Stop. Are you daft, boy? Do you want to lose your soul?'

Cedrin stopped dead and looked around him into the gloom of the dome, sweeping his gaze across the temple floor. There was nothing. Just night and shadows.

'It's there. *There.*'

The hermit bent forward as he pointed to the centre of the design, his manic eyes catching the gleam of the fire, his grey hair sticking out in patches. The man was clearly mad. Cedrin would have laughed if not for the well-kept greatscythe at the man's side.

'If you want to reach the fire, you have to walk *around* the Iris design, not across it. You see?'

'I understand,' said Cedrin.

The man relaxed, indicating a path around the outside of the mosaic.

When Cedrin reached the fire, the old hermit gave Cedrin a slap on the back and laughed. 'That wasn't so hard, was it, lad? Now you can sit if you like. You don't have to stand there like a frightened narsell.' The hermit indicated a place by the fire, just outside the mosaic. Cedrin noted with some amusement that the man himself did not leave the patterned floor, the fire having been set at the border of the design. He thought about pointing this out to the man then changed his mind – he did not look like someone who appreciated irony.

Cedrin sat by the fire. The man laid aside his greatscythe and turned the spit.

'Caught plump and juicy, these were. Straight from their burrows. Want some?'

Cedrin smelled the cooking flesh, which had been basted with spices and oil. It was a tantalising aroma. 'Yes – if you have some to spare.'

'Plenty for everyone,' said the hermit.

The man carved off pieces of the succulent meat, passing them across, and they ate in silence. Although he seemed relaxed, Cedrin could tell the hermit was watching him carefully.

'Do you live here?' asked Cedrin.

'Of course, of course. I'm the Captain of the wall. Where else would I be but still here at Blackthorne?'

Cedrin looked at the man, trying to gauge him. How far gone into madness was he? He feared to say the wrong thing – particularly as the man's weapon never left his side.

'Where're you headed, lad?'

'North,' he said. 'North to Searn. I'm working a caravan as a mercenary. Everybody is fleeing Raynor, the Eath –'

He stopped, realising the man's delusions could run very deep. What if he believed the Empire was still intact?

'I knew it. I told Linnas the Eathal would advance on Raynor. That's another two rubies he owes me.'

Did the hermit really know Linnas or was it another delusion? 'What's your name, lad? You've an Athrian accent but have Anacian looks. A refugee, eh?'

Cedrin smiled. 'They used to call me *mainlander* in Athria; that was supposed to be an insult. I'm called Cedrin by my friends.'

The old man screamed as though struck by an arrow. Cedrin leapt to his feet, looking into the darkness for an attacker. He felt the man's grip on his shoulder, spinning him around to face him. He was surprisingly strong.

'Who is your father, boy? Quickly. Tell me!'

Cedrin relaxed, realising there was no intruder. 'Tarral ... the ... the glassmith.'

The man's eyes widened. He gripped Cedrin's harness, pulling him in close and looking into his face. 'No. *No.*'

The man stiffened suddenly, crying out in pain. He released Cedrin and staggered back, his left hand held to his head, the other still holding his greatscythe. He stepped off the mosaic onto the dusty floor beyond. He recovered quickly and looked down at his feet. 'There were no lights and yet ...'

He looked across at Cedrin. 'It's gone. You're here. And it's gone,' muttered the hermit.

Cedrin had to get out of here. He gathered himself for a sprint straight across the mosaic and out of the temple. The hermit sensed the move and leapt between him and the mural. For one intense moment Cedrin thought he would have to fight his way free against a greatscythe. The man was fast, and he was not sure he could get close enough to grapple with him before he released the blades.

'Go, quickly! But if you value your soul, do not touch the Iris,' shouted the hermit, his head turning to watch the centre of the mosaic with an insane intensity.

Cedrin ran around the edge of the mosaic and out of the dome, stumbling into the darkness. The tumbled ruins were like a maze. He grunted as his head struck stone. He reached blindly, waiting for his eyes to re-adjust. Cedrin jerked as a hand fell onto his shoulder.

'*This way.*' It was the hermit. 'To the right.'

He could see it. He blinked. He could see everything. The light was rising, flooding out from the temple. He turned back to the dome and froze. Through the arch a brilliant light had risen from the Iris like a small sun. He could now see the full extent of the patterned floor, a symmetry of five that danced and turned on itself. His eyes followed the glowing ball as it rose within the dome, hovering above the floor. It flared outward to the edges of the mosaic, then began to turn, faster and faster. A song rose at the edge of his hearing ... no, five songs, all sounding together, growing louder as the whirlpool of light spun faster.

The hermit grabbed his arm. 'Don't look! Come.'

Cedrin fled with the hermit through the ruins and out beyond the ruined outer wall. The song had risen, pounding through his head. Inside his mind he could hear an echo. Hidden within the fabric of each song was a part of the echo. This was where the five songs overlapped and fell around each other. The echo drew him ... back towards the Temple of the Iris.

The hermit backhanded him across the face. 'Don't listen to it! Run, damn you. While you still can.'

Cedrin's mind cleared, and he saw the hermit still had his greatscythe. His cheek stung with the blow.

Cedrin edged away from the strange man, then ran down the darkened slope until he found the path. The small moon Rea had risen full, and lit his way. He kept running until the path levelled out and he could see the lights of the mansion in the distance.

Only then did he turn back to the dark shape of Blackthorne tower behind him. There was no hint of the light that had grown inside the dome, and no trace of that strange song. There had clearly been some powerful magic at work. As to whether the Iris was dangerous, or if that was yet another aspect of the man's madness – it was impossible to say.

'Crazy hermits and paranoid Suul,' whispered Cedrin. The whole trip to the Kaidell estate had been a waste of time. The sooner he was back to Kranor's company, the better.

Chapter Seventeen

The outskirts of Seyt lay ahead.

As they drew closer, the reality of her situation began to dawn on Ellen. Her plans were in ruins, a return to the comfort and position she enjoyed in Raynor now impossible. Instead she faced life on the road, trying to unravel a mystery and build an alliance with a man who had no reason to trust her. Rescuing Raphal had been a reckless gamble – and now she was paying the price. The only thing left was her promise to Myan, and the quest for the Scion.

She reached up to her head and checked that her mought bracer concealed her Suul mark. Now that both she and Raphal were fugitives, she had to be doubly careful. She remembered her defiant excursion to the Seyt market with a feeling of sick dread. By now the Warlord's spies would have heard of the Suul woman who travelled with a Priest. Perhaps rumours had also reached the agents of the Athrian Temple, which sought her under edict.

Last night she had barely slept, constantly alert for an attack by Linnas' men. When she did drop into an exhausted sleep it was to dream of being led naked into the Warlord's court imprisoned in a torc of mercury glowmetal, while the ranks of Suul sneered and laughed. 'Ah. Uran's new bed-slave,' the Warlord had said, leering at her. She had woken just as Uran was leading her from the main hall on a silken leash ... Ellen shivered. She looked up at the distant walls of Seyt. Was someone even now watching for her return? She gritted her teeth in defiance. *Let them come.* They would not find Ellen

Cintros an easy conquest.

The road descended towards Seyt from the hills, giving her an excellent view of the harbour, which was filled with tall sea-going vessels. Any one of them could take her back to Athria within days. She knew that was impossible, but even so she longed for home; for the familiar faces and sights of Regent's Hill and the Cintros mansion. It would be good to see her brother Torren, even though he now sat on her throne.

They had left the Kaidell estate before dawn. Cedrin had taken the news of Linnas' refusal stoically, thanking her for her efforts on his behalf. He now rode ahead with Marken, his broad shoulders swaying slightly with his amelak's movement. He had said nothing more; nothing at all. She found it infuriating. Somehow she had to broach the issue of her travelling north with him. If she could somehow make it seem his idea, that would be ideal. He was a man who valued his independence and needed to feel as though he was taking the lead. She had given the issue of approaching him a lot of thought through the night and had decided to tell him Raphal was a fugitive. Nothing built trust like sharing a secret.

'Raphal. Did you say you wanted to talk to Marken?'

The ride back from Seyt had been a quiet one, and Raphal was absorbed in his own thoughts. 'Hmmm? Oh, yes. Such a talented young man working as a mercenary. Such waste.'

'Perhaps now might be a good time for a private conversation?' suggested Ellen.

Raphal's eyes lit with understanding. 'I see. Very well.'

The old Larus Priest and Druid urged his amelak up along the track to Cedrin and Marken. There was a brief conversation, then Cedrin dropped back to give Marken and Raphal privacy. Ellen clicked her tongue, increasing the pace of her own beast. She soon drew up beside Cedrin. Her heart leapt then beat faster.

'We have made good time,' said Ellen.

'Aye. Xyanthius will be pleased to see us back. We leave tomorrow for Ceta along the north road,' said Cedrin. 'Look ... Ellen. Before we part I just want you to know that I bear no ill will towards you. I always suspected that Linnas would act as he did.'

Always suspected the mission to the Kaidell estate would be a failure? Did he have so little faith in her? She ruthlessly squashed a sharp reply.

'It was my fault, Cedrin. I should have found out more about Linnas before I approached him so directly,' she said.

'Don't worry. We all made it out in one piece. In fact I think Marken rather enjoyed himself.' A brief flash of amusement passed through his eyes, then he became serious once more. 'I always knew my place was not with the Suul. But at least now I know the truth about my father. For that, I thank you.'

Ellen nodded, not sure what tack to take next. Talking to someone like him was so different to a Suul. *He* was so different. Rough, yet direct, with an honesty and conviction that was almost palpable. His grey-blue eyes met hers steadily, looking right into her. Something squirmed inside her heart, blossoming into a hopeful joy.

'I know I have been suspicious of you and that I was slow to trust. For that, I hope you will forgive me,' said Cedrin.

'There … is nothing to forgive,' said Ellen. The day was warming now, and beads of sweat glistened on his taut pectoral muscles.

'So where will you go now? Back to Raynor?' he asked.

The truth was, she had no place to go, but a tearful confession was not what she had in mind.

'Can I tell you something in confidence, Cedrin?'

Cedrin's face was stern for a moment, his eyes hard. She felt a little frightened of him in that moment. 'Yes. You have earned that.'

'Raphal is a fugitive. He was with the false-Scion's delegation and was imprisoned by the Warlord.'

'Then …'

'He is an old family friend and I could not bear to see him treated like that. I secured his freedom and helped him flee Raynor,' said Ellen. There was much more to it than that, but nothing he needed to know. She was not about to tell him she used her own Sorcerous powers to free him, or that she herself was being sought by the most powerful man in Kelas. 'But he remains in danger as long as he is on the road. Raphal needs to get to Olcis. I will travel north with him.'

Cedrin was quiet for a moment. 'Well, you will be making for Searn before you strike east on the Olcis road. Why don't you travel with Alechul's caravan? The road north is dangerous and even though we travel slowly, you will be well protected. Much easier for you to hide in a group like that, than travelling alone.' He paused as though deciding something. 'Besides, I may not be Suul, but you are the closest thing I have to a blood relation. Linnas was no kin – that I could see. I will do my best to protect you both.'

Ellen could see he was sincere and was touched by his offer of protection. Now was not the time to point out that she was an expert scythewoman. She allowed herself a small smile as her stomach fluttered. 'You're right. I will talk to Xyanthius.'

Ellen was overcome with the sense of solid strength that Cedrin possessed. His innate ability to lead and inspire. What was it about him? Her leg brushed his, and she realised she had unconsciously manoeuvred her amelak closer to his.

'Oops … sorry,' she said.

Cedrin gave her a rare smile. In that moment Ellen was acutely aware of her loneliness. She suddenly wanted nothing more than to be embraced, to lose herself in his strong grip, bury her head into his shoulder and forget. Simply forget.

Her hand tightened on her reins, and she moved her amelak away. The road had descended from the hills and the city gates were close now. With a shock she realised she had forgotten the threat of the Warlord's guards. She looked up along the battlements for any suspicious observer.

'Is something wrong, Ellen?' His eyes were narrowed as he watched her. He had noticed her sudden tension.

'No. Of course not. I have much to organise. I'll see you tomorrow.' Ellen's court mask descended easily. She gave him a brief smile then urged her amelak up to Raphal and Marken. She had to be careful. Cedrin was far too intelligent to be fooled for long.

'Raphal?'

The old Priest broke off talking with Marken and nodded in

reply.

'I will be at the Temple of the Two Moons until midnight. All will be ready – should you choose to come,' said Raphal to Marken.

Marken was uncharacteristically serious. 'I will come – and give you my answer there.'

Marken's reply puzzled Ellen, but she had no time to consider it now. She wanted to get through the gates and lose herself quickly inside the city. There would be no repeat of her mistake this time. She and Raphal would stay well hidden.

'Farewell, Suul Cintros. It has been a pleasure,' said Marken.

'You will be seeing me tomorrow,' said Ellen.

Marken raised an eyebrow.

'I will be travelling north with you on Alechul's caravan. But not as a Suul. Can I trust you to keep my identity, and that of Raphal, secret?'

'Of course.' Marken's face lit up with a dazzling smile.

'Tomorrow then.'

'I look forward to it … Ellen,' he said graciously.

Ellen urged her amelak forward, Raphal keeping pace beside her. 'Draw up your hood,' she said. Raphal pulled up the cowl of his robe, drawing it down over his face. The city gates were wide open, a sporadic stream of traffic passing in and out under the bored gaze of the guards. Her stomach tightened as they passed beneath the arched gates and she looked up at the wall behind her, alert for archers … or pipemen. Nothing. The guard nodded to her and they were through.

Just inside the gates, a group of men were gathered around a wagon. A small harena stood in the harness, snorting impatiently as the men tried to lever off a broken wheel. One of them looked up as they approached, a small man with a series of hideous burn scars on his face. Ellen flinched at his ruined face and turned away.

'Where to now, Ellen?' asked Raphal.

'Anywhere we can stay out of sight until nightfall. Then I need to pay Alechul a visit,' she said. If there were spies watching for her, they would be searching the inns. She hoped they had not yet made the connection between her and a certain caravan that had recently arrived from Athria with a Priest and Priestess of Mythar among the travellers.

'I know a small Temple near the harbour – the Sea Wind Temple – many of the tillermen learn Navigation magic there. It will suit nicely,' said Raphal, turning his amelak down into one of the steep lanes leading to the water.

'It's too late to disguise you for the trip north – Kranor's men know you too well,' said Ellen as she followed. Raphal's face would be familiar to them by now, since he had acted as her spokesman and shield for the journey from Raynor. Hopefully the refugees who had witnessed her healing would have all been left behind in Seyt. She knew she could trust Cedrin and Marken, who were the only other witnesses. Apart from that one incident, she had kept her face concealed for the whole journey. 'It needs to appear as though we don't know each other, at least at the beginning. The border of the Yasser States is technically fifty leagues south of Searn, but patrols only extend a day's ride north from Seyt. Once we are on the road, we should be safe.'

Raphal nodded with approval. 'Let's hope we can leave Seyt unobserved. How long will you travel with Cedrin?'

Ellen frowned. 'As far as Searn initially. Then as long as it takes for the mystery of the Scion to reveal itself. Myan always believed Cedrin was vital.'

Raphal was thoughtful. 'An unusual man. He would be a fierce ally to the cause of the Scion – should you win him over. You will have plenty of time on the trip north.'

Ellen stretched her back, tight from hours in the saddle. The suns were past the zenith now, and falling in the west. A heavy weariness was descending on her, the lack of sleep beginning to tell. She would have liked nothing more than to find a good inn and command a hot bath, but that was impossible now. Her hands closed to fists on the reins. Behind her in her saddle-bags was a small fortune in coin and gems. Even so, she would have to spend the rest of the day hiding in some dusty temple back room, with nothing more to look forward to than another sleepless night as she sought out Alechul.

Needing to distract herself, she thought back to Marken's

puzzling reply to Raphal.

'What were you and Marken talking about?'

Raphal straightened in the saddle, his eyes glistening as he looked out into the distant harbour. 'I cannot say too much, Ellen. I was … acting as confessor.'

She did not want to pry, but needed to know what Raphal was up to. 'And?'

Raphal was silent for a moment, gathering his thoughts. 'Marken was a gifted student. Passionate about the Druidic arts and healing. When that Hendian slave lay dying, he knew he could have saved him … if he had the knowledge. That truth has been eating away at him ever since. He realised then that his desire to heal had never lessened, and he asked me to teach him.'

'Then the trip to the temple?'

'I have agreed to teach him on one condition. Marken must agree to be inducted into an Order of itinerant Moon Druids based at the Temple of the Two Moons – one of the few healing temples the Temple of the Sisters does not control. He must give an oath to return for one month each year to give service as a healer – no matter what position he achieves in the world. If he takes that oath, I will teach him what I can on the road.'

'But you are a Larus Druid,' said Ellen.

'I know healing, Ellen. For the most part the magic is the same, merely a different Essence is used. Even though Marken only ever passed his Initiate, there was little more Crephis could have taught him regarding the gathering of the Moon Essence – he is a natural. He lacked only the knowledge.'

They rode on in silence, her thoughts tumbling over each other. The lids of her eyes drooped, and she leant forward over her mount. As they passed an alley on her left, she caught a glimpse of a small man running parallel to them down towards the harbour. There was something about him – some alertness. Her heart hammered. She kept watch on the left, waiting for another alley to open up.

There!

It was Scarface from the gates. Just for a moment their eyes met and he knew she had seen him. He ducked away and was gone. When the next alley mouth opened up, he was nowhere in sight. Damn! There was something about him, something about the scars. They were long and straight as though he had been … branded. Her stomach gave a sick twist as she remembered the two Templemen questioning the Brotherhood men from the raid on Regent's Hill; the sickening sound of the red-hot clearglass rod as the torturer touched it to the skin of the chained man. The screams. That man had been tortured by the Temple of the Sisters.

'Raphal. How long to the Sea Wind Temple?'

'Not long now. It's up on that rise.' Raphal pointed to the small swelling of headland on the north end of the harbour.

Ellen measured the distance to her sheathed scythe, then looked around her, alert for anything. Every dock worker, sailor, merchant and beggar seemed to be watching her, and anyone could be a spy. There was no sign of Scarface. One thing was for sure – she was no longer tired.

* * *

Kalyth blew the dust from the flagstones then sat back on his haunches, his greatscythe balanced on his knees as he worked the dust from the handholds with an old knife. It had been years since he had disturbed the memories buried below, and he knew pain waited for him. He tucked the knife into his belt and slung his greatscythe across his back. Outside Uros had fallen below the horizon, Larus following as second twilight began. He had scouted the area thoroughly and knew he would not be disturbed.

To his right, the Iris lay silent. He knew the Ward would stir again. He no longer thought of it as Belin, but as the *thing* that controlled Belin, the Ward. When it did return, he would be gone. Last night the Compulsion that had compelled him to return each day to the Iris had broken. As soon as he realised Cedrin was here – in Blackthorne – and not in Athria, it had snapped like a twig, releasing him. He knew nothing about Sorcery. The only thing that mattered to him was that he was free.

He bent to the stone, taking a firm grip. Slowly he lifted, grunting with the effort, the solid muscles beneath his faded robe straining. With a shout, he tilted the slab over and jumped back. It fell with a dull thud, revealing the trapdoor and mought ring concealed beneath. The years had taken their toll on him, but the strength remained. He gripped the ring and wrenched the trapdoor open, coughing as a cloud of dust billowed up. Stairs descended into darkness.

Kalyth lit a brand from the fire and made his way down a tightly spiralling stair, cut into the stone. When he reached the vault, the flame glittered on precious relics of glass and crystal, draped with ancient, dust-filled webs. He lit the torches on the walls and extinguished the brand, then waited for light to fill the chamber. It had been twenty-eight years since he had stood in this room. His gaze moved to five big mought-bound chests against the far wall.

'You never found Belin's treasure, Linnas, you blood-sucker,' said Kalyth.

The seven glowmetals housed here always filled him with dread. He had half-expected them to take on a life of their own in his absence, but he thanked the Sisters they had not. The covers he had placed on them had not been disturbed.

Then he turned to another chest, small and plain, set back in the shadows. His throat tightened. A pain grew high in his chest. The casket had once rested in his rooms in the ruined Blackthorne manor. Its sides were still blackened from the fire that had gutted the structure; the same flames that had claimed his wife, sons and daughters.

He made himself walk to it, though the strength had vanished from his legs.

'Open it, you coward,' he said.

He reached out, his fingertips brushing the clasp. His hand trembled, and he snatched it back.

The pain in his chest was even more intense now. He tried to shout, to bring some strength back into himself, but the sound emerged like the groan of some tortured animal. He wanted to turn and run, but he could not back away from this, not now. He sank to his knees, his eyes aching as he fixed them on the chest.

War had given him no time for grief. He had lost so many comrades, shovelling the cold earth onto their still forms even as the next battle was upon him. When he returned to Blackthorne and dug his family from the ruins, his heart had been filled with the same ashes that had buried them. He had lain them to rest and locked the memories away, hoping that time would dull the pain. Yet some pains cannot be dulled.

His hand shook as he released the catch, then opened the lid.

'Ahhh.' A cry of pain tore from his lips as he gazed at what lay inside.

On top of the pile of clothes within, just as he had left it, was the delicately rendered depiction of his wife Mari. The years fell away, and he could not believe she was gone.

The pain in his chest welled up now, releasing in a flood of tears half a lifetime in the coming. He could not even recognise the high keening sound he made as he reached for a tiny painting, lifting it from the pile like a sacred chalice. There she was, young and full of life, brown hair swept over her shoulders, eyes sparkling with humour and deep with love.

'Why?' He covered his eyes.

He had not even been here when the tower fell. Blackthorne had been under attack from within. The warriors of the Sarlord of Hend – who had allied with the Eathal to betray the Empire – had forced their way inside the gates. An Eathal Sorcerer had set the internal structure of Blackthorne aflame.

On the crest of the hill, he had turned his narsiit to see the tower engulfed in flames and the fighting pressing harder, the screams of the dying muted by the distance. How his heart had urged him to turn and fight, to forsake the mission Belin had charged him with and return to those he loved. But he had been a soldier too long. He turned and galloped away, taking the young babe with him, trusting that Belin and his men would see his family safe.

He pressed the picture to his lips, kissing it. 'Mari, I am sorry. So sorry.'

The grief poured from him. For long years he had lived in its shadow, trapped in Blackthorne with the ghosts of his past, yet not daring to look them in the face. Now it passed through him in a flood. He saw the laughing faces of his children … then their stiff, blackened bodies as he lowered them into the earth. Years stolen. Wasted. Vanished.

At last he was spent. He laid aside the picture and drew a breath, amazed at how free and light he felt – as though a stone had been tipped from his shoulders and constricting leather bands cut away from his chest. He lifted the clothes and put them aside. Beneath was a jacket covered with mought scales, a tough set of leather leggings and military issue boots. He lifted the greatscythe off his shoulders, discarded his patched and faded clothes and donned the armour. He selected new clothes from the pile by the chest and pushed them into an oilskin backpack he had stored with them. The rest he returned to the chest. Then he took a mirror and razor from the chest and closed it, setting the mirror on the lid.

A stranger looked back at him. His hair was unkempt, his beard completely grey. Taking the knife, he tested its edge. It sliced through a piece of cloth with ease. He began to carefully shave off the beard. Eventually his face felt the air for the first time in decades. He looked and felt as though the years had suddenly fled from him. With new energy, he attacked his hair, cropping it close to the skull. The warrior he remembered appeared in the mirror, older, but with the pride he had once felt.

Kalyth extinguished the torches, lighting a single brand to guide his way up to the Temple of the Iris. He shut the trapdoor and pulled the stone back into place, carefully filling the joints with dust and laying debris over the lid. *Linnas will never have Belin's wealth, even if the secret goes with me to my grave.*

He ran from the Temple, and his feet found an easy rhythm as he loped up the road. He did not look back. If he did, he knew he would see the ruin of Blackthorne and the ruin of his life abiding together as though interred in the same grave. He looked forward, taking the air of the evening into his lungs like the promise of new life. *Onwards to Seyt.* He had a caravan to join, one heading north. He could not leave Cedrin to his fate now, not after all that had passed. Perhaps if he could help him, protect him … his life would have meant something after all.

Raziin struggled against his warriors' restraining hands. Once he had laid eyes on the Shattered Temple, the force of the Compulsion had become overwhelming. Every moment he was delayed increased the pain. He would not be able to fight against it much longer.

'Should we release you, Lord?' asked Merceth.

'No,' hissed Raziin. 'As I said – wait until the suns are at the zenith.' If all was to go as planned, they would have to act when the Sisters were at their greatest strength.

They were deep inside the Crusox, a hilly remnant of the ancient primal forest of Tupur that had been too steep to clear for farming, always resisting the efforts of men to claim it. The Eathal military strength in Tupur surprised Raziin. He had watched them over the last few years as they had worked within the old mountains and caves of the Crusox, improving supply routes and creating stockpiles, yet that had always been a hidden thing. For days now they had been passing command posts and new fortifications, built using human slaves. They had been allowed through because the Eathal commanders recognised Raziin and his men as agents of Hukum – yet even so there had been something in their eyes. Word had spread that he was travelling to his death.

His eyes were drawn to the big dome at the centre of the Shattered Temple complex. In ancient times there had been three domes, nestled beside a temple of soaring columns. Now massive trees towered over the ruins and the stately pillars lay tumbled; two of the domes nothing but empty, broken shells. The Eathal, hating the brightness of the suns, were attracted to the comforting darkness inside the dome and used it as a base. Raziin had been here many times to report to Hukum's agents and to gain his rewards of knowledge.

It was to the mountainous crags and deep valleys of the Crusox that the armies of Raynor, Athria and Armon had pressed the defeated Eathal after the Battle of Raynor. The Warlord Daran, Myan Cintros and Raziin's father Leith Cinnor had smashed them here. The Eathal had scattered, fleeing to Maht through the many tunnels and fissures that connected the Crusox to their home caverns.

The Shattered Temple was a mystery. It had been deserted long before the fall of the Bulvuran Empire and many rumoured it had once been a stronghold of the Cioans before the coming of Carris.

'The suns are at the zenith,' said Merceth.

'Do it,' commanded Raziin.

Merceth nodded to Kyal and they released their hold. Raziin stumbled from their grip. He fought down a clawing hand of fear as his feet moved without his conscious control, taking him through the trees towards the dome. He was soon propelled into a shambling run, moving like a tortured mannequin. He fought the impulse and managed to slow to a fast walk. The last power of the Compulsion was pulsing red within him, rising in a last urgent flame. A quick glance confirmed that his men were well hidden inside the trees.

He was less than six paces away when the Eathal warriors standing guard outside the dome saw him. They immediately called out a warning to those inside. Under the light of the suns, Eathal eyesight was poor, and they squinted against the glare as he stepped closer. Typical Eathal, they were bald and squat, heavily muscled and dark skinned. They each carried a small shield and a heavy axe of darkglass. Used to the warmth of the caverns, they were heavily clad in leathers and furs, heavy boots on their feet, the dim insignia on their chests like a blur in the sunlight. Two of the Eathal stepped forward and took him by the arms. Raziin had left his greatscythe with Merceth and appeared unarmed. He knew they would be confident and would not be expecting any trouble from him. They did not search him or find the lanedd calv concealed in his boot.

'Here is the Northman, come to meet his fate,' said one in the Eathal tongue.

'His ugly human head will look good on a spike,' said the other, ending his joke with a deep-throated chuckle. Beneath Raziin's pain, a savage anger stirred.

They led him past the other guards and through a set of

wooden doors into the dome. Raziin cried out as he entered the dark – not with pain, but with sudden release from it. The first part of the Compulsion had run its course. Once more he had full command of himself. His fate hung on a razor's edge. He let them drag him forward. In the second part of the Compulsion, he was to lay his head down on an executioner's block, while an Eathal Lord killed him with an axe of darkglass. Who was it to be? One of the Inner Circle? Perhaps even Hukum himself?

As his eyes grew used to the darkness, he peered forward. He could see faintly glowing stands of *lungii* growing from piles of bat guano. He heard plaintive sounds from the ceiling above and recognised the calls of bats, no doubt complaining at the sudden brightness from the opened doors. Raziin knew they were more for decoration, and to provide the Eathal a sense of familiarity, than to serve any function.

They led him to the altar in the centre of the dome. As they approached, Raziin saw that since his last visit, Eathal craftsman had carved a throne from the massive stone block. He could vaguely make out a big Eathal lounging back into the old altar's embrace, dark and forbidding, as though he too were made of stone. The carvings of the four Old Races remained at each corner of the old altar, now merely decorations on a seat of power. The Eathal guards paused three paces from the throne's base, and Raziin finally caught a glimpse of his adversary.

Staraz. Hukum's own son was Raziin's appointed executioner. His stomach twisted with a desire for violence. *No. Not yet.*

Staraz stood, leaning forward eagerly.

'Ahhh. The mighty Raziin,' said Staraz, his deep voice mocking. His eyes glinted beneath his heavy ridges, showing his savage enjoyment of Raziin's plight.

'Let him come forward,' said Staraz in the Eathal tongue. 'He has to kneel to me.'

The guards let Raziin go, ready with their heavy axes for any betrayal. Raziin threw himself forward at Staraz's feet, feigning the Compulsion that would have forced him to kneel, awaiting death. Set just before the throne was a finely dressed cylinder of stone. Raziin recognised it as a section from one of the fallen columns of the Shattered Temple, now in use as an executioner's block. He trembled with hatred.

'Look. He shakes with fear,' said Staraz.

The guards grunted in contempt.

Raziin's hand flexed, waiting for the moment. Above him Staraz gloated.

'You should have been killed long ago,' said Staraz in the Eathal tongue. 'You and your kind are fit only to be slaves, and slaves you will be until your labour for us is finished. Then you will die.'

Raziin heard the sound of an axe drawn across stone and knew Staraz had hefted his weapon. He measured the distance to his booted calv.

'Stretch your neck out, Northman, like the pitiful and pale creature that you are.'

As though compelled, Raziin complied. From the corner of his eye, he watched as the axe rose, its faint shadow dark and twisted against the curved wall of the dome.

'*Die*,' hissed Staraz.

The axe fell, striking down with a force that would have slain a harena. In an instant, Raziin was on his feet, the long knife in his hand before the axe had completed its deadly arc. The axe struck stone, and Staraz had time only to widen his eyes before Raziin stabbed him in the throat. He locked his left arm around Staraz's right in a wrestler's grip, trapping his weapon, and cut expertly with the knife, the razor-sharp lanedd slicing through the tough, leathery skin and muscle with ease. Blood sprayed out, sticky and warm. He could taste it on his lips. His tongue darted at it. Staraz's left arm pounded at him, his feet kicking, but Raziin held fast.

The guards ran forward, ready to strike with their axes, but Raziin used Staraz as a shield.

'The human has attacked Staraz!' called one of the Eathal guards. The doors opened, and more Eathal warriors ran in.

'Yes. Yes! Bring them all,' yelled Raziin.

The guards spread out. Soon one would get behind him. Staraz's breath gurgled and bubbled, air hissing from his opened neck. Raziin felt the Fire rise in Staraz and continued to work the calv, sawing deep. He had only moments. *There!* The sharp lanedd found the Eathal's spine.

Staraz gave a last sucking sound of horror. With a final cut, Raziin severed the spine and sent Staraz's hairless head flying from the body. Raziin released the headless corpse with a shout of triumph. A gout of Fire erupted from the torso, flaring to brightness, then guttering out like a snuffed candle.

With an enraged shout, the guards rushed at Raziin, but he leapt high, landing with a foot on either side of the throne, where the flat surface of the old altar remained. Blood soaked his chest and hands, the bloody calv clutched tightly like a charm in his fist. He laughed, lost in a rapture of power as he drew on the Fire. He raised a Shield above himself, then shot a silver ball of Force at the apex of the dome.

There was a booming impact. A handful of blocks tumbled from the ceiling, bouncing from his Shield as the dome opened to the sky. The bats shrieked as the sunlight flooded down, calling out shrilly as they launched into flight. The Eathal warriors flinched back, blinded. He had taken out the apex stones. Now there was nothing to support the structure's massive weight. There was a sound like distant thunder, and Raziin laughed as the rest of the dome collapsed. Light bathed Raziin as he stood on the old altar, a new god, given birth.

'Die, you Eathal scum!'

More stone bounced from his Shield as the dome fell into ruin. His breath came fast as he watched the heavy blocks crush more than a hundred Eathal warriors. Then it was over. He stood alone above the carnage, covered in Staraz's blood. Uros' divine messenger.

'Eeeohhya!' He gave a primal scream of joy. He was free.

Outside the dome, Raziin's men had attacked the Eathal warriors who had been outside the dome when it collapsed. The dark-skinned warriors were skilful, but in the light of day they were easy targets. They fell quickly.

With a burst of Force, Raziin leapt from the altar, flying through the air to land outside the dome amid his men. Above them bats circled, shrieking and looking for the dark cave they had lost. Another time he would have struck them from the sky with a sheet of flame, but instead he laughed at their confusion.

'What now, Lord?' asked Merceth.

'Now we journey to Olcis,' said Raziin.

Merceth nodded, withdrawing the bloody blades of his greatscythe. 'Getting back through the Eathal forces in Tupur will not be easy.'

Raziin's satisfaction at the death of Staraz was fading. His general was correct. The destruction of the Shattered Temple would not go undiscovered for long. He looked up at the suns. They had to be well out of the Crusox before dark.

'Let's move,' commanded Raziin.

Merceth signalled to the men. Silently they broke into a steady run, back along the path to the vale where their amelak mounts were hidden.

A savage smile touched Raziin's lips, and he gave silent thanks. *I will keep my promise, Uros. Once I have the Spear, and Cedrin is dead, blood will flow over Kelas.*

Chapter Eighteen

Ellen rode in the caravan's vanguard.

Now that the refugees were gone, Xyanthius had organised the caravan like a military column. The two guards, forward and rear, rode in formation around the harena-borne wagons. Each covered vehicle was protected by two men with spears or bows. Raphal rode in a wagon near the rear of the caravan. Ellen had glimpsed him earlier. As they had agreed the prior night, Raphal had left the Sea Wind Temple before dawn to approach Xyanthius on his own. As she suspected, Xyanthius did not pass up the opportunity to take on a talented healer. Ellen herself had sought out Alechul, and the merchant had been well compensated for her passage. She had explained she was the daughter of a wealthy miller in Raynor, travelling to family in Searn. Her Suul mark had been well concealed beneath her bracer, and he did not question her story. Cedrin and Marken remained in the rearguard, riding together on the left flank.

Ellen and Raphal were not the only travellers going to Searn with the caravan. She had been surprised to learn that the Suul Azel and his servant, refugees from the court of Hianer who had travelled with the caravan from Raynor, had joined the warriors in the rearguard. The Suul must have come on hard times indeed to take Kranor's pay. Thankfully she had never travelled to Hend and did not know Azel. Her identity was still a secret.

The north road followed the coast. As the suns dipped towards the sea on her left, the waters grew brilliant with reflected glare. After a day of travel, Seyt was still on the horizon behind them. She was exhausted, but not from fatigue, from boredom! *On my narsiit I could be halfway to Searn by now.* Many of the warriors of the vanguard riding nearby had tried to engage her in conversation, but the talks were short-lived – ended abruptly at a sharp glance from Xyanthius. She would be glad when tomorrow dawned. As agreed, Raphal would ride beside her from the second day, after they happened to 'meet' this evening.

In the thirty years since the Empire's fall, the heavily-trafficked road had fallen into disrepair. Potholes and ruts opened where there had once been a flawless surface. They had passed many small forts of stone along the road, built by the Empire. All were now deserted, serving only to provide warmth and shelter to travellers, squatters and the occasional animal.

Ellen looked across the broad valley to the east. The countryside was rich and fertile, yet dotted with deserted farmsteads, the orchards grown wild, the fields lying fallow. Her image of the old Empire was of towering spires and grand courts, enclosed by the magnificent walls of big cities. The centres of trade and craft were vital she knew, but the real wealth was in the land. This was decay.

The road curved to the east, then dipped. The sea was lost from sight as they entered a low valley. Nestled into one of the hills on the eastern side was an old road fort. Larger than the usual garrisons, it had a natural spring and the yard around it was fenced in stone. Here Xyanthius raised his hand and called a stop. Ellen broke away from the caravan and dismounted, sore from a long day in the saddle and relieved to be on her own feet at last. Around them wagons, harena and men broke from formation into seeming chaos. Not knowing what to do, she joined a queue of men waiting to water their amelak. There were a series of stone troughs, each filled from the spring through a stone channel. She searched through the crowd for Cedrin and saw him and Marken at one of the other lines.

'Nice night?' asked one warrior.

'Very pleasant,' she said, giving him a quick smile. The warriors were powerful men, heavily muscled and stinking of sweat. They seemed to crowd around her as she waited for her turn at the trough. Her nervousness communicated itself to her mount, and the amelak grew skittish.

'Whoa, there,' said a short, dark-haired warrior, taking her amelak's bridle. He stroked the beast's neck and made a series of soothing sounds. The mount settled, and he led it to the water for her. Ellen stayed close to him.

'Thank you,' she said as she watched her exhausted mount drink.

'My pleasure. I'm Lann,' he said.

'Ellen.'

'Athrian, eh?' he asked.

'Err … yes,' she said, realising that her accent made this obvious. Why then had Alechul not questioned her story of being from Raynor?

As she returned from the trough, a warrior from the rearguard galloped past her on an errand.

'Good evening, Madam,' he said pleasantly as he passed. Ellen was surprised at the cultured tone and looked up to see it was the Suul Azel. She smiled and nodded to him as he passed, a warm but non-committal encouragement.

She was struck by how fragile the order of the world was. All her life she had dwelt comfortably with the Suul, secure in the knowledge she would always rise above others, always have a place in the citadel of power. Yet what was a Suul without a court? Nothing. A chill ran through her, thinking of the Suul who fled Hianer. Their lives as lords were over unless they were wealthy or well-connected enough to be received into the court of another nation. She had been forced from Athria and had thrown away the chance to enter the court of Raynor by marriage to Uran. What if she became like these refugees? Drifting across the world at the mercy of others? Impoverished? No. *That will never happen to me.*

She led her amelak to the old fort and the wide yard beyond. The wagons had been drawn up and a score of warriors and servants were preparing Alechul's pavilion. Others tethered the harena and led their amelak to graze on the thick grass. The harena were omnivores, but preferred a diet rich in meat. They were being fed a thick gruel and would also feast on the collected scraps from the fires later.

Groups of warriors were gathering to practice with their weapons, some sparring without blades. Others sat cross-legged in meditation, their scythes across their knees. She could see Cedrin and Marken amongst them. She knew these were the devotions of the Way of the Scytheman: a discipline followed by many warriors in the Athrian garrisons. Myan had considered the devotees of the Way as the solid core of his forces, although many Athrian Suulvey mistrusted the cult, since it also advocated individual conscience, and they feared warriors who could potentially disobey orders if it conflicted with their personal values.

'Excuse me, Lady?' Ellen turned to see the thin figure of Raphal. It was good to see a familiar face.

'Hello, worthy Priest of Mythar. A nice evening,' said Ellen neutrally. People were walking past on various errands, and their conversation was drawing no attention.

'I could not help but notice you were travelling alone. Would you like to share a fire?' asked Raphal, his eyes glinting with amusement.

'That would be good,' she said, smiling. *It would be.* She had yet to learn how to set up a tent – Raphal had done that for her since Raynor. Adapting to life without servants was difficult.

'Evening, Father,' said a passing warrior.

'How are you, my son?' said Raphal.

'You no longer travel with the Priestess?' asked the warrior. Ellen tensed. She studied the warrior and recognised him as a slightly-built man who had been on sentry duty the night she had healed the former slave.

'No. She had other duties at a temple in Seyt.'

'Pity. It least we have you, eh? I'll pass the word.'

The warrior looked across at Ellen and nodded politely in greeting. There was no recognition.

'Good evening,' said Ellen.

As the man walked away, she let out a long sigh, rolling her shoulders to relieve the tension. She should hardly be surprised. She had only shown her face once on the whole trip north – and then only to Cedrin and his friends and a handful of refugees.

Ellen and Raphal lit a fire some distance from the centre of camp in the lee of the old fort, then set up their tents. They hobbled their amelak and let them graze nearby. Xyanthius had set up a large central hearth in the main yard, and most of the warriors were setting up their tents around it – although some of the warriors chose to light their own fires on the edges of the guarded perimeter. Ellen noted that Azel had also set up his camp near the fort's wall. He sat alone looking distantly into the flames as his servant prepared a meal. The fearsome and silent Sindar was nowhere to be seen.

'Ho there!'

Ellen turned to see Cedrin and Marken walking towards them. She sat straighter.

'Good evening,' she said, brushing a loose strand of hair away from her face and wishing she had gone to the spring to wash.

'Some strong tea is called for, I think, don't you agree, worthy Druid?' said Raphal to Marken.

Marken grunted and smiled. 'Yes, worthy Druid.'

Raphal had said little about the ceremony at the Temple of Two Moons, only to confirm that Marken had gone through with it. In the firelight, she could see the new tattoo, high on his right shoulder, depicting the two moons of Yos, Asic and Rea. It declared to all that he was sworn to the Essence. It was not unlike those carried by the Temple Guardians and many would simply assume he had once served within the Temple. An honourable mark. Those who knew would see the detail was different, revealing him as an Itinerant Moon Druid, bound by oaths but not by place.

Raphal had told her that many wealthy men and Suul were granted this mark, allowing them to gain knowledge yet escaping the strictures of the Temple. That Marken had been accepted into this order was unusual to say the least. However, there was always a price to pay. The vows were strictly enforced.

'I'll fill the bladders with water,' said Marken.

Raphal stood. 'I will join you.'

The two walked into the night, leaving Cedrin and Ellen alone. He slowly packed a pipe and lit it while Ellen busied herself with the fire.

'The amelak must be more comfortable for you than the wagons,' said Cedrin, drawing on the long-stemmed pipe and exhaling the smoke with a deep sigh of satisfaction.

'Yes. But not near as comfortable as my narsiit ...' She was suddenly conscious of the fact that to own a narsiit was the privilege of the Suul, and only wealthy Suul at that. She braced herself for an uncomfortable silence, but Cedrin took the comment in his stride.

'I dare say they would be the best mounts, if you are fortunate enough to have one. Tarral often told me about his narsiit.' His face darkened. 'When I was much younger.'

'Yes, of course. The Emperor's One Hundred travelled on narsiit,' said Ellen, remembering Tarral as she faced him that morning in Athria. He was a tough and confident man – with a complete lack of awe for her rank as Suul. Not surprising given that he had once served in the Emperor's bodyguard. The warriors of the One Hundred had been men of ultimate skill, drawn from the Suul and the ranks of the army alike, with no concern given to rank or family. Their skill with the greatscythe and their passionate loyalty was all they had in common.

'You knew?' said Cedrin, his eyes narrowed.

'I met Tarral, after the attack on Regent's Hill,' said Ellen. She saw him tense at the mention of the rebellion. *Idiot!* They had never had a chance to talk frankly about the failed civil war in Athria, which had seen them on opposite sides of a bloody conflict. It was far too raw a subject to bring up now.

Cedrin cleared his throat. 'Yes. Well – they are a fine beasts. Tarral once told me he reached Raynor from Seyt in one night. They must truly fly.'

Raphal and Marken appeared out of the night, rapt in some conversation in ancient Cioan. Ellen knew the language intimately, but on the page. She had rarely heard it spoken and she could only pick out snippets, and even those seemed obscure and meaningless. Still arguing, or so it looked, they set the water boiling and began to prepare the meal, hardly noting what they did. Marken laid the filled skins nearby.

'Warm night,' said Ellen.

'Mmmm,' said Cedrin. He took a long draw on his pipe and looked out at the vast canopy of stars.

Ellen fought down a feeling of panic and forced herself to relax, resisting the temptation to fill the silence with chatter. She looked across at Cedrin. He *seemed* relaxed. Perhaps that was what you did on the road, sat in silence, making only occasional comments. At court it would be unthinkable, the dance of conversation was ever-present, like a trap for the unwary. Things will flow more naturally in time, she reassured herself.

The food was welcome. Cedrin said little and Marken and Raphal – though they had ceased their talk during the meal – stayed silent as they ate, obviously still thinking about whatever esoteric lore they had been discussing. As soon as the meal was finished, they fell straight back into Cioan.

The grime of the road was thick on her skin, and after the weariness of the day's riding she did not have the energy for a strained encounter. Ellen seized one of the water skins and disappeared inside her tent to bathe and refresh herself. As she approached the entrance, she was sure she could feel his eyes on her and smiled. Maybe the night was not such a loss after all.

* * *

Cedrin watched her walk away. Suul Ellen Cintros. Nothing brought that fact home clearer than remembering where they both came from. In Athria, he had been on the lowest rung of the tightly-controlled Sardom, living under the feet of the rich, while she had lived in palaces, destined for greatness. They could never be more than two strangers sharing a fire, as if meeting by chance on the same road. In the end, she would return to her world and he would make the best of his life. In the end, they must part forever. Still, he could not help but want her. He would never meet another woman like her as long as he lived. Even now, every woman he met, he compared to her. He knew all this, and had resolved numerous times to keep his distance, and yet ... every time he came near her his heart sang.

A tall warrior ran up to their fire. As he drew closer, Cedrin recognised him as Rastor. The young warrior had healed well, and the bout with Kanis had seen him lose none of his enthusiasm.

'They're telling stories at the main hearth,' said Rastor.

'Thanks. We'll be there,' said Cedrin.

Rastor flashed him a smile and ran on to the next fire.

He would go to the fire with Ellen. He would be polite, but restrained.

A few moments later, Ellen emerged from her tent, still dressed in her riding leathers. She straightened, tilting her back head, and Cedrin's breath caught in his throat. She really was stunning. His eyes dropped to her waist, and he wondered what it would feel like to put his arms around her. She stepped forward, breaking him out of the spell. He bent to tap out the embers of his pipe, then stood up. He slung his greatscythe across his back. Xyanthius had given the warriors instructions to keep their weapons with them at all times.

'They are telling stories by the main hearth,' said Cedrin. 'Do you want come along?'

She smiled, and just for a moment he thought he saw relief there. 'I would be delighted.'

Cedrin's face split into a wide grin. It seemed it had been a long time since he had smiled quite so broadly. It felt good. Just watching her felt good.

'Err … shall we then?' he said.

'Why not?'

'What about you two?' said Cedrin, calling over to Raphal and Marken.

'What's that?' asked Raphal.

'Are you coming to the storytelling?' asked Cedrin.

'You two go … we'll be along shortly,' said Marken. Cedrin doubted it. When Marken told Cedrin he was going to the temple last night to take vows as a Moon Druid, he thought he was joking. He had never seen his golden-skinned friend more serious about anything. Having to watch that dying slave, knowing he could do nothing, had really shaken him.

Cedrin and Ellen left Raphal and Marken to their discussions and walked together to the big fire. The former Brotherhood calvanni and the disguised Suul, enjoying the warmth of the night, and each other's company. Neither dared speak in case the spell was broken. Cedrin glanced at the woman beside him, noting the gleam to her skin, her fairness of face and the way she held herself: so self-possessed, intense.

She looked up at him, her green eyes soft, yet striking. He knew he was staring, but could not help it. He tried to come up with something to say – any inane fragment of conversation – but could think of nothing. He turned away, hoping Ellen did not guess his thoughts. It would seem so natural to take her into his arms, raising her lips to meet his in a kiss, tasting her … but it was never to be. He had to enjoy this for what it was, for as long as it lasted.

He heard bursts of laughter from the main hearth as they approached. There was already quite a crowd, and he searched for a gap in the circle around the hearth. *There.* They pushed through and sat, finding themselves next to the shaven Anacian, Sindar. No wonder there was a gap – people always left room for the grim warrior. The man exuded tension, and a barely suppressed anger. Cedrin nodded to the silent man. Sindar returned the greeting then watched Ellen with a strange intensity for a long moment before turning away. The look unsettled Cedrin, although he could not say why. What history could possibly exist between those two? Ellen *was* a beauty. Perhaps it was merely lust.

Across the circle, he saw the new leader of the rearguard, Kalyth. He was a strange one, dressed in old-fashioned legion armour with mought plates. There was something familiar about him Cedrin had been unable to place. Lann had told him Kanis was furious at being replaced as leader of the rearguard and forced to serve under the old warrior. Even now Kanis was glaring at Kalyth, his eyes dark and murderous as he drew on a skin of wine. Cedrin liked to think the demotion was retribution for Kanis' illegal strike on Rastor in the tournament. Whoever he was, the old warrior was highly placed. He had seen Xyanthius and Kalyth greet each other like brothers at the mustering that morning. Cedrin wondered if he too had been in Emperor Riin's bodyguard. If so, it was odd he did not remove his leather armour and show the honours on his chest. He had worn it all day, come to think of it, even in the heat of Larus noon.

A humorous story was being told by one of the older warriors, and Cedrin and Ellen were soon both laughing with the crowd. Even Sindar smiled at some points, obviously enjoying the distraction from his secret and dark thoughts.

'… and there ends the tale,' said the warrior, sitting down to applause.

Another of the older warriors rose from the circle. He had a scar that ran from his left eyebrow down across the left side of his face to his chin. This made his left eye seemed to squint and gave him a savage appearance.

'Some say we live only in the shadows of what has gone before,' said the old man, turning around with arms spread to the crowd.

Some of the younger warriors snickered. Cedrin looked across to them and saw Rastor jab one of his friends in the ribs to quieten him.

'Once there were great cities, high in the clouds. The Old Races built wonders there. The winged Verial, the Tahistil – the great spiders of the south – and men and Eathal.'

A ripple of uneasy talk spread through the crowd at the mention of the Eathal. Men living and working together with those dirty cavern-dwellers? It was hard to imagine when Hend lay in ashes under their legions. Many of the warriors here had lost uncles and fathers in the first Eathal conflict a generation earlier.

'In the south is the fabled Ciofran-Ac, built by the Jakir – ancient guardians of Yos. Where even today the Seer lives with fearsome beasts at her command.'

'More like swamp-dwellers,' muttered someone, and there was a ripple of laugher.

The old warrior fixed the man with a sharp glare and increased the power of his voice.

'Great temples, the like of which have not been seen in Kelas again. Great domes and bridges, and towers that soared as high as the suns. Mighty works, built with arts that have been lost. This and more, the Jakir wrought.

'Cities built deep under the mountains, lit with the power of magic.' He had the full attention of the crowd now and dropped his voice.

'And from their number, the Old Races would choose the greatest: beings who could mould the very world in their hands. And these were the Jakir, the guardians of Yos. Beyond dispute, beyond question, unparalleled in power, they sought justice in the land.'

The Jakir were said to have been so powerful the barriers between worlds had opened to them. As a child, Cedrin had always loved to hear tales of them. They were heroes who held the very balance of the universe in their hands.

He looked across at Ellen and saw her sitting with her hands on her knees. Her head was tilted up slightly, her eyes glittering as she listened. The mought bracer covering her Suul mark reflected the light of the fire. Cedrin leant in towards her, resting his hand on the ground behind her and just touching her back with his arm. He could smell her delicate perfume. He leant in a fraction closer, his chest now brushing against her shoulder. His heart thumped in his chest. Any moment he expected her to turn to him with a look of wariness, or disapproval, and move away. He turned back to the storyteller, but all his attention was on her.

She looked up at him. He looked back, as innocently as he could. She smiled and leant into him, resting her weight on him. She felt warm and soft. He moved his arm closer, until it circled her back. A wave of desire rose inside him. He knew he should move back, let himself cool off, but he could not. She reached across and laid her hand on his thigh. He looked at her carefully. All her attention was on the storyteller. It was no more than an unconscious gesture.

Cedrin turned back to the storyteller, his head pounding. A Suul lady was in his arms and it felt ... easy. Wonderful. The only problem was he wanted more.

The storyteller was well into the tale of the ancient Jakir Nevris, who battled the dark Priest Moscran and his warriors of the Red Feast. It was a tale Cedrin knew well, and the man told it beautifully. He took a wineskin from the warrior next to him and swallowed a few mouthfuls. He offered it to Ellen, who shook her head. He passed it on to Sindar, who took it without a word.

Moscran held the whole of ancient Tupur in a grip of fear. Using dark blood rites, he had given power and strength to the warriors of the Red Feast while extending his own life. Any who opposed him were taken for the rites, their drained bodies thrown into a fire pit that burned day and night. Inside his Red Temple, ancient Anan-Ac, Moscran was invincible. Many Sorcerers and warriors had tried to destroy him, to end his reign of terror, yet all had failed. Those left in power in Tupur had already taken gifts of extended life from Moscran, and his warriors were under his spell. Then the Jakir Nevris, leading a small group of warriors, broke through into the Red Temple. He defeated Moscran's attacks and dragged him from his inner sanctum. Nevris threw him into the burning charnel pit. Outside the sphere of the Red Temple's power, Moscran could not resist the flames and was burnt alive. The Red Feast was disbanded and the people saved.

The man got an enthusiastic round of applause. Cedrin had always liked the poetic justice of the tale and had once seen a fine painting of Moscran being thrown into the flames by Nevris, the eyes of his burning victims strangely alive as they looked up from the pit to welcome him.

'Then there is the tale of the Fall,' said the storyteller. 'Little known and seldom told. This I got from a Meadrel whose line stretches back to the dawn of time ...'

Cedrin smiled. It was pretty standard for storytellers to wax on about the lineage of their stories. He had heard variations on the Fall of the Jakir many times. Even so, he was happy to hear it again. The man was a fine storyteller, and he did not want to break the contact between himself and Ellen. *Uros!* This was Ellen Cintros! He tensed for a moment. No. He could not think about her like that, not now. She was just ... Ellen. A woman.

'It was the time of the Jakir's greatest pride. They had travelled between worlds and opened up the doors to knowledge unimaginable.'

The man went on to tell of three of the Jakir, driven by ambition and a thirst for power, who fell into temptation, abandoning their vows to protect and serve. Together they banished the other Jakir to a shadow world by trickery and seized power. But they had sown the seeds of their own destruction, and one by one were drawn into the darkness they had created.

'Yet their downfall came too late. By the time the Three passed from the world, the time of the Jakir was over.'

Again the man was given a round of applause and he sat down, beaming at the praise.

The night had grown late, and the circle around the fire began to break up.

Ellen pulled away from Cedrin and stood up, stretching.

'Did you enjoy the stories?' asked Cedrin, rising to his feet.

'Yes. I always enjoy tales of the Jakir. My father … I mean. I have many books of their tales,' said Ellen. A cloud passed across her face.

'It's always good to hear fanciful tales,' said Cedrin, eager to keep the light-hearted feeling between them. 'Great spiders and winged Verial building cities with men and Eathal!' He laughed. 'If only they existed, I would love to visit them.'

'The Jakir did exist. That's history. There is a ruined city on the peak of Asgod-Ki that was built by the Verial. There is strong evidence that it was a major Jakir enclave.'

'Verial city …,' Cedrin exploded into laughter. He had no idea Ellen had such a good sense of humour. Everyone knew the Verial – like the great Tahistill spider-beings – were just the stuff of legend. He suddenly realised she was not laughing and abruptly looked back at her. She was serious … and angry.

'I'm sorry,' said Cedrin. 'I thought you were joking.'

Her eyes flashed hot, and she transformed from a genial travelling companion to a Suul in an instant; her head tilted up, her poise regal. It was like being stabbed in the heart. Even so, he sought to make amends.

'I agree, who is to say what existed in the distant past? Perhaps these Verial did exist. Marken even thinks that real phoenix actually existed,' said Cedrin.

A calm descended on Ellen, her face smoothing into a pleasant smile, the light in her eyes masked. Immediately he sensed the distance between them. He had seen this expression on her face before and now knew it was some sort of shield, the sort no doubt employed by Suul courtiers.

'It was an enjoyable night, but it's late. I will see you tomorrow,' said Ellen.

'Of course. Good night. I look forward to sharing the fire again,' he said, watching her walk away.

'Damn,' he muttered to himself. What had he been thinking? She was from a different world. There was no future for anything but a distant acknowledgment between them.

Those remaining around the fire now gathered into small groups and the old warrior Kalyth started practising greatscythe forms near the fire. Sindar stood alone with his arms crossed, watching Kalyth, and Cedrin walked over to him.

'Do you know anything about him, Sindar?' asked Cedrin.

The tall Anacian roused from his thoughts. He looked at Cedrin, then at the others gathered close by.

'Where is ... your lady friend?' asked Sindar.

'She's turned in. Why do you ask?' said Cedrin.

Sindar ignored the question. 'I know nothing of Kalyth, I'm afraid,' he said turning back to watch the old warrior. 'If Xyanthius has given him control of the rearguard, you can be sure he held significant position in the old Empire. The way he manipulates that greatscythe, I would say he has great familiarity with that class of weapon.'

Cedrin nodded. It was the longest thing he had ever heard Sindar say, and he was struck for a moment at how refined Sindar's speech was. He had very little accent, and what there was he could not place. Cedrin looked sideways at the man and his fearsome tattoos. He would have thought someone like him would be ... coarser. From the hard side of the city.

They both watched the old warrior in silence. Cedrin marvelled at the formal, elegant patterns the man was using. The blades flashed from the haft and disappeared with precise control. The best comparison he could think of was some sort of deadly dance. As Kalyth worked, sweat fell from him. Even so, he did not remove the vest of his heavy leather armour and Cedrin wondered what marks he was hiding. More warriors came to watch him, the crowd forming into a ring of curious onlookers. Lann joined the circle next to Cedrin and Sindar.

'Pretty good, eh?' said Lann.

'I've never seen anything like it,' said Cedrin. 'Have you, Sindar?'

The grim warrior looked at Cedrin, but said nothing.

A wave of excited talk rose amongst them as the warriors discussed his precise technique. Kanis pushed into the ring of watchers, and the conversation dipped immediately. Kanis' small, dark eyes narrowed as he watched Kalyth. Xyanthius also joined them, the warriors giving their captain a respectful distance.

'Technique can be as pretty as you like. The only thing that counts in a fight is being able to fight,' said Kanis, his voice low and dangerous.

The old man worked through two more patterns, then locked his blades away. He turned to acknowledge the crowd for the first time, sweeping his eyes across them. Cedrin felt the man's gaze pause on him for a long moment. The hairs on the back on his neck rose.

'Very impressive, old man, but can you defend yourself?' asked Kanis, sneering.

Kanis broke away from the circle and walked in towards Kalyth, greatscythe in hand. Kanis looked back briefly at Xyanthius, as though checking his reaction, but the mercenary captain merely watched. Although his face was impassive, Cedrin thought he saw a glint of anticipation in Xyanthius' eyes for a moment, but it was gone too quickly to be sure.

'A leader should be an example to his warriors. I know for a fact, *old man*, that I can best every warrior in this camp with a greatscythe.' A bold boast, thought Cedrin, considering Sindar defeated him the tournament. Kanis paused three paces away from Kalyth, trying to stare down the old warrior. Kalyth seemed relaxed as he met his gaze. 'Eh? Nothing to say? Do you know anything else besides those little dances?' Kanis fluttered his hand in the air in a mocking gesture.

They were a match in height but Kanis had twice the muscled bulk of the older man. Still, the old warrior did not seem put out.

'What's this about?' asked Kalyth. 'Xyanthius is in control of this caravan. If you have a problem with the way he runs it, you need to talk to him, boy.'

Cedrin's heart raced. *I know that voice!* His eyes widened as he looked at the man, imagining patched clothes and unkempt hair in the place of the armour and close-cropped hair. *It is the hermit from the tower.* The beard was gone, but it was him.

'My name is Kanis, old man, and I'm not your *boy*,' said the thicket warrior, his chin jutting out aggressively.

'Kanis is trying to provoke him into a match,' said Lann.

Cedrin nodded. Kanis could not attack Kalyth, who was now his superior. But if Kanis could provoke Kalyth into a match and humiliate him ... he stood a chance of convincing Xyanthius to restore his place. It was a dangerous tactic – provoking an unknown warrior – but Kanis would also be driven by the need for revenge.

'I don't wager, but If I did – I would lay funds on the old man,' said Sindar, giving a rare smile.

'Wouldn't bet against you,' said Cedrin, remembering how fast the old hermit had moved that night in the ruined tower.

'Nothing to say, *old man*?' said Kanis.

Kalyth sighed. 'I supposed we may as well get this over with. A round with no blades?'

Kanis' face split into a savage smile, and he looked back once more at Xyanthius, perhaps to make sure he was watching. He stepped forward, approaching the old warrior casually. Then Kanis' greatscythe was swinging through the air, heavy blows falling towards the old man. It seemed the sheer force of the strikes and their suddenness would end him, but Kalyth turned every strike. Then the old warrior deftly side-stepped. His greatscythe jabbed forward in a blur. Kanis collapsed to his knees, wheezing for breath. *A strike to the solar plexus.* He looked up at the older warrior, his face pale with rage. Kanis twisted the haft of his greatscythe and the deadly lanedd blades shot out from both ends of his weapon. He pushed his greatscythe up into a blocking position then planted one foot on the ground, the other leg still in the kneeling position. He was ready to launch into an attack.

Kalyth looked over to Xyanthius, an eyebrow raised in a silent question.

'If he attacks you with blades, Kalyth. You have my permission to kill him,' said Xyanthius.

Dead silence fell on the group. As the words sank in, Kanis' face flushed red. He blinked rapidly as he looked between Kalyth and Xyanthius. Kanis slowly withdrew the blades, rose to his feet and backed away. Then he pushed through the circle and disappeared into the night. Xyanthius watched him leave with savage satisfaction on his face. The mercenary captain nodded once to Kalyth, who returned the gesture, then left. *So there is justice after all.*

The circle exploded into talk, the warriors crowding around Kalyth in congratulations. Kanis was a hard man, often cruel and vindictive, and there was no shortage of warriors who delighted in his comeuppance. Kalyth accepted the compliments with good grace, but soon left the camp.

Cedrin followed him into the darkness. He had to find out what he knew of Belin. Just beyond the circle of light, he found him waiting. Cedrin paused, matching the old warrior's gaze, once more trying to reconcile this armoured veteran with the hermit of Blackthorne.

'It *is* you,' said Cedrin. 'But you have changed. It's like you are a different man.'

'A different man?' Kalyth shook his head. 'I am the same man. Just beardless and in the company of men for the first time since I care to remember.'

'Were you truly Belin's man?'

'I was. I served Belin in many things. Now I serve no-one but myself,' he said, extending his hand. Cedrin reached out, and Kalyth took his arm in a warrior's grip, forearm to forearm. 'I am Kalyth.'

'Cedrin.'

Kalyth turned and walked out into the night, and Cedrin matched pace with him. They passed through a gap in the stone fence where a gate had once stood, then climbed a path behind the fort to the crest of a hill. As they walked, Cedrin's head was swimming with questions. All his life he had cursed Belin, yet he had always dreamed of finding out more about his mysterious father. They sat at the top of the hill, looking out over the sea. Both Asic and Rea were crescent moons, their light glittering on the distant waters. The sea breeze was cool as it swept back into their faces. Cedrin was unsure what to make of Kalyth. It was hard to reconcile the crazy hermit of Blackthorne with this warrior.

'Tell me of my father.' Cedrin's stomach clenched with tension as he waited for the answer.

Kalyth gave him a sharp look. A moment later he seemed relieved, as though perhaps he had expected some other question.

'Belin was my Lord – but we were also friends. I served *him*, not his Suul blood.'

'Did he perish in the Last Days?'

'He was lost, long ago – only days after you were born,' said Kalyth.

Cedrin nodded, his suspicions confirmed. A tremendous weight lifted off him. Then he asked a question that had haunted him for years. 'Kalyth, who was my mother? Was she a Suul, a commoner or … a whore?'

Kalyth sat still for a moment. He laid aside his greatscythe and turned to grip Cedrin by the shoulders, staring right into his face. To Cedrin's surprise, he saw tears glistening in the old warrior's eyes.

'Your mother was a Suul, and a great woman, but she is dead and gone, as is your father and your family. You must not look back. Promise me, Cedrin, you will never look back, only forward.'

Surprised by Kalyth's reaction, Cedrin could only nod. Remembering his visit to the Kaidell estate with Ellen and his paranoid half-cousin Linnas, he decided perhaps it was better to leave the past alone. He still had to know.

'Who was she, Kalyth? At least tell me that. What can it matter now?' said Cedrin.

Cedrin saw the muscles work on Kalyth's jaw. 'Lad … I can never tell you. I know that's hard, and it's not what you want, but no good will ever come of knowing it. Believe me when I tell you that. Look forward. Only forward.' Kalyth released him.

Cedrin struggled with his disappointment, but looking into Kalyth's determined face, he knew there would be no shifting him on the issue: at least for now.

'These long years have been ... a torment, for me,' said Kalyth, looking out over the sea. 'But that's over now. The Suul have no hold over me anymore.' The old man struggled for words.

'I loved Belin. Like a brother. And I feel some debt to him ... and to you,' said Kalyth. 'I saw you watching me before. Would you like to learn those greatscythe patterns? Would you like me to train you as Belin once trained me?'

Cedrin leant forward, excited by the prospect of learning those beautiful movements and having the skill to defeat Kanis as easily as Kalyth had.

'Yes. I would be honoured,' said Cedrin.

Kalyth's eyes narrowed, his face creasing into a tight smile. 'And would you be willing to follow my instructions without question. To do as I bid?'

Cedrin considered it. 'Yes ... as far as the training goes.'

Kalyth nodded. 'Done then.' The old warrior picked up his greatscythe, taking in a deep lungful of the sea air. 'Yes. A fine night. A fine night for a run ... I think the two crescents should give us enough light. No point in delaying what can be started in the moment. Do you run?' said Kalyth, turning towards him.

'Err ... when I have to,' said Cedrin, conscious of his weary limbs.

'There is nothing better to build up stamina in a warrior,' said the old warrior.

Kalyth sprang up, surging into motion. Within a heartbeat, he was loping over the hill track, jumping moonlit hollows as easily as a narsiit.

'Come on!' yelled Kalyth.

Cedrin grabbed his greatscythe and set off after the old warrior. He could only just make him out in the darkness. Cedrin pushed harder, gaining slightly. Soon his lungs were burning, the heavy tar taste of tobacco rising in a sickening wave. Cedrin's breath was coming in ragged gasps now, and his head throbbed from the after-effects of the wine. Far ahead, he heard Kalyth's laughter. Maybe the old man was crazy after all.

***

Ellen woke with a start. She looked around the dark confines of the tent and wondered why she was not in her rooms in the Cintros mansion. Out of instinct. she reached for her scythe. Then she remembered the road to Searn, the caravan – and her stiff overreaction to Cedrin's unmeaning jibe, which sat like a heavy weight on her heart.

'Ellen, I have it!'

'Who is it?' she asked fearfully, her heart beating fast.

'It's Raphal. It's taken me all day, but I finally remembered who he is!' He was standing just outside the entrance to her tent, his voice muffled by the fabric.

'Raphal ... What are you talking about?'

'He's Belin's lieutenant!'

Ellen could hear the excitement in Raphal's voice. With a groan, she struggled out of the tent, the thin white silk of her nightdress falling loosely around her naked body. Outside, the fire was low and Marken lay asleep by its dying embers. Cedrin was nowhere to be seen. Puzzled, she looked at the stars. It was late.

The closeness she had felt at fire had been like water to a woman dying of thirst. She could not forget how she leant against Cedrin as she grew weary, delighting in the feel of his rough shirt and the hard muscles beneath it.

She beckoned Raphal over to the fire, stepping close to the embers to warm her legs. 'Start from the beginning. Who is Belin's lieutenant?' she asked, keeping her voice low.

The scholar grinned. He had obviously been thinking about this for hours.

'The man who joined the caravan in Seyt, the one Xyanthius put in charge of the rearguard. I knew his face, but could not place his name or remember how I knew him. I have been puzzling over it all day – tonight it finally came to me. He is

Kalyth, Belin's lieutenant! I thought him dead, as did many others. After the Last Days, Myan looked for him but he had vanished. Now, out of nowhere, here he is!' He took Ellen's hands, barely able to barely suppress his excitement. 'If anyone knows the identity of the true Scion, it is this man.'

The last webs of sleep blew from Ellen's mind. *Kalyth!* The man who brought Cedrin to Tarral as a babe. All this time he had been languishing in some backwater while others struggled to keep the Empire's shattered fragments together. One word from this man could have ended a lifetime of searching. Myan, Leith and Daran could have rebuilt the Empire for the Scion, and Cedrin could have claimed his birthright and been raised as a Suul. *Damn, him.* There was only one word for his actions: betrayal.

Sensing Ellen's anger rise at the news, Raphal's excitement faded. 'You don't think he will help us?'

Ellen let out a long breath. 'I think if he wanted to help, he would have done so long ago.'

'You must question him though.'

'I will,' said Ellen. 'You can count on it.'

Chapter Nineteen

Raziin woke from a deep dream, roused by inhuman screaming. It was his glowmetal pendant, transforming the energies of yet another of Hukum's Compulsions into meaningless sound. He felt the dark will of his master surround him like a suffocating blanket. Still his former master sought to subdue him. He smiled. Such attacks would come to nothing while the Seer's pendant hung from his neck.

'Too late, Hukum,' he said.

The crescent moons were high in the sky. Behind Raziin, the dark shape of the Crusox loomed like a titan. They had ridden hard from the Shattered Temple, using little known paths to skirt the main Eathal emplacements. He and his men had ambushed two small patrols, killing them swiftly. So far they had avoided the main armies of the Eathal. The legions had pushed further ahead into Tupur, leaving only minimal forces behind them to support the supply lines. When they approached the rearguards of the advancing Eathal legions, they would face their toughest challenge. They would need to pass through their lines to get to Olcis.

Raziin sensed the energies of the Compulsion as it sought purchase in his mind. It was the final act, which would have seen him kneel and accept his death. Anger flared inside him, as well as the fierce satisfaction of knowing he had defeated the Compulsion and killed Staraz. Perhaps now was the time to tell Hukum? To even the score? He knew he should wait until they were safely out of Tupur, but the temptation was too great. For years he had hated Hukum and the service he forced on him.

Now, at last, he was free of it. Free to reclaim his own destiny.

Raziin rose from his place near the fire and walked between his sleeping warriors and out in the night. The sentries nodded to him in deference as he passed. Some distance from the camp he knelt, opening his mind to the Bridge, seeking Hukum.

'Master,' he called out with his mind. 'Master, if you seek me I am here.'

At once he sensed Hukum's presence, as though the Eathal Sorcerer was standing next to him. He could feel his hot anger. Raziin laughed.

'You have failed to snare me, Hukum. You are weak,' sent Raziin across the Bridge.

There was a surge of energy towards him. Hukum was attacking with the Final Matrix, trying to crush him, punish, as he had before. Raziin blocked it with the Barrier. Then Raziin formed the Final Matrix himself, thrusting back into Hukum's mind with a focussed attack. For a moment he had a glimpse of a deep cavern, filled with glowmetals. He felt surprise, then anger, before Hukum's own Barrier slid into place.

A warmth filled him. At last he had measured Hukum's strength on equal terms. The Eathal had no greater power in this contest than he. Raziin laughed again. 'Great Sundar of the Eathal, you are nothing before me,' taunted Raziin.

I don't know what foolish half-Blood gave you the Final Matrix, but you are a dead man, Raziin. A walking corpse. You shall fall to me. Death awaits you at the Shattered Temple.

'I have been to the Shattered Temple and returned. Look to your son, *master*, for I have taken his head.' Raziin's heart beat faster as he felt Hukum's doubt and frustration turn to fear.

'Yes, I have slain him. You will be next. Live in fear, Hukum. The Spear of Carris is about to be raised again – in my hands. You will be the first to die.'

Impossible. Empty threats.

'You are the one who is empty, Eathal. Empty of power.'

Raziin withdrew from the Bridge. His attack with the Final Matrix had given him a taste of what was possible, and a sense for how he was limited by distance. Once the Spear of Carris was his, he could destroy Hukum's mind from the other side of

Yos. For now he was content. He knew Hukum would reach for his son's mind and find only silence. It was good. Very good.

'Free!' he shouted to the night.

His warriors came running, alert and ready to face an attack. The glowmetal shrieked around his neck as Hukum tried once more to snare him with a Compulsion, and it ripped the carefully wrought Sorcery to shreds.

The Seer had served him well indeed, the fool. When he held the Spear, he would return to destroy her as well.

* * *

Hukum crushed the message capsule in his clawed hands, his fist shaking with anger and grief. *Staraz and his whole command, slain and destroyed.* His son, his firstborn – the strongest and most powerful of his children – dead at the hands of a *human*.

'Ahhhh!' he screamed in muted pain and rage.

Around him servants backed away. The messenger stood uncertainly before the Sundar, his slitted green eyes widened in fear.

Hukum cast the message away as though it had burnt his hand and stood in shock, his powerful muscles tensed in impotent rage. He seized the messenger, lifting him off the polished marble of his apartment floor.

'Find my son and bring him to me.' His voice was low and thunderous.

The messenger, a young thal, trembled in his Lord's grip, fearing death. 'L ... Lord Staraz ... my Lord?'

Hukum howled and threw the messenger across the room. He hit the wall with a *thwak* and fell winded to the floor. The Eathal bone structure was solid, and although stunned and bruised from the force of the impact, he was otherwise unhurt.

'I have but one son,' shrieked Hukum, his body trembling as he sought to get control of his rage. 'And his name is, Faivel.'

Faivel. He ground his teeth. The name was like a curse on his lips. 'Why, Kallor? Why did you take my son when I have worshipped you faithfully? Why grant me the Vengeance only to take away my true Blood?'

Hukum's servants had retreated to the walls, their gazes fixed to the floor as he began to pace. Not a flicker of emotion showed on the faces of his bodyguard.

Somehow Raziin had defeated the second phase of the Compulsion. He cursed loudly, but nothing could ease the pain he felt. He had to face the truth. Raziin, the human tool he had trained himself, was now out of his control. From some unknown source, he had gained knowledge of the most powerful of the Matrices – the Final Matrix – enabling him to focus a mental attack across the Bridge. He also had some other tool or magic that defeated Hukum's Compulsions. There was only one way now to end this … terrible mistake. A Sorcerer must meet him in the field, destroying him and his band of mercenaries once and for all.

Humans. They had killed his beloved Staraz.

'Damn them all.' He could wait no longer. He would issue orders for the Tupur attack to begin. Yes! He would not rest until he saw all the cities of men in flames. Olcis, the city of mirrors, would be shattered; Raynor brought low, then the other cities would fall one by one. The Vengeance would burn bright as it consumed Kelas in cleansing fire. Perhaps then the pain of loss would ease.

The broad doors creaked open, and Faivel entered, led by one of Hukum's servants. Gone were the scholar's robes. Faivel was dressed like a warrior in a finely-tailored outfit of *jakka* hide. The habitual stoop was gone, and he carried himself erect. Hukum was surprised to note the boy was slightly taller than he was. His thin frame had filled out, showing the beginnings of lean muscle. An angry scar on his chin showed where a blade had sliced at him in one of his training sessions with the bodyguard. Yes – a definite improvement. Still, the boy was a pale shadow of his brother. Faivel's eyes, detached and wary, showed none of Staraz's fire. Hukum grunted as another wave of grief washed through him. It seemed impossible that Staraz was gone.

The messenger had – wisely – decided not to return.

* * *

Faivel met his father's gaze, keeping his face neutral. He had been dragged from an exhausted sleep, his shoulders and arms aching from the gruelling weapons training. That was not the worst of it. The long hours had kept him away from his precious books. For this, more than anything else, he cursed his father. What was it to be now? More punishment thinly disguised as training? All because he did not share his brother Staraz's love of combat and slaughter?

For a long moment Hukum stared at him. Faivel saw the usual disgust there, but now there was something else in his eyes; a savage light he had never seen before. He noted the crumpled message capsule on the floor and tensed.

'Staraz is dead. Killed by Raziin,' said Hukum.

Faivel took a step back, holding onto the frame of the door for support. He had never gotten on with his brother, but blood was blood. His thoughts flew immediately to his mother. She would be heartbroken.

'You are now the only son who remains,' said Hukum. 'And there is one thing I know in my heart. I would rather our House perish than this murder go unanswered. Blood must avenge blood. You are to seek out that human scum Raziin and fight him – Sorcerer against Sorcerer. I know I have never had time to complete your training, but you have the Barrier Matrix and a good command of the Fire, and that should be enough. All you need do is resist him long enough to cut him down.' Hukum looked him up and down then snorted in disgust. 'Even your failure will be more of a comfort to me than your indolent and wasted life.'

Out of long practice, Faivel ignored the insults. 'But … how am I to find him?'

'Staraz was killed at the Shattered Temple. Raziin and his men will be close by. I will give you the best trackers, the fastest mounts. You will easily catch him before he can leave Tupur. If you succeed, I will complete your training and you will take Staraz's place in the Circle.'

'Such an honour,' said Faivel. His mind worked rapidly, trying to tease out the problem. Why this need for direct action?

'But ... why not destroy Raziin across the Bridge?'

Hukum's lips drew back in a snarl. Faivel had never seen him so enraged. 'He has the Final Matrix.'

'How?' asked Faivel.

'Enough whining, you snivelling coward! Get out of my sight! Do not return to Maht without Raziin's head.'

Faivel bowed and backed out through the doors. He always disappointed his father. Faivel had been resigned to his father's contempt and happy with his life. Then had come that summons to Hukum's chambers and the beginnings of his torment. He thought this would be a passing phase. He would perhaps be stationed in some outpost as a governor for his father, and would be once more free to follow his scholarly ways. But now this: he was to meet Raziin in the field to avenge his brother's death. The tunnels took on an unreal quality as he made his way back to his chambers. It was as though he had stepped into someone else's life. Who would have guessed that Staraz would be the one to fall, and he would be the one sent to avenge him?

Faivel's early life had been a misery, always in the shadow of his brother. Never as strong, never possessing the savagery and lack of introspection that made a warrior. Then had come a miracle when Venan, a cousin to his mother, had given him a book. Knowledge and its pursuit had consumed him. It was when he refused to forsake his studies for the spear and axe that Hukum had disowned him. If Hukum were to learn that Faivel now secretly worshipped gentle Lidu, like his mother ... his father would kill him.

As he walked through the dark tunnels, deserted this late into the sleep cycle, he struggled with his fear. The traitor Raziin had been fearsome enough – yet now someone had given him new weapons. What else did he now possess? There were too many unknowns, and Hukum was acting too much out of his need for revenge. *Lidu give me strength.* Faivel's jaw set with determination. He had grown in wisdom and knowledge and his own supporters had increased in number. Even so, they were still in the minority. Hukum could slay him at will and go unchallenged. He had no choice but to walk in the world of men and light, on this foolish quest for death.

He was not without his own weapons.

As with all adept Junta, Faivel had been trained in the basic Matrices from an early age by the Firemasters. The training of most Junta ended at this point and would only go further if they were chosen to form the Bridge with a Master. In the Sundar's family, that honour had gone to Staraz.

Hukum imagined Faivel as untrained, but he had underestimated his son's desire for knowledge. Long ago, Faivel had secretly convinced Venan to train him and he was now the equal of any Master, including Hukum. He knew of the secret glowmetal Hukum used to construct his Compulsions. He had discovered a reference to it by chance during one his researches into the properties of the Maht glowmetals. He would never allow Hukum to Bridge to his mind. Never. Even so, a place in the Circle had been beyond his dreams and promised power and influence he could use. *That* would be a worthy prize.

* * *

Cedrin winced as he swept his greatscythe down. For three nights now they had been training, and he had practiced this one simple movement for hours while Kalyth watched him critically. Left side, right side; left side, right side, until his muscles quivered with strain. Not once had Kalyth even asked him to extend the weapon's blades. He raised the greatscythe above his head, then down again. They had picked a spot just inside the ring of sentries and lit their own fire to give them enough light for training. Cedrin's camp, where he, Ellen, Marken and Raphal had pitched tents, was hardly visible through the darkness. Alechul's pavilion dominated the centre of the encampment, lit from within by oil-lamps. This was surrounded by the circled wagons, then the warriors' fires.

'You still have too much tension in the shoulders, it's cutting your speed,' said Kalyth. 'Let the greatscythe's weight become part of you. An extension of your will.'

Cedrin tried to relax, but lost his grip in the middle of the swing.

'No. No! Your hand position is all wrong.'

Cedrin lowered the greatscythe, his breath ragged.

'What? Why have you stopped? The moons are not even above the horizon,' said Kalyth.

'When are we going to start some real training?' asked Cedrin.

Kalyth's face hardened. 'Three nights and you've had enough. And tell me – what exactly is real training?'

'Sparring. Getting a feel for the ebb and flow of conflict.'

Kalyth's mouth stretched into a grim line. 'You think you're ready?'

Cedrin straightened, putting himself into a blocking position.

'Very well,' said Kalyth. The old warrior took his right hand off his greatscythe, holding the weapon one-handed. 'Well, *master*. Attack when ready.'

Cedrin shuffled his feet, then feinted in, trying to get Kalyth off guard. The old warrior ignored the attack, and stepped forward, jabbing him in the forehead with the end of his greatscythe. Cedrin growled in frustration and swung at Kalyth's head with all his power. Kalyth swayed back, sweeping his greatscythe above his head and down in a swift arc that took out Cedrin's leading foot. Off balance, Cedrin thudded into the ground, his greatscythe flying out of his hands as reached back to break his fall. He lay stunned for a moment, partly winded. Kalyth stepped forward and put his boot-heel on his throat. Cedrin reached up to pull off the foot, but Kalyth smacked his hand away with his greatscythe – which he still held one-handed.

'Ready for more, *master*?' asked Kalyth.

Cedrin choked with the pressure against his windpipe. He shook his head, holding his hands out in surrender. Kalyth's attack had been so fast and focussed, his movements economical and deadly. Cedrin's blow must have missed him by a hair's breadth, yet Kalyth had known exactly how far to move.

Kalyth let him up, eyeing him carefully as Cedrin retrieved his weapon.

'The Way of the Scytheman is more than just the perfection of martial skills, Cedrin. You must also learn to empty yourself of emotion. As soon as you lashed out at me you stopped thinking,' said Kalyth. 'Have you been practising the meditation?'

'No,' croaked Cedrin. 'Haven't really seen the need for it.'

'Well, you should start – at least until you learn the patterns. Your mind must be focussed. Clear.'

'But how can I ever improve if I waste my time sitting around with my eyes closed?' said Cedrin.

Kalyth's eyes narrowed. 'I know you are determined to learn, Cedrin, and that's good. You need that level of commitment. But what's driving that, under the surface, can be insecurity – a feeling of weakness. All will come in time. You must practise the meditation.'

'I will – if I can find the time.' Cedrin was still stung from the defeat and defiant despite himself. He knew Kalyth was right. He had learnt the importance of mental focus in calv combat long ago. Something about the greatscythe broke his cool. It was not just the difficulty of the weapon – he felt the stakes were much higher now. The pressure to master the weapon, to live up to Belin's memory, hovered over him constantly.

'Remember our agreement, lad. You are to do what I ask without question. In return I give you the sort of training that not one of these idiots could dream of,' said Kalyth, waving his greatscythe at the other unseen warriors in the camp.

'Aye,' said Cedrin, rubbing his throat.

Kalyth gripped his shoulder. 'Patience, lad. The greatscythe is an unforgiving weapon, with no margin for error. Your technique must be faultless, your timing excellent. Your mind razor-sharp.'

A woman's scream cut through the night. Immediately his thoughts flew to Ellen. Cedrin turned and ran. He wove through the tents towards his camp. Kalyth ran at his side, the old warrior's gaze keen as he searched the night.

Cedrin heard a man's angry yell, cut off abruptly. Then the howl of another man in pain.

Their small camp slowly resolved out of the darkness. The side of Ellen's tent was shredded – cut neatly with something sharp-edged. Marken was battling a dark-clad man, scythe to scythe. Raphal was sitting on the ground by the fire, holding his head. Cedrin saw Ellen with her scythe, holding two men at bay. As he drew closer, he saw one man lying prostrate across the shredded ruins of Ellen's tent. Another man was trying to crawl away, his side dark with blood, dragging himself forward with one hand.

One of the two men attacking Ellen cut in. She blocked and sent a cut back at his head that he narrowly escaped. The other darted in to take advantage of her lowered guard, but Ellen was too quick, blocking his attack with a lightning fast movement and forcing him to leap back as she riposted.

'Gods in heaven,' said Cedrin. She was incredible. Each of the attackers was highly skilled, but Ellen fought like a master; cool, balanced and intuitive.

They attacked again, this time together. She blocked both of their scythes, her movements too fast to see. One of the men cried out as her blade sliced the skin beneath his chin, missing his throat by a thumb's breadth. The two attackers fell back. One circled to her left, the other to her right. They were used to fighting as a team and were trying to split her defence. The thought of her being injured or killed tore at him. He had been so enthralled by her skill, he had forgotten she was in real danger. He extended the blades of his greatscythe with a snap.

'Cedrin. No,' said Kalyth. 'They are too skilled for you.'

Cedrin fixed his gaze on the closest of her two assailants and rushed forward.

'No, my lor—' yelled Kalyth running after him. The old warrior took point ahead of him, shielding him from danger. Cedrin growled in frustration.

Ellen shifted her grip. Her right hand swept out and the attacker on her left gasped as a knife shot into his throat. The man dropped his scythe, reaching up to pull the knife free. He sank to his knees, his tunic darkening with blood. The other attacker turned to run, but Ellen was faster. Her scythe swept down, cutting through the back of both calf muscles. The man howled, falling face-forward to the dirt.

Cedrin stopped, unsure who to help. He turned back to Marken. He saw his friend step in to block an attack with the haft of his scythe, the blade pointed down. He then reversed his weapon, the blade cutting up into the man's chest to sever the heart. The man stiffened, then fell soundlessly.

Ellen closed on her opponent.

'Don't kill him. Xyanthius will want him questioned,' said Kalyth.

Other warriors arrived. Marken knelt to examine Raphal, while the newcomers checked the fallen attackers. The wounded man, who had been trying to crawl away, had stopped moving.

A breeze swept through the camp. Ellen's loose gown fluttered around her. Only then did Cedrin realise she was dressed in a nightshirt. The man at her feet had released his hold on his weapon and was lying motionless. As she bent forward, he suddenly flipped over. The man's face was horribly disfigured with long parallel scars that looked like burns. He raised one arm, his fist held straight out in front of him. Then he opened his palm, blowing a cloud of dust straight up into Ellen's face.

'Ahhh!' called Ellen in pain, her free hand going to her eyes as she staggered back. *She was blinded.*

The man reached into his tunic and pulled out a blowpipe, swiftly bringing it to his lips. Poison! Cedrin watched helpless as he raised the weapon.

'*Ellen!*' He was already in motion, but he would not reach her in time.

He felt something flowing nearby, like a dam released. He could almost taste it on the back of his tongue.

The dart shot out of the pipe – straight for her heart. It struck an unseen barrier a little more than one pace from her and dropped to the ground.

Cedrin attacked, one of his greatscythe blades cutting the pipe in two. The man reached for his sleeve. Kalyth jumped in front of Cedrin, his weapon flashing down. His first blade sliced at the man's hand, his second stabbed in to take him low in the chest. It was over in a heartbeat. A small throwing knife tumbled to the earth from the attacker's bloody hand. Kalyth kicked the weapon away and pushed Cedrin back with his arm.

Ellen had recovered, and although she blinked back tears, her vision had cleared enough to focus on the attacker. She stepped forward and rested the point of her scythe blade on the man's throat, her expression grim.

'Let me live,' gasped the man. His accent was Athrian. He coughed, and blood darkened his lips.

The other warriors formed a ring around the fallen man. Kalyth's arm jerked away from Cedrin, as though he did not want to be seen protecting him. Nothing showed on his face though. The old warrior's eyes were as hard as stone.

'We need to secure the camp,' said Kalyth. 'These men may be part of a larger force. Ahhh … Cedrin, you stay here and watch this one. You others – with me,' commanded Kalyth. The old warrior ran off into the night, followed by the other men. Cedrin watched him go, thinking how odd the old warrior's behaviour had been during the attack. He had not let Cedrin engage any of them. What was it he had called out just after he moved in to help Ellen?

'Let me live,' said the fallen attacker again. There was little chance of keeping the man alive even if they wanted to, thought Cedrin.

Cedrin twisted the mechanism of his greatscythe, withdrawing the twin blades. The weariness in his muscles had vanished.

'Let me live. *Please.* I had no choice,' pleaded the man. The point of Ellen's scythe did not waver.

'I saw you following me in Seyt. Who sent you?' demanded Ellen.

The attacker swallowed, his eyes rolling in fear.

Marken walked up to them.

'The other attackers?' asked Cedrin.

'All dead,' said Marken.

So this man was their only possible source of information.

'Who!' demanded Ellen.

'The Athrian Temple,' said the man.

'What did they tell you?' asked Ellen.

'We were told to watch for a rich woman matching your description – that you might be travelling with a Priest.'

'And?'

'After we reported to the senior agent in Seyt, we were sent after you. He told us to take you at night. To … attack … when you slept.'

'To kill me. To *kill* me while I slept.'

The man's face glistened with sweat. 'Yes,' he said, his voice harsh.

'You said you had no choice,' said Cedrin. 'What did you mean?'

'My wife and children are in the debtor's prison. I was a trader – I supplied the Athrian Temple in spices and delicacies. I … cheated them … and they took everything. They tortured me.' The man shuddered. 'If I don't pay the debtor's fee … my family will die in that stinking hole. If I did this, they promised to wipe the debt and secure their release. We would have all been free of the cursed Temple.' The man's eyes flashed with hate and fury. His breathing was growing more laboured.

'I don't believe you. The Temple would send Druids,' said Ellen.

The man sank back, trying to escape the reach of Ellen's weapon. 'No. The Athrian Temple has …' he winced in pain, '…few agents outside of Raynor and Athria. None further north than Seyt.'

'You are one of the Warlord's agents. Admit it!' said Ellen.

'No. I am no Warlord's man. They were told to let Xyanthius' caravan pass.'

'To let it pass?' asked Marken.

'Yes. The word was out to all the guards in Seyt and the Warlord's spies. No one was to look too closely at Xyanthius' caravan. They were under orders to let it pass – no delays – no inspections for contraband.'

The man trembled with pain.

Ellen lifted her weapon, and Marken knelt at his side. He closed his eyes and began a soft chant. The man's face showed relief, and his breathing became easier.

'Why should we believe you? Why should we let you live?' asked Ellen.

The man looked from Cedrin to Ellen. 'Let me live and I will tell them I killed you.'

'It won't work,' said Cedrin. 'The Temple will have him

Tested.'

'Please. Don't kill me. Without me, my family will die in that diseased pit.'

Cedrin flicked the Kaidell signet ring with his thumb, turning it on his finger. He stepped back behind the man, away from his line of sight and sought out Marken's gaze. When Marken looked up, he jerked his head towards the attacker in a silent question. Marken looked up at the sky, then with a grim line to his mouth, shook his head. There was no question. The man was dying. Ellen had seen the exchange and understood.

'We won't kill you,' said Ellen, her face softening. 'Lay back and rest.'

The man's face was deathly pale now. 'Thankyou ... thank ...'

Marken laid him back onto the ground and the dying man's eyes fluttered. Marken stopped his healing chant and took away his hands. Immediately the man jerked in pain. He gasped once, then lay still.

Across the camp, Cedrin could see a group of warriors approaching, led by Xyanthius and Kalyth. The old warrior had finished securing the perimeter.

'What's happened here?' asked Xyanthius as he reached them.

'Thieves,' replied Cedrin. 'A bad night for them. This man's four friends lie dead back at our camp and he has just joined them.'

'My men tell me they were a little more skilled than typical thieves,' said Xyanthius, his eyes narrowing. 'No matter. It seems they were alone. There is nothing to be done now but to bury them. At least none of our own were harmed,' said Xyanthius. 'Let's hope that's all the excitement we have for one night.'

Xyanthius nodded stiffly to Ellen, then led the warriors away.

'I'll send some men to help deal with the bodies,' said Kalyth, as he turned to follow Xyanthius.

'Are you all right?' asked Cedrin, looking over at Ellen.

'Err ... yes. Thank you,' she said.

Marken looked to the east. Cedrin followed his gaze and saw

that Asic's crescent was rising.

'I need to attend Raphal. I'll see you back at camp,' said Marken, walking back towards their fire.

Ellen shivered, trembling with cold. She hugged herself with her free arm. 'I need to get some clothes on.'

'It's a reaction from the combat,' said Cedrin. Without thinking, he stepped in and circled his arm around her shoulders, drawing her in. Ellen resisted for a moment, then leant in. She felt small and slim as she shivered against his chest. The woman was an enigma. He remembered how fast she had moved with her scythe and how she had taken out one of the attackers with a deadly-accurate knife throw. And the dart – he had not stopped to consider it in the heat of the moment – but it had stopped in mid-air. Sorcery?

'The Warlord is not just after Raphal, is he?' asked Cedrin.

Ellen looked up at him, her eyes glittering in the moonlight.

'No. He seeks me also – for rescuing Raphal.'

'Then why this order to leave Xyanthius' caravan untouched? Wouldn't the Warlord want every caravan searched?' asked Cedrin.

'I don't know. Perhaps Kranor paid for the privilege, as a way of protecting Alechul's wealth. Xyanthius might know,' said Ellen. Her trembling eased as a warmth grew between them.

'Hmmm. Probably best not to ask too many questions,' said Cedrin.

Ellen's nightshirt had slipped off one shoulder, revealing the curve of her left breast. Her skin glowed in the moonlight. She put her palm on his chest, covering one of his Brotherhood tattoos. 'I saw you step in with your greatscythe. Thank you,' she said.

A cool wind whipped her nightdress around her. This close he could see the tiny hairs standing up on the skin of neck. Her nipples, hard from the cold, pressed through the thin material.

Cedrin swallowed. 'I was not about to let them harm you.' She was so beautiful. He longed to crush her against him.

She smiled, and her hand lingered for a moment longer on his skin. 'I better get dressed before Kalyth's men arrive,' she said, breaking away from him.

'Of course,' said Cedrin.

He followed her back to camp, a sense of unreality closing in around him. What had Kalyth been doing, defending him like that? He had talked about his debt to Belin, but his actions seemed beyond this. And what exactly had he sensed just before the dart shot towards Ellen? Was that what Sorcery felt like from a distance? All his impressions were coloured by his desire for Ellen, and the lingering warmth of her, still fading from the skin of his chest. It was all supposed to be so straightforward. A new life on the road as a scytheman, the future open before him. Now ... now it was anything but simple.

Chapter Twenty

Ellen had been unable to confront Kalyth. The warrior was always surrounded by men or in the company of Cedrin. His eagerness to teach Cedrin the greatscythe and the former calvanni's sudden loyalty to him was puzzling. She felt the gap between her and Cedrin widening inexorably, all the while conscious that their time on the road together was slipping by. Frustrated, she realised she was no closer to winning him as an ally to the cause of the Scion than when they started out from Seyt. Every time they seemed to develop a level of rapport, he would pull back. She sensed it was her Suul rank that created the distance, but had no way to change it. That was why she had been so eager for him to become a Suulqua. That door was closed.

She looked up to the front of the slow-moving caravan, where Kalyth rode with Cedrin and Marken. In a further show of confidence, Xyanthius had moved Kalyth to command of the vanguard, putting him in charge of overall defence of the caravan. Cedrin and Marken had also been moved from the rearguard to the vanguard – no doubt at Kalyth's request. After the night attack, Kalyth had ordered all the warriors into full armour. They sweated under the suns, cursing the heat.

Command of the rearguard had been given to the Suul Azel, in deference to his rank and experience in leading men in Hianer. Kanis, as Azel's chief lieutenant, rode beside the Suul in sullen silence. Azel saw her watching him and waved. She responded with a polite smile and turned away. He made no secret of the fact he was courting her and often halted his amelak near her to converse, passing by on whatever pretext he devised. He was not a man who excited Ellen's interest, but he was polite and knew the ways of the Suul. She found him good company on the long nights when Marken and Raphal were secreted together away from the fire; and Kalyth and Cedrin were practising greatscythe drills. Wearied by travel, Ellen could hardly wait until the small city of Ceta rose on the horizon and with it, all that civilisation brought: clean clothes, clean skin and privacy.

As the suns dropped to the horizon, Xyanthius gave the command to halt. The wagons were drawn up on a small hillock by the road. Ellen dismounted with relief. The familiar sounds of camp surrounded her as she watered her amelak. Thinking to catch a few moments alone with Cedrin, she quickly chose a spot and built a fire. She sat alone, enjoying the warmth while she waited for the others to arrive. Dark fell swiftly, and still the others had not appeared.

A tall man appeared at the edge of camp and she smiled, thinking it was Cedrin. But as the shape grew more distinct in the glow of the fire, she saw it was Kalyth, his greatscythe strapped across his back.

'Good evening, lady,' he said, bending to warm his hands by the fire.

'Good evening,' she replied stiffly.

'Is Cedrin here?' he asked.

'No,' she said, her voice hard. The old warrior raised his eyebrows and watched her for a long moment. His eyes moved to the mought bracer on her head.

'I don't believe we have met,' he said.

'No. I am Ellen ... Caso. My father is a merchant,' she said.

He nodded, clearly unconvinced. 'I am Kalyth.' Ellen could sense his alertness, an intensity that could leap in an instant to lethal action. It frightened her. A fact that only served to increase her anger.

'I know who you are, Kalyth Orin,' said Ellen, using his full name.

Kalyth squatted back on his haunches and regarded Ellen thoughtfully. 'So you do.'

'You served Belin Kaidell at Blackthorne,' she said.

Kalyth's face remained impassive, his dark blue eyes like mirrors, showing nothing. 'I did serve Belin – although I would have thought that before your time.'

Ellen was no stranger to word games. 'So you would be in a better position than anyone to tell me if Belin was alive.'

For a long time Kalyth's face did not change. Slowly the man rose, meeting Ellen's gaze with the cool analysis of the weaponmaster.

'Who are you, Ellen *Caso?*' His eyes flickered to the headband. 'A *Suul.* Of course.'

Ellen surged to her feet, standing tall. This man had betrayed her father, betrayed the Suul he served. She ripped off the mought bracer, revealing the brightly-inked Suul mark beneath.

'Yes, I am a Suul,' she said, her voice low. 'I am Ellen Cintros, daughter of Myan.'

Kalyth's jaw dropped, and he took a step back. 'Myan's daughter …' His face paled.

'Yes. Myan. Belin's cousin and friend. Riin's confidant and councillor. The Sorcerer whose Fire turned the tides of war in the last Eathal conflict. The same man you deserted, traitor!'

Ellen tried to get a grip on her emotions, but they were surging out of control.

Kalyth swiftly regained his composure. His gaze narrowed. 'So you have come to sway Belin's son to the Suul's ways,' he said, watching for Ellen's reaction.

'Yes. Yes I have come. To help give Cedrin the future his blood demands,' she snapped.

Kalyth's lips curled, his confidence returning. 'You Suul are all the same. Power and manipulation – it is all you know.'

Myan had worked for the good of Kelas. She needed no more proof than the war and division that had arisen in the Empire's wake to know its fall had been an evil thing. Civilisation and order – she believed in those as her father did before her. Kalyth could have helped to prevent three decades of chaos.

'Do you have any idea what your betrayal has cost? Myan spent a lifetime searching against hope for the Scion, then for Belin's son. His friend's only living child.'

Kalyth's face twisted in pain. 'Don't talk to me of betrayal. It was *I* who was betrayed. I carried one child to safety while Hend's elite razed Blackthorne before my eyes. My wife and family lay dead in Blackthorne's ashes, and I was ordered to run from their side. Abandoning honour, hope and love, all for one *Suul* child!'

Ellen took a step back, stunned by the intensity of his emotions. 'Both the Suul and their servants made great sacrifices for the Empire.'

He advanced, his eyes moist with tears. He raised an accusing finger. 'You *Suul* talk of duty so easily. But it is your servants who make the sacrifices. I did my duty, and all I loved was laid waste. My duty to the Suul ended that day at Blackthorne.' Kalyth turned to walk into the night.

Ellen watched him go, her mind ringing with his words. *The child.* He had carried the Emperor's child to safety. The skin on the back of her neck crawled, the hairs standing on end. Belin rescued the Scion – and Kalyth took the child to safety. She sat heavily by the fire, stunned by the enormity of what she had discovered. If Belin trusted the man enough to bring his own son to Athria, then it made sense he would trust him with the Emperor's child.

Kalyth knew the identity of the Scion, perhaps even where he was. He was out there, in Kelas somewhere, with some noble family. Perhaps never even knowing the truth of his own birth. She had to find him! But how could she get Kalyth to tell her? What leverage could she possibly apply to a self-sufficient warrior who had rejected the Suul and everything they offered? Ellen picked up a stick and moved a branch over into the centre of the fire. The flames flickered then swarmed across the dry bark.

She would find a way.

* * *

Ellen pulled gently on the reins of her mount, slowing the amelak to a standstill. 'Two hours on the road and we are already slowing down.'

The level plains of the Delta province had given way to the Mulisar foothills. Just ahead of them the north road narrowed as it cut through the gap between two low hills, forcing the caravan to slow. The day was bright and clear, the two suns having just risen above the eastern peaks to sweep away the last shadows.

'Life is a journey,' said Raphal, looking west across the distant sea.

Ellen bit back a short reply. By now she knew better than to argue with the old scholar.

They were riding in their usual place in the middle of the column. Ellen watched Cedrin as he passed through the gap with the last of the vanguard. The drivers on the lead wagons shook their reins, urging the big harena into motion. She had seen it all a hundred times.

The rearguard outriders protecting the middle of the column had been forced to ride up against the wagon as the cuttings on either side of the road closed in. Sindar and three other warriors sat on their stationary mounts nearby. He was a strange man. She had greeted him twice as she passed him in the night-time camp, but he never returned the greeting. In fact he had never once even met her eyes. The fearsome warrior looked at her briefly, perhaps sensing her gaze, then looked away. He tugged gently on the reins of his mount, turning his back to her. Perhaps it was not so strange. She had never seen Sindar talk with any of Kranor's warriors either.

A battle horn blasted across the valley.

Ellen jumped in the saddle, her hands tightening to fists on the reins. Her amelak bleated. The horn sounded again – closer this time – and the harena bellowed in fear, pulling against their harnesses and dragging the wagons out of the line despite the curses of the drivers. Shouts and battle-cries filled the air as the horn continued to blow. Two wagons collided as the beasts surged forward, trying to pass the narrow gap.

Ellen swept her scythe out of its saddle sheath, turning her amelak in a circle. A mounted force of more than forty men had crested the hills on the eastern side of the road and were thundering down towards them. Almost half of them had bows. Sindar, and the other rearguard warriors already on the right flank of the caravan, turned their mounts. Another eight rearguard warriors from the left flank urged their frightened amelak through the close-packed caravan to join them. Sindar immediately took command, directing the men into a fighting line. Arrows hissed through the air as the mounted archers sent shaft after shaft into the rearguard warriors and their mounts.

'Raphal! *Down*,' shouted Ellen. Raphal slid off his mount, using the beast for shelter.

One of the rearguard warriors took an arrow to the shoulder, the shaft punching through a gap between the mought plates of his armour. He screamed in pain, then hit the ground hard as his amelak went down. Another man fell with an arrow through his cheek, another in his chest. The air was rent with the bestial screams of amelak as two more mounts fell. An arrow flashed past Ellen's face and thudded into a wagon rail. The Window flashed into her mind, the Fire ready to follow. The harena screeched and pulled at their harness straps, turning to bite at each other in their panic. Up ahead, the vanguard were trying to push through the gap in the hills, but were hampered by the wagons stuck there. She looked behind. Azel was coming up with the rest of the rearguard, but he was blocked by the narrow road. The attackers had chosen their spot carefully. Ellen and Raphal were trapped between the high verge and the close-packed wagons.

The wagon riders scrambled for their bows. One or two managed a shot, but the bandits were coming fast and the defenders' shafts failed to find a mark.

The battle horn was deafening; alien. Ellen traced the sound to a mounted bandit, high on the crest of the hill above them, who held a trumpet-like instrument to his lips.

One moment the bandits were galloping down the slope, the next they were on them. Only seven of the rearguard warriors remained to meet the onslaught. Men shouted and cursed. The scrape and clatter of battle filled the air as they met blade to blade. Sindar was using a cavalry scythe, slashing left and right with deadly accuracy, controlling his amelak with ease. Two bandits surged at him from either side. He ducked beneath one attack, extending his scythe in a stabbing lunge that took the second bandit in the throat. As he straightened, he swept the scythe back at the first bandit in a tight arc that took the man's head from his shoulders. Ellen blinked. His technique was perfect. Beside Sindar, another rearguard warrior fell, a lance punching through his leather armour into his chest. Another was slashed across the face with a scythe and screamed, losing control of his mount and tumbling to the ground. He disappeared under the hooves. There was a gap in the defending line. Sindar saw it immediately.

'Fall back!' Sindar commanded. He retreated closer to the caravan with the four remaining warriors, where they reformed their line.

The archers in the wagons loosed shafts into the attackers, picking their targets. The mounted archers of the bandits responded instantly. Two of the lightly-armoured caravan archers tumbled to the ground, peppered with arrows. One cried out as an arrow took him through the arm. The others ducked for cover.

Azel and his rearguard attacked the bandits' flank, making them split their forces. She could see Azel and Kanis fighting furiously in the front ranks, but the bandits were experienced warriors, and Azel could not use his numbers to good effect in the cramped confines. Ruus and the four rearguard warriors from Kranor's One Hundred held the line steady on either side of Azel and Kanis, fighting with steady precision.

Kalyth led a group of warriors from the vanguard back through the disarray of close-packed wagons towards the fighting. The animals were still panicked, the wagons shifting and crashing into each other as the harena tried to pull free. The bandits split their attack again, turning to engage Kalyth's men. The old warrior guided his mount expertly with his knees, his greatscythe cutting into the bandits. Three fell in a matter of moments, shrieking in pain as the lanedd blades sliced and cut.

'Shoot the horn-blower!' shouted Kalyth.

The caravan archers, finally given a single target, drew their bows and loosed. Shafts dropped out of the sky around the horn blower. Most of the arrows were badly aimed as the archers loosed quickly and dropped back under cover, but one struck the flank of the bandit's mount. The amelak screamed in pain and reared. The sound of the horn abruptly ceased as the man struggled to control his mount.

'Again!' yelled Kalyth.

The horn blower had turned to flee as the second barrage of missiles hit. An arrow struck him in the throat. He fell, his foot tangled in the stirrup as he tumbled from his mount. The amelak fled, dragging his corpse back over the hill and out of sight.

With most of the bandits' mounted archers engaged, the caravan archers came out of cover. They stood with bows drawn, but the fighting had become a furious mass of constantly moving warriors, and it was now impossible to pick a target without endangering one of their own.

Neither Kalyth nor Azel had managed to force the bandits back. In the middle, only paces from her, Sindar and his warriors were hard pressed. She could see they would not hold. If they broke, the bandits would take the centre of the caravan. The drivers and archers would be dead in heartbeats, and she and Raphal would be fighting for their lives. She tensed, ready to join the fight.

Raphal reached up to grip her wrist. 'Ellen. You must not use the Fire. Even Kranor's men fear it. Xyanthius will not pardon you, even if you save the wagons.'

She shook his hand free and urged her mount forward. She could not stand by while others gave their lives to defend her.

Ellen shouted and pushed her way into the middle of the line next to Sindar. The tall Anacian saw her coming and made space for her. A bandit rode at her with a lance levelled at her throat. At the last instant she knocked the spear tip past her, reversing the blocking movement into a cut at the warrior's head. The scythe's blade slashed into the bandit's face, cutting up and across his eyes. He screamed and fell, blinded.

A bandit galloped through, his lance levelled at Sindar's back.

'Sindar!' she called.

The tall Anacian looked back, but he was already engaged scythe to scythe with another warrior. If he turned to meet the new threat, the man would cut him down.

'Cintros!' Her family's battlecry sprang to her lips. She galloped her mount straight at the bandit. Her amelak collided with his, breaking his line of attack. He turned towards her, but she was ready. Her scythe cut down into his shoulder, right into the lung. The man gasped and fell.

Her charge had taken her right out of Sindar's fighting line. A dark-skinned Meadrel tribesman surged at Ellen, cutting in with his scythe. She blocked and attacked, but found her strikes easily turned. Unlike the other bandits, he did not shout or bellow warcries, but fought in silence; his dark eyes fixed on her. None of her attacks were getting through his guard. Her stomach tightened in fear. She paused for a moment, wondering if she should use the Fire. The bandit grunted and stabbed in. Instinctively, she blocked. A feint! His blade cut at her throat. She ducked and winced as his blade hit. She felt the impact, but no pain. The blade had been turned by her mought bracer.

Ten warriors of the rearguard, led by Azel, joined them with battle-cries and a clash of weapons. Riderless, one of the bandit's amelak collided with the mount of the Meadrel warrior. The man's thrust went wild as his amelak struggled to turn beneath him. Ellen's blade swept through the gap. The Meadrel's eyes widened as he saw the blade coming. An instant later, it took his head from his shoulders. Blood gushed out in a warm geyser, splashing across her face and vest. She could taste it in her mouth. The bandit's scythe tumbled from his fingers, and his body followed it to the ground. In that moment, she was acutely aware of every sound; each cry of animal fear and aggression, each blade of red-stained grass. All movement around her seemed to slow.

Kalyth led his men into the line, easing the pressure.

'Ellen!' Cedrin cried. 'Are you injured?' He was searching her face and body. Of course. She was covered in blood. He was looking for injuries.

Ellen was too exhausted to reply, but shook her head. Relief showed on his face, followed by determination as he turned back to the fight. Cedrin and Marken pushed past her, joining a new fighting line in front of her and taking her out of the combat. For a moment she was furious, but she could sense the tide of the battle had turned. No longer needed, she dropped back.

A horn sounded somewhere above them on the hill and the bandits fled. She looked up to see who had sounded the blast and caught a brief glimpse of a man on a narsiit before he vanished beyond the crest.

It was over.

'Get the dead and wounded into the caravans,' commanded Kalyth. 'And let's get these damned wagons out of this gap.'

Nearby, Sindar flicked the blood from his scythe and sheathed it in one fluid motion. He turned his amelak to ride by her. Ellen smiled, thinking Sindar would thank her for coming to his aid. He turned away, riding on without a word. The demon tattoos on his shaved head seemed to leer at her.

He was not the only one to ignore her. The other warriors also seemed distant as they spurred their amelak past. Some bowed their heads, others showed signs of uncertainty. Even Lann, who had always been friendly, greeted her coolly and kept riding. Ellen was at a loss to explain it until Azel rode to her side holding her mought bracer in his hands.

'My Lady,' he said with a smile, bowing slightly, his eyes alight with delight and recognition. 'Or should I say, Suul Cintros?'

Ellen took the mought bracer, feeling self-conscious, and slipped it back into place on her head. The wagons were beginning to move once more and the guards were forming. Ellen felt eyes on her and turned to see Sindar watching, his pale-blue eyes filled with a strange intensity of fear and longing. He turned away, spurring his amelak to the front of the caravan. Just briefly, Ellen had thought ...

'Is there anything I can do for you, my Lady?' asked Azel, his eyes alight with triumph.

'No, but thank you, Azel,' she said, then turned towards the caravan to find her place beside Raphal. The old scholar had remounted, and was waiting for her.

'I've done it now, Raphal,' she said.

Raphal was thoughtful but said nothing, the palm of his free hand moving across his bald head absently.

'As soon as we reach Ceta the whole of Kelas will know where we are,' said Ellen.

'We are in a well-defended caravan, surrounded by allies. For now, we are safe. Perhaps this will be for the best,' he said.

Ellen cleaned her bloody scythe blade and sheathed it. Then she rubbed the drying gore off her skin as though it were acid.

At least in Ceta, she could get a bath.

* * *

Ellen looked across the fire at Cedrin. Like Marken and Raphal, he ate in silence. The words of a slow dirge drifted across to them from the main hearth as the warriors mourned, drinking and singing of the life of those lost. Five of their number had fallen, another later dying of injuries. Many were injured. It would have been far worse had Kalyth not given the command to don armour. Xyanthius was pleased with the outcome. He and Alechul had toured the camp earlier, congratulating the warriors. It did little to ease the tension – at least for Ellen. The attack had destroyed the illusion of lazy travelling, making her acutely aware of the danger they were in. The caravan had barely left the Delta and only half the wagons were full. It was north from Ceta, with a full load of valuable wares and coin, that they would face their greatest threat.

Ellen had washed with obsessive thoroughness, determined to rid herself of the taint of blood. Even so, the shock remained. The fighting had affected her deeply. After the battle of Regent's Hill, she had felt sick with relief and triumph, but had felt no regret. To her, the men who had fallen beneath her blade during the failed rebellion had been casualties of war. Now? Her life on the road had forced her to recognise the attackers not as faceless warriors, but as men with hopes and dreams. Only now did she understand how much she had changed. She sat by the fire, comfortable in the company of the former calvanni she had once been prepared to execute.

Even so, she was still out of place. A Suul among common people; feared by them, respected, yet hated for her privileged background.

Marken and Raphal rose from the fire and disappeared into the night, leaving Ellen and Cedrin together by the small hearth.

'You took a great risk today, Ellen,' said Cedrin.

'I was trained as a warrior. I could not sit by,' she said, watching the flames.

Cedrin tapped an empty pipe against his palm in irritation.

'You have been playing with that damned pipe for two hours. Are you going to smoke or not?' said Ellen, trying to distract him.

'Ahhh.' Cedrin looked at the pipe and put it down beside him. 'I never thought the habit would be so hard to break. But I have to – with all this running Kalyth has me doing, I feel like my lungs will burst. I need to clear them.'

'My father always used to say the smoking weed was seditious. "Like a bad-tempered lover who knows the arts of pleasure too well",' said Ellen.

Cedrin smiled, then grew serious. 'I am not destined to be part of the Suul, Ellen. I have to be my own master, wherever that leads me.'

She knew he would be leaving any moment, to train with Kalyth. It was foolish, but she resented the time he spent with the old warrior. Sudden anger flared up inside her, overriding her reason.

'If you are so much your own master, then why let Kalyth poison your mind against me and the Suul? He was the one who betrayed you!'

'What has Kalyth to do with this? Belin was my father; it was his responsibility. What could he have done if he lay dead all these years? I do not blame *anyone* now. The past is done.'

'Kalyth was Belin's right arm. He was the man who gave you to Tarral at Belin's bidding. He was the one who kept you away from us, keeping you hidden because of his own bitterness!'

Cedrin was silent for a moment as he absorbed what she said. 'So it was Kalyth who took me to Belin. Well – if that is so, I owe him the debt of my life. But again, that is in the past. What does it matter now?'

Ellen walked around the fire to Cedrin. 'If not for Kalyth, we would have been side by side. Both Suul, fighting together instead of worlds apart. Why can't you see I am your blood? That the Suul are your brethren?'

'I am not a Suul. I want my own destiny. If I bow to the Warlord, or to your brother Torren, or to you, my destiny is no longer my own. I am a man, Ellen. Just a man.'

'And I am a woman!' she said, taking the bracer off her head and pointing to the Suul mark. 'Do you think this makes my blood run cold?' She shook, overtaken by emotion. She knew she should stay cool, keep silent. But she could not. Perhaps it was the shock of the battle. It was like she was watching herself from a distance as it all poured out of her.

Cedrin stood. 'I think the blood in your veins runs anything but cold ...'

He stepped in towards her, and her heart leapt. Her breath was coming quick now. She just wanted him to take her. Rank be damned! She pushed herself into his body. His hands reached to encircle her waist, sending a frisson of pleasure up her spine. Ellen knew she should step away. Instead she pressed herself deeper into his embrace.

'Would that it could have been different,' he said. His breathing too, was ragged. And she felt the hardness of him against her. She looked up into his face, into his grey-blue eyes and saw the desire there. He wanted her – and it felt glorious!

'I am just a warrior, not a Suul,' he said, his voice hoarse. 'Not a fit ... suitor ... for the daughter of the Sarlord.'

'But—' she started.

Cedrin put his finger gently on her lips to silence her. She reached up, her hand sliding across his hard pectoral muscles. Warmth flooded her groin. She did not want to think, did not want to break from the warmth and strength that surrounded her.

He gently held her away from him, breaking the contact. 'Did you ever stop to think your debt to Myan is fulfilled? How much would he have expected? The friendship of our fathers has been rekindled in us. Even if we never meet again after Searn, that will always be true.'

Brought back to reality, Ellen stepped back. Her heart was

racing. For a moment she had completely lost herself, awash with the pounding of blood and his desire for her. The night swam around her, filled once more with the knowledge of who she was. Her quest for the Scion. Her unquestioning faith in Myan. The barriers she had built over a lifetime of court life slammed into place. Yet, her need remained. It burned inside her, and like a rising fire that deepened the shadows beyond it, it only increased her sense of isolation.

'I understand,' she said. 'Things could have been different. *Should* have been different. You will always be a Suul to me, Cedrin. A Kaidell – and the son of a great man.'

She turned and walked off into the chill of the night.

Out of sight, she sank to her knees and burst into tears.

Chapter Twenty-One

Cedrin's powers of Sorcery had slumbered since Seyt, but Marken was more anxious than ever. If – when – his friend's powers emerged, they would endanger them both … of that he was sure.

'There's no end to these damn hills,' said Cedrin. His friend had adapted well to the saddle, riding easily on his amelak, greatscythe strapped across his back.

'True. But at least these ones don't block the view,' said Marken, thinking of the narrow defile in which they were ambushed yesterday.

So many times, as Marken and Raphal discussed the glorious abstracts of magic, he had come close to revealing everything to Raphal, but he could not. The old Druid and Priest was his friend and mentor, but still owed his allegiance to the Temple of the Sisters in Olcis. How far could Marken push the old scholar's loyalty? He could not risk it. He had no wish to watch Cedrin executed at the hands of the Temple. What would he do if Cedrin destroyed himself? Or was taken by a Temple-incensed mob in some lice-ridden town?

The suns were climbing in the east, but were hours from the summit. *Another long day.* He increasingly found himself wishing the days away, waiting for Raphal's insightful instruction and the evenings spent puzzling over the various techniques of Essence magic. Taking his vows at the Temple of Two Moons had brought something back to life inside Marken. There had been a time, when he first entered the Temple in Athria, when he had fully embraced the calling of Druid and healer; a time before the slow pace of learning, the discipline and the rigid moral code had led him to reject that life. Becoming part of the Two Moons' order of itinerant healers had re-ignited that flame. His time with the Brotherhood had always been just a stepping stone to buying his way into the ranks of the Suul. And all that ambition had come to nothing. It was good to have something else in his life, in his mind, rather than that. Being able to help someone, to heal someone, to have the Moon Essence flow through him – it was an indescribable feeling. He never wanted to have to again feel that frustration of kneeling beside a dying man and being helpless.

The low hills stretched out on either side of the road, all the way to the Mulisar ranges to the east and the steep coastal cliffs to the west. The closer they came to Searn, the greater the temptation to approach Ellen grew. It was obvious she wanted to win him as an ally, yet Cedrin refused to even listen to Marken when he talked of his Sorcerous blood – calling it his *curse*. The idea that Ellen would simply walk away after Searn infuriated Marken. Cedrin needed a teacher! The more he learnt of the Realms, the more certain he became.

Marken patted the neck of his amelak absently, his fingers running through the beast's woolly coat. On the road to the Kaidell estate, Marken had nursed high hopes for Cedrin and for himself. The unexpected appearance of Ellen Cintros had promised to open doors that had always been closed to them. He saw himself at last a part of the Suul, standing by Cedrin's side as he entered their ranks. Anything would have been possible then.

At the front of the column, Xyanthius rode with Kalyth. As usual, Alechul travelled in the lead wagon, well away from the dust of the road. Ellen and Raphal were somewhere back behind them, in the middle of the caravan. Marken studied Kalyth, trying once more to puzzle out the presence of the old warrior and his interest in Cedrin. Kalyth was a man of action. Such men do not do anything without good reason.

'He's got to be more than just an old greatscytheman who knew Belin,' said Marken.

'Who? Oh, Kalyth. You're not on about him again, are you?'

said Cedrin.

'His reasons must run deeper,' said Marken.

'Why should they? Why should Kalyth be anything more than what he seems?'

'There are too many coincidences, Cedrin. A master scytheman, once a respected warrior, spends half a lifetime in obscurity then suddenly appears. He leaves everything to join this caravan, and he is teaching you the greatscythe, guiding your every step.'

Cedrin's amelak snorted and gave out a series of grunts, falling out of step. 'No-one is guiding my way,' he said.

Marken had known Cedrin long enough to realise he would achieve nothing by confronting him.

'Rather odd sense of fashion though, hasn't he, the old lad,' said Marken.

'True. I've never seen him without that armour.'

'Maybe he's been wearing it since the fall of the old Empire,' said Marken, pinching his nose with his fingers and screwing up his face as though from a bad smell.

Cedrin laughed, relaxing.

Images of the Spire still haunted Marken. That terrible moment when they had been frozen in place by Raziin's Sorcery, only a heartbeat from a vicious death. Then the power had burst out of the Cedrin – a vast wall of Fire – breaking the spell and knocking them all from their feet. It had been too late for Jaso. Raziin had already gutted the little Athrian like a fish … taunting them with his death. How under the Suns was Marken going to get Cedrin to admit he needed Ellen to teach him Sorcery?

'Answer me one question, Cedrin,' said Marken.

Cedrin looked suspicious, but nodded. 'Aye. One question.'

'That night at the Kaidell estate. You walked to Blackthorne Tower, didn't you?'

Cedrin was silent for a time. 'Aye,' he said at last.

'And you met Kalyth?'

Anger flashed across Cedrin's face and Marken knew he had hit the mark.

'You said *one* question!'

Marken laughed in triumph. 'You don't need to tell me anything else. I can guess the rest. He was in the Tower all those years, living in the ruins. In walks Belin's son, and for the first time in almost thirty years, he walks away. To follow you. And you tell me he doesn't have a reason? You are the reason, my friend.'

Cedrin looked out over the sea. 'He can go where he wishes – he is a free man.'

Marken sighed.

'So I wonder how Morec will run Smuggling in Athria now he is Mouthpiece?' said Cedrin, deflecting the conversation.

Marken took the bait and they talked of Athria, then the cities ahead of them and the dangers of the road. Cedrin avoided all mention of the old Legion warrior who rode ahead of them.

* * *

Cedrin winced as his fingers were caught between his greatscythe and Kalyth's. He tried to blank out the pain and keep his concentration. One slip and the old warrior would have him. After the endless hours of drills, something had clicked for Cedrin. Where once the heavy weapon had seemed awkward, now it was light in his hands – like an extension of his arm – freeing him to focus on the combat. The meditation had also helped, freeing his mind from the anxieties of the past and future.

They fell apart and circled, the deep glow of the fire framing them in red. Kalyth came forward again, the greatscythe falling in the same pattern of attack. Cedrin blocked, moving the greatscythe faster in his hands as the blows quickened in pace. His arms ached and his lungs burned, but he kept his mind empty, watching every movement of the greatscythe as it turned and cut, swung and drove forward. The mought hafts met with rapid, staccato thuds as he turned the blows. Kalyth broke away and Cedrin was surprised to see the implacable warrior actually out of breath. Kalyth still wore his armour, despite the gradually warming nights.

'Well done,' said Kalyth. 'We will make a greatscytheman out of you yet. Your eye is improving.'

Cedrin doubled over, his lungs pumping as he struggled to catch his breath. He smiled at Kalyth's compliment. As if he had a choice! It was improve or get hit, and he knew from experience a strike from a greatscythe haft was not pleasant.

'Let's cool off on the beach,' said Kalyth, jogging off towards the path.

Cedrin forced his aching legs into motion, grimacing at the pain as he followed Kalyth. To his surprise, the running eased the ache in his lungs and he fell into a comfortable rhythm, leaping across the path from stone to stone as it descended the cliff to the beach below. With soft sand beneath his feet, he stopped to remove his boots. He looked around for Kalyth and was surprised to see him already in the sea, diving between the slowly crashing waves. The old warrior's armour was neatly piled by the shore. Cedrin stripped naked, following his teacher into the waves. He revelled in the refreshing coolness.

He made his way out past the breakers to where Kalyth was swimming. The smell of the sea was strong here, reminding him of simpler days in Athria. He lay back in the water, moving his arms and legs to stay afloat as the waves rose and fell. The stars stretched out overhead. Ellen's face floated into his mind. Did the stars care who was a Suul and who was a peasant?

'I'm a fool,' he said.

'What's that?' called Kalyth.

Cedrin found his feet on the sand and stood up in the water. Kalyth was making his way back to the shore.

'The water's cool,' said Cedrin.

'It is that,' said Kalyth.

They swam through the breakers and waded back up onto the shore. There was a natural spring here, tumbling from the cliff, and they showered and drank the cool water. Kalyth's chest was covered with tattoos, indistinct like dark bruises in the night. They flicked the water from their bodies and dressed, sitting on the shore to watch the silent waves. Above, the sky was clear and bright.

'Kalyth, why did you follow me?'

The warrior was silent for a time, then replied with conviction. 'I had languished in that Tower too long, with memories, and ... spectres.' He clapped Cedrin on the back. 'It was time to leave.'

A wave crashed softly to the sand. Somewhere down the coast a seabird shrieked and another answered it.

'You were the one who took me to Athria after Blackthorne fell, weren't you?'

The silence was heavy and Cedrin could sense Kalyth's sudden intensity.

'Who told you?' said Kalyth.

'Ellen.'

Kalyth cursed. 'The Cintros woman. I should have known.'

'So it's true then?'

'Yes. Yes! I was the one,' said Kalyth, rising to his feet. 'Come, let's walk.'

They set off down the beach, breathing the sea-tangled air deep into their lungs, watching the shore and the sea. Clouds passed overhead, blotting out the moons, and the night grew darker.

'Why didn't you tell Myan I was in Athria?'

'It was a dark time,' said Kalyth. 'The Empire was falling, powers were shifting and the Eathal were on the march. I had done as much as Belin asked. I'd brought you to safety.'

'But a simple word. A letter ...,' said Cedrin.

'Do you think you would have lived better as a Suul? Do you think you would have been happier? I let the matter lie because that was best. Belin was gone. Blackthorne was in ashes. Things were never going to be the same again. If you had known ...' The old warrior's voice was hoarse with fury. 'You would have spent your life seeking to be something you could never be.'

Lightning lit the sky, thunder crashing overhead. The sky above them was swollen with dark cloud. In a silent consensus they turned back to the camp, quickening their step.

'Once I would have died for the Suul. For Belin. I believed in the Empire and the rule of Raynor. But I lost everything I loved when Blackthorne fell. Nothing but ashes remained ... I owed Belin nothing more.

'I know the Cintros woman. I know her kind. Duty is all they talk about, but it's duty to them. Talk about their responsibility to the people and you see another face of the same coin. They are born above us. They seek to stay that way even if we die by the thousands.'

The rain lashed down in a sudden squall, soaking them.

Kalyth raised his voice above the storm. 'Don't you see it, Cedrin? She wants to use you! Stay your own master. Live your own life. They will try to lure you with wealth, but for us it means a leash.' Kalyth gripped Cedrin's arm. 'While you are free, Cedrin, I live again.'

The rain grew heavier. 'Come on!' yelled Kalyth, breaking into a run and leading them from the beach to the path. The rain was blinding. Cedrin's calf muscles screamed at the effort of pushing through the sodden sand. In the torrent, the path had become a small fast-flowing stream. They scrambled against the current, conscious of the treacherous footing and deadly fall below.

Kalyth's words had a deep effect on Cedrin. All his life he had possessed a fierce streak of independence. Who can say what might have been? He had always worked with the here and now. Kalyth had proven himself a friend and teacher, and whatever his motivations, Cedrin trusted him. He had answered the seeds of doubt that Marken had succeeded in sowing in his mind. As for Kalyth's warnings about Ellen ... He was not sure he could shun her so easily. She was more than just a Suul to him now.

* * *

Ellen sat back in her chair, listening as Alechul continued his never-ending chatter. The rich merchant was enjoying the company for its own sake, and Ellen amused herself with the notion that the man completed business deals by mesmerising his associates.

The caravan lay less than a day from Ceta and was within the city-state's patrolled territories. The lights of the city could be seen faintly from the main hearth, although the warriors, relieved to be able to relax at last, were more interested in wine and song.

Alechul had organised a feast in his spacious pavilion. All the company leaders were present; Xyanthius, Kalyth and the Suul Azel. The canny merchant had also invited Ellen and her companions, knowing of Kalyth's special interest in Cedrin and Ellen's rank as a Suul. He had no doubt also heard that Cedrin was the son of the legendary Belin.

The feast had gone smoothly, all present enjoying a change from the plain foods of the campfire. Marken particularly had been in his element, praising the food and spicing up the conversation with witty banter. Kalyth, though, had remained tense and silent all night. The old warrior grew more impatient as the hours lengthened. It had been impossible to do more than smile at Cedrin. She certainly did not feel like talking freely with Kalyth sitting between them like a grumpy chaperone. Raphal had eaten sparingly and said little, but clearly enjoyed the company.

'It was bravely repelled,' said Alechul, waving a leg of meat in his hand. The man clearly enjoyed his food. His overweight frame was cunningly concealed by his voluminous, richly decorated robes. 'Even Lady Ellen fought with the warriors.' He bowed to Ellen. 'You are braver than I, Suul Cintros.'

Ellen's stomach churned at the mention of her name. She smiled and nodded, her neck tight with tension. For the last hour she had forgotten how much danger she was in. With Ceta so close, she would need to be alert once more for agents of the Athrian Temple and the Warlord of Raynor.

'We owe everything to the valiant efforts of the rearguard and vanguard,' said Alechul, nodding to Azel and Kalyth.

'They were just testing us,' said Kalyth, bursting in on Alechul's banter. 'We must be wary from now on.'

'Nonsense!' said Alechul, brushing aside Kalyth's warning with wine-induced bluster. 'We are safe and they are far gone. Drink! Eat!'

The big merchant waved at his servants, and they came forward offering wine. Azel refilled his cup and watched Ellen with a glassy stare. It made her uncomfortable.

'All we have is chaos. Since the Cinanac fell, the provinces fight like rabid dogs. Now the Eathal march again. Who could have believed Hend would fall? These are dark times. It's bad for business. Give me a strong Emperor to rebuild Bulvuran,' said Alechul, draining his glass with a sigh of satisfaction.

'Hear hear!' said Azel, lifting his glass.

Kalyth growled in disgust. 'Are you so eager to be a slave to the powerful? At least now a man can make his own way. All the Emperor did was put the provinces in chains. From Carris to Riin, all they wanted was *power*. Jewels and coin for a bigger palace and a richer court.'

'How can you say that?' said Ellen. 'We are living in the ruins of the Empire, waiting as it falls about us. Who do you think built the road that we are on? Or the port we are making for? If the Emperor was still a power in Kelas, perhaps we could travel from Seyt to Searn without a small army.'

Kalyth and Ellen faced each other across the table. She bristled at Kalyth's cool contempt. Alechul winced, realising his error in broaching the topic.

'These roads were built using coin taken from the provinces, just like the Cinanac palace and all the mansions that line the Palardos,' said Kalyth.

'Come now,' said Alechul. 'Let's not spoil our feast. I daresay these are good times for warriors and generals, eh? Each province pitted against the other, each seeking wealth and land.'

Raphal cleared his throat and smiled at Kalyth like a kindly father. 'There will always be evil and greedy men, just as there will always be good men. But chaos will ever breed chaos. Who will unite Kelas against the Eathal now? The Warlord who struggles to rule his own fractured capital? Armon, who has ever been inward looking, caring only for Cioan traditions and gods?'

Kalyth nodded gravely. 'There is some truth in what you say, Priest, but it is absolute power that frightens me. The rise of another Carris.'

Azel laughed. 'You cannot mean the Destruction of Carris. That is a myth, something invented to tarnish the memory of a great man.' The Suul's cheeks were flushed with wine, and he held his head arrogantly as he regarded Kalyth.

Kalyth's eye narrowed, his deep blue eyes cold as they fixed on Azel. 'Who knows what is fable and what is history. Many believed the Eathal a myth only thirty years ago.'

Azel's sneer disappeared at the mention of the Eathal.

Raphal rose, raising his voice to fill the tent, his face grave. His right hand clutched his staff and the robes that fell around him seemed to increase his size.

'From the Fire of Olcis
by Carris' hand
the Spear rose
and fell on the land.'

Raphal's voice was compelling, and the company was silent in the wake of his words.

'The saga of Carris?' asked Marken. Raphal nodded without turning, but the spell was broken.

'Superstition. If the Spear ever existed, where is it now? These artefacts have a convenient way of disappearing. In my opinion they are only good for frightening children,' said Azel, pleased with himself.

Cedrin laughed. 'I agree, Azel.'

Ellen looked across the table at Kalyth. The man remained silent, his eyes distant.

'Do not doubt the Prophecies, Azel,' said Raphal. 'The Spear of Carris is indestructible. It will rise again, as will the Phoenix of Bulvuran. Since the forging of the blade, the two were linked throughout time.'

Azel pushed the wine from him with a violent motion, tipping the glass goblet and spilling the heavy red across the cloth. Alechul clapped his hands and a servant ran forward to clean it. The red stain spread like an ill-omen. They all watched in silence as the servant sponged the spill. More than wine had been lost. The light mood of early evening was gone.

Defiant, Azel surged to his feet, swaying slightly as his chair fell to the ground behind him. 'I cannot support your superstitions, Priest. They are designed to scare the faithful, not rational men.'

Azel left the tent, his servant rushing to help him as he neared the exit.

'But surely the Cinanac line is finished, Riin and all his kindred slain?' asked Kalyth, his face guarded.

'The Scion will rise,' said Raphal, as though giving a statement of fact. 'More than one false-Scion will come before him. Even so, many prophets have seen the Scion of Carris and his Nemesis rise together.'

Kalyth's face showed a flash of anger, but it was gone quickly, the cool reserve back in place. 'I tell you, Priest. It is better for Yos if the Cinanac line never rises again.'

'How can you say that with the Eathal massing at the borders?' snapped Ellen. Alechul and Xyanthius murmured agreement with her.

'Aye, surely an Emperor of any description is better than a disunited Kelas,' said Cedrin.

Sensing the mood was against him, Kalyth rose and retrieved his greatscythe. He turned to Cedrin before he left. 'Don't forget, Cedrin. Empires are built and raised on the blood of others. Another Cinanac would mean the death of thousands.'

Ellen looked between Kalyth and Cedrin, noting the respect Cedrin had for him. A hot rage overtook her. Who was Kalyth to make pronouncements like this? She surged to her feet, shouting at his back. 'The Scion would be the saviour of thousands!'

Kalyth stopped, turning slowly, menacingly, to face her. 'Suul Cintros. So much your father's daughter.' He turned to swiftly exit the tent.

Ellen sat, the feeling of the man's contempt like acid.

Alechul clapped his hands. Immediately the servants began clearing away the table. 'I believe the feast is at an end.'

She gave brief farewells and left the tent quickly, seeking calm and solace in the night. What did he mean? How could the Scion be the death of thousands? She walked aimlessly, not heeding her path. The loneliness of the past weeks, the uncertainly, was suddenly overwhelming. The notes of a merry song drifted towards her from the main hearth. Laughter and joy seemed like dim, unattainable memories.

She felt a gentle touch on her arm and jumped in surprise, turning to see Cedrin there. *He moves so damn silently.* He laid his hands on her shoulders, looking deeply into her eyes.

'I know I should not be following you like this,' he said.

In that moment all the isolation crashed in on Ellen, and she buried her face in his chest, desperate to hold on to someone. She was proud of being a Suul, proud of who she was, but her quest for the Scion had left her nothing. And despite all her sacrifice, she had failed to win Cedrin to her cause.

* * *

Cedrin felt the warmth of Ellen's body and was seized with the desire to protect this woman, to give her his strength. Yet how could he, a lowly scytheman, protect a Suul? A Sorceress? He pushed aside his thoughts and gave in to the moment.

Ellen looked up at him. Her eyes glistened with tears and her voice was hoarse. 'Kalyth despises everything I am. But there is good in the Suul, Cedrin. Don't let him turn you against me.'

Cedrin touched her cheek. Her eyes shone like jewels.

'Kalyth has never forgiven himself. He cannot forgive anyone else. He believes he was betrayed by Belin. You can hear it in his voice.'

Her lips were dark and wet, inviting.

'I can't believe Belin would have betrayed him,' she said. Cedrin felt her body tremble.

He leant down, and she rose to meet him. Then they were kissing. Her hands moved across his toned pectoral muscles. He drew her in, his hands sliding down her back to her slim hips. Heat rose between them in a wave, and he grew hard. He pressed himself against her.

Ellen broke away from the kiss, breathless. 'I … can't let this happen. Not now.' She pushed out of his arms. 'I'm sorry,' she said. 'I'm sorry.' She ran into the darkness.

Cedrin sat heavily on the ground and looked at the stars while his desire slowly faded.

'You *are* a fool,' he said to himself.

What did he think he was doing, seducing a Suul? He shook

his head. Perhaps it was too long since he had a woman. He had to do something to break this spell. He could not let himself desire her. She would always be beyond his reach, and after Searn they would part forever.

Even so, he knew he would never meet another woman like her. Not like Ellen Cintros.

Chapter Twenty-Two

Raziin watched the distant pillars of smoke rise into the northern sky. *A glorious sight.*

'It must be Talis, my Lord,' said Merceth.

'Yes. Hukum's armies have been unleashed. He has set the whole city to the torch,' said Raziin. Judging by the smoke, the city had been burning for less than a day.

He and his men were positioned on the top of a low rise with a good view in all directions. Their eastern back-trail emerged from wooded hills into a flat, empty valley. To the west, the land gave way to a maze of steep hills that Raziin knew intimately.

Both suns had risen long ago, yet the morning remained dark, the sunlight dimmed by the heavy smoke. They were still trapped in Tupur, between the armies of Hukum and freedom. Late yesterday they had encountered a small detachment of warriors from the rearguard of the main Eathal army. They had dispatched them quickly, but not before one of them had released an *efreet* – an Eathal messenger bat – alerting the main force.

Then had begun a night of running battles as they faced the Eathal in their element: darkness. Units swept around them, trying to pin down their position. Twice they broke free of the net, using their amelak to evade the Eathal foot patrols. Raziin had seen a pattern to their attacks. They were trying to drive them north-east, not to the main body of the Eathal army, which was north of them, but to somewhere else – or towards *something* else.

Raziin summoned the Window, channelling Fire into the

Lens Matrix. Immediately the view before him swept away in a blur. Where before the distant Eathal legions had been a dark smudge north of Talis, they were now transformed into the packed ranks of Hukum's forces. He could see individual Eathal, marching with dark cloths wrapped around their heads to cut down the light of the suns. He made a slight adjustment to the Matrix, pulling back his vision. Like a long, dark snake, the whole of the main Eathal force was striking north towards the city of Valleth. Excellent. This would leave a gap open behind them, allowing he and his men to move west, then north along the Asog river to Olcis.

Raziin released his hold on the Fire, and his vision returned to normal. He looked critically at his men. All were powerful warriors of Cioan stock; golden-skinned with hair from golden brown to gold. He himself was a Cioan albino, his skin pale, his hair silver. He was a purist, and despite the men he had lost over the years, he refused to let anyone serve him unless they were pure-bred Cioan. Two of his men were badly wounded, faces pale with pain as they sat astride their amelak, but they kept up the pace. Raziin would expect nothing less from his chosen. Two others were forced to ride double, their amelak having fallen to Eathal spears. Supreme warriors, once leaders in his failed rebellion against his father, they looked to him to command them. Soon, with the power of the Spear, he would return to Armon and smash the forces of his brother Ralin, seizing the throne. Then the loyalty of these men would be rewarded. He would need strong leaders when the time came – men willing to do anything at his bidding.

'My Lord! The Eathal have closed the gap,' said Kyal. His thick-set lieutenant pointed back along the trail.

Raziin pulled on the reins of his amelak sharply, causing the animal to bleat in pain as it turned. He was too angry to enjoy its torment. Eathal warriors jogged into view in the valley below – hundreds of them. Too many to deal with by Sorcery alone. His own men numbered less than thirty.

'No matter. We will soon be out of Tupur,' said Raziin. Their amelak, although exhausted, would easily increase the distance.

He was just about to give the command to turn and retreat,

when the Eathal slowed down and began to form lines. They split into two flanks, leaving the centre free. He wondered at this until he saw what emerged from the trail.

'*Jakkund*,' snapped Kyal.

Jakkund were the only mounts the Eathal possessed. Their thickset bodies were covered in short, dark fur, their small eyes almost sightless. They had long, sleek legs, mobile snouts and big, constantly moving ears. Selectively bred from the docile jakka – cavern-dwelling cattle – for the Eathal nobility, they were big, powerful and fast. There were no more than a thousand of them in the whole Maht cavern system, and only a handful trained for war.

'Hukum's elite,' said Merceth. The giant's eyes narrowed as he watched them forming up. 'These should be in the vanguard of Hukum's army.'

'It seems our former master has learned the truth of his son's demise,' said Raziin.

There were more than sixty of the jakkund-mounted troops. They spread out in the gap, lowering lances as they formed their lines. Now Raziin knew what the Eathal ground troops had been pushing them towards.

The Eathal line began to move, the jakkund lancers riding slowly, keeping pace with the ranks of the foot soldiers.

If he was to make it out of Tupur, he needed to destroy the jakkund detachment. First he needed to separate them from the Eathal infantry. He would be risking everything, but surely Uros would not allow him to fail. Hadn't the Red Goddess led him to the Seer of Ciofran-Ac? Given him the means to free himself from Hukum?

'Be ready, Uros, to receive your gifts,' said Raziin, lifting his greatscythe from his back. Across their line, his men did the same. Raziin cantered down the slope towards the Eathal, his men following, steering their mounts with one hand on the reins. In the midst of combat, they had been trained to keep control of the amelak with only their knees, freeing both hands for their greatscythes. Only limited control was possible this way with untrained mounts, but it should be enough in close quarters – and he planned to get close.

At the sight of them approaching, the jakkund centre pulled out. On either side, the rest of the jakkund lancers followed, automatically keeping formation. A gap had begun to form between the lines of the Eathal foot soldiers and the jakkund.

'Turn!' called Raziin, pulling his amelak around. The tired animal almost stumbled, but Raziin wrenched at the reins, forcing it up. His men followed him, Kyal on his left and Merceth on his right. He increased the pace, making it seem as though they had baulked from combat and were trying to flee the field for the warren of valleys and hills to the west.

Raziin looked back and grinned savagely. *It was working*. The jakkund lancers, fearing they would escape, had pulled ahead of their infantry, leaving them far behind. A little longer ... *Now. It was time to put an end to this.*

'Attack!' commanded Raziin, turning back towards the jakkund and pushing his amelak to a gallop. He reached for the Fire, his breath coming fast as he anticipated the carnage to follow. Raziin flicked the reins, pushing more speed from his mount. He opened the Window, channelling the Fire into a Force Matrix that would release a long scything blade through the jakkund, cutting the legs from the beasts. Already he could imagine the blood. He was just about to release the bolt of Force when he sensed something. *Fire.* His eyes flicked to a tall figure in the centre of the jakkund line. An Eathal Sorcerer!

He only just had time to raise the Barrier as the force of the Final Matrix slammed into his mind. His Barrier wavered, but withstood the onslaught. With Hukum as his master he was well versed at fending off mental probes. Still – the power of the attack surprised him. The Sorcerer was stronger than even Hukum.

The jakkund were closing fast, the lancers picking their targets.

'*Die!*' Raziin release the bolt of Force. His heart raced, watching the glittering silver blade materialise in the gap between the lines and shoot towards the jakkund. The Eathal Sorcerer raised his arms. The bolt of Force slammed into a Barrier. Yet the Sorcery did not protect the whole of the mounted Eathal line. On the left and right flank, the blade of

Force continued on, cutting into the legs of the jakkund. The beasts squealed in panic, collapsing. Those behind them crashed into them at full pace. Yet the centre of the jakkund line swept onward, protected by the Eathal Sorcerer's Barrier. Again the Sorcerer attacked with the Final Matrix, trying to find a way into his mind. A barb of pain lanced into Raziin's left temple. The jakkund were so close he could see their small, dark eyes.

The eyes.

Raziin laughed as he channelled power into the Light Matrix.

A brilliant flash erupted from his hands. Across the line the jakkund screamed, the well-disciplined formation dissolving as the animals bucked and pulled away.

Then they clashed. Raziin dropped the reins. The twin blades of his greatscythe extended in a snap. A moment later they were cutting into flesh.

'The mounts!' Raziin yelled in Cioan.

His men fought with unleashed fury. Trained to use their lances, the jakkund troops were unprepared for the close-quarter fighting. For the moment Raziin and his men had the advantage. Through the chaos of combat, Raziin could see the Eathal foot soldiers closing in. They had to be free before they arrived.

Raziin raised the Fire, unleashing it in a gout of hot, hungry flame. It hit a Barrier and exploded harmlessly before it reached the jakkund troops. As the flames died, he saw the Eathal Sorcerer in the midst of the fight, defended by four jakkund-mounted troops.

'Yaa!' Raziin pushed his amelak towards the Sorcerer. One of the mounted bodyguards stabbed at Raziin with his lance. He swayed aside, letting it pass him harmlessly as he swung the right blade of his greatscythe through the Eathal's neck, taking his head from his shoulders. His left blade sliced up, taking another bodyguard's right arm off just below the shoulder. The Eathal screamed as his lance tumbled to the ground.

The Sorcerer held no weapon, but looked at Raziin calmly. 'You must die, Raziin. For the death of Staraz. Blood must answer blood,' called the Eathal Sorcerer over the tumult.

Raziin knew that voice!

Faivel.

The second son of his former master, Hukum, Faivel had been one of the many Eathal he met in the Caverns of Maht. Even though he was Staraz's brother, Faivel was the last Eathal he would have expected to exact Hukum's vengeance.

A bolt of Force shot at Raziin like an arrow. Hastily he raised a Barrier, blocking it. The power of the bolt knocked him backwards. With both hands on his greatscythe, Raziin could only gasp as it swept him out of his saddle. He landed on his feet, but tumbled backwards. He turned the fall into a roll and sprang up onto his feet, just in time to duck beneath the lance of one of the remaining bodyguards.

Half the jakkund were down, but the rest had reformed behind the tall Sorcerer. For a moment Raziin could not believe what he was seeing. His recollection of Faivel was of a skinny scholar, terrified of his domineering father.

The Eathal foot soldiers were closing fast.

'Dismount!' Raziin yelled over the chaos.

His men obeyed instantly, jumping down from their amelak.

The Eathal and their mounts shared one thing – sensitive hearing.

He felt Faivel raising the Fire to attack, but had no time to consider it.

Raziin let the Fire fill him, channelling it into the Matrix of Lightning. He released it in one massive bolt. There was a blinding flash – followed instantly by an ear-splitting detonation of thunder.

Both the amelak and the jakkund went crazy, bolting in every direction. One or two of the jakkund riders had kept their seats, but were struggling frantically with their mounts. The Eathal were crying out in pain, hands clamped to their ears. The ranks of the advancing foot soldiers had faltered.

Then the Force bolt hit Raziin.

It sliced through his leather armour, cutting deep into his ribs. He staggered back, losing his grip on his greatscythe as a flood of warmth trickled down his side. He looked down and saw blood, the white of bone showing beneath. *Pain.* The world swayed, then Merceth was at his side, lifting him. Another warrior supported him from the other side and they were running.

Holding grimly to consciousness, Raziin formed a Barrier over them. He felt an impact on the Sorcerous shield and steadied his concentration. Then Faivel attacked with the Final Matrix, the Eathal once more trying to find a way into his mind.

'Run for the hills, Merceth. West. West,' gasped Raziin.

He saw his warriors running beside him, the pillar of smoke from burning Talis in the sky to his right. As they topped a rise, Raziin looked back to see Eathal following them on foot. But a man can run faster than an Eathal. Only three jakkund riders had managed to capture their mounts. He smiled. It would take them at least a day to reform their cavalry, and by then he and his men would be in the maze of steep valleys that riddled western Tupur.

'Do you want to stop and heal yourself, my Lord?'

Raziin shook his head, saving his breath. He could still feel Faivel's mind seeking his. As long as he was within sight of the Eathal Sorcerer, he would be in danger if he dropped his Barrier. He needed to use all his power to counter him. Once they had lost their pursuers he would be free to use the Matrix of Form to heal himself.

'How many?' asked Raziin.

'Twelve lost, my Lord.' Almost half his men.

Raziin grimaced at the pain. So few now. But it would be enough.

* * *

Ellen looked down the road at the gates of Ceta. The caravan had bunched up, forced to slow this close to the city. Riding just behind the vanguard, Ellen and Raphal had moved their amelak up beside Cedrin and Marken. Out on the open road, Xyanthius would have told them to move back, being non-combatants, but this close to the city the rules were relaxed. Raphal was lost in thought, looking up at the clouds.

In less than an hour, they would be inside the city. Cedrin and Marken would be billeted with the warriors and once more

Ellen and Raphal would take their own rooms somewhere else. It brought back to Ellen the fact that she really had made no progress in winning Cedrin as an ally. When it came down to it, he would go his own way. In less than a week they would arrive at Searn just like this – and part ways for good. At some point on the road she would have to confide in Cedrin. Otherwise this quest would be meaningless. Yet how could she convince someone who mistrusted the Suul, someone who was determined to make their own way in the wider world, to join her quest for the Cinanac Scion? Then there was the threat of the Warlord and the Athrian Temple. Were assassins even now watching the gates as they had been in Seyt?

Ellen groaned, the same thoughts had been circling her head for hours. At least the time on the road had opened an easy dialogue between her and Cedrin. They had both come a long way since her galley overhauled his ship on the Sea of Mists, when she had been prepared to take him into chains for his part in the failed rebellion.

'What will you do in Ceta?' Ellen asked Cedrin.

'Take some free time with coin in our pockets. A decent meal would be good – and a real bed. You?'

'I'm looking forward to a bath,' said Ellen.

Cedrin laughed. 'That too.' His gaze lingered for a moment. 'Perhaps …'

'Pull the wagons over!' shouted Xyanthius from the vanguard.

Damn it! Ellen felt sure Cedrin had been about to ask her to share a meal.

'Uros' tits!' said Cedrin. 'We're only minutes from the gates.'

Cedrin looked sideways at Ellen. 'Err… sorry.'

'I've heard men swear before, Cedrin,' she said.

'This makes the third time,' said Marken. Twice before, the flagman on the walls had signalled them to clear the road. Both times it had been as important entourages left the city, moving south towards the Delta province.

'What is it?' called Cedrin.

Kalyth, riding just in front of them, squinted at the flag signal. 'An approaching Suul.'

The drivers struggled to shift the harena-borne wagons onto the side of the road. The harena were tireless, but disliked interruptions and changes in direction. The great beasts bellowed in protest and pulled against their tethers.

Ellen's amelak danced nervously and she patted its neck. 'It's all right, girl. Shhhh.'

Once on the side of the road, they looked back to study the approaching rider. He was mounted on a narsiit, the wings spread to catch the air as it flew. *What a sight.* Ellen missed her own narsiit, which she was forced to leave behind in Raynor.

'Grace in motion,' said Cedrin, his eyes alight with admiration as he watched the sleek beast approach.

'You have never seen a narsiit run?' she asked.

'No. Wow, what a beauty!'

The hooves moved in a blur, the narrow head tilted into the wind. In moments, the Suul had gone from a blur on the horizon to a fully visible figure. The suns glinted off his jewelled finery and harness. They were not the only ones watching – all eyes were on the winged mount as it passed, and to their surprise, the rider reined the animal in as he reached them.

The narsiit reared and snorted in protest, flapping its wings in irritation. It watched the warriors and beasts with wild, intelligent eyes.

'*Cedrin! Marken!*' called the Suul.

'By the suns … I know that voice,' said Cedrin.

Ellen looked at the Suul. He was thickset, his blonde, almost white hair drawn back in a single tail, the half-Meadrel features split in a wide grin. Something did not seem right. She looked at his forehead. There was no Suul mark.

'*Skye!*' shouted Cedrin and Marken together.

Xyanthius spurred his amelak down the lines to meet this mysterious rider. As he approached, his eyes narrowed. 'You have a fine mount, sir,' said Xyanthius, appraising the cut and expensive inlays of Skye's rig. 'But I have a caravan waiting for the gates.'

Skye bowed to Xyanthius from the saddle. His narsiit snorted and folded its wings with a snap. 'Please, gain the gates by all means. And allow me to travel with my associates here,' he said, pointing at Marken and Cedrin.

'Very well.' Xyanthius turned his amelak and rode back to the vanguard. 'Form lines! *Let's get this caravan moving!'*

The drivers coaxed the harena back onto the road. Skye manoeuvred his narsiit in beside Cedrin and Marken, and Ellen fell back behind them, immediately sensing the distance between herself and the three friends. In that moment, she knew her and Cedrin would be going separate ways for their time in Ceta. Just like that: the arrival of this man, Skye, had closed that door.

'Cedrin. How are you, my friend?' said Skye, leaning down from the high saddle to grip forearms enthusiastically with Cedrin, then Marken. 'Well met!'

'Unbelievable,' said Cedrin. He and Skye looked at each other and burst out laughing. Ellen had never seen Cedrin smile like that before. His whole faced was transformed, making him younger, more relaxed.

'How under the suns did you come by all this? You didn't steal it, did you? And a narsiit!' said Marken.

'So many questions!' said Skye, his dark eyes twinkling. 'Let's just say the Temple gave *me* a donation.'

The three friends burst into laughter as they fell in formation with the caravan. For the first time, Skye noticed Ellen behind them. His smile froze for an instant. 'Ellen Cin—'

'For the sake of Larus, Skye,' said Marken cutting him off. 'Not so loud. Yes, we know, she has been travelling at our hearth.'

'That's the Sarlord's daughter ...'

'Skye!' said Marken, stopping him once more and nodding to the nearby warriors to caution him. 'It's a long story.'

'After Raynor, why should anything surprise me?' said Skye.

Skye bowed to Ellen from the saddle. She returned his civil greeting. With a shock, she recognised him as the same calvanni who had been with Cedrin on the trader during Storm Season. In all the finery she had not recognised him as the same man. How did he come by a narsiit? It took years to train one of the wild plains runners – and they would *never* carry a stranger.

Cedrin and Marken, their amelak dwarfed by Skye's narsiit,

pulled ahead and she let them go, riding back with Raphal.

'It's impossible,' mumbled Ellen under her breath.

'What was that, Ellen?' said Raphal.

'Oh. A narsiit can't just be ridden like any other animal,' she said, turning to her old friend.

'There *are* ways to charm a narsiit,' said Raphal.

Ellen looked at him for a long moment, wondering at his cryptic answer. Nothing more was forthcoming.

She turned to watch the three former calvanni and was suddenly aware of how different they were from her. They had lived a different life in a world she did not understand. There was still time to bridge the gap. Between Ceta and Searn anything could happen.

The caravan lumbered towards the low walls of Ceta. The domes and towers were undressed stone, the tiles coloured with dull cream and brown pigments. There were no brightly-coloured spires here. It was a small provincial city, the like of which could be seen throughout Kelas. A trade and financial centre for the surrounding agriculture.

Ellen felt tired. As they entered the city she led her amelak away from the caravan. She looked back once to see Cedrin and his friends rapt in conversation. They did not notice as she and Raphal disappeared into the crowd.

* * *

Marken slid his empty glass across the table. He could hardly believe what Skye had just told them.

'So Raziin is alive.' Cedrin drained his glass and waved to the bar servers for another.

The tavern was crowded and was growing more bawdy as the night drew on, the buzz of conversation deafening. Skye's tale had left Marken and Cedrin both amazed and sombre. His robbery of the Temple had been brilliant, making them wish they had stayed in Raynor. But other news overshadowed this triumph. Raziin was in Kelas. Skye's brush with death at his hands had reawakened their memories of Regent's Hill. Looking at the swarthy Athrian now, it was hard to believe he had been so close to death.

'You were healed at a temple, you say?' asked Marken.

'I searched for it again, but it was gone. Nothing but a dead-end alley,' said Skye.

A serving girl laid three new ales on the table. She could hardly take her eyes off the flashy Athrian and his jewelled harness. Skye palmed a coin into her sweating hand and winked. Her eyes lit up, and she gave him a nervous smile before hurrying back through the crowd.

'This one lodged deep.' Skye ran his hand down a long scar on his left side. There were others on his arms and chest. The scars had all healed cleanly and begun to fade, and if he had not known better, Marken would have thought they were two years old at least.

'I can hardly believe you survived. If I had not seen a man cured by magic I would *not* believe it,' said Cedrin.

'I almost had him. I was as close to Raziin as I am to you,' said Skye to Cedrin. '*Closer*. But I hesitated.'

'Why?' asked Cedrin and Marken together.

Skye was silent for a moment. 'Fear,' he said, matching each of their gazes in turn, as though to challenge them.

'How can you claim that when you came so far? I don't know a single man who would have had the nerve to challenge a Sorcerer with a long knife,' said Cedrin.

'It *was* fear. That and superstition. I could have had him, so easily.'

Skye hit the table with his fist. 'He is just a man, Cedrin. A mortal with a weapon we do not have. That I know. It is like fighting a spearman, you must learn the reach of his blade and wait for your moment.'

'There must be more to it than that,' said Cedrin, reaching for his ale.

Skye gripped his arm to stop him and met his gaze. 'No. There is nothing more. That's why I came back to find you, Cedrin. I realised your power is only a weapon and that it does not make you an evil man.'

Marken leant forward eagerly. Of all the people he might have imagined would help Cedrin confront his powers, Skye would have been the last.

'I want no part of it. Not of Sorcery.' Cedrin wiped sweat off his forehead with his free hand. 'Damn this smoke. It's hot in here.'

'Don't be a fool, Cedrin. If someone attacked you and I threw you a calv, you'd use it. You cannot close your eyes. I have learnt that magic lays all around us, even if we fear it, even if we don't see it. What if Raziin were to challenge you again, or another Sorcerer or Druid?'

Cedrin broke Skye's grip on his arm and took a draught of his ale. 'It may be a weapon, but it is a dangerous one. People are killed for using it. The greatscythe is my weapon now.'

'The decision is yours,' said Skye. 'But you cannot make the choice in fear, Cedrin. That much I know.'

Marken prayed silently to Larus in thanks for whatever spirit had possessed Skye. The man was changed. Perhaps there was some hope that together they could persuade Cedrin.

Skye suddenly laughed, looking from him to Cedrin. 'By Uros, you have become a cheerless lot since the last time I saw you. The night hasn't even started yet!'

Skye stood and whistled across the room to the tavern prostitutes. They waited by the bar, breasts revealed tantalisingly through open blouses, rings on their fingers and large bangles around their necks and wrists. Each were marked with the flower tattoo declaring their profession.

'Hey, little flowers. Over here!'

A thickset Anacian woman in a loose, brightly-coloured dress picked out three women and sent them over. They moved slowly from the bar, fixing them with sultry smiles as they came.

A lithe young woman of Myrian stock sat on Marken's knees. She had small, firm breasts and a tight body. She would be fun to play around with, but he had seen too many men slink into the Athrian Temple to have their privates healed of weeping sores to lay with a common prostitute – he would only go so far. Skye's woman was plumper, and he was already teasing her, making her laugh. Skye had been a calvanni for the Mask of Courtesans in Athria, and he knew his way around women like this.

Cedrin's woman was a half-Cioan beauty – easily the choice of the bar – curvaceous, with long red-tinted hair. But Cedrin's eyes were back across the room, on one of the other prostitutes.

'What's the matter, lover?' The half-Cioan whore followed his gaze across the room. 'Her? She's skin and bone. You want me to get her for you? Poor choice – but whatever you need, sweetheart.'

Marken looked over towards the bar. The other whore who had caught Cedrin's eye was short and lithe, with honey-blonde hair. Marken wondered at it, until he saw the other whore's resemblance to Ellen. *Ahhh.*

'No,' said Cedrin finally. 'It's fine. More than fine. In fact you're just what I need to clear my head.'

The half-Cioan whore ran her hand through Cedrin's hair. 'You're a serious one, aren't you? Don't worry, love, I'll take care of you.'

The men soon forgot Raziin, Athria and Sorcery amid a haze of alcohol and heated lust.

* * *

Ellen sat on the balcony in a plain dress of white silk, refreshed but restless. Below, the city was alive. People shouted to each other across the crowded thoroughfare, milling in groups and walking from one lighted tavern to another. The scene was so foreign: frightening and enticing all at once.

Only now, after all her time on the road, did Ellen realise how sheltered her life had been in Athria. The whole sphere of her world had consisted of Regent's Hill, the palace and the Cintros mansion. The secrets she had shared with her father had underpinned her life, yet also trapped her, limiting the depth of her relationships. At the time, her life had seemed so full. It had taken the condemnation of the Temple to reveal how shallow her friendships with the Suulqua were. How quickly they turned away when her grasp on power slipped.

Now she longed to see more, to understand more of life. Walking to the balcony's edge, she allowed her thoughts to wander. What were Cedrin and his friends up to? No doubt they would be making the best of their pay somewhere, enjoying themselves while she sat alone in a tavern room. She loved Raphal, but his idea of a good time was reading a history book or praying. No. She had to get out there, into the bustle of life.

She regretted not being able to bring Valdas and Mendor, her two Suulqua, and some retainers with her on this journey. She had paid the servants well to alert her to anyone suspicious, but that meant nothing. A determined assassin, or a squad of Temple Guardians would still reach her, and she would be once more fighting for her life.

'Let them come!' she snapped. She was sick of living in fear. She was Ellen Cintros. Was she not a Sorcerer and a warrior in her own right? On impulse, she channelled the Fire, feeling the familiar flow of power. She no longer feared to use her Sorcery. Any Temple agents would already know she was here – by now every warrior in the caravan would have repeated the story ten times.

She leapt into the room, rolling as she hit the floor. As she rose, her hand swept out to seize her scythe. At the same time, she drew on the Fire, forming the Shadow Matrix, and vanished. *Myan did not train me to sit inside a room.* She could do anything like this, move anywhere. Ellen smiled. She knew what to do. As far as the tavern staff and Raphal were concerned, it would be as though she had never left the room.

She ran to the balcony and leapt into mid-air. Immediately she plummeted five stories to the cobbled street below. She swiftly drew a Matrix and halted her fall with delicately applied tendrils of Force. As her feet touched the ground, a feeling of intense freedom filled Ellen.

A laughing reveller staggered away from his friends and stumbled into her.

'Heat take you!' snapped the man, rounding on her with a drawn knife.

When he saw no one, he made the circle of Larus above his heart. 'Demons,' he muttered.

His companions burst out laughing, thinking it a great joke.

Ellen stayed motionless, waiting as they passed her by. Still exhilarated, but cursing her lack of care, she walked through the crowd, enjoying the night and her freedom; dodging amelak, carriages and people as she went. Before she knew it, she was looking for Cedrin and his friends, her heart beating fast. She watched every group passing by and peered into every tavern. She wondered what she would do if she actually found them. Should she watch them for a time? That seemed wrong in some way. Unfair.

Perhaps she could let the Shadow Matrix fall in some dark corner, then come upon them as though by accident? She was hardly dressed for a tavern, but she had not thought about it before leaping to the busy street. Ellen wove through the crowd, enjoying the atmosphere. She stopped to watch a street performance by a trio of jugglers. It was fun, but staying out of people's way was proving to be a challenge.

Ellen was distracted by a chorus of loud laughter and turned towards a nearby tavern entrance. Cedrin and his friends were leaving the place, their skin glistening with heat and sweat, faces flushed with ale. Each had a woman under his arm and it was obvious they would have their way with them tonight. Ellen's throat tightened.

Cedrin was with a half-Cioan woman, a beauty, with light golden skin and dark bronze hair. Her breasts were full and high, and like the other women, she did not conceal herself as she moved onto the streets. Hot rage pulsed through Ellen. Great bolts of Force and Fire waited just beyond her touch. In that moment, she wanted to lash out at that slut with every force at her command. Her head swam, and for a moment it was as though she stood at a precipice, ready to step forward into nothing.

The three friends and their women climbed a stair to the rooms above the tavern. At last she turned aside the Fire. Her mind was filled with Cedrin and the woman who would have him tonight. Ellen felt cruelly betrayed, more so than when her Suulqua lover Palsus had rejected her, but she knew that was absurd. Where, in all the leagues she had travelled, had Cedrin stopped being part of her oath to Myan and become something more?

The fun of her illicit adventure had soured. Ellen slipped into a darkened alley and let the Shadow Matrix fall. The spinning form of energy dissolved around her, and she turned back towards her rooms, sullen and deep in thought.

'Grab her!' called a rough voice.

She looked up, startled. Four men had fanned out around her, two in front and two behind her.

'Grab her, idiot! Let's get her back into the alley.'

One of the men made a grab for Ellen.

She would never allow a repeat of what happened in Seyt. Ellen swung the flat of her scythe-blade into the man's temple, reversing the weapon and striking him in the groin with the haft. He let out a whoosh of air and collapsed, clutching himself and yelling in pain. A small crowd gathered, watching but not intervening.

Ellen turned slowly to face her attackers. She deliberately tilted the scythe blade to catch the torchlight.

'I'll kill the next man who takes a step towards me,' she said.

The leader looked from the lanedd blade to Ellen, then ran. The other two paused for a moment then ran with him, leaving their unfortunate friend to his fate. Ellen walked back her rooms, shaken yet exhilarated. She had faced them, and *they* had run.

Only weeks ago, the same experience had truly shaken her. Now her hands shook slightly, but the incident had not struck to her core. The agents of the Warlord, the Athrian Temple – they no longer frightened her. She had been operating on faith: faith in the cause of the Scion, faith that Myan knew something about Cedrin that she would eventually discover – something that would make him vital. Soon, things would become clear. When they did, nothing would hold her back from reclaiming what was hers.

* * *

Cedrin sat on a rooftop with Marken and Skye. They watched the sea as it broke on the distant shore and the traders leaving Ceta on the morning tide, spreading their sails to the wind. The morning suns glinted from the glass windows and mought roof-tiles of the city, surrounding them with a bright haze of light. Below, the streets were beginning to fill with people.

Marken tapped Cedrin on the shoulder with the stem of his pipe. Cedrin shook his head, a feeling of sickness rising in him at the thought of any more se or tobacco.

'No, I've had enough,' said Cedrin.

Skye accepted the pipe. 'What's the matter, Cedrin, lost your stomach for it?'

Cedrin could only nod. He always though he was a fit man, but during the weeks with the caravan, Kalyth had shown him differently. Nights sparring and running had cleared his mind and opened a new awareness in his body. Now the ale did not taste as good and the tobacco smoked last night in the grip of the drink sickened him.

He had changed since Athria. A night like last night would have been a good time for Cedrin. He enjoyed the company, but found himself increasingly restless. So he drank more, but the ale had not cheered him and the se failed to lift his mood. And the Cioan woman ... despite her charms, the act had left him feeling empty. Something was missing. A piece of him had been cut off.

He rubbed his eyes, and looked down at the waking city, struggling with melancholy. Was this what he wanted for his life? A scytheman was an honourable profession, but there had to be more. A sense of something higher, a connection to the world beyond his own ambition.

He had longed for weeks to be in Ceta, to spend his pay. Now he wished for nothing more than to be back on the caravan, duelling with Kalyth, and passing the odd hours at the hearth with Ellen.

Cedrin brightened as he turned his thoughts to the Suul woman, wondering where she was. Even as he did, a different sort of pain began. She was forbidden, he reminded himself. He could never touch her, never take her in his arms. Never meet her lips again nor hold her like she was his own. Hussies like the Cioan half-breed were his kind. Like Kalyth, Ellen would leave his life soon. It was inevitable, and he saw no way to change it.

If this was the future, then so be it. He looked out to the sea and the horizon, determined to rid himself of this dark and unfamiliar feeling. Kranor would have need of leaders, and in time he would join the One Hundred. That was no small thing. Yes. He would stay with Kranor's company, continue to improve with the greatscythe. It would be up to him to build his skills and wealth, then look for the opportunity to start his own company. He would need connections first, and that meant time spent learning the ropes.

'You seem a little sombre for someone who has just enjoyed a night with friends, Cedrin,' said Skye.

'Too much se,' said Cedrin, realising he had been staring out to sea, lost in thought. 'Err... What will you do now, Skye?'

'Well, I've seen Raynor and I'm not too keen on going back there. I would like to see Olcis – and it's far from the Eathal and the coming war in the Yasser States. There must be opportunities there. How about we all go to Olcis together?'

'Do you want to rob the Hesguit now?' said Marken, blowing out a stream of smoke.

Skye laughed. 'Maybe,' he said. 'What about you, Cedrin? It's obvious the Cintros woman is here for you. Are you returning to the court in Athria with her? She is a Sorcerer, so they say. Perhaps you would make good allies.'

'I'm no Suul,' said Cedrin. His shoulders tensed.

Skye laughed. 'Cedrin, what is a Suul? Nothing more than a man or woman with a mark on his forehead. Take any person from the streets, give them a Suul mark and a chest of coin, convince them they are better than anyone else and put them in charge of something. Nobody would know the difference. By Uros – I made Xyanthius' whole caravan pull over just because I rode a narsiit.'

Cedrin shook his head. 'I have to stay my own master. I don't want to bow to a Sarlord or any Suul.'

'Cedrin, who do you think has to bow the lower, a Suul or a common mercenary? I know who is richer, and that's a *fact*.'

Cedrin's face became determined. 'Aye, but who has to bow more often?'

Skye nodded. 'So you'll not seek an alliance with her.'

'No.'

Marken remained silent, watching the exchange with intense interest. The silence drew out and finally he spoke. 'Cedrin, the Fire that runs in your veins will always be with you.'

Cedrin looked at Marken defiantly, but said nothing. A part of him wanted to hear.

'You have to train your powers before they kill you – I've told you this before. You have to tell the Cintros woman. Your talent is rare, Cedrin. You cannot let this opportunity pass.'

'It will take more than vague warnings from Druids to make me change my mind. I'll learn to control it myself, in my own fashion,' he said.

'Cedrin's powers could kill him?' said Skye.

'Yes,' said Marken. Cedrin looked away.

Skye gripped Cedrin's shoulder. 'I did not realise the danger you were in, my friend.'

Cedrin was warmed by the renewal of friendship. He could see that Skye was determined to make up for breaking his trust after they arrived in Raynor.

'I will travel with you to Searn,' said Skye. 'If you come with me to Olcis. How about it, eh?'

'Yes!' said Marken, tapping the last embers from his pipe.

'Aye, that's a deal,' said Cedrin. 'I will need Kranor to agree to a temporary leave from the company, though. I've made a commitment to him.'

The three held their fists together to swear the oath. Cedrin's heart lifted at the feeling of the bond between them.

'To Olcis!'

'What are you louts doing up here?' came the voice of an old woman. They turned to see a solidly built Anacian lady climbing from the upper windows onto the roof with a broom handle clutched in her fist. *'Be off! Or I'll give you a knock you'll not forget!'*

They laughed and scrambled from the roof, amused at the old woman's fearlessness. Cedrin and Skye raced down the side of the building onto the street, Marken close behind them. He felt like a youth again, running with his friends on the streets of Athria, free and wild.

Chapter Twenty-Three

Cedrin laid down his greatscythe and knelt by the stream. All was quiet. Above him, the sky was scattered with stars, the two moons falling apart as Rea left the slower Asic behind. He splashed some of the cool water on his face then ducked his head under. He threw his head back with a gasp, the clear, cold water falling over his bare shoulders and chest as he rose. He felt alive. Vital. His mind keen and clear. He picked up his greatscythe and made his way across the rolling heath towards the hearth.

Ceta was two days behind them. Once they cleared the walls, Kalyth had begun his training with renewed vigour. They were still concentrating on 'basics', according to Kalyth, and Cedrin had not yet learnt the elegant forms the old warrior used to train his power, speed and control.

Despite this, Cedrin felt he was beginning to master the weapon. Long years of calv fighting had taught him much; concentration, speed and co-ordination, the dynamics of movement in close quarters. Even the reluctant Kalyth admitted he showed promise. *Life was good.* His reunion with Skye had rekindled a part of him which had died since Athria, and he looked forward to their journey to Olcis. It would be as he had always dreamed. A life of adventure, free on the roads, bowing to no man, friends at his side ...

He approached the small circle of fires beside the main hearth and searched out the familiar figure of Skye's narsiit, unmistakable, even in the night. Nearing their campsite, his thoughts turned to Ellen. There had not been a word spoken between them since before Ceta. At first he thought nothing of it, but as the sullen silence stretched into the second day, he knew something was amiss.

The last night before entering the city they had come so close … as man and woman, not Suul and warrior. She was always in his thoughts and despite Kalyth's warnings, he had decided the bond between them was too important to see finished. He considered everything at length and decided there was only one thing to do: ask her to come to Olcis with him.

Cedrin walked into the light of the fire, ready for a good meal and a long postponed conversation with Ellen. Skye sat alone at the hearth, smoking a pipe. Ellen's tent was nowhere to be seen.

'Finally. Some company. This is one dull campsite with Marken off doing Larus-knows-what with Raphal. I'd been thinking I smelled like a fishing-boat or something,' said Skye.

'Where's Ellen?'

Skye exhaled, the pungent smell of tobacco enticing Cedrin, even though he had sworn off it. 'You mean Suul Cintros?'

'Aye, Ellen Cintros.' Cedrin squatted by the fire, breaking open a loaf of bread and taking a plateful of the rich stew from the crock that lay heating on the fire.

'She and Raphal lit their own fire tonight,' said Skye.

He ate rapidly, hardly tasting the food. Skye silently puffed on his pipe.

Cedrin picked up his greatscythe and stood. 'Which fire is it?'

The stocky Athrian sighed and pointed out Ellen's small hearth. 'For Larus' sake, let me come with you. The fire is warm, but a bit low on friendly talk, if you know what I mean.'

'I have to do this alone.'

'I understand,' said Skye. 'Best done swiftly then. Good luck, my friend.'

'I'll be back as soon as I can,' said Cedrin, guilty about leaving Skye alone after all his friend's efforts to rejoin him.

Cedrin walked away, determined yet apprehensive. As he approached Ellen's fire, he could see she sat with two others in the dim light. At first he took them to be Raphal and Marken, but as he neared, he saw it was the Suul Azel and his servant. *Azel. Azel is always pursing her. And he is a Suul.* In that moment, Cedrin wanted to turn away. A lifetime of social conditioning told him he had no right to intrude on these two nobles. Then his determination reasserted itself.

As Cedrin walked into the light of the fire, Ellen's face lit up. He quickened his pace. Yet no sooner had she seemed glad to see him than her face was transformed into anger. She seemed so furious that he stopped short. Had he done something to offend her?

'Missing your new friends in Ceta already?' Ellen's mouth was set and there was a fierce glow that enhanced her beauty.

'Evening, Cedrin,' said Azel.

'Azel,' said Cedrin. The Suul had instructed all the men not to call him Lord, since technically he owed allegiance to no court. Cedrin had always liked the plain-faced Suul. His manner was a little stiff, but he instinctively felt Azel to be honest and honourable. Right now he was furious that the man was monopolising Ellen's attention.

'Ellen. I would like to … talk to you,' said Cedrin. He felt like a fool.

'There is nothing stopping you.' Ellen forced a laugh, turning to Azel as though it was a joke, although Cedrin could see her eyes were still hard.

'Ahh … alone,' said Cedrin.

'I'm entertaining presently,' she said.

Cedrin gripped his greatscythe with white knuckles. 'Well then. Perhaps another time.'

He stalked off into the night, embarrassed and furious.

* * *

Ellen watched him go. With every step, the life seemed to drain out of her.

'Yes. It is often best to keep the lower ranks at bay, Suul Cintros,' said Azel. 'That sort can be trouble.'

She knew her treatment of Cedrin had been churlish, but the image of Cedrin with that Cioan half-breed … it would just not leave her mind. It was like a knife stabbing at her. The fact she had watched from the concealing shield of the Shadow Matrix, like a guilty thief, only fuelled her anger.

Azel cleared his throat. 'You need a man of character to accompany you to Olcis. A Suul, like myself for instance.'

Telling Azel of her plan to travel to Olcis had been a mistake. But the portly Suul was always there, trying to engage her in conversation, asking her plans, hoping – obviously – to win her favour.

Ellen forced a pleasant smile. 'Thank you for your company, Azel. But I wish to be alone.'

Azel could not hide his disappointment. 'Of course.'

The former Hend Suul gathered his greatscythe and waved to his servant, bowing slightly as he left. His efforts to win her over had increased manyfold since they had left Ceta. Behind the arrogant exterior, he was desperate. Penniless and dispossessed, he would do anything to regain a place at court.

Ellen stared into the fire. The embers shifted and became a rose, wilting, falling, dying. She had come so far in search of the Scion and was no closer than when she started. How much *would* Myan have expected of her? She had lost too much, given too much already.

* * *

Cedrin shifted in the saddle. His skin itched beneath his black leather armour, which relentlessly soaked up the suns' heat. It felt wrong to have his chest covered, but once more Kalyth was taking no chances. They were all in armour, and almost all of the mounted troops had been issued cavalry scythes: shorter than a normal scythe with a thick curving blade. The only exception were the handful of warriors like Kalyth who had been trained in mounted greatscythe combat. Cedrin's own greatscythe was strapped to his back. Most warriors had also been issued spears, or lances if they had been trained to use them. Like the cavalry scythes, these could be fitted into a special sheath on the saddle and secured with a series of hooks.

He could feel Ellen's eyes on his back, but refused to turn

around. They were still not talking.

The north road followed the coast here, and to their left there was a sheer drop to a shoreline of jagged rocks. Skye rode with them in the vanguard, a finely-crafted horn bow and quiver in his saddle, a well-made scythe in his hands. The narsiit had settled well beside the amelak, but Cedrin had not grown used to the height of the animal. Skye loomed above them.

'Anyone for a dip?' said Skye, peering down at the foaming waters below. He mimed a dive off the edge into the sea.

'The water might be nice, but I'd doubt you'd feel it when you got there,' said Marken.

The three of them burst into laughter, earning a sharp look from Kalyth. The old warrior had warned them twice to keep their voices down.

Two wild narsell ran across the hills to their right, moving fast with their wings spread. A relative of the narsiit, they were small-limbed and delicate, and seemed to glide through the air as they leapt over hollows and fallen branches.

Kalyth reacted immediately. 'Stop the caravan! Defensive formation!'

The caravan shuddered to a halt. The ranks pulled tight, turning to face out from the wagons. They gripped their weapons, suddenly alert, watching for attack. Cedrin could hear a sound like distant thunder, and he scanned the road and hills. The sound grew louder. Hoof beats. Hundreds of them. An attacking cavalry force? Cedrin adjusted his grip on the cavalry scythe. A herd of narsell swept into sight, fleeing north-east across the hills.

Laughter broke out in the ranks.

'Savaged by a group of narsell!' joked Skye.

Those near him laughed again. Throughout the troop, the tense silence was replaced with sporadic conversation.

'*Silence!* Hold ranks!' Kalyth's voice demanded instant obedience.

They waited. The narsell were almost lost from sight when a troop of palgur appeared. They ran with frightening speed, the backs of the great cats undulating as they came, closing fast on the last of the fleet-footed narsell.

'Ferocious – and hungry,' said Skye.

A harena bellowed, and the amelak danced in place, the animals scenting the powerful predators. There were fifteen of the great cats. Even against a hundred mounted warriors, they could wreak untold havoc and death.

'*Spears!*' yelled Kalyth. 'Ready bowmen!'

There was a rattle of movement as Cedrin and the other warriors put away their scythes and hefted the longer weapons. A forest of lanedd blades now extended beyond their ranks. Bowmen stood high on the wagons and drew their shafts to their cheeks, holding at the point of tension, seeking aim. Against beasts like the palgur, close-combat weapons were useless.

Down the lines, the warriors readied for attack. Amelak began to snort and pace. The harena wailed. Skye's narsiit bucked and reared, throwing the tight lines into confusion as it sought to break free. Skye struggled to keep his place in the saddle.

The palgur turned. They raced straight for them. Then inexplicably, they turned away, following the narsell as they fled inland.

A wave of relief spread through the ranks. Cedrin let out a breath he did not even know he was holding. Marken wiped sweat from his eyes. Thinking it was over, they readied themselves to move forward again. But the animals grew more restless. Skye's narsiit screamed: a powerful, fearful cry that sent the animals into total frenzy.

'Ahhh! *No.*' Skye could only hold on as his narsiit spread its wings and vaulted *over* the ranks, clearing the amelak and riders in a single, powerful leap. The animal ran north with explosive speed. In moments, Skye was a blur on the horizon.

'Keep the lines!' called Kalyth.

But it was useless. The warriors had lost all control of their mounts. Xyanthius, Kalyth and Azel shouted for order. The harena broke from formation and ran into the hills to the east of the road, dragging the wagons with them. One harena screamed as it ran over the high cliff, taking the wagon and the driver with it. Wagons were being overturned as they collided. The warriors, trying to control their amelak, watched hopelessly.

Then the sky split with an explosion of sound like thunder. The amelak bolted. Cedrin lost his grip on the saddle and fell hard to the earth, winded and blind with pain. Screams. Shouts. Confusion. He opened his eyes and struggled to rise, but a great shadow covered them, and he looked up to see a massive shape against the suns.

'*Drakon!*'

Cedrin scrambled to his feet. He had lost his spear and had taken a savage hoof-blow to the leg. His greatscythe was still strapped to his back. Trying to escape the chaos, he made for a low hillock to the east of the road. Then he looked up.

The drakon was huge. Easily the size of a small galley. Its pitch black, armoured scales drew the light from the sky. It swivelled its angular head towards them, its glowing amber eyes watching them without emotion or mercy. The drakon had been pursuing the palgur and narsell, but when it saw them it banked sharply, immediately shortening its wings to dive. The air screamed as it touched the red-hot gills beneath the beast's wings. Its claws reached out towards them, glittering like diamonds, razor-sharp and stained with blood.

'Sweet Larus,' said Cedrin.

All semblance of order in the caravan had disappeared. Across the ground lay scores of injured, crippled amelak. They cried in pain and fear, still struggling to run. Marken was down.

'Ellen. Where's Ellen!' he shouted.

And the drakon struck.

Cedrin winced at the heat as it passed. Vapours ripped at his lungs and stung his eyes. The drakon clutched at one of the warriors, but he dived under a wagon. It seized the harena and wagon in its claws and bellowed in rage. Its breath roared out, hotter than a furnace. The wagons nearby exploded into flame. The harena roasted alive. Cedrin's breath caught in his throat as the acid vapour was blown back at him by the sea wind.

The drakon ripped the harena in two in its jaws as it climbed, feasting on the wing. As it crested, a high blur of darkness in the sky, it ate the rest and threw the wagon to the ground.

It dove again.

'Cedrin, you have to flee!'

He turned to see Ellen beside him, her face blackened with soot.

'Get down! You cannot stand on a hilltop. It prefers humans and Eathal over all other prey!'

He gripped her arm, relieved to see her safe. 'Let's get out of here.'

Cedrin looked around, searching for somewhere to hide. He looked back up into the sky. The drakon filled his vision. *It was coming.*

'Save yourself!' he yelled, pushing her away.

Its eyes shone with cold cognition. Its jaws opened, revealing the cavern of its mouth. He would be melted in the fires of its heart in an instant. Even so, he refused to run. Let the drakon come.

'Cedrin! *No.*'

The beast had seen him. He looked at Ellen, who was squatting down beside a wagon. She was frantic. The wagon would provide no protection for the two of them. But he could distract it. He could save her.

Cedrin ran away from Ellen, waving his arms.

The drakon plummeted straight for him. The scream of the air beneath its wings was deafening. The sun glinted from its reddened claws.

'I am ready,' said Cedrin. *Ready for the Drakon. Ready for annihilation.*

Something collided with him, knocking him from his feet.

Ellen.

She stretched out her arms. Once more Cedrin sensed something moving. *Flowing.* Now he knew. The Fire.

Something shimmered in the air in front of Ellen, taking shape.

'Ahhhh!' she gasped, her face contorted in pain. A silver bolt shot from Ellen's outstretched arms. The size of a battering ram, it reflected the light of the suns as though its sides were mirrored. As it streamed from her, she continued to create it, and it pumped skyward in a vast silver column. The point of the Sorcerous ram struck the drakon like a spear, ripping armoured plates from its belly. Yellow blood splashed out. It vaporised instantly into a cloud, dropping to the ground. It set the grass to flame, charring the earth black.

The drakon lost control. It tumbled, plummeting towards the earth. It seemed it would strike, but at the last instant it righted itself and extended its wings, fanning out the red-hot gills beneath. The air roared as it passed through the gills, sweeping across them in a hot gust. It gathered speed, racing just above the ground. It swept past them with roar of defiance, its breath sweeping over them like a foul wind. Then it shot skyward, rising until it was gone from sight.

Cedrin scrambled to his feet. Ellen had saved him. Ellen and her Sorcery.

He raced to her side. Her face was drained of colour, her eyes pale and sunken.

'Cedrin,' she said, reaching to touch his face. She staggered, and he caught her as she fell, sagging into his arms. Cedrin lifted her off the ground, surprised at how small she felt, how fragile. Her bracer was gone, lost in the chaos. He carried her down the hill to the remnants of the caravan.

Warriors were riding back. Most of the wagons had returned, albeit crippled, drawn by the now complacent harena. Many had been overturned and were strewn about the ground like broken toys amid the mess of their scattered contents, some still burning. Five harena had been lost: one to the drakon, one to the cliffs and three to the beast's incendiary breath.

Marken jogged up beside him, leading their amelak.

'Let's get her to Raphal,' said Marken. 'This way.'

Marken led him through the chaos to Raphal, who was using his skills to heal the warriors.

'Raphal!' called Cedrin. His stomach tightened. Had Raphal seen Ellen use her Sorcery? Would he still heal her?

The Larus Druid straightened from examining a warrior's leg, which had been crushed beneath an overturned wagon. The warrior was fighting to stay conscious.

'Quickly,' said Raphal, waving his arms.

Cedrin laid her down gently on the turf and the Druid firmly pushed him out of the way. After a frantic examination he relaxed, obviously relieved, then laid his hands on her. A golden glow suffused her body, shining brightly in her face like sunshine.

'The Essence of Larus,' whispered Marken.

When the glow faded, the pale, sunken look had gone and Ellen's breathing was deeper and easier.

'Thank you, Raphal,' said Cedrin.

'Do you think I would need thanks for healing Ellen?' said Raphal, frowning.

'I —' started Cedrin.

'I am not the Temple, Cedrin. Just part of it – for good or for ill,' said Raphal.

For Cedrin the meaning was clear. Despite Raphal's allegiance to the Temple of the Sisters, his loyalty to Ellen came before any concerns over her use of Sorcery.

'I understand,' said Cedrin.

Raphal returned to healing the warriors.

'Will you join the healing?' Cedrin asked Marken.

'No. There is nothing I can do until the moons rise. With Larus high in the sky, Raphal can use his skills. We are lucky. Larus Druids have great skill with sudden injuries, such as broken bones and wounds. They can strengthen and quicken the natural pace of healing in the body.'

'Why not other types of sickness?' asked Cedrin.

Marken nodded towards Raphal. The Druid was walking down the line of men, pausing at each. 'Do you see how he examines each of the wounded? Raphal is checking each of the injured carefully for signs of other disease.'

As they watched, Raphal waved two warriors away, refusing to heal them. One had a slash across his cheek, the other was nursing a broken rib.

'I know these two. One has the wasting disease in his lungs. The other has a fever, likely a water-borne parasite picked up in Ceta. They came to see us the other night. Each would have worsened under Raphal's touch. The power of Larus enhances all life – even that of a parasite or growth. Fortunately, their injuries are minor.'

'And Moon Essence?' asked Cedrin. Cedrin looked down at

Ellen, wondering what more he could do.

'The Moon Essence is more subtle. A Moon Druid can target the disease.'

Cedrin looked around at the chaos, seeing the extent of the damage with a cool head for the first time.

'We better help,' said Cedrin

They left Ellen sleeping beside the Druid and tethered their amelak to a makeshift picket line. They then joined in the hard work of salvage. Most of the wagons could be repaired, but three were little more than firewood. So began the laborious task of gathering goods that had been scattered and strapping them to the backs of harena. Alechul was frantic and galloped from one ruined pile to the next, amending his inventory. The merchant was more upset about the lost wagon loads than the men dead on the rocks below. Alechul persuaded Xyanthius to send men down the cliff to gather the fallen goods before the tide ruined it. Recovery of the bodies was incidental. The merchant's lack of concern for the men rankled Cedrin. It brought home to him exactly what he was, a hired soldier, paid to take a chance with death. He consoled himself with thoughts of the Way. He had the right to refuse any order that went against his judgement of what was right.

They worked hard all day, finally piling the ruined wagons to make a pyre for the two dead. The warriors paused by the burning pyre in reverence, watching as the sooty, dark-yellow flames engulfed the crushed remnants of the men.

An amelak galloped up to them as they watched the flames.

'Back to work, there is no time for this now!' said Alechul from the saddle. 'There is much more to be done ...'

It was poor timing, but Alechul was right. They would be vulnerable to attack until they restored the caravan. In grim silence, the warriors turned from the flames. As dusk fell, the caravan was back to a semblance of order. Marken left to join Raphal.

The main hearth fire was lit, and Cedrin shared a simple meal with the other warriors. For a time he walked through the men, checking all were well. Rastor had come through it without a scratch. Lann had a broken leg, which had been quickly healed by Raphal. The talk revolved around the strange events of the day and the politics of who would be given mounts, and who would ride in wagons until they reached Searn. Mounts were in short supply, many of the amelak having been either lost or crippled.

Cedrin stretched out on the ground. There had still been no sign of Skye. The flames of the pyre danced in his mind. There was no glory in this, Cedrin realised. He loved the skill, the feeling of mastery, but to die a sudden, meaningless death defending a merchant's wealth seemed without honour or purpose. He tossed and turned on the hard ground while the men around him snored, already in exhausted sleep.

Then he saw Ellen walking towards him.

* * *

Ellen had roused an hour ago. She had lain in a sort of trance state for a while, listening to two warriors near her talk of the 'silver arrow' that had struck the drakon on its last plunge. This had brought her back to awareness. Her head felt like it was splitting in two. In her desperation to save Cedrin, she had channelled far too much of the Fire. She listened carefully to the talk of the men around her. Although word had spread, few had seen the spear of Force strike the drakon.

Ellen pushed herself to her feet and walked over to Raphal, who watched critically as Marken worked under the light of the moons, healing a man with a cut to the forehead.

'Is Cedrin all right?'

'He is fine,' said Raphal. The old Druid had dark circles beneath his eyes. 'He is by the fire.'

It was one thing to be told Cedrin was unharmed, another to actually see him. A wave of relief flowed through her as they saw each other across the main hearth.

Cedrin started to sit up, but Ellen waved him back, sitting wearily beside him.

'It's good to see you well,' he said.

'And you.'

Cedrin looked around at the sleeping men, then leant in

closer to her. 'You risked a lot to save me, Ellen. Thank you.'

'The road has become a dangerous place. And we are still a long way from Searn,' she said.

'Do you still plan to go to Olcis?' he asked.

Ellen's breath came fast. Her head was a mass of pain. 'Yes. I have vowed to see Raphal safe.' *And I have a mission to complete for my father.*

'And after that, will you return to Athria?' he asked.

'It's a little early to say,' she said evasively. 'The Templemen are strong in Athria. They have mercury torcs that suppress ... a Sorcerer's power.'

She saw Cedrin flinch at the mention of mercury glowmetal. Ellen wondered what his reaction to the glowmetals in the Cintros labyrinth might be.

'For now I think I will just concentrate on recovering,' said Ellen. One thing was for certain – she did need to recover. It would be days, perhaps weeks before she could safely reach for the Fire again. Her father had warned her of the dangers of opening the Window too far and until now she had heeded him. But never had she felt the need of power as she had today.

'Ellen. I have been meaning to ask you —'

'*To arms! To arms!*' The call rang through the camp.

They sat in stunned silence.

The sentry's horn blasted through the night, then ceased abruptly.

Kalyth swept past the hearth on his amelak. '*To arms! We are under attack!*'

Before they could rise, mounted bandits were rushing through the camp on amelak and narsiit, screaming warcries in a score of languages and casting spears from the saddle. Ellen struggled to stand but fell back, overcome with pain and faintness. *I am defenceless!* The Fire was closed to her and she hardly had the strength to raise her own arm. 'Sweet Larus!'

A javelin took a warrior in the chest, and he was knocked from his feet, shouting in pain and surprise. Cedrin snatched up his greatscythe. A rider spurred towards him, lowering a lance. He swayed aside, his weapon cutting up and through the man's bicep. The attacker yelped in pain and dropped his lance, turning his amelak back the way he came. All around them, warriors milled in confusion. Xyanthius, Azel, and Kalyth were nowhere in sight.

'To the hearth!' called Cedrin, his voice booming through the chaos. Instantly the warriors responded, rallying to him. Ellen ran with them. They formed ranks around the central fire, protecting the wounded. Ruus and two others from Kranor's One Hundred were there, following him without question.

'Cut at the legs!' commanded Cedrin.

They obeyed, slashing with scythe and greatscythe at the bandits as they rode at them. The bandits fell back, giving them some breathing space.

Ellen looked up to Cedrin. He seemed to stand taller as he stood beside the fire. The phoenix on his chest flexed as he turned into the light.

'Archers!' shouted Cedrin.

Men disengaged from the ranks and ran to the hearth to change weapons. The mounted bandits drew back and formed a wedge. They were led by a military man, there was no doubt.

'Where are Kalyth and Xyanthius?' said Cedrin. 'They could not have fallen already.'

The men looked at Cedrin, waiting for his next command. The archers held their bows ready. In a battle, timing was everything and they were trained to wait for the command, for that crucial moment. The bandit leader shouted a warcry and raced towards them. Soon they would be in the light of the fire. *The time to fire is now! Why is Cedrin hesitating?*

'Give the command!' she said.

There was something wrong with Cedrin. His face, his body, were frozen in place. Magic! But where? Standing on a ridge above the encampment was a Moon Druid, arms raised to the moons. The magic-user had identified Cedrin as the leader and frozen him in place. Cedrin was trapped, and there was nothing she could do. Then she felt something stirring. Something impossible. She felt the Fire rising *inside* Cedrin.

'Let fly!' yelled Ellen, with all the command her life as a Suul had given her.

The air was filled with the thrumming of bow-strings, then

the screams of bandits as the shafts found their marks.

Then Fire exploded from Cedrin. A tongue of flame sped across the intervening space from Cedrin to the Moon Druid. The Druid barely had time to widen his eyes before the flames engulfed him. His scream was brief and agonised. The Fire flowed from him for moment longer, then guttered out. Cedrin and the charred corpse of the Druid fell to the earth together. The concussion sent the mounts of the attackers into a frenzy and stunned everyone, bandit and warrior alike. But the bandits regrouped quickly and rushed back to the attack.

The battle swirled around Ellen as the bandits and Xyanthius' warriors went head to head. She knelt at Cedrin's side. He shook violently, his left side twisted with muscle spasms. She cradled his head in her arms. This was her fault. If she had only looked further than Myan's cryptic words, she would have seen the danger. *This* was why Cedrin had to be sought. Myan had known of the Fire in his Blood!

A warrior fell near them, and a man stepped over the body. He towered above her. His greatscythe blades dripped with blood, his face grim and impassive. Her eyes were drawn to the Suul mark on his forehead. *The bandit leader was a Suul.* His eyes showed no pity as the greatscythe began to move. She had no power and little physical strength.

'At least you will die at the hand of a Suul,' he said.

She reached for her concealed knife, but knew she would never get to it in time.

There were two dull thuds. A gasp of pain. Ellen blinked. Two arrows had appeared in the bandit leader's chest. He dropped his greatscythe and reached for them. Another shaft struck him in the neck, and he sank to the ground with a strangled sigh. A narsiit whinnied and Ellen could see Skye high on the hilltop, a horn bow in his hand as he aimed for another of the bandits.

'Form lines!' called Kalyth. She saw him and Xyanthius running towards them, Azel close behind. Then she realised: the Druid must have also held them in his spell. With his death, they had also been released.

The men gave a cheer and fell into formation around the

leaders. The bandits fell back, and seeing their leader dead by the hearth, retreated, leaving their dead and wounded behind. Skye galloped down the hill and sent volley after volley of arrows after them until they had vanished from sight.

It was over. Only the moans and cries of the wounded and dying remained.

Ellen felt a hand on her shoulder and turned to see Marken beside her. His face was pale and drawn. 'Is Cedrin all right?'

'I don't know. He may never rouse again. The raw Fire can destroy the mind.'

Marken winced in pain as he knelt. She saw blood on his shoulder. He had been wounded. He touched his friend's fevered brow.

'I warned him,' said Marken. 'But he wouldn't listen. If only he had come to you earlier.'

Ellen's stomach twisted. 'He knew? All this time you both knew?'

Marken nodded. 'Yes. We knew. It happened on the Spire, when we faced Raziin. The Northman held us all with Sorcery. Cedrin released the Fire. The pitch beneath the Siren was lit and we were freed. We owe him our life.'

Ellen was furious. 'Why didn't you tell me?'

Marken sighed. 'It was his wish.'

They looked at Cedrin, fearing the worst.

'I could have helped him,' she said, tears rising in her.

'Will he live?' someone asked in a deep voice. They looked up to see Kalyth towering over them.

'Only time will tell,' said Marken. 'There is no physical wound.'

Ellen looked at Kalyth with an unspoken accusation, but when she met the old man's eyes, she saw only concern for the young man he had taken into his care. There was no way Kalyth could have known about the Fire.

'Is he...' Kalyth asked Ellen, looking openly into her eyes as an equal for the first time since they had met.

'Yes,' said Ellen, reading the question. 'He is Old Blood.'

The words seemed to crush something in Kalyth.

'How bad is it?' asked Ellen.

'Eighteen men lost, with three others close to death. Eleven wounded too badly to fight. And all the while ... I could do nothing. Struck from my amelak by some magic, then held in place, unable to speak or move.' Kalyth looked at Cedrin with a strange mixture of fear and concern. 'There is much to do.' Kalyth walked off into the night, issuing orders as he went.

Skye arrived, mounted on his narsiit and carrying a passenger behind him. He leapt swiftly from the saddle, dragging his dark-skinned companion after him. The man appeared to be Meadrel, squat and heavily built, but completely bald. A thick mought chain dangled from a slave-ring around his neck.

Skye knelt at Cedrin's side, his face grim. 'What is it? What wound did he take?'

Ellen could say nothing.

'It was the Fire, Skye. It happened again, just like the Spire,' Marken said.

Skye bowed his head. 'So you were right, my friend. He could not control it.'

Ellen was infuriated, but was too outraged to speak. They had all known.

The dark-skinned man knelt at Cedrin's side, close to Skye. This close, Ellen was shocked to see the heavy brow ridges and leathery ears. He was no Meadrel. The man was a minitil, the ill-fated progeny of Eathal and Man. The strange skin colour and build now made sense.

'Where did you find him?' said Marken.

'I followed the bandits as they fled, but they soon scattered in the dark. I found *him* wandering around the hills. I can only guess he was their slave and followed them from their camp. He speaks some archaic dialect of Cioan. As far as I can tell, his name is Bovosan,' said Skye.

'Why did you bring him?' asked Ellen.

Skye looked puzzled and then smiled. 'I'm not sure. It seemed the right thing to do. I can't imagine one of their slaves holding too much loyalty to *them*.'

'Well, no-one in chains is any use to us,' said Ellen.

Skye smiled. 'That is easily fixed.'

The stocky Athrian beckoned the minitil to his feet. Using a tool from his pouch, Skye deftly picked the primitive lock on the minitil's collar. The chains fell to the dust, and Bovosan lowered himself to the ground in prostration. He bowed to each of them in turn, and to the still form of Cedrin. He gave praise in his tongue to Yosini then moved to Cedrin's side.

'*Makdiron Suphus*,' he said, looking at each of them as though to be understood. '*Makdiron Suphus*!'

Skye looked from Bovosan to Marken and Ellen, who both knew ancient Cioan.

'What is he saying?'

'Master of ...' said Marken. 'I can't make out the pronunciation.'

'Master of Fire,' said Ellen. 'He is calling him the Master of Fire.'

'Marken!'

They looked up to see Raphal staggering towards them, holding a cloth to a light head wound. Ellen's heart leapt in concern. In all the confusion she had forgotten Raphal!

'Are you all right?' said Ellen, torn between Cedrin and her old confidant.

'Yes, yes,' said the old Druid impatiently. 'But there are many others who are not.'

Raphal turned to Marken. 'Come, Moon Druid. It is time for you to start using your powers again.'

Raphal pointed a long, thin finger at Marken's shoulder. 'Start with yourself.'

Marken touched the wound then paused to concentrate. It was surrounded with a glow of milky light, rising to the brightness of a full moon. It faded, leaving the wound healed.

'By Uros,' said Skye. 'You *are* a Moon Druid.'

Raphal nodded with satisfaction.

'Come! We have need of more Moon Essence tonight!'

Chapter Twenty-Four

Ellen looked back into the wagon where Cedrin lay prostrate and barely breathing. He had not roused since the Fire had ravaged his mind and was weak from lack of food and water. The thought that he might die here, after all they had been through was like a massive weight hovering above her, ready to fall. Despite Marken and Raphal's efforts, spasms still ravaged his left arm. The strange minitil Bovosan had not left Cedrin's side and sat beside him in the wagon, occasionally touching his brow with a damp cloth or gently massaging his arm. The devotion was puzzling, but welcome. Cedrin's destruction of the enemy Moon Druid must have had a profound effect on him.

The noonday suns beat down.

The harena were piled high with casks, barrels and crates, some drawing improvised sleds, bowing under the weight of goods and wounded warriors. The wagons ran awkwardly and bore the signs of hasty repair. Dust rose in clouds, kicked up by the sleds. The men in the rearguard covered their faces with cloths to keep it from their throats.

The light banter of the road had ceased as they struggled on, waiting for the bandits to strike again, or the drakon to return in redoubled fury. The caravan had not ceased to be a worthy prize. Alechul's wealth in coin and gems lay intact, hidden in his wagons. They were still days from Searn and another full scale attack was possible. The guard numbered barely sixty warriors, and fatigue weighed heavily on all of them. Ellen had taken Cedrin's place in the vanguard and rode with Skye and Marken. After the losses they had sustained, Xyanthius was not inclined to protest.

'*Impersiolos! Impersiolos! Majus maxicans!*' it was the minitil, crying out in his strange tongue. This time even she could not quite catch the meaning of the obscure Cioan dialect.

'Kalyth. Can I check on Cedrin?' asked Ellen.

The old warrior's eyes lit with hope. 'You can all go – but return quickly. We need to stay in formation.'

Ellen rode back to Cedrin's wagon with Marken and Skye. The voice of the minitil was raised in some incomprehensible salutation.

As she neared her heart jumped. *Cedrin has woken from his fever.* He was looking up at the strange face of Bovosan above him in bewilderment.

'Who, by Uros, is this?' he said, pushing himself into a sitting position. Bovosan was attempting to prostrate himself in the cramped confines of the wagon, his rapid oration continuing without pause.

Ellen burst into relieved laughter, the others joining her.

'His name is Bovosan,' said Skye. 'And I think you'd better get used to him.'

Less than an hour later, Cedrin rode alongside Ellen. He had insisted on returning to the vanguard. Raphal and Marken could find nothing wrong with him except fatigue. The dark-skinned Bovosan ran at a steady pace beside Cedrin's amelak, a heavy mought hammer in one hand and a small hide shield on the other. They were Eathal weapons. There was no doubt from the way he held them, he knew how to use them. Bovosan was not born a slave. His incredible endurance won the admiration of many of the warriors. He had also chosen three short javelins from the caravan armoury, which he slung across his back. The minitil made some of the warriors uncomfortable, but Xyanthius had given his approval so they held their tongue.

'Why didn't you tell me sooner?' asked Ellen, trying to keep her voice level. It was still hard not to be angry.

'I had hoped I could control it.' Cedrin looked around nervously at the nearby warriors, but no one except Skye and Marken were within earshot. 'I know how close I came to disaster. I remember the Window. The way it melted, bursting outwards. The Fire – it flowed through me burning everything.'

Cedrin flexed his left arm, wincing at the pain.

'Your arm will recover,' she said. 'Considering everything, you have been lucky. To survive raw Fire once is a feat. Twice is the luck of the gods.'

Ellen shivered. Even though her physical strength had returned, she dare not touch the Fire for days yet. 'You will have to learn to control it. To channel it.'

'Aye. It's high time I learned that.'

'And I cannot teach you properly on the road,' she said.

'You're right, Ellen. But I can't go back to Athria and Raynor will soon be under siege.' He paused. 'Skye, Marken and I are also planning to travel to Olcis. Perhaps we can travel together?'

'I will come with you to Olcis,' said Ellen, suppressing her sudden excitement. At last things were falling into place. Finally she had found the thing to link Cedrin to her, and it was the last thing she expected. Sorcery. And he was coming with her to Olcis. Cedrin was *Old Blood*. She would teach him to use the Fire, and as time drew on, she would make him a Suul in everything but name. Then she would win him to her cause.

'Ahhh. The gods have mercy after all,' said Marken.

'What's got into you?' said Cedrin.

'Oh, nothing,' said Marken, looking entirely pleased with himself. 'Perhaps Raphal could get us apartments in the old city of Olcis. The Eathal are unlikely to strike that far north, and the city is defended by the Temple Druids and a full legion of warriors. We would be safe there.'

'Perhaps,' she said. The idea of teaching Cedrin Sorcery in a city ruled by the Temple of the Sisters sent a chill down her spine. Given the Warlord's open attitude to Sorcery, Raynor would have been the obvious place to take Cedrin, yet the city was closed to her. In time she would be able to open a dialogue with the Warlord through Estle and come to some compromise, but that did not help her now. If only the Athrian Temple could be persuaded to change their stance – to turn a blind eye to her powers as they had for her father Myan. A wild thought came to her. There was one person in Olcis who could make them see sense. The Hesguit himself. As head of the Temple of the Sisters in Kelas, he could force the Athrian Temple to rescind the edict against her. A sick feeling grew in her stomach and her limbs felt heavy. Would she dare? To walk into the centre of the Temple's power in Kelas? The Olcis Temple had never formally declared against her, but would they hear her petition or simply take her for execution?

They crested a rise, and Ellen saw the sea and Searn itself in the distance. She would be glad to see the caravan journey, with its discomforts and perils, come to an end. Yet she was not eager to return to a life at court. Without realising it, she had come to revel in the freedom. She looked across at Cedrin and smiled. The idea of travelling to Olcis in the company of three former calvanni would have appalled her a month ago; now she had come to think of them as friends.

It would be a strange group, she mused. Three warriors, who were anything but typical men, an old Druid who would be more at home in his dusty chambers in Olcis, and a minitil who served Cedrin like a bodyguard.

She watched Kalyth, his back as straight as an arrow as he rode. She would be glad to part company with him.

* * *

Cedrin glanced over his shoulder again, always surprised to see the silent Bovosan only two steps behind. The half-breed's eyes shone faintly red in the dark, but otherwise the night took him in as though he were part of its substance. Despite the minitil's heavy build, he walked with remarkable economy. Cedrin had spent two frustrating hours with Ellen as translator, trying to convince Bovosan he could go free, much to the amusement of his friends. The whole exercise had been a waste of time. The minitil continued to follow him like a second shadow, his weapons always held ready. At least Raphal had been able to use his powers as Priest to read the minitil's intentions. It seemed the strange fellow was dedicated to protecting him.

Bovosan himself remained grave and withdrawn, as though responding to some important duty they failed to comprehend. Despite the language barrier, he had proven a master of evasion.

Marken told Cedrin he had the uncanny sense the man was a courtier. But what strange court would employ a minitil?

Cedrin muttered to himself as he continued his climb. The path rose from the protected hollow where they had made camp, up through the steep hills to the cliff top. It was a challenging ascent, yet even when the path grew steeper and Cedrin found himself stumbling on scree, the enigmatic Bovosan climbed with little effort, making no sound, always just behind him. He felt glad the minitil was not his enemy.

When he reached the top, he pushed the half-breed from his mind and paused to take in the view. The stars spread out across the clear sky, the bright moons touching the swell with delicate tendrils of milky luminescence. The ocean breeze was brisk, and he revelled in the strong blast of it as it whipped against him, pushing back his hair. The sea never failed to lift his spirits. He inhaled its cool freshness and felt life and vitality flow through him. That same breeze had touched the wave-caps and coursed the leagues of silent blue.

Cedrin walked along the narrow cliff top. He saw Kalyth ahead, moving through his ancient greatscythe forms, careless of the wind or the perilous fall below him. Cedrin paused ten paces away, wary of the blades as they spun and flashed.

Kalyth finished his pattern. He locked his blades into the haft and looked across the cliff top towards him, taking in the shadowy form of Bovosan with a rapid flick of his eyes.

'It's good to see you to back from the halls of Llors.'

Cedrin smiled. 'It's good to be back, although ...' He flexed his left arm. 'I could be better.'

Kalyth smiled wickedly. 'The only way to beat an injury is to work it,' he said, extending the blades of his greatscythe.

Cedrin smiled and swallowed, taking his own greatscythe from his back as Kalyth advanced. 'I thought I would wait a while to start training again,' he said, slipping off the leather sling.

Kalyth launched an attack and Cedrin hastily moved his greatscythe to block.

'So what are you going to do? Tell your enemy to wait until you're better?' said Kalyth.

Cedrin looked across at Bovosan as though for support, but the minitil laughed. He sat cross-legged, speaking rapidly in his own tongue and laughing again as he settled himself to watch.

Kalyth smiled. 'I think I could grow to like your companion.'

Cedrin drew breath to reply, but was soon too busy matching blades with Kalyth. The old warrior fell on him with enough ferocity to convince him this was no drill. He was hard pressed to turn Kalyth's attacks, let alone speak. Usually it seemed a game. A fast play of wits where the loser bore no more hurt than to be winded, or perhaps knocked to the ground. A hard game, but still a game.

Kalyth hit him with everything. This was real. Cedrin fought his fear of the razor-sharp lanedd, and his anger, pushing aside anything that would cloud his mind. Even a warrior with Kalyth's control could make mistakes. Their blades met with a rapid staccato. He was breathing hard. His left arm ached.

Each moment seemed a lifetime, the fragile bridge between life and death as thin as a blade's edge. Kalyth broke free and circled, his movements formalised like a slow and graceful dance. Cedrin studied the old warrior's face, the shining eyes of deep blue and the grim smile. Kalyth had barely raised a sweat, while Cedrin glistened with hot moisture and shook with fatigue. Then he was blocking again, moving backwards towards the cliff and cursing himself for the loss in concentration. Desperately he feinted and side-stepped away from the perilous fall, blocking deadly blades with every step.

They sparred for almost an hour, until Kalyth stepped back and withdrew his blades. Cedrin bowed forward, exhausted. His hair was slicked back to his scalp with sweat, his heart thundering ahead of a burning ache in his lungs as he struggled to breathe.

Kalyth laughed and loosened the top catch on his armour. 'Exhausted already?' he said. 'Then how would you expect to fight from dawn to dusk? Or stand guard duty all night then do it all again the next day? Really, I would have expected a young lad like you to have more endurance.'

Cedrin looked at Kalyth in mortification.

'Still it wasn't a bad drill. You have got the basics at last.'

'Drill?' said Cedrin, still too exhausted to straighten.

Kalyth smiled. 'You didn't think it was the real thing, did you, lad? I could have given a mortal blow over thirty times. I lost count of the times I could have sliced you to pieces along the way.'

Cedrin looked at Kalyth in dismay. He had been pushed to his utmost limit and still he was as vulnerable as an unarmed man to this old warrior.

Noting his despondent look, Kalyth stepped up to Cedrin and gripped his shoulder. 'Don't lose heart, lad. You are now ready to learn the real art of the greatscythe. A journey that will take the rest of your life.'

Kalyth stepped back and hefted his greatscythe. Wary, Cedrin stepped back, ready for another attack.

Kalyth merely smiled. 'Grace is economy of motion. The most power for the least effort.'

The old warrior demonstrated a series of blows. The movement was executed with no more effort than a wave to a friend across a crowded room, yet with two simple body swings his greatscythe had accelerated to a deadly velocity on each arc. For the first time, Cedrin really saw the elegance of the movement.

'You try.'

They had performed this drill a thousand times. It was one of the first Kalyth had shown him. He moved the greatscythe through the twin arcs and felt his heart labour once more under the strain, his tired muscles taxed with the effort. He felt like a child compared to the older man, the movement impossibly clumsy.

'Too much effort. The power comes from speed not muscle,' said Kalyth.

Cedrin tried again and was confounded by the difficulty of what seemed such a simple movement. 'Curse Uros!' said Cedrin, fumbling the movement in mid-swing and dropping his greatscythe.

Kalyth laughed and clapped him on the back. 'Enough for one night. Let's walk.'

Cedrin picked up the greatscythe and locked the blades

away, falling in beside the older man as they made their way across the top of the cliff.

'Maybe I'm not cut out to be a scytheman,' said Cedrin.

Kalyth laughed. 'Rubbish! You have done well. If you master that simple movement alone, you will be a better scytheman than anyone in the company.'

Cedrin looked at Kalyth in disbelief. 'Surely not?'

Kalyth smiled. 'Don't doubt it – but then again, I'm not saying it would be easy.'

Cedrin looked over his shoulder and saw Bovosan moving behind him with his mought hammer, his face impassive. The minitil gave him a slight bow. Cedrin turned away, baffled.

He and Kalyth walked in silence, enjoying the fresh air.

'I saw you destroy that Moon Druid,' said Kalyth, his voice sombre. 'Do you know what that means?'

Cedrin sighed heavily and could not resist another look over his shoulder to make sure Bovosan was out of earshot. 'It means I'm a Sorcerer.'

Kalyth laughed bitterly. 'You're a long way from claiming that title, lad. No. What it means is you are Old Blood, descended from the ancient rulers of Kelas.' He spat, showing his disgust.

That gave Cedrin pause.

'So, Old Blood,' said Kalyth. 'Where does your path take you now?'

The words were like a challenge, and Cedrin hoped he would never bear the full brunt of the bitterness that underlay them.

'I have no choice,' said Cedrin, as though to justify his actions. 'I have to learn to control this ... this Fire. Only Ellen can teach me. She has agreed to journey with us to Olcis from Searn.'

Kalyth spun suddenly, gripping his shoulders. 'You must listen to me, Cedrin,' said the old warrior, his voice low and dangerous. 'You must *not* go to Olcis. Learn as much of the art from the Cintros woman as you may, *but do not go to Olcis!*'

Kalyth's eyes were wild. Cedrin looked at him for the first time since the warrior had joined the caravan and saw again the madman from the tower. 'You must not go anywhere near the Temples!'

Cedrin was lost. 'The Temples? Of what?'

Kalyth shook Cedrin as though he were a child. He was amazed by the old man's strength.

'The Iris!'

Cedrin shook himself out of Kalyth's grip. 'You make no sense!'

Kalyth pointed a finger at him, as though in accusation. 'All that was ever evil in the Cinanac Emperors has taken shape and it lays within the Iris. It will take you and change you. Pervert you. Use you as it will. Kelas will fall beneath it!

'Carris was an evil man, yet he was sane. The power that lies in wait for you will show no mercy. It will drive you insane. Once unleashed, that insanity will spread like a flame until everything is consumed!'

'What has this to do with me?' he raged back at Kalyth, meeting him eye to eye.

'It has everything to do with you, *Old Blood.*'

'This is crazy. I am nothing more than an old warrior's bastard son. You know that!'

Kalyth's eyes met Cedrin's with frightening clarity. 'You are not Belin's son,' he said. 'All Belin's heirs died in Blackthorne's flames.'

It was like his heart was ripped out of him. 'What?' said Cedrin, almost at a whisper. He found himself shaking. *'Then who am I?'*

Kalyth did not flinch as he replied, but tears filled his eyes and his voice shook.

'The child I carried with me to Athria was the Cinanac heir, brought through the Iris by Belin while his mother's blood lay cooling within the palace. This child should have stayed lost, Cedrin. Should have become a memory like all shining moments of the past.'

Kalyth was crying openly. Even though Cedrin heard the words, the implication was so fantastic it was lost on him.

'What are you saying?'

'You were that child, Cedrin.' Kalyth shook with emotion.

'Cedrin Cinanac. Son of Riin. *Old Blood! Suul!* Heir to an Empire that is dead! Heir to the cancer of destruction that always dwelt in your family's line. Heir to the evil that now lives in the Iris.'

Kalyth exhausted himself in his fury, and Cedrin could not help but laugh at the absurdity of what the old warrior was saying. The heir to the throne of Bulvuran? A Suul? *The Scion?* It was impossible. He was nothing more than ... what?

Of all men alive, Kalyth should know the truth of it. The pieces fit themselves inexorably into place. Why would Belin order a bastard son saved while his own grandchildren perished? Why would a warrior such as Kalyth leave his own family to die in flames to save a child? Only an oath that bound the heart and mind closer than life could command that sort of act. The oath a warrior gives to his Lord ... or his Emperor.

Cedrin looked out at the dark sea. 'Sweet Larus! I *am* the Scion.' He turned back to Kalyth. 'And Tarral?'

'Tarral never knew,' said Kalyth. That made sense. Tarral would not have lied to him, it was just not in the man's nature.

Cedrin's mind flew back to Raynor. A city torn apart because of one man claiming to be what he was: the lost heir to Bulvuran. Why? Why should he be cursed with so much unwanted power? First the power of the Fire, now the power to alter the course of history. As Scion, he could command men's lives, change the fate of nations. He had seen enough to know once he was recognised, his supporters and enemies would number in the thousands. The hundreds of thousands! He shuddered. The Warlord of the Yasser States would be his *personal* enemy.

'You must deny it, Cedrin. You must leave Kelas and never return. If you can convince the Cintros woman to go with you, so much the better.'

Cedrin was perplexed. So much that Kalyth said did not make sense. 'What is the Iris? Why is it evil?'

Kalyth grimaced. 'The Iris is little more than a doorway. The Temples of the Iris are linked through magic. It is a mystery and in itself is harmless. It is what lives *within* the Iris that must be feared. If you stand within any of the Temples, we are all lost. Your mind will be forfeit and flames of destruction will engulf us all.'

'What is it? What lays in the Iris?'

Kalyth became wary. 'The Ward. It is a work of High Sorcery and contains ... immense reserves of power. But there is something else, some other mind at work. Something of unspeakable evil.'

He spun to face Cedrin. 'That force would possess *you*, Cedrin. Now it is trapped within the Iris. But should it find you ... You would become the instrument of its evil. Within you, it would walk the land.'

Cedrin shook his head. It sounded so unreal, so contrived. 'And all I have to do is stay away from this Iris?'

'Yes, but—'

'Enough! You were the one who told me to choose my own path,' said Cedrin, his fury rising. 'I have chosen. From Searn I travel to Olcis. I will learn the ways of the Fire and then I shall see.'

Kalyth was shaken but straightened to face him. 'But Cedrin, things can never be the same, now that you know ...'

'This changes nothing!' said Cedrin. 'I will still bow to no-one, Kalyth. Not even you!'

Cedrin turned and strode back along the hill-top towards the path, gripping his greatscythe like a club. The truth tore at him. So many had died so that he could live. The Kaidell signet ring had been transformed in an instant from an object of pride to a constant reminder of Belin's sacrifice, right there on his right hand. He struggled under the weight of this awesome debt. He did not understand what that meant yet, although in some ways it changed nothing.

He was still going to Olcis.

* * *

The minitil, who had been watching the exchange from the ground, rose swiftly and turned to Kalyth.

'Kalyth Orin,' said the dark-skinned fellow in his heavy accent. Kalyth wondered how much of his lack of understanding was feigned and how much was real.

'*Impersiolos,*' said Bovosan, gesturing at the retreating figure of Cedrin. 'Iris evil. I protect him.'

Kalyth locked gazes with the half-breed for a long moment and came to feel a mutual bond of concern for the young man who had been so heavily laden with the unwanted truth. Bovosan extended his hand in the ancient gesture of friendship. Kalyth responded and they gripped forearms.

'We protect *Impersiolos* together,' said the minitil.

Kalyth wondered if it was chance that brought the strange warrior to the caravan or design. And yet, what could the minitil do against the power of the Ward, or the *Beast*.

As though reading his thoughts, Bovosan smiled. 'Kalyth. I know Iris.'

Before Kalyth could question him, the minitil was gone, racing after Cedrin at a steady run.

Who was this minitil? Kalyth shook his head, pushing the mystery from his mind.

He watched Cedrin disappear into the night. He was strong, that one. The expression on the young warrior's face when he had defied him had sent shivers running down his spine. That tone – that rage – had been Riin's. If there was ever any doubt in his mind that Cedrin was the Emperor's son, that ended it.

*　*　*

As the old warrior left, Osterac scrambled to the cliff top and wiped a sheen of perspiration from his bald head, grimacing as he thought of the garish demons inscribed there. The ugly tattoos had been the Warlord's parting joke, even so, they provided an excellent disguise and one he could rid himself of easily; by simply growing his hair. The Warlord had assured him Xyanthius' caravan would pass swiftly – and unquestioned – through the Yasser States. And it had. The Warlord would be furious if he knew Ellen Cintros had been protected by his own orders.

He had sought the cliff for the solitude he relished, fleeing the coarse warriors and their inane conversation. When Kalyth and Cedrin had appeared, he had quickly concealed himself, preferring to remain undiscovered. What he had overheard chilled his blood. *Cedrin Cinanac, heir to the throne of Bulvuran.*

Osterac reached into a concealed pocket in the undervest beneath his armour and took out the bulky signet ring of the Cinanac. He had stolen it from Daran's own pocket. No, not stolen, taken back what was his.

For so long he had believed, made himself believe, there was a chance. Even after the humiliation of Raynor, the forced confession, he had kept the dream of sitting on the Emerald Throne alive. The Resius family were the only Suul in Olcis who could trace their ancestry back to the founding of the Empire – to the First Consort of Carris himself. He had traded a certain future of power in Olcis for a chance at the Bulvuran throne, convinced by the Hesguit to go through with the elaborate deception.

He closed his fist around the ring. A wound opened in his palm. Osterac ignored the pain. He imagined the blood was Cedrin's, the shape within his grasp the calvanni's crushed body. *The throne is mine!* No other was fit for it. Certainly not some gutter-scum from Athria. What would he know about being a Suul? Or ruling? *Nothing!* He deserved to die like his father before him, then he, Osterac, would at last fulfil his destiny.

He slipped the signet ring onto the first finger of his right hand and held it up to the moonlight.

'Emperor Osterac of Bulvuran,' he said. Yes. He liked the sound of that.

Chapter Twenty-Five

Cedrin watched as the Land Gate of Searn drew closer. Within sight of the city, the tense silence had broken, replaced by the welcome sound of laughter and friendly talk. Cedrin had approached Xyanthius on the road, and the mercenary Captain had given him leave to travel to Olcis. As for what he had learned from Kalyth – that was something almost too fantastic to contemplate – and it did not alter his plans one whit. He had no intention of becoming the pawn of the mighty, like the doomed false-Scion Osterac. The fact that his claim was legitimate would not protect him in the slightest. It was a secret best left buried, for his own protection and the protection of those close to him.

He leant forward in the saddle eagerly. Arriving at Searn marked the end of his first period of service in Kranor's company. He looked across at Ellen riding beside him in the vanguard. Like Marken and Skye, she looked at the city. They had all agreed to take lodgings together so they could plan their trip to Olcis. It was going to be an exciting few weeks.

The wide sweep of Myos bay spread out before them, and he drew in a breath of the air, salty with the tang of the sea and the faint rotten smell of the harbour waters. So much like Athria.

'Smells like home,' said Cedrin.

'It does,' said Ellen, laughing.

They could hear the faint noise of the city as they drew closer – the buzz of talk and clatter of wagons and commerce. The main part of Searn was not visible above the walls, set as it was into the hewn rock of the steep coast. What they could see was the traffic streaming in and out of the Land Gate – and none of it moving fast.

A challenge rang out from the wall and Xyanthius called the caravan to a halt. A Searn official, mounted on an amelak, rode out to talk to him and Alechul. The discussion between the man and Alechul was brief, punctuated only by covert bribes. Minutes later, the official was halting the major traffic to make way for the caravan.

'Alechul is wasting no time today,' said Cedrin.

'It's surprising how free he is with his money now he has Searn's harbour in his sights,' said Marken.

'You'll get no complaints from me,' said Skye. 'The quicker we get into Searn, the quicker I can buy an ale and get this dust out of my mouth.'

The harena lumbered into motion. Once through the gate, they had a tremendous view down the stepped terraces of the city to the docks. Thousands of galleys and sailing ships lay at anchor in the narrow but deep waters of the enclosed harbour. Other ships stood-to at the mouth, oars pushing against the tide as they waited their turn at the Sea Gate. The buildings were a mixture of mud brick and the local white-grey stone, hewn from the surrounding cliffs.

The caravan slowed as they pushed through the packed, narrow streets of the city, working their way down to the docks. After the danger of the road, the routine normality of the city streets was a stark contrast.

Reaching the docks, the laborious task of unloading began. It seemed an anti-climax after what they had come through. He watched the warriors as they moved crates and barrels from the battered wagons and sleds into Alechul's warehouse. Their life was facing death and for the most part, they thought nothing of it. These men had done it a hundred times and would be ready to do it again tomorrow. Although pleased at his own achievement, in some ways the completion of his first mercenary tour was a hollow triumph. Risking death should mean more.

An hour later, the company had parted ways with Alechul and his wagons and harena. They made their way back up the slope to Kranor's headquarters in Searn, now guarding only a small chest of coin containing their payment. The crowd parted before the group of proud warriors as they made their way into the drab sprawl of the Old City. The pace was slow, and most of the warriors walked beside their mounts, although the wounded continued to ride. Easy, friendly talk passed between them, and even Kalyth and Xyanthius laughed together at the head of the column like new recruits. They all felt the expectation of a free night in the city with their pay heavy in their purses.

'There's Kranor's headquarters,' said Lann, who was walking beside them. He pointed to an ancient, yet defensible five-storey stone building just ahead. A tall stone wall enclosed the building and its adjacent training yard. A small group of warriors, another of Kranor's companies, exited the gates as they approached. Catcalls and jibes passed between old friends and rivals as they moved past. The mood was lighthearted, but there was a serious undertone. It was understood that the next time they met there would be faces missing, warriors who had fallen by the way. Some of the men from the other company called out for news of friends, only to be told they had died on the road from Raynor.

As they passed through the gate, stable hands ran to take their mounts. They shied away from the narsiit, which paced uneasily and would let no one approach. Skye stabled the tall beast himself. The wounded were taken to the infirmary while the rest of the warriors milled about in the walled courtyard waiting for Alechul's coin.

Cedrin and his friends, together with Ellen and Raphal, sat beneath a big tree in the centre of the courtyard. The thought of splitting up after so much shared danger simply not occurring to them. The suns fell over the headland, plunging the city streets into twilight and they instinctively moved closer to each other.

Marken lit a pipe, sharing it with Skye to pass the time. Ellen and Raphal were deep in some whispered argument. Cedrin wondered silently if he should go in search of Kalyth. The old warrior had given him so much. He needed to say goodbye properly. He made a mental note to return the next day. Tonight was a time for celebration.

Cedrin looked around for Bovosan, wondering if the mysterious minitil had slipped away, but he soon found him leaning against a wall nearby. The dark-skinned warrior bowed his head at Cedrin in deference, a small smile touching the corners of his mouth. The other men ignored the strange warrior.

Kanis emerged from the command room, a disapproving sneer on his face as he swept his gaze over the warriors. Behind him followed a clerk carrying a small chest and ledger, and two aides with a small table and chair. Now that they had reached Searn, the temporary rank that Azel and Kalyth had been given as commanders on the road was meaningless. Neither had been members of the company. Once more Kanis was senior, a favoured member of Kranor's One Hundred. And he knew it. As Cedrin met his mean eyes, he was taken straight back to the training yard in Raynor.

They formed a line leading up to the small table, the members of the One Hundred first. As each man took their pay, the clerk marked them off in the ledger. Ruus was the first to take his pay, and nodded a farewell to Cedrin before disappearing inside the headquarters.

'Well, we earned this,' said Marken, standing in the line just behind Cedrin.

'We did,' said Cedrin, thinking of the drakon, the bandit attacks and the men who had fallen. 'Skye will have to miss out though.' He looked over to where Skye waited with Ellen and Raphal. He was gesturing as he told a story to Ellen, who looked back at him with an amused, but disbelieving expression.

'I don't think he needs the coin, somehow,' said Marken.

'No,' said Cedrin.

The line shuffled forward as more warriors took their pay and left the courtyard.

'If I don't see you again it will be too soon, Suul,' said Kanis to Azel as he took his pay.

The tension rose across Cedrin's back. A silence had fallen on the courtyard, filled only with Kanis' sarcastic voice. Hardly a man collected his pay who did not bear a jibe from him.

Lann was well ahead of him in the line, and Cedrin waved a

farewell as the warrior took his pay and left with his friends. Lann had already signed on for a return trip to Raynor.

Rastor stepped up to the table.

'I suppose you think you are a warrior now?' said Kanis.

Rastor ignored him.

'How is your jaw? Come back for another lesson any time,' said Kanis.

Something snapped inside Cedrin.

'What for, Kanis? So you can show him how to break the rules of a contest?' Cedrin's voice rang out across the courtyard. If he thought it had been quiet before, now it was deathly silent.

Kanis' dark eyes fixed on Cedrin. Rastor took his coin and raced out through the gates. Cedrin thought that was a little strange, but was glad to see the lad go without more torment.

Two more took their pay, but Kanis ignored them, waiting for Cedrin. The thick-set warrior unslung his greatscythe, his face split into a savage grin. As Cedrin stepped up to the table, Kanis' greatscythe slammed down, making the chest of coin jump and sending the startled scribe's stylus flying.

'No pay for this one,' said Kanis.

'The pay is my due,' said Cedrin. 'I'm sure you will agree. Or do you want me to ask Xyanthius?'

The scribe looked from Kanis to Cedrin. His hands shook as he reassembled his papers.

Cedrin met Kanis' gaze across the table, refusing to back down. Kanis' greatscythe swept up at Cedrin's face. Cedrin swayed back, narrowly avoiding the blow.

'So you want Xyanthius to fight your battles now that old Eathal-fucker Kalyth is gone?' said Kanis.

Across the courtyard, Ellen was on her feet, her face pale. Raphal had a restraining hand on her arm. Skye was on his feet beside them, his face grim.

'You sure about this, ami?' said Marken.

Cedrin stepped back, lifting the greatscythe off his back and letting the leather sling slide off the haft and into the dust. Marken and the other men in the line moved back, giving them space.

'I need no one to fight my battles, Kanis. I'm taking my pay.

If you think you can stop me. Do it!'

Kanis laughed. 'You all heard the challenge!' he called across the courtyard. 'There is no rank here. Not with this.'

Kanis walked around the table. 'This has been a long time coming, *Kaidell*. I'm going to give you something to remember me by.'

Kanis' blades snapped out, and his greatscythe surged into motion.

Cedrin blocked twice, then leapt aside, giving himself time to unlock his own blades. Rastor ran back through the gates, followed by Lann and all the warriors who had already taken their pay. Word had spread fast. Ruus led a group of other warriors out from inside Kranor's headquarters. By their tattoos, at least sixteen were members of the One Hundred. Up in the highest storey of the building, Cedrin saw a curtain flick open. Xyanthius and Kalyth watched from above.

Then he had no time to think of anything.

The attacks came fast. Low. High. Cedrin blocked them as they came. He circled, then feinted, falling automatically into the trained pattern that Kalyth had drilled into him. The greatscythe felt light in his hands, moving with all his natural speed. Kanis tried a low feint then pushed forward using all his strength. Cedrin met him blade to blade, using his height and strength to first halt him, then push him back. Kanis was fast and powerful, but his range of attacks was limited. Already Cedrin was seeing a pattern. Cedrin feinted again, low, then high, then swept in with a straight lateral cut, taking Kanis by surprise. Cedrin's left greatscythe blade whistled past Kanis' face, nicking the skin of his nose. Kanis' savage grin vanished.

Kanis grew more defensive, falling back and circling. Then he stopped his attacks, backing away and holding up his left hand in supplication.

'All right, all right. That's enough, eh? You made your point. You earned your pay,' said Kanis.

Cedrin relaxed, dropping his guard. Kanis' greatscythe immediately cut at his throat.

Cedrin leapt back, off balance. He lost his footing and tumbled backwards. As he fell, he saw Kanis' face looming closer, twisted with hate. He rolled, coming up into a blocking position. Kanis was there, his blades cutting at him, left then right.

Once more they were in the thick of it. Cedrin gritted his teeth, trying to focus. He was no stranger to dirty tricks. Every time he had challenged someone in the Circle of Blades he had come up against a bastard like Kanis. *Concentrate!* Sweat was thick in his eyebrows. It dripped down and stung his eyes.

The fight continued, slowing as exhaustion set in. After a while he saw that Kanis' left strikes were faster than the right. In an instant Cedrin saw the opportunity. As Kanis attacked, Cedrin blocked the left blade and darted in, attacking *before* Kanis' next blow. His blade slashed along Kanis' chest, right through his right pectoral muscle then his shoulder.

Kanis yelped in pain.

Cedrin used the haft of his greatscythe to knock Kanis' weapon from his loosened grip. Then he kicked out Kanis' leading leg. The man fell heavily, landing on his back. Within a heartbeat, Cedrin's right greatscythe blade was at his throat. He paused there, his eyes locked to Kanis' – long enough for the man to know Cedrin could kill him if he chose to.

'Like you said, Kanis. This has been a long time coming.'

Then he swept his blade up, cutting off the tip of Kanis' left earlobe. The man gasped at the pain.

'Something to remember me by,' said Cedrin.

Kanis pushed himself to his feet, blood streaming down his chest and the side of his head. Collecting his greatscythe, he staggered back to the building. The crowd parted to let him go.

As soon as Kanis disappeared inside the headquarters, the courtyard erupted into cheers. Men swarmed around him. Marken and Skye were there, clapping him on the back. Ellen watched from across the courtyard, her face flushed red, her eyes hot.

Cedrin looked up to the top storey of the headquarters. He saw Kalyth and Xyanthius briefly before the curtain was drawn once more. He twisted the mechanism of his greatscythe, withdrawing the blades.

'Well done, Cedrin. I've never seen anything like it,' said

Lann, gripping forearms with him and pumping vigorously.

'You really are Belin's son,' said Rastor, his eyes wide with awe.

Cedrin tensed. The knowledge that he was the Scion, the son of Emperor Riin Cinanac, flooded into his mind like an unwanted tide.

'Thanks, lad,' said Cedrin, squeezing the young man's shoulder. 'Kanis had it coming for what he did to you.'

'You can say that again,' said Ruus. 'I never thought I would see Kanis get his comeuppance like that. Make sure you come back to the company. I'm sure Kranor will offer you a place in the One Hundred before the year is through.'

'Thank you, my friend,' said Cedrin, gripping forearms with Ruus.

Gradually the crowd dispersed, and Ruus took over the distribution of coin. The grim silence was gone, replaced by excited talk and laughter. Eventually though, the courtyard emptied as the men took their pay and left.

Ellen and Raphal came to join him and his friends.

'Are you all right?' asked Ellen, touching his arm in concern.

'Yes. Unharmed. In fact I've never felt better,' said Cedrin.

'You could have been killed!' said Ellen, her eyes flashing.

Raphal raised his eyebrows, while Marken and Skye exchanged a knowing look.

Cedrin sobered, seeing the real concern in her eyes.

'Sometimes there is no backing away from a fight,' said Cedrin.

'And that's the truth,' said Skye.

Ellen glared at Skye and stormed off through the gate. 'Come, Raphal. Let's find a tavern. Preferably somewhere with no posturing warriors!'

Cedrin and his friends followed Ellen and Raphal through the bustling alleys into the heart of the city.

'Do you think she will cool down?' asked Cedrin.

'Cool down? Why would you want her to cool down? I like my women hot,' said Skye, winking at Marken.

Ellen looked back at them and her face flushed red. Just for a moment Cedrin saw relief on her face, then she turned away.

At the tavern, Ellen soon had servants and maids rushing around the building attending her needs.

'Come on, lads. I'm eager for a bath after all this travelling,' said Cedrin.

'Sounds good,' said Skye.

'Will you join us, Raphal?' asked Marken.

'Err … very well,' said the old Druid, rather stiffly.

Even Bovosan laid aside his weapons and joined the warriors in the hot tubs, his grim demeanour leaving him as he lowered his body into the steaming waters. He spoke rapidly to himself in his own tongue, expressing delight.

'What is he saying?' said Skye, as the four lounged together in a row of tubs.

Marken shrugged. 'Larus only knows. It's hard enough to follow him when you try and listen.'

Bovosan burst out laughing, and they all turned to watch the strange man as he soaped himself.

'Sometimes I have the uncanny feeling he hears everything we say,' said Cedrin.

Skye smiled. 'He's a wily one, there is no doubt about that.'

Refreshed, they dressed in clean clothes.

'We are going down into the city. Do you want to come with us, Raphal?' asked Marken.

'No. I think not,' he said primly. 'It is time for some long neglected contemplation and study. Remember, Marken, drink reduces the Essence.'

'Yes, Master Druid,' said Marken seriously. 'I will keep that in mind.'

They left their larger weapons in the care of the inn-keeper and went into the city. It was exciting for the three former calvanni, like a homecoming. The people were of the same Myrian stock as the Athrians, slight and mostly fair. If not for the accent, it would have been as though they had never left Athria. The sights and smells of a port city, the bustle and the open buildings, all reminded them of home. They followed the slope of the hill towards the docks district. They knew if the city was anything like Athria, the docks would be the centre of the night life.

If not for the presence of Bovosan, constantly a step behind them, it would have been much like old times. In the country, the dark-skinned man's silence and grace made him unobtrusive; not so in the city. Insults and comments flew at the minitil and his companions. Some took him for an Eathal, others a Meadrel. In every case, he was immediately picked as an outsider.

When two inns turned them away, his presence became a sore point between them, but there was no helping it. It was said that being freed from slavery was an intense experience. Clearly it was a debt his self-appointed bodyguard took seriously. Cedrin made a note to buy the half-breed a robe that would conceal his features from view. He was on the point of seeking out a market to buy one when they found an inn where the proprietors gave little heed to the nature of their customers. They eagerly pushed their way through the crowd to claim a space. They dropped their newly earned coin on the table and as if by magic, a serving woman appeared.

'Three ales, No ... make that four,' said Cedrin, watching Bovosan. 'Let's see if we can loosen his tongue a little, eh?'

They laughed at the thought, but the minitil was unmoved and eyed the crowd with intense vigilance.

When the ales arrived, Bovosan eagerly accepted the amber fluid. He took a small draught, shrugged his shoulders and smiled.

Cedrin lifted his glass. 'To Olcis.'

'Olcis!' they said together.

As Cedrin drained his glass, he could not help noticing Bovosan's grim look, his deep-set green eyes urging caution. When they had downed their glasses, the minitil's still stood on the table, untouched. Kalyth's voice came back to him. *You must leave Kelas and never return.* Cedrin tried to push the memory from his mind and join the fun, but forgetting Kalyth's warning was not so easy. Bovosan's serious manner was a constant reminder of unseen danger.

'So how long will we stay in Olcis?' asked Marken.

Skye waved down a serving woman for another round of ales. She smiled at him across the room and walked back to the bar to fill their glasses.

'I have funds enough, and you two have your pay jingling in your pockets. We could stay for months,' said Skye. 'Are you still planning to rejoin Kranor's company, Cedrin?'

'That option is still open. But I could not do that until I have at least learned to control … my power,' said Cedrin, checking no one else was listening.

'Wise,' said Skye. 'It need not stop you in the long run. Look at Raziin himself. He has worked as a mercenary for years in Kelas, and his powers are widely known.'

'But he never worked for the Temple and he has to keep constantly on the move,' said Marken.

'True,' said Skye.

The second round of ales arrived. They disappeared as quickly as the first.

'Let's plan to stay for a few weeks in Olcis. By then I will have an idea how long it will take to learn to control the Fire. Ellen seemed unsure about Olcis … she may want to move to another city.'

'Oh, it's "Ellen" now,' said Skye. He looked across to Marken and gave him an exaggerated wink.

'It's not like that,' said Cedrin defensively.

'Sure – we believe you,' said Skye, chuckling. 'Truly though, I am glad Suul Cintros has agreed to teach you. That was a real stroke of luck, right there.'

'Absolutely. If Ellen had not followed you from Raynor…,' said Marken.

Cedrin felt a warmth in his chest as he thought of her. He remembered the drakon closing in, then Ellen pushing him aside to deal with the beast. She had saved him. By teaching him Sorcery, she would do so again. Without her help, it would only be a matter of time before his power rose again, killing or crippling him or his friends.

'Whatever you decide, Cedrin. We are with you,' said Skye.

Marken laid a hand on his shoulder. 'To the end.'

Cedrin's heart soared. These two men were his closest friends. To have them with him as he tried to grapple with the Old Blood inside him meant more than he could have said. The knowledge of his true identity hovered in his mind like a heavy weight. If he could not trust Skye and Marken with the truth, then who could he trust? They deserved to know. But was now the time to tell them? After all the perils of the road, this night should be for celebration. They had done enough, sacrificed enough for him already. He decided to wait. There would be plenty of time for confessions on the road to Olcis.

The conversation went on in a light banter and the night turned as a thousand others had in the smoky back-rooms of Athria.

Yet Kalyth's warnings gnawed at him. Should he tell his friends about the Temple of the Iris in Olcis? If so, would they argue against travelling there? The thoughts swirled around in his head. His natural independence rallied, and with it his determination to travel to Olcis despite the warnings. He might be the Scion, but he was still his own man.

He took a sip of the ale and found he had lost his taste for it. He put the glass back on the table and pushed it away from him. His thumb played over the Kaidell ring in irritation. All the introspection had taken the edge off his mood.

'Want something stronger? Bakta?' Skye raised his hand to the barmaid.

Cedrin shook his head. 'No. I'll wait a while.'

Marken packed a pipe of se and offered it to Cedrin. As the night grew late, the air in the tavern had come to reek of the weed. Cedrin waved away the pipe, memories of the strange mood that had gripped him in Ceta all too vivid. Marken shrugged his shoulders. He and Skye shared the bitter smoke between them while Cedrin thought ahead to Olcis, wondering if the danger Kalyth saw there was real. If so, all he had to do was stay away from the Iris.

Bovosan's strange green eyes met his for a moment, as though sensing his thoughts. For a moment he though he saw disapproval there. Cedrin glared back at him. Bovosan soon looked away, his attention back on the men and women as they walked past. Always alert, always seeking for danger.

* * *

Ellen fell back onto the feather down mattress, revelling in the soft feel of it against her clean skin. *Paradise*. At that moment, she never wanted to leave the feel of silk. Her dresses and clothes had been washed and pressed, and she wore a soft shift of white. Happy and satisfied, she drifted towards sleep.

After all the doubt and indecision, at last she was making progress. She had succeeded in winning over Cedrin, and in time the cause of the Scion would have a strong advocate: another Sorcerer and warrior. An Old Blood. She could no longer deny her feelings for him. The discovery of his power, of his links to the Old Blood, had burst the flood-gates of emotion. All that could never be, was now possible, together ... She was dizzy with the prospects of the unknown road opening up before her.

She floated into fantasies, daring to dream of a time when they could live together within the embrace of the Suul, in the luxury of privilege. A rough voice intruded upon her thoughts. *What of the Scion?* Ellen opened her eyes, the mood suddenly gone. Wishful thinking was all very well, but the fact remained her quest had barely begun. She had yet to find the Scion, and Cedrin's place in this was still a mystery. Was Cedrin's Old Blood the only reason Myan valued him so highly?

Ellen rose from the bed and paced her room, trying to remember everything Myan had said. *Cedrin must be found. He bears Belin's signet ring. You must find him and protect him.*

Ellen froze in her tracks. At no time did Myan claim he was Belin's son, only that he carried the signet ring. She tried to put herself in Myan's place. There were only minutes of life left, time only to whisper a few words. The joining of minds had been a last desperate effort before he died. That he had found the strength of will to summon the Fire at all had been remarkable. With so little time, he had spoken first of Cedrin, then he had gone on to talk of the Scion and the Iris.

'Uros!' cursed Ellen in frustration. It was impossible. How could she discern the truth from only a few words? All she knew beyond a doubt was Myan's belief; his absolute certainty as the final words were given, mind to mind, that Cedrin must be found.

Suddenly uncomfortable in a simple shift, Ellen changed into a dress and paced the room once more, her fatigue banished by her agitated thoughts. If Cedrin was so important to the cause, then perhaps she was not the person to teach him. If he could command even a fraction of the power he had channelled at the Druid, he would grow to become the most powerful Sorcerer in modern history. Perhaps he needed a teacher like Erioth. A Master of the Fire.

Ellen stopped pacing. She pulled at the dress, straightening and rearranging it. She had become leaner on the road, and no matter which way she righted it, the dress did not seem to fit. In desperation, she threw off the dress and put on her leathers, which had been cleaned then softened with special creams and waxes. Finally dressed in the leathers she had worn for the last few weeks, Ellen could not stifle a laugh. She had come a long way since Raynor if she preferred them to dresses.

Ellen sat down and stilled her mind. The time had come to contact Erioth. Ellen knew nothing about his winged race. In the time she had known Erioth, their conversations had strayed very little beyond the arts of the Fire. The Verial Sorcerer owed his life to her father and his time with her had been the repayment of that debt. Ellen knew he risked the wrath of his people by leaving their hidden Domains north of the Ranmyden ranges, but the personal bond between him and her father had been deep.

When Erioth had left Athria, he had warned her against reopening the Bridge between them.

'This is the end of our time, Ellen. I have already done much to deserve punishment from the Elders.'

'But ...,' protested Ellen.

'I give you one final boon. At one time, when the need is great, you can contact me. But think on it well, for that will be the last time I acknowledge you, or anyone in Kelas.'

Concentrating her will, Ellen opened the Window and channelled the Fire, keeping the flow small and focussed. She spun a Matrix in her mind and transformed it with the raw power of the Fire, sending it out from her like great voice, calling Erioth. As it flew northwards, the Bridge between them reawakened.

A great relief spread through her. He was still alive! Her greatest fear had been that he had perished in the years since she had last seen him. As the Bridge strengthened, she fought a giddy expectation that threatened to break her focus. The distance was great, and passed through leagues of solid rock to a deep place. Finally a picture began to resolve. There was one final barrier, a subtle resistance like a curtain. She pushed through it and a cascade of images flooded through her mind; a deep hall within the earth, an old man, a golden-tipped spear, a great spider-being cowering before a fountain of power.

There was a moment of recognition, then Erioth's thought reached her.

Ellen, flee!

'But, Erioth, I have to talk to you ...'

Then there was something else. The Bridge between them was being invaded by another mind. Whipping tendrils of blue lashed out at her. One tendril touched her briefly, failing to make full contact, yet even that brief contact stunned her. The intruder's power was immense.

Ellen, break the contact! Quickly!

Another tendril lashed out at her across the Bridge, stabbing into her. Ellen struggled to break free, to raise a Barrier, but it was too late. More tendrils snaked across the Bridge, invading her mind. One moment she was in her apartments in Searn, the next she was there, under the mountain, looking through Erioth's eyes at an old warrior with silver hair.

The warrior was glowing with power, surrounded by a luminous sheath of crimson and yellow flame. Beneath his feet turned the unmistakable five-fold symmetry of the Temple of the Iris. A vast cavern opened up around her, piled with shattered columns and fallen masonry. The ruins trembled with the power of the Fire. Great blocks tumbled, sending clouds of dust up into the darkness. Hundreds of bats circled above. The huge spider-being stood at Erioth's shoulder, its legs tense, its multi-faceted eyes reflecting the Sorcerous flames.

Just beyond the circle of light were scores of Eathal dressed in well-crafted, yet simple skins. They lay face down and prostrate around the Iris.

This is a ruined Eathal city.

The warrior was dressed in old-fashioned leather armour that could have been the twin of Kalyth's. Beneath the sheath of flame, she could see a tracery of blue tendrils surrounding him, linking him to a spear that was strapped across his back. She gasped as she saw the golden blade. *Forged metal.* The blade glowed so brightly she could hardly focus on it. This was the source of the power.

The Spear of Carris.

The tendrils tightened their grip on her mind as the man advanced across the Iris.

'Fight it, Belin! Break the grip of the Ward.' It was Erioth's voice, seeming to come from her throat.

The man was Belin!

Ellen felt the magical grip tighten on Erioth, silencing him. She was trapped with him.

The old warrior was now only a single pace away. His eyes danced with blue lights. Through the Bridge she could sense that Belin's mind had been taken over by something else, something that drew its power from the Spear. What had Erioth called it? The Ward?

The tendrils searched her mind. Memories swept past her: Myan dying on the floor of the throne room, her quest for the Scion. Finding Cedrin. Suddenly the flow ceased.

The Ward laughed, a dry, unnatural voice issuing from the throat of Belin.

He comes. The Ward's thought shot across the Bridge, along with its triumph. *And he is Adept.*

The tendrils continued searching. From the very depths of her mind, they drew forth a spinning gem of blue. Some sort of magical construct. Ellen's stomach constricted in fear as she saw this thing in her mind's eye for the first time. *It had been hidden in her mind all this time. Even before Raynor.* Always there had been hints of it, but her mind had slipped from it before the point of recognition.

The Ward examined the construct carefully. *Intact. Function confirmed.*

Ellen felt sick with a sense of violation. That *thing* had been inside her mind. And it had come from the Ward.

The Ward turned away from her, walking to the centre of the Iris.

'You will soon be reunited with your protégé, Erioth,' said the Ward.

Ellen fought the grip of the Ward, struggling to raise the Fire, to form a Barrier – any sort of Matrix to combat it – but its grip was like a vice. The Ward's power, flowing from the Spear, was too great to challenge.

Ellen. You are in terrible danger here. You must keep Cedrin away from the Iris. Do you understand? Away from the Iris at all costs! Erioth's thoughts were charged with fear and anxiety. *We came in search of the Spear, to take it and hide it in the deep north.* An image of Erioth and the Tahistill – the spider-being – travelling through the mountains flashed past. *Instead the Ward imprisoned us.*

But the Ward is not the danger.

'Silence, Erioth!' commanded the Ward. The old warrior's hand waved and Erioth's thoughts were sealed from her.

Ellen struggled in its grip, trying to break free.

She looked out through Erioth's eyes, searching for some clue, something to help her. The Ward had his back to her, walking over to the far side of the cavern.

Her eyes fell on the Spear. In distant Searn she shivered with a sudden chill. A rippling distortion swelled up through the air from the spear, a miasma of darkness fixing her with its gaze.

There was a sharp pain in her chest, and her throat constricted as the thing struggled to take shape.

She had felt its gaze before. In the Athrian Iris. *This* is what had seen her that time in the darkness. This is what had frightened her.

It reached for her, sliding like rancid oil into her mind. She heard distant laughter, two voices speaking together. *Soon. Soon.* It peered into her with brutal lust, its touch like diseased hands on her skin, forcing themselves inside her. It began to take shape in her mind, a head like a great hound, with a single yellowed horn, the eyes bloodshot and rheumy. One eye was grey-blue, the other golden. The features swam, and now two sets of eyes looked out of the huge head, both filled with lust. Both insane.

The Ward gestured once more, without turning. A wall of blue overtook her vision, wiping all away. *You will remember nothing.*

There was a brilliant discharge of energy. She was released and pushed back, a Matrix shooting towards her. Instinctively she reached for the Fire, deflecting most of its power.

Ellen fell to the floor shaking. Around her, the richly woven mat was ash, the floor beneath charred to black.

She struggled to her feet, shaking, trying to think ... to think. Think! She could not remember. Everything was covered with a great darkness. She had tried to reach Erioth then ... nothing. Just pain. With agonising effort she pushed against the hold on her mind, struggling against *something* that held her. Slowly it began to reveal itself. It seemed she would pierce the veil that concealed it, which covered her mind, when a fountain of blue exploded in her mind, sending her staggering into darkness.

* * *

Ellen woke, shaking her head as she rose from the floor. There was a strong smell of smoke and a wave of sickness threatened to take her.

She did not know how long she had lain in the dark. In a daze she made for the bed, her mind numb. As she fell onto the mattress, she smiled. There was nothing to worry about. She knew all she needed to know. *The Scion must stand in the Temple of the Iris.*

But Ellen fell into a troubled sleep. She ran through dreams of darkness with the hot breath of the beast on her neck, and through them all, Cedrin was in mortal danger.

Chapter Twenty-Six

Kalyth ate a plain breakfast of cheese and bread. As he finished the last of it, a serving woman came to clear it away.

'Would you like anything else, sir? Ale or mulled wine?' she asked.

'Hot tea would be good,' said Kalyth. After his years in the Tower, he had lost his taste for alcoholic drinks.

As soon as Cedrin had told him of his plans to travel to Olcis, he knew he had no choice but to follow him. Early this morning, he had asked after Cedrin and his friends from inn to inn until he found them. Now he waited in the warmth of their tavern's common-room for them to appear. Xyanthius had already released him from service, thanking him for his help. Being part of a body of men as they travelled north had made him feel alive again, and he left that life reluctantly. But he had a duty to Belin, and Riin's son, that he would never be free of. And it was not just duty – coming to know Cedrin, the man he had become, the man he could become, had filled a void inside him. He had come to treasure the times they spent training together, as though in passing on his knowledge, his life had begun to fall into perspective; to mean something again.

The woman put a cup of hot herbal tisane on the table before him and he pressed a coin into her palm. She smiled in response and left.

He was sipping the tea when Cedrin came into the common room with his Athrian friends Marken and Skye.

Kalyth tensed, not knowing how Cedrin would react. The tall young scytheman stopped as he saw Kalyth and walked straight over to him.

'Kalyth,' said Cedrin.

'How are you, lad?' said Kalyth, rising to grip forearms with him. 'Well met.'

'I had meant to see you today. To say goodbye and thank you for training me.'

Kalyth cleared his throat. 'Well. There is no need to say goodbye.'

Cedrin raised his eyebrows.

'I want to travel to Olcis with you. To continue to teach you the greatscythe. I owe your father and Belin that much.' *And I want to be there to keep Ellen's Suul claws off you.*

Cedrin's face split in a wide grin and he stepped forward to grip Kalyth's arm. 'That's brilliant news. You will be more than welcome. We plan to set out tomorrow morning.'

Relief flowered in Kalyth. Cedrin had accepted.

'Come have breakfast with us,' said Cedrin.

'No thanks, lad,' said Kalyth, pushing his half-finished tea away and standing. 'I have other things to attend to. I will see you here tomorrow, before dawn.'

'Good,' said Cedrin.

Kalyth saw Ellen moving down the stairs with her usual poise. She looked stunning in a loose silk dress of pale cream. Time to make an exit.

'Keep well, lad,' said Kalyth, slapping his arm.

Kalyth walked out into the new day. He gritted his teeth as he thought about all that lay ahead. One Face of the Temple of the Iris lay in Olcis. Nothing could be more dangerous to both him and Cedrin. He prayed that their sojourn in Olcis would be a brief one. Memories of the years spent trapped close to the Blackthorne Iris sent a chill down his spine that not even the warmth of the morning suns could banish. Nothing could entice him near the Iris again – not an Emperor's fortune. All he had to do was keep Cedrin away from it until they left Olcis. An easy task, after all what reason would the lad have to seek out such an esoteric temple?

* * *

'It's no use,' said Cedrin. 'It's just an image.'

Ellen sighed. 'Be patient, Cedrin. It took me years to master this, you cannot expect to gain anything quickly.'

Cedrin and Ellen sat together on a small hillock late at night while the rest of the company slept.

They were four days travel from Olcis.

He grimaced.

'Try again,' she said.

Cedrin drew a heavy breath. He was bone weary. The days and nights since Searn had been both exhausting and exhilarating for him, but the pace was beginning to tell. Despite his weariness, the punishing training schedule Kalyth had devised grew even heavier. His brief hours of sleep passed in an eye-blink. Only snatches of rest gained in the saddle were keeping him going. Despite his vow to tell Skye and Marken the truth of his birth, the time had never seemed right. Yet he had to tell them. Just being who he was put them in danger. He would tell them tonight, he vowed, after he finished training with Ellen. He wished he could confide in her as well, but he knew that telling Ellen would propel him on a course he was not ready for.

Cedrin pictured the Window. He opened it inside his mind but found only darkness. The power – the immense flow of the Fire that had soared through him on the Spire and facing the Druid – was absent.

He looked over at Ellen, who was sitting silently, concentrating. Suddenly he could feel something; sense it in the air. It was like a high tone, just beyond hearing. He shuddered with fear and anticipation, closing his eyes once more.

The Window was there, but unlike the other times, he could sense the Fire behind it. Not the torrent he had felt before, but a buffeting force, like a gusty wind against a closed shutter. Striving to keep his mind focussed, he opened the Window. The Fire filled him. It seemed he rode at the head of a flash-flood. He was soon lost in the sheer joy of *power*. Distantly he heard Ellen's voice and opened his eyes.

'Channel it, Cedrin,' she said quickly. 'Let it flow along your arms into the night.'

He looked down to find himself sheathed in a nimbus of red. He raised his arms and it flashed from his fingertips in rough balls of flame, roaring as it soared higher into the sky. *He was channelling the Fire!*

Beside him, Ellen glowed with the same power. She seemed so alive, so alluring. Cedrin reached across and took her into his arms, kissing her as the Fire coursed through them. She gasped in shock as they met. Instantly, their minds were laid open to each other, their spirits touching in emotional embrace.

As they kissed, Cedrin drank her spirit like honey, awash with images and thoughts, dreams and fantasies. He trembled with the desire to know her completely, to enter her totally. Something whipped past him, into his mind, then back. A moment later, a blue shape passed between them in the wash of images, flying beneath the surface of the mental contact and into the soft darkness of his mind, burying itself deep. For that long moment, they shared as only two Sorcerers could, the Bridge slowly forming between them …

Ellen pushed away from him, breaking the contact.

'No, Cedrin,' she said breathlessly. 'We cannot.'

She let the Fire fall from her. 'Close the Window.'

With a mental effort, he closed it. The flow ceased and he was empty. A terrible disappointment filled him.

'What happened?' he asked.

Ellen was breathing rapidly, her chest heaving. Her skin glistened, her lips still wet from their kiss. 'We were Bridging. Much longer and ...' She shivered. Her pupils were wide and dark, and her eyes flicked between his lips and his eyes.

'Bridging?' he asked, perplexed.

Ellen ran a hand down the side of her thigh. 'We were ... linked.'

'In mind?' he asked, remembering the indescribable joy he had felt.

She shook her head. 'In mind and spirit. Two spirits. One mind.'

'Is that possible?' he said.

Ellen nodded. 'Yes. But only Master and Apprentice link in

such a way. Once Bridged with a Sorcerer, you are linked until death. It is the only way the more complex Matrices can be learned ...' She swallowed. 'I think that's enough for one night.'

She turned and walked into the night, leaving Cedrin bewildered and alone.

Something squirmed, deep inside his mind. Had he really considered telling Skye and Marken he was the Scion? Strange. *The less who knew the better, at least until he reached* ... Cedrin shook his head. His fragmented thoughts, swirling around the image of an Iris, drifted away.

'I must be more tired than I thought,' he said, making his way through the camp to his blankets, where he fell into an exhausted sleep.

* * *

Total abandon terrified Ellen.

A tremor ran through her body and she hugged herself as tears of frustration rose in her eyes. She wanted Cedrin with such a passionate desire it frightened her. She had been immersed in him, filled by his presence, and she longed for it again. She knew she had to run before she did something foolish, before she reached for his mind again and forged the Bridge between them regardless of the consequences. She had the power. She could force him to submit, use her powers to open his mind and establish the Bridge. Then she would own him forever ...

But there was something else. After the mental contact with Cedrin, something in her mind had changed. When she had left Raynor, she had been so convinced of everything. She would find the Scion and ensure he stood within the Iris, as her father had commanded her. Now ... there was some terror eating at her. She looked out into the same darkness that had been so comforting less than an hour ago, strangely fearful. What was it? What had changed?

Searn.

She felt it in her gut.

Something terrible had happened to her in Searn. Some ...

violation. What though? And why think of it only now? Her mind rebelled, but her heart screamed at her to listen.

Ellen thought back, following her instincts. Why had she never talked of the significance of the Iris with Raphal? What could it mean? She brushed the tears from her eyes and composed herself, walking through the camp towards her tent. None of her training as a Suul could completely quell the numbing fear that now possessed her. Ellen could not shake the feeling that something terrible was going to happen.

She reached her tent and fell into an uneasy sleep, trying to push the fear from her. But in her dreams it took shape. Free at last from the restraining hand, it surfaced.

She ran through the labyrinth beneath the Cintros mansion, lost in the dark, her heart hammering. Behind her the Beast growled and grunted, driven by lust and a need to kill. Three times it almost had her, but she escaped, running blindly, deeper into the maze than ever before. The dark fuelled her terror.

Her outstretched hands struck a wall and she screamed in fear, searching feverishly for a way out.

She was trapped!

The Beast was close now. She could hear it snort in triumph and spun to face it. Its eyes glowed in the dark, one grey-blue, the other gold, filled with hate and a lust for destruction. They burned into her, draining her strength. She experienced a jolt of recognition. She knew this thing – she had seen it before – but the memory slipped away.

A Cintros bitch. Its thoughts echoed in her mind.

In the glow, she could see the cracked horn, wickedly sharp, stained with blood.

'What are you? What do you want!'

We are Behemoth. We want – All.

A soft golden light grew in the corridor behind it. Ellen blinked as a winged shape hurtled towards her, a sea-raptor, sheathed in golden light, with eyes of deep green.

Follow me, quickly, pulsed the bird into her mind.

The bird swept past her, shooting off to the left, where a narrow passage was revealed. She sprinted after it, racing up a steep set of stairs there.

Behind her, the Behemoth roared.

* * *

Ellen woke with a gasp.

It was still night, and through the open doorway of her tent she could see the moons were low in the west.

Memories filled her mind, rising like wreckage to the surface of a storm-tossed sea.

She had tried to contact Erioth!

A cold fear settled in the pit of her stomach as she remembered facing the Ward. It had possessed Belin and held the Spear of Carris, tapping into its immense power. Erioth and the Tahistill were its prisoners.

All within the Iris.

How had this been hidden from her for so long?

The Ward had subdued her mind with the same ease a father subdues a child. Ellen saw again that shape of spinning blue, recognising it for what it was: a magical Compulsion. That *thing* had controlled her mind, guiding her thoughts. Yet why had its hold on her lessened now? She gripped the rough blanket to stop her hands from shaking.

The Ward was the guardian of the Spear, yet within the Spear lurked something even more terrible.

The Behemoth.

And she knew what it wanted.

The Scion.

* * *

Cedrin stopped his morning run to watch the suns rise from a hilltop, his heart pumping with exertion. It seemed as though life had taken on a new purpose. He knew beyond doubt his destiny awaited him in Olcis. Once in the city, there would be something he had to do, he was not certain what it would be, but fate would guide him.

He spread his hands to the rising light of the Sisters,

laughing with a sudden feeling of power.

I am the Scion.

* * *

Ellen rode beside Raphal, silent and withdrawn. The truth was she was frightened. When she began her quest, it had seemed a game, an adventure; she had to find the Scion and take him to the Iris, following the dying words of her father. For the first time in her quest, she saw forces and minds at work older and more powerful than either her or her father. Now she knew the Iris contained a force that wanted to make the Scion its own. Remembering the touch of that dark mind, she suppressed a wave of nausea. To be Bridged against your will to that power would be a soul-destroying torment that only death could sever. Still its touch lingered on her.

Cedrin rode ahead with Kalyth. There had been a change in him, something subtle, almost impossible to pin down. The dark-skinned Bovosan rode just behind them, a silent watchful presence.

'There! The Great Lake of Olcis,' said Kalyth as they topped a rise.

They paused on the hillock and looked out across the lake as the morning sun glittered on the waters, turning the surface to shimmering silver. Fed from sources below the mighty Mulisar range, the lake stretched for over fifty leagues at its widest point. From it, the Asog river flowed south to join the Yasser at Raynor. It teemed with fish and bird life. It was easy to see why the first Anacians, rowing up the Asog past the mighty Cioan cities in search of a new land, had chosen the freshwater lake for their settlement at Olcis. Scores of small craft poled through the shallow reeds in search of game and fish, and she could see small sloops and galleys far out on the water.

On the shores of the lake was the small port town of Rybol, busy with river traffic moving up the Asog between Olcis and Raynor.

'If we move quickly, we will be well past the bridge at Rybol by suns' fall,' said Kalyth.

422

'Lead on, General,' said Skye.

Kalyth smiled at Skye's playful jibe and pushed his amelak forward, Cedrin keeping pace by his side.

'Are you all right, my dear?' asked Raphal.

Ellen realised she was trembling. She tried to give him a reassuring smile, but without success. 'A slight fever, nothing more.' She turned away to hide her disquiet.

Never once had she questioned what lay within the Iris, or what meaning it could possibly have. Had Osterac been the Scion, she would have taken him to the Iris – straight to the power that waited. Her father had also been convinced of the need to bring the Scion to the Iris. Had he known of the danger? Or had he, like her, been magically compelled? Ellen remembered the first time she stood near the Iris in Athria, the magnetic presence that drew her towards it, closer to the dark gaze that watched her from that distant place ... The more she remembered, the more certain she became. Something had entered the mind of Myan as surely as it had entered her mind, using them both to get what it wanted. But why had its influence waned only now?

Ellen pushed the circling thoughts out of her head. She still believed in her father's vision of the restoration of the Empire – this had always been her father's quest, and now she shared it.

The day drew on, the companions making fast time. The stark fear that had plagued Ellen dulled to a vague uneasiness. Beside her, Raphal's face was creased with worry and he continually looked across the lake towards the distant seat of the Hesguit, supreme ruler of the Temple of the Sisters. Raphal had his own concerns, and she would not burden him with her own vague fears.

They came to Rybol in the early afternoon and passed across the ancient drawbridge over the Asog without challenge. By late afternoon, they had crested the last of the low hills that bordered the river and were travelling across the wide flatlands of Tupur, making for the main Olcis road. As they drew closer, they could see a large group travelling north on foot.

'Is it some sort of patrol, Kalyth?' asked Skye, riding his narsiit up beside the old warrior.

Kalyth shook his head. 'It's not a military column. And look,' he said, pointing to the rear of one group. 'They are driving livestock.'

'Where are they from, do you think?' asked Cedrin. 'I would not have expected refugees from Hend to be on this side of the Asog.'

Kalyth shook his head. 'They are not from Hend.'

As they drew closer, they saw it was less an organised column than an undisciplined press of people, ragged and travelling in small groups. Many led heavily-laden amelak, others drove small wagons piled with belongings. Whole families together, dejected and miserable beneath their burdens. When they reached the main way, Kalyth hailed a man on an amelak.

'Ho! Who are all these people?' yelled Kalyth.

People looked enviously at their mounts as they rode past, their hope soon overtaken with despair and fear. Ellen had seen that look before, on the faces of the thousands who had sheltered the Storm Season in Raynor. Homeless. Driven.

The man did not rein his amelak, shouting back across his shoulder. 'The Eathal are driving north into Tupur, ten legions strong. Talis is already doomed.'

Ten Legions.

The hairs stood up on the back of Ellen's neck.

'The sooner we are in Olcis, the better,' said Marken.

They pushed past the ragged group of refugees and increased their pace.

'I, for one, will feel happier inside the walls of Olcis,' said Skye.

Ellen galloped forward to ride beside Kalyth. Cedrin nodded a greeting, which she returned with a strained smile.

'Do you think the Eathal will strike at Olcis?' she asked Kalyth.

The old warrior looked grim. 'If they are ten legions strong, nothing in Kelas could stop them should they choose to push north. The Warlord may be able to hold them at Raynor, but he will be powerless to force them out of Tupur with his own troops trapped in his city. I only pray the traveller's words were an exaggeration.'

'But surely they dare not hit Olcis yet? The Warlord could strike at their forces from behind – break their supply lines,' said Cedrin.

Kalyth shrugged. 'Perhaps they lay siege at Raynor already. With ten legions, the supply lines could be well defended. It is pointless to speculate until we get to Olcis, then we can discover their real strength and deployment from reliable sources.'

* * *

Cedrin ducked as Kalyth's blade whistled past his head. He felt the blade tug at his hair. He knew better than to stop and think. Immediately Kalyth's second blade swept up, changing path at the last minute. He caught it on the flat of his right greatscythe blade and feinted in with his left.

Back and forward. Strike. Block. Counter.

He fell back and circled, his heart thumping, but his breathing easy. At last his fitness had increased to match the old warrior's.

Kalyth pushed forward, both lanedd blades cutting in with uncanny skill. One blade cut for his neck. He swung his haft to block. Too late! It was a killing stroke. Kalyth stopped his blade with expert control, leaving Cedrin with a stinging cut on the skin above his jugular. It had not been the first. He had a score of cuts across his neck, arms and torso where the blades had kissed, but not bitten deep.

'Break!' said Kalyth, stepping back.

Cedrin lowered his greatscythe, drawing in slow, even breaths.

'Good,' said Kalyth, leaning on his greatscythe. 'You are ready to learn the lanedd dance.'

'The forms,' said Cedrin breathlessly.

'Yes, the forms.'

Kalyth walked across the trampled grass to a level patch of ground and held his greatscythe in the ready position, his hands placed firmly on the release mechanisms.

Cedrin copied him. Kalyth corrected his stance and hold

until he was satisfied, then began the first move. Slowly he followed Kalyth's movements, shadowing the graceful path of his hands and feet, the mought and lanedd. It was like a dance, an expression, and in its pure form was completely divorced from violence.

The perfection of the forms was an art in itself, beyond death, beyond conflict: a focus of the mind on the present. As they joined in the ancient movements, they were together, sharing in that simple joy of physical expression. The hours fled, fatigue banished by a feeling of peace.

When the training was done, Cedrin sought out Ellen. She had been withdrawn since that night on the road when they almost Bridged. He wondered what had come to trouble her so deeply.

He found her sitting silently by her tent, her arms wrapped around her knees in a rare, vulnerable pose. She was lost in thought and did not hear him approach.

'Ellen,' he said softly.

She started. 'Oh ... Cedrin.'

'Are we training tonight?' he asked.

Ellen paused, letting out a sigh. 'No. I don't think we should do anything more until we reach Olcis.' Although her voice was level, her face was tight with tension.

Cedrin laid aside his greatscythe and closed the distance between them. 'What is it?'

Ellen stepped towards him, the tight mask of her face dissolving into need, then suddenly she backed away from him.

'You should leave,' she said, failing to bring the usual command into her voice.

Cedrin took another step, and this time she did not back away. He took her gently into his arms and she sagged into him. Suddenly she was crying, shaking with tears, gripping him as though he were the only thing that could hold her together.

'What is it, Ellen? Was it the Bridge?'

She looked up, her eyes large and soft in the moonlight.

'No, it was Searn. Something happened there. I tried to contact my old teacher, Erioth ...'

'Mind to mind?' asked Cedrin, a little awed.

'Yes, but something went wrong. There was another being, something evil ... Erioth is in danger. We are all in danger.'

'We will be safe in Olcis,' he said with conviction.

He reached to brush her hair from her face, but she pushed his hand away angrily.

'We don't know that. I feel danger everywhere,' she said.

Cedrin smiled. He had been feeling increasingly confident over the last few days, ever since he had mastered the Window for the first time.

He laughed and held her tightly. At first she struggled, then she relaxed into his chest.

'I'm not sure how safe Olcis will be for me,' she said. 'If the Olcis Temple ratifies the edict of the Athrian Temple, they will take me prisoner and force me into some sham of a trial before executing me.'

'We'll stay a week or two and get the lay of the land. If it's dangerous, we'll all go to another city, far from the Eathal and the Temple,' he said in a soothing voice.

'I will need to see the Hesguit. It's the only way. But the risk ...,' said Ellen. She felt warm and soft against his chest.

'Be at peace, Ellen. Everything *will* be fine,' he said, running his broad fingers through her soft hair.

'Part of me wants to believe that,' she said.

Cedrin was hardly listening. He could not wait to get to Olcis.

His vision flashed blue.

I must stand in the Temple of the Iris.

Strange thoughts, he had been having lately. As if he was going to travel back to Tower Blackthorne just to stand in a ruined Temple. No. Olcis was his destination, and that felt so right.

The moment passed.

'Yes. Everything will be as it should,' he said.

* * *

'*Cedrin is the Scion?*' The disbelief in Xyanthius' voice was palpable.

Osterac shifted uneasily from foot to foot.

'Yes. He is the Scion, the son of Riin Cinanac. Carried to safety after the fall by Kalyth himself,' said Osterac, silently cursing the itching of his scalp where his hair was growing back.

Xyanthius shook his head. 'Yes. Kalyth may have had a hand in it, all those years ago. Yet if Kalyth has known all this time, why did he not bring the news to Kranor or any of his officers? It's maddening! And now the boy is gone and Kalyth with him.'

Osterac knew that the leaders of Kranor's company were all sworn to the cause of the phoenix, and many like Xyanthius had once served the Emperor Riin.

'This would explain Kalyth's interest in Cedrin. And his appearance after vanishing for so long. But what proof do you have?' asked Xyanthius.

Xyanthius looked at Osterac's covered chest. 'The agents of the Warlord paid us well to take you – no questions asked. But who are you, Sindar? Where do your loyalties truly lie? You are not even sworn to the phoenix, why should we believe you?'

Osterac had hoped it would not come to this, but now he knew he would have to play every card at his disposal. He *had* to get close to Cedrin, had to be part of his inner circle as he grew in power.

Osterac tore the shirt from his chest, revealing the intricately worked and richly-coloured totem tattoo and phoenix crest.

'I am the greatest of patriots,' said Osterac, his charismatic voice ringing through the room. 'Only the restoration of the line of Carris can save Kelas now. Only Cedrin Cinanac. That is the truth.'

With a flourish, Osterac produced the Cinanac ring. 'Behold the ring of Carris. Last worn by Riin Cinanac as he fell to the Eathal assassins at Serpent's Tongue.'

Xyanthius was clearly shaken. He stepped forward, white-faced. He trembled as he took the ring from Osterac's fingers.

'The signet ring of the Cinanac,' he said, his voice little more than a whisper. 'I swore service to Riin when he wore this.'

Osterac bowed his head, fighting the contempt that threatened to break his demeanour. *Patriots!* Fools like Xyanthius would give him what he wanted, he reassured himself. He had but to bide his time in the ranks of Cedrin's supporters until the moment was right.

'How did you come by this ring?' said Xyanthius with sudden force.

'It was given to me by the Hesguit,' said Osterac. 'To support my claim to the throne.'

Xyanthius' wide face lit with comprehension.

'*You!* You are Osterac the Pretender!'

Osterac nodded. 'Yes, I was the puppet of Olcis. But no more. I escaped the clutches of the Temple Druids. I renounced my false claim and fled Raynor.'

Xyanthius' eyes grew sharp with distrust. 'Then how did you come to know the true identity of the Scion?'

Osterac met Xyanthius eye to eye and told the truth with absolute conviction. 'It was chance. Only days from Searn, I overheard Kalyth confess the truth to Cedrin.'

Xyanthius looked at Osterac for a long moment then nodded. 'So the lad himself had not known?'

Osterac shook his head. 'No.'

'Yes, that would explain much. Much.' Xyanthius grew animated and waved an aide to his side, passing the ring to him.

'Send a small company of warriors to Raynor at once, mounted on narsiit. Give this to Kranor and tell him, "The Phoenix is reborn in Olcis, but the plumage is dull and the claws are blunt." Go. Quickly!'

'Your will, commander,' said the young officer, fighting to suppress his excitement as he ran from the room.

As the young officer left, Xyanthius turned and gripped Osterac's shoulders in his strong hands.

'You have won a place among us, young Osterac. You have proven yourself a patriot and a supporter of the Empire's cause. You will ride with us as we seek out the Scion.'

Osterac knelt quickly at the old commander's feet, using the motion to conceal his sudden elation. 'Thank you, Lord!' he said, in all sincerity. 'Thank you for your trust.'

Chapter Twenty-Seven

Ellen had never seen so many people packed together. Even though it was only just after midday, the carnival crowd of Asic's Blessing swarmed around them, already well into drink. Being a feast day of the Sisters, all work had been given away in favour of the traditional celebration. The buzz of excited talk reverberated between the tall stone buildings of Olcis as though they were steep-sided canyons. Bovosan pointed at a costumed figure walking on stilts and laughed, his deep-set green eyes glittering with tears as he slapped his thigh. It was the most animated she had ever seen the usually stoic minitil. In contrast, Kalyth seemed even more tense than usual, and had been since they entered the city gates. Passing under the gaze of the Olcis gate guards – and the unknown eyes of other watchers – had been the tense moment for Ellen. Here in the chaos of the crowds she felt far less exposed. She marvelled at the elaborate, and often hideous, masks and costumes. Asic's Blessing was celebrated throughout Kelas, but she had never seen anything like this. Almost every person in sight was dressed as one of the myriad lesser gods and goddesses that sheltered beneath the Sisters. Costumes of the senior deities themselves – Larus and Uros – were forbidden by the Temple.

A drunk woman stumbled on the hem of her oversized goddess costume and pitched sideways into Ellen's amelak, the woman's shoulder jabbing painfully into her leg. Ellen bit back a sharp retort.

'Are you all right?' Ellen asked the woman.

'Huh? Sorry, love,' said the woman, swaying back to her

friends. The woman had lost her mask, while the masks of her three companions had been pushed up onto their heads and sat at odd angles atop their elaborate hairdos.

'Moons' Blessing,' said Ellen to her retreating back.

'I'll 'ave a drink for ya'' said the woman, lifting a terracotta jug in salute without turning.

'I doubt she even felt the impact,' said Cedrin with a wry smile.

They pushed their amelak through the costumed revellers and down to the lake shore and the main city streets. As they neared the centre of the city, the buildings rose in height. They looked up in awe as they passed a magnificent spire of glittering glass. Olcis surely was the jewel of the old Empire.

'Look at the colours in that!' said Cedrin.

It was called the City of Glass for good reason. Thousands of spires and coloured kiln chimneys rose on either side; a forest of glass, shimmering in the suns. Here the crowds were thicker than ever. Their mounts had slowed to a walking pace. Clearglass was everywhere, even in the windows of the most meagre dwellings. For centuries, the wealth of the Empire had come to Olcis through the thousands of Temples that had fallen under its sway. Even the cobbles that lined the streets were cast in durable mought and stood out brightly in hues of gold, blue and green. Soon the Bulvur itself came into view: the Citadel of the Temple, inner sanctum of the city and the seat of the Hesguit; a city in miniature where only the Druids of the Sisters, and the rich and influential, were shown entrance.

'Hard to believe we were worried about the Eathal advance,' said Cedrin, raising his voice above the din of the carnival crowd.

'They certainly aren't,' said Skye.

After the riots of Raynor, it was a startling contrast.

'Tonight the two moons rise full together,' mused Marken.

'A rare and lucky occurrence coming so soon after Storm Season,' said Raphal sombrely. 'A sign of the favour of the Sisters.'

'They certainly seem to be enjoying themselves,' said Ellen, pointing at a costumed figure of Kallor dancing down the street.

She burst into laughter as the man tripped over, landing in a comical heap.

It was late afternoon before they found a tavern. They stabled their mounts and crowded eagerly around a table in the common room, eager for a kitchen-cooked meal after so many days on the road.

'The wealth here is staggering,' said Marken, between mouthfuls.

'The population is easily double that of Raynor,' said Ellen, taking a sip of watered wine.

'The kilns of Olcis make the best lanedd blades in the whole of Kelas and, many would argue, the whole of Yos,' said Cedrin. 'And the Olcis guilds guard their secrets closely.'

'As closely as the Druids guard the mysteries of Essence,' said Marken.

Raphal's bushy brows drew together at that comment.

'Are you pleased to be back, Raphal?' asked Skye.

The old Druid rubbed his bald head absently, lost in thought for a moment. 'I'm pleased that I am not sitting in the Warlord's prison. But I suspect there will be little joy in this homecoming. I will be taken before the Hesguit as soon as I show my face in the Citadel.'

'Do you have any idea how he will react?' asked Ellen.

'Only the Sisters know what his judgement will be. But there is no point putting it off.' The old Druid pushed his empty plate away and rose to leave.

Ellen knew that, rightly or wrongly, the Hesguit's wrath at the failure of the Raynor mission would fall on the old Druid's head. Although it was unlikely he would be harmed, there were many ways a Druid could be made to suffer. Mindless acts of penance would be a torture for Raphal, whose brain was so acute and active.

Ellen pushed aside her half-finished plate. 'I will come with you to the Citadel,' she said, realising as she said so that she still wore her travelling leathers.

Raphal waved her back. 'That is unnecessary, Ellen, and possibly dangerous. I must face the judgement alone.'

'I don't know why you are so eager to see the Hesguit, Ellen.

Why don't you come out and enjoy the carnival with us?' said Cedrin. He and his friends were eager to be out with the crowds. It was hard to understand how they could be so carefree when there was so much at stake for her.

'No. I will accompany you, Raphal. I want to formally come before the Hesguit and ask him to rescind the edict of the Athrian Temple,' she said.

Ellen had thought hard about the risks, and had decided that she could not pass up the chance to put things to rights in Athria. Being forcibly exiled from her home had been hard. At some point she had to return, and she would rather do so openly, and without the Temple as an enemy.

Raphal smiled. 'As you will. I wish you success, but be careful. The Hesguit is a Templeman, and even though he cannot act without the sanction of the High Council, he has wide powers.' Raphal sighed and straightened his robes. 'Be that as it may, I must leave now.'

Kalyth stood. 'I will come with you also,' he said, draining the last dregs of his beer with a sharp tilt of his glass. 'I want to send word to an old friend in the Citadel.'

Raphal nodded. 'Very well then. But I can make no promises. I am a lowly Larus Druid in the eyes of the Temple. A scholar. They will listen to no petition from my lips.'

'Can't this all wait until after Asic's Blessing?' asked Cedrin.

'No,' said Ellen. She wanted nothing more than to take a bath and change her clothes, but instead followed Raphal from the tavern. She was determined to face the Hesguit, hoping to call on the alliance Olcis had made with her father. There would be plenty of time for merry-making later. Besides, she could not simply abandon an old friend like Raphal to his fate.

'I'm sure you lads will enjoy yourselves well enough without either old warriors or ... female company,' said Kalyth, slinging his greatscythe across his back.

Cedrin and his friends laughed. Bovosan, who had eaten in silence, was unmoved.

* * *

433

It was dark by the time Ellen, Raphal and Kalyth rode through the gates of the Citadel. The amelak had certainly made Raphal's journey to the Hesguit's fortress quicker and easier, and Ellen knew he was grateful both for that and her company.

Just inside the gates, a squad of Temple Guardians blocked their path with levelled spears. The leader of the squad stepped forward, a Razor by the insignia on his uniform.

'Declare yourself,' demanded the Razor.

'I am Raphal, Larus Priest and Druid. With me are Ellen Cintros of the Athrian court and Kalyth Orin.'

Ellen gripped her reins tightly, suddenly feeling she had made a terrible mistake. What was she doing walking right into the clutches of the Hesguit? No. It was worth the risk. She needed long-term options. Re-establishing herself in Athria would give her a position of strength in Kelas. As Sarla she could command Estle and force the Warlord to back down. She would need that sort of leverage to bring the Scion to power.

The man nodded curtly, waving the Guardians back.

Stablemen ran forward to take their mounts away, then they were led through into the Citadel. Despite Raphal's assertions he was a lowly Druid, the servants and many of the Suulqua of Olcis deferred to him as they entered the Hesguit's court. They were ushered into a small but pleasantly appointed antechamber flanked by six Temple Guardsmen.

A thin, nervous, court steward entered. 'Light refreshments?' he said, waving forward servants bearing platters of sweetmeats and pitchers of water and fruit juice.

They seated themselves on a plush lounge while the servants laid out the food on a low table.

Before the steward left them, Kalyth took him aside. 'Can you pass a message to Lempar?'

The steward looked perplexed and ill at ease. 'Not everyone has the ear of the general,' said the man, a cunning look coming over his features. 'But there are those who can be paid to carry a message.'

Kalyth smiled sardonically as he opened the drawstrings of his purse, drawing out a sizable coin. Ellen saw a flash of red. *A ruby.* A substantial payment for a simple message. The steward's eyes gleamed as his hand closed over the coin. He drew himself up with self-importance, a posture that bordered on the ridiculous given his balding head and emaciated frame.

'And what message?' asked the steward.

'Tell him Kalyth Orin wants to see him.'

The steward bowed then hurried away.

The three barely had time to compose themselves when the carved wooden doors of the chamber swung open again. Three Templemen swept into the room, their red robes swirling around them with whispered menace. The leader wore the insignia of a High Druid of Uros. Ellen leapt to her feet, the Window flaring to life inside her mind. She forced herself to relax. Uros Druids could have no power over her while night ruled outside.

Raphal rose slowly to his feet and faced his brethren in silent defiance. The High Druid studied Raphal much as a butcher might assess the virtue of a fattened harena.

'Neanin! High Druid of the Hesguit's court!' announced one of the High Druid's Templemen aides.

The High Druid turned to Ellen. When she met his cold, calculating gaze, Ellen shivered involuntarily, remembering how close the Athrian Templemen had come to taking her. Torren was not here to protect her this time. For a long moment they took each other's measure, Ellen keeping a pleasant mask over her features.

'Greetings, Cintros,' said Neanin. 'I am surprised to see one of your ... lineage, seek to come before the Hesguit,' he said smoothly, obliquely referring to the Fire she and her father shared.

'My father was a friend of Olcis,' said Ellen, recalling to Neanin's mind the Battle of Raynor where the Druids of the Temple and two Sorcerers, Leith Cinnor and her father, had wielded magic together to turn the tide of war against the Sundar's army.

Neanin nodded slightly. 'Indeed. Yet your father is gone and times change fast. The edict of the Athrian Temple still stands?' he said with the quiet smoothness of spilt acid.

Ellen's throat tightened. 'Yes, but of course I was falsely

accused. I had hoped the Hesguit would force them to rescind,' said Ellen, infuriated that a slight tremble had entered her voice.

Neanin gave a cold smile. 'Unlikely. But of course, the edict has no force here ... until it is ratified by our own Council of High Druids.'

Ellen forced a smile, but found nothing to say. Neanin was threatening her, and a man like this Templeman could not be ignored.

'But be assured, Cintros,' he said finally. 'We will meet on the matter.'

Neanin turned back to Raphal. 'You will come with us,' he said, summoning the old Druid with a curt gesture. 'The Hesguit will see you immediately.'

Raphal bowed stiffly, resigned and silent as he walked forward to join the group of Templemen. Neanin waved to his two aides and they positioned themselves quickly on either side of him. Nodding in satisfaction, Neanin led his small entourage to the doors without a backward glance.

'And my audience?' said Ellen, taking a step forward. 'When will the Hesguit see me?'

Neanin halted briefly in mid-step. 'You will be advised.' Then they were gone. Two of the Temple Guardians closed the door behind them.

'Uros' Blood!' snapped Ellen, stamping her feet.

Kalyth looked sidewise at her, raising his eyebrow.

'What!? Never heard a woman curse before?'

A slight smile curved the corners of Kalyth's mouth. He casually leant in close to her. 'I wonder if we are being observed?' he whispered.

'No doubt,' she replied. She sat on one of the plushly cushioned chairs and stared balefully at the platters of food that had been untouched since their arrival. She would trust nothing provided by the Hesguit.

Ellen tapped the cushion impatiently. After all they had been through, she realised she may never see Raphal again. Fear gnawed at her resolve and panic threatened to overwhelm her. Even now, the High Druids could be meeting to issue an edict for her arrest. How long should she wait before forcing her way out of the Citadel? Two hours, four hours? Dare she even use the Fire this close to the Hesguit's seat of power? Grimly she forced those thoughts out of her head. She had taken the risk. There was nothing to be done now but to see it through.

They made occasional strained conversation as the time crawled by. Kalyth was the last person she wanted to wait on the Hesguit's pleasure with. The doors opened once more and Ellen stood in anticipation of her audience, but instead of the court steward, an old warrior appeared. The six Temple Guardians snapped immediately to attention.

'At ease, men,' he commanded. The warrior was of Anacian stock, yet short and thickset, his hair greying but full, his face pleasant despite the long thin scar that ran down his right cheek. When he saw Kalyth, his blue eyes sparkled with delight. Ellen felt an instinctive like for the man.

'Kalyth!' he said, coming forward to take the old warrior's forearm in a vigorous grip. 'By all the gods, I thought you were dead.'

Kalyth gave a rare laugh. 'I may as well have been, old friend. I have been to Llors and back.'

'What's all this?' said Lempar, pointing to Kalyth's heavy armour. 'Why are you covering your honour like a thief? You haven't been rotting in some foreign prison, have you?'

Kalyth's smile faded. 'The Empire is dead, Lempar. My honour died with it.'

'Rubbish,' said Lempar. 'The Fall can never change the deeds of the past ... or their worth.'

The two stood silently for a long time, sharing something that went beyond Ellen's ability to catch. Despite the years of separation, they shared a deep bond. Eventually Lempar turned to Ellen.

'So, who is this pretty scamp, Kalyth?' he said, running his eyes over the tight curves of her leather outfit. 'Not your wife?' said the general with a laugh.

Ellen stiffened in outrage, cursing herself for not taking the time to change her clothes. She also realised that out of habit she still wore the bracer that covered her Suul mark. She swept the bracer off her head and hitched it onto her belt, tilting her head back with regal poise.

'I am Suul Ellen Cintros, daughter of Myan,' she said.

The old warrior's face showed surprise and he took a step forward and bowed. 'The pleasure is mine, Suul Cintros.'

'Ellen Cintros, meet Lempar, Supreme General of the Legions of Olcis,' said Kalyth.

The old general smiled. 'Not as impressive a title as it once was. I hear you made quite a fuss in Athria,' he said, laughing once more. 'I must say you show remarkable ... nerve, seeking an audience with the Hesguit.'

Ellen was rankled and changed the subject. 'I hear the Eathal are marching north?'

Lempar nodded. 'Yes. They are advancing on all fronts. I'm afraid we underestimated their military and magical strength from the outset.'

'What is their strength? How far north are they stopping?' asked Kalyth.

'Stopping?' said Lempar with a cynical laugh. 'They have put ten Legions into Tupur, five of which are advancing to Olcis. They show no signs of stopping, my friend.'

'So it will come to a siege. You must be already looking at fortifications. You have a wide perimeter to defend here,' said Kalyth.

Lempar's smile vanished. 'No fortifications. They have already destroyed Talis and the Hesguit has ordered the entire legion into the field to meet them.'

Kalyth cursed. 'The fool! You have barely ten thousand men against a force of over fifty thousand Eathal and their Sorcerer-Lords.'

Lempar shrugged. 'The Hesguit has spoken and we obey.'

Kalyth shook his head. 'Larus help Olcis when the Eathal legions reach it – it will be undefended. The Citadel and the Druids will be the only things left to stop them.'

Lempar and Kalyth continued to talk of the coming battle, considering tactics, troop numbers and fortifications until Ellen grew bored and restless. She paced the room, deep in thought. The dark foreboding that had gripped her on the road to Olcis emerged once more, redoubled, and she was drawn back to

Searn, back to the confrontation with the Ward and the Behemoth. Her vision darkened as she remembered the Behemoth's loathsome touch.

'Are you all right, my Lady?' asked one of the Temple Guardians.

Ellen came back to herself. She had stopped pacing and her hands were trembling. Gods! Her stomach churned with nausea.

'I'm fine, thank you,' she said, forcing a smile.

She walked to the low table and poured herself a glass of water, managing a sip. Even the *thought* of the Behemoth was enough to bring it all back. She need not fear though. Its evil lay contained in the Iris. Then she froze at a sudden thought, the glass poised halfway between her lips and the table. What if there was a Temple of the Iris in Olcis? What if it could reach her here? Raphal had told her there were six Temples of the Iris. There had been one in Raynor and another in Athria, why not another in Olcis? 'No, there couldn't be,' she said, under her breath. Yet even as she said it, fear gripped her. Carefully, she put down the glass. Why had she not talked to Raphal of this? She returned to pacing the room, ignoring the two old warriors, still locked in their conversation.

A wave of panic swept over her. In that moment she was convinced Cedrin was in danger. Then her reason slowly reasserted itself. *No. The Iris would have no interest in a warrior's bastard son.* Cedrin was safe with his friends, and Bovosan would never leave his side. Ever since Searn she was finding it increasingly hard to control her fears.

The Temple Guardians were replaced at their station, and she asked the new guards the hour. It had been well over three hours since their arrival, and still there was no word. She had forgotten the arrogance of the Temple.

Her sense of uneasiness increased, her thoughts flying faster. The Ward and the Behemoth were far too powerful to be underestimated. She had to find out if there was an Iris in Olcis. She had to find Raphal and ask him before she left the Citadel – audience or no audience. He was the only one she could trust.

She thanked the Sisters the Scion was not in the city.

Cedrin watched the suns go down from the tavern porch. They slipped majestically behind the low hills that bordered the lake, touching the stilled waters with a red-orange blaze. He, Marken and Skye had joined five spearman on leave from Rybol. The buzz of the crowd was deafening. Clouds of se-tobacco drifted past. The festive crowd spilled from every tavern and bordello into the streets, jugs of ale and bottles of bakta passed from hand to hand. Now that the suns had gone down, he felt the excitement of the crowd increase, as though the dark sanctioned what had been unthinkable under the watchful eyes of the Sisters.

'… and I said, "Honey, that's what a spear's for!"' said one of the spearmen, delivering the punch line of his story.

His friends burst into laughter with the other spearman. Cedrin joined them half-heartedly, his gaze drifting once more to the temples beyond the Citadel. There was something eating at him, like something he had planned to do, but could not remember. A restlessness had been building in him for hours that the ale could not ease.

Bovosan stood silently in the street, watching him. Cedrin had become so used to the minitil's presence he hardly noticed him anymore.

'… *my fair lady sang for love, not sorrow …*' sang a passing musician, strumming a lute as he walked through the crowd. He wore an enormous blue hat, shaped into a five-pointed star.

On impulse, Cedrin put his ale down on the porch railing and walked down into the crowd, following the musician.

'… *she said she would find for me an orange rose …*' he sang.

Laughing faces loomed in front of Cedrin, blocking his way. The musician moved on, his voice booming above the crowd. '*My love was like a hungry fire …*' Cedrin caught one more glimpse of the musician before he stepped into an alley. Once more the frustration built inside him. It had felt good to be moving.

Above him, the full moons of Asic's Blessing were livid and swollen.

He pushed through the crowd. He saw a skinny street-youth skilfully cut away the strings of a man's purse and reflexively reached to his own belt. Cedrin still had his money. The young man looked across at him with a triumphant gaze and slipped away with his prize. *Cutpurses would be everywhere tonight.*

He walked back in the direction of the tavern, intending to rejoin Skye and Marken. For a moment the crowd parted, giving him a view of the distant Citadel. There was a taste of something in the night – like the swell of the Fire, but at the same time more powerful and distant. He walked towards it through the deepening twilight, leaving his friends in the company of the five drunken spearmen. The noise of the crowd fell away as he wandered into the maze of temples and quiet contemplation groves that nestled against the walls of the Citadel.

He avoided the main Temple complex, drawn instead into a darkened and deserted precinct. These were the lesser temples, holy places given over to the many other small deities. He stopped at one, recognising the shape of the Tree. Here an elderly Priest and Priestess were kneeling in prayer. Sensing his gaze, the Priestess looked up at him. He nodded back respectfully. A moment later he realised her gaze had moved past him and he turned to see what had caught her attention. For a moment he saw movement in the shadows behind him, then it was gone.

'Now I'm seeing things,' he muttered under his breath.

When he looked back, the Priestess had returned to her prayers.

He kept moving, soon reaching the outskirts of the temple precinct that bordered on the steep, barren slopes of the Mulisar range. Everything here was built of the same grey rock as the Citadel and had never been in favour enough to warrant facing with tinted mought. Cedrin ran his hand over the rough stone of a temple shrine. These were built by his own ancestors, the ancient Anacians. He climbed up the slope, moving past shrine after shrine carved into the face of the mountain itself. His feet moved faster.

Come.

For a moment, he felt hot breath on his neck. Heard the

growl of a beast. His vision collapsed to a single point. It was close now, like a glowing ember in the night. He walked onto a jutting outcrop of rock, high above the city. Here, as before, there were many temples and shrines, but these were old, the gods and heroes neglected and ravaged by time. A young Priest was walking by, swinging an smoking incense bowl and praying silently under his breath.

'Priest!' called Cedrin.

The young man started, eyes wide and fearful as Cedrin approached.

'I mean you no harm,' said Cedrin.

The Priest blinked. 'My apologies. The remote parts of the Temple precinct are rarely visited, except by devotees such as myself who tend the shrines.'

'What is this place?'

'The square of Cinanac,' said the young Priest, hurrying past him. Incense spilled from the bowl as he clattered away.

The place was deserted, but even so there was *something* here. It drew him to a carved stone wall. He followed the wall, tracing his hand over the smoothed relief. A section swung open under his touch, and without hesitation he ducked through the shadowed entrance.

Tall, elaborately faced columns rose above him, glowing white in the moonlight. There were five columns, enclosing a complex mural. Cedrin was drawn forward.

He sucked in a breath as he saw it.

The Iris.

Like a blossoming flower, something rose to the surface of his mind. An elegant construct of shimmering blue energy.

The Scion must stand in the Temple of the Iris.

He, Cedrin, must enter the Iris.

Filled with this new sense of purpose, he closed on the Iris, his eyes fixed to its five-fold symmetry. Even now the pattern was starting to shift ...

To awaken.

Chapter Twenty-Eight

Skye tossed the dregs of his beer out into the street. An intelligent man can only take so much conversation from a spearman, or for that matter five spearmen from Rybol. The first time he heard a story repeated he hardly cared, the third time was definitely one time too many. He had watched Cedrin slip away earlier and had assumed he had gone to find a privy, but that had been almost an hour ago. He looked across to Marken and saw that his smile seemed a little strained.

'Shall we go, eh?' asked Skye.

'Good idea,' said Marken.

'Hey! You fellows aren't leaving us, are you?' said one of the spearmen. 'It's still early.'

'We'll be straight back. Don't worry,' said Marken, patting the man on the shoulder, then turning to wink surreptitiously at Skye.

They walked out into the torch-lit street.

'Where do you think Cedrin has got to?' asked Marken.

'No idea. But that lad sure has been acting strangely,' said Skye.

The crowd swept them down towards to the lake shore, past jugglers and clowns, musicians and poets, all raising their voices above the din. One man hung perilously from the gutter of a building, shouting out some alcohol-inspired wisdom. 'It's the Moons, don't you see? They rule Yos, not the Sisters!' Two men were trying to hit him with empty bottles, laughing as each exploded against the side of the building. Their drunken aim was terrible.

Fights broke out sporadically. The city guardsmen stopped some of them, but were usually content to watch. Frequently only drawn blood or worse would end it. Sometimes, grim-faced bouncers, sober and ready for action, would leave their establishment doors to break up the fights. But mostly these were isolated incidents, and the crowd was making merry, laughing easily and loudly.

Near the lake docks, Skye, always alert, saw a flicker of movement at his side and looked across to see a young lad trying to cut his purse. His hand swept out, taking the boy's wrist in a vice-like grip. Skye watched the play of fear and anger across the youth's face. Another boy, probably the thief's friend, hovered nearby.

'If you're not quick enough, lad, don't try it,' said Skye. 'You'll end up cut, or worse.'

The youth knew enough to hold his tongue.

'I didn't even see him move,' said the boy's friend, referring to Skye.

The thief looked at Skye's Brotherhood tattoos, marking them in his memory. Skye knew he would not forget those symbols.

'Where can a man gamble around here?' asked Skye, releasing the boy.

The youth backed well out of his reach and pointed up an alley. 'Up there, demon-spawn!' He gave Skye a rude hand-sign and ran off into the crowd.

Skye and Marken laughed and shuffled through the crowd to the narrow alley mouth.

'Hey, pretty boys. Want some fun?' called a whore from a window above, pressing her ample breasts together in display as they looked up.

'Maybe later, little flower,' called back Skye as they passed.

As they rounded the corner, Skye saw two black-clad warriors outside the entrance to a gambling house. They leant casually against the wall, a painted woman on each arm, greatscythes slung across their backs. He pushed Marken into the shadows.

'What is it?' asked Marken, his hand automatically reaching

to check the scythe slung across his back and the calv in his harness.

'Look at the back of the alley,' said Skye. 'Do you see those two warriors? The Cioans?'

Marken tensed as he saw them.

'They were with Raziin in Raynor. If *they* are here, Raziin is here,' said Skye.

Skye checked his knives, loosening the catches on his harness sheaths. He studied the two warriors, a plan forming quickly in this head.

'Follow me,' said Skye. 'And be ready to cut.'

Marken's breath was rapid and uneven as they walked casually along the narrow alley, skirting debris and rotting rubbish.

'Act drunk,' whispered Skye. He knew Raziin's warriors were expert scythemen and wanted every advantage.

Skye bowed his head and walked unevenly, looking across to see Marken aping him. He faked a stumble, drawing close to one of the warriors. Marken followed. The warriors watched them as they neared. Skye continued on, as if he were walking past. As soon as the warrior's eyes left him, Skye drew his calv and darted in, cutting the straps that held the man's greatscythe across his back. The second warrior reached for his greatscythe, but found the sharp lanedd of Marken's calv at his throat.

The first warrior bent to pick up his weapon, but Skye flashed his calv in front of the man's face. 'No so fast.'

The women screamed and ran.

Seeing his companion trapped, the first warrior kicked out savagely at Skye's groin. Skye was forced to step back to avoid the blow. The warrior drew a concealed calv and lunged at Skye, forcing him to give ground. A man staggered from the entrance of the gambling house, right into the middle of the fight. The warrior grabbed the man and pushed him at Skye, using the distraction to flee into the alley.

Skye drew a throwing knife from his boot sheath and threw it, aiming for the neck. The warrior dodged aside just before it struck and the knife hit his shoulder instead. The wound did not slow the warrior's pace, and within moments he was lost in the crowd.

'Uros' tits!' cursed Skye.

Marken tightened his grip on the second warrior, his calv drawing a thin line of blood from the man's neck. Skye gritted his teeth, absently testing the edge of his blade on his finger.

'Why are you in Olcis?' asked Skye, leaning forward to trace a cut across the warrior's chest, drawing blood. 'Why is Raziin here?'

'Uros take you, gutter-scum,' said the warrior, his breath ragged with pain as the knife cut deeper.

'Gutter-scum?' said Skye in a sudden rage. He grabbed the man's hand, forcing it closer to his razor sharp calv. The man struggled, but Skye was stronger. The lanedd edge of his blade touched the Cioan's finger, opening a wound. The warrior winced in pain.

'I won't play games with you. *Where is Raziin?*' asked Skye.

A small crowd gathered to watch. Skye did not care as long as they did not interfere. His heart pounded as he remembered Jaso's death on the Spire. How he was butchered like meat. 'Uros fucker,' hissed Skye. The edge began to cut into the man's finger. The warrior struggled, but Skye's grip was as hard as mought.

There were those who said revenge was not the obsession of great men, even so, Skye had never aspired to anything higher than the next dawn. Jaso had been a brother to him.

'Argh!' The man's severed finger fell to the cobbles.

The warrior's arm trembled.

'Raziin,' said Skye coolly. 'Where is he?'

A sheen of sweat broke out on the warrior's forehead. 'No,' he said, his voice tight with pain. The blade began to cut once more. Into a second finger.

'I don't know,' pleaded the man. Skye sensed truth and eased off the pressure.

'Then why is he here?' demanded Skye, giving vent to his rage.

'To meet the Athrian, the other one. The one who drew the Fire.'

Skye and Marken met each other's gaze with sudden fear.

Cedrin was alone.

'Go on,' said Skye.

The man looked up with bleary eyes, the pain taking its toll. 'He had to be here at the time of Asic's Blessing. The Seer foretold it: the Athrian would be here in Olcis, in the plaza of Cinanac. Raziin has gone to meet him. It's all I know … I swear it.'

Skye released the warrior's arm and the man sagged into Marken, as though weak with pain or exhaustion. Marken was forced to take his blade away from the warrior's throat as he caught him. *A trick.*

'Watch him!' said Skye.

The warrior exploded into action. He tripped Marken and drew his own calv, the long knife stabbing at Skye's heart. The warrior was fast, but Skye was faster. The warrior's blade met only air. Skye feinted in. The warrior raised his blade to block the cut and gasped as Skye's calv flashed past his guard and through his throat. The warrior staggered forward two steps. He dropped his weapon as he reached to his throat in disbelief. Slowly he sagged to his knees, his life-blood pumping from his throat and soaking the front of his leather armour. The look of shock on his face faded and he fell forward, dead.

Marken pushed himself to his feet.

'Are you all right?' asked Skye.

'Yes. But it is not me we have to worry about. It's Cedrin.'

'Let's try back at the tavern first,' said Skye.

They hurried back towards the tavern, pushing against the crowd. They were surrounded by drunken fools with painted faces and masks askew, and groups walking arm in arm, blocking the way.

'Damn this crowd,' said Marken.

Finally they reached the tavern. The five spearmen were still there, but there was no sign of Cedrin.

Skye looked around him, searching the faces. Nothing.

'How can we find him in this crowd?' shouted Marken over the din. 'It's impossible!'

Impossible? *Not if we had magic.* 'We may not be able to find him, but what about a Sorcerer?' said Skye.

'Ellen!' said Marken, gripping Skye's arm.

'Now all we have to do is get into the Citadel and find her,' said Skye, stepping over a snoring man, a spilt glass of ale still gripped tenuously in his hands.

Marken smiled. 'That part will be easy.'

Skye raised his eyebrow.

'Your Lordship,' said Marken, bowing. 'A narsiit is better than a Suul mark when it comes to bluffing!'

'Yes! Come on,' said Skye.

* * *

'Finally,' said Ellen, pushing herself to her feet. With Lempar gone, the room had become a prison, her long wait with Kalyth a torture of uneasy silence.

A middle-aged court functionary approached them across the patterned marble.

'I am Suulqua Melor of the Olcis court,' said the man. He coughed and brushed a piece of lint off his shoulder, watching Ellen with insolent, dull eyes. 'Ellen Cintros, the Hesguit has declined to see you today.'

Ellen gritted her teeth. 'When can he?'

'The Hesguit has not set a firm audience time. Apply again tomorrow,' said Melor.

'*Tomorrow?*'

'The Hesguit faces many pressing matters,' said Melor in a bored voice.

That was the end of her scheme. If she had been able to see the Hesguit immediately, she would have had a chance of forcing a decision before the High Council could meet and ratify the Athrian edict. By tomorrow night, orders could be issued to take her. Her gamble had failed.

'Take me to Raphal the Larus Druid,' she commanded.

The Suulqua snorted. 'Quite impossible,' he said with a superior sneer.

Ellen had known too many courtiers to be bluffed.

'Now!' she snapped, her voice ringing with the command of a Sarlord's daughter.

Melor started, taking an involuntary step back. 'I'm sure if you return tomorrow ... arrangements could be made,' began the man, his whole demeanour changed from aloof to subservient.

'I shall not be returning tomorrow. Take me to see Raphal the Larus Druid. *Immediately*,' she said.

The courtier bowed and spread his hands in supplication. 'But, my Lady. The emissary was given over to the High Druid of Larus for penance.'

'Where is he?'

Melor looked up, clearly mortified. 'He would be in the Brown Robes contemplation chapel, but not even another Druid dare disrupt him without permission from the High Druid.'

Ellen suppressed a feeling of triumph. In the court of Olcis, she had absolutely no authority, yet panderers like Melor never failed to blow with the wind. Had he chosen, the Suulqua could have had her thrown out of the Citadel with one word. As it was, she had taken command.

'Take me to the contemplation chapel,' she said, her shoulders and head tilted in her best Cintros poise.

Melor met her eyes and bowed in deference. The Suulqua waved irritably for the doors to be opened for him and signalled for Ellen to follow.

Ellen allowed herself a brief moment of respite and looked across at Kalyth, who fell in step beside her. She was surprised by the poignant sadness she saw in his face, mixed evenly with open admiration for her. All this from a man who had only ever expressed contempt. Kalyth turned away and the moment was gone.

They followed Melor through the vast hallways of the Citadel, flanked by two Temple Guardians. They soon reached the vaults of the library, an extensive labyrinth of interconnected rooms that ran deep into the very heart-rock of the Mulisar range, each lined with books, scrolls and tomes, and countless artefacts of antiquity and power. Her father had often said the Olcis library was the finest in Kelas, containing documents written before the founding of the Cioan Empire.

'There is the entrance,' said Melor. The Suulqua pointed to a small opening in the dressed stone of the corridor between two chambers. There was no marking of any kind, and Ellen first took it for a natural fissure.

'Let it be known I warned you against entering and led you here under duress,' said Melor.

Ellen gave him a withering glance. 'Thank you for your help, Suulqua.'

Melor walked away, leaving a single Guardian. By leaving, he had absolved himself of responsibility for what would happen.

Ellen walked through the small opening into the chapel, forced to stoop even though she was not tall. Kalyth had to bend almost double to pass the tiny opening.

She gasped in surprise as she straightened. 'Oh, my ...'

It was a natural cavern, the walls and ceiling covered with thick translucent deposits of a water-borne mineral that had solidified over the years, draping in sheets, columns and conical pillars of tremendous complexity and beauty. Dominating the chamber was a rough-hewn altar, shaped and sculptured around a single glowmetal of gold. The violet streamers of light from the glowmetal were the only illumination in the room and loaned the place an alien aspect that sent chills down Ellen's spine. After a moment of awe, she reminded herself she was not here to sightsee and continued into the room.

A thin man lay prostrate on the cold ground before the altar, partially hidden in its shadow. Her heart leapt as she recognised him.

'Raphal,' she said, hurrying over the uneven surface to him.

Raphal raised himself stiffly off the stone. As his eyes focussed on Ellen, they widened in alarm.

'Dear Ellen! You should not be here. The Hesguit could order you imprisoned for such an act,' said Raphal in a stern whisper.

'Raphal, I had to come,' she said.

She trembled, remembering the evil power that had overcome her and sent her into darkness.

'What is it, Ellen?' he said, concerned.

'There is no time to explain everything. A dark force is at work within the Temple of the Iris. I need to know if there is a

Face of the Iris in Olcis.'

Kalyth suddenly tensed. He seemed about to question her, but at the last moment held his tongue, waiting for Raphal's answer.

'That question leads to a thousand others – but I can tell you are in urgent need.' He tapped his head. 'By the Yellow Sun, it's hard to think! After all the hours on that cold floor my mind is in a fog.' He rubbed his chin absently as he paced back and forth before the altar.

'Yes. Yes, there once was a Face of the Iris here. As to where it lays ...' He shook his head. 'I once knew. If only I could remember.'

Her worst fears had been confirmed. The Iris, and the evil within it, was here.

'It would take me days to find out, perhaps weeks. Searching old journals, records, or something could simply jog my memory ...'

A wave of nausea swept through Ellen, leaving her with a pounding headache. She leant back against a stone pillar as memories bubbled up through her mind like a black flood. She saw the Iris turning at the feet of the Behemoth as it reached for her.

'Are you all right, Ellen?' asked Raphal, extending a thin arm to steady her as she swayed on her feet.

Tears flowed down her cheeks and her brain was slowing, as though immersed in a thick, dark fluid like molasses. Raphal's brow creased in concentration. Abruptly a bolt of warm, golden Earth Essence flowed through her, dispelling the darkness like mist driven away by the summer sunshine. She gasped and fell into his arms, weak yet finally free of the taint of that dark memory. The old Druid led her to a rough-cut seat of stone and she sat, pausing a moment to regain her strength.

Raphal looked at her gravely. 'Why did you not tell me of this, child? The touch of darkness on you would have become a cancer of terror in your mind, slowly swelling with your fears, had I not dispelled it.'

The Behemoth ...

Ellen began to thank Raphal, when a familiar voice echoed

through the chamber.

'Yes, but *Lord Skye* ... I am obliged to remind you it is forbidden to enter and that I led you here only under duress ...'

The faintness had passed. Ellen stood up, turning to see Skye and Marken enter the room, almost unrecognisable in the court finery they wore, the ill-fitting nature of which lent questions as to its origin.

Marken ran across the chamber to Ellen, "Lord Skye" close at his heels.

'Thank the Sisters we found you, Ellen,' said Marken. 'Cedrin is in danger.'

Kalyth seized Marken by the shoulder. 'What danger! Where is he?'

Marken looked from the old warrior to Ellen, unsure what to say.

Skye responded. 'It's Raziin. We found two of his men near the docks. Apparently a Seer told Raziin he must meet Cedrin in the plaza of Cinanac at Asic's Blessing. Why, I have no idea. No one can even tell us where it is.'

'That's it!' said Raphal. 'The Iris is in the plaza of Cinanac, I can remember reading that somewhere. Damn ... but where is the plaza of Cinanac? This is infuriating! I can't remember. But I could find it in the records, perhaps by morning.'

Raphal's face suddenly grew slack. 'It's the Prophecy. The Scion and the Nemesis together in the Iris.'

'Raphal! What are you saying?'

'Ellen, it's obvious. Cedrin is Old Blood. He must be the Scion!'

Skye and Marken gasped in shock and Kalyth's gaze grew hard, flicking between each of them defensively.

The fear turned her spine to water. How could she have been so stupid? As Myan lay dying he would not pause to tell her anything that was not vital. His first words had been of the Scion. Of Cedrin. She had been blinded by Cedrin's links with the Brotherhood, his origins on the streets, all too ready to believe what they had all believed, that he was the bastard son of Belin.

All along she had expected the Scion to emerge from hiding,

dressed in finery, the Suul mark glowing for all to see. What a fool she had been! *Cedrin is the Scion.* The Cinanac heir. It was incredible – unreal – yet the more she thought it through, the more the pieces began to fit. Would a bastard son have the Old Blood? Would a bastard son be saved ahead of legitimate children ...

Ellen spun on Kalyth, a wild fury overtaking her. *'You knew!'*

Kalyth backed away as she advanced. 'You knew all along he was the heir! And you held your tongue to make your betrayal of Riin complete!'

Kalyth flinched.

'Well — see what your bitterness has earned. Now he is being drawn to his own destruction!'

'This is what I hoped to prevent!' stormed Kalyth, anger breaking though his cool reserve. 'I was protecting him. Don't you think I knew the danger? I was enslaved by the Ward – the same force that took Belin. I was forced to lurk like a beggar near the Iris; forced to watch time and again as Belin appeared, possessed by the Ward, wondering when the darkness in the Spear would poison my mind.' Kalyth acknowledged their shocked looks. 'Yes. That's right. The Ward holds the Spear of Carris,' said Kalyth, his voice desperate. 'If one of the Old Blood is taken by the Ward, we are doomed. The Spear is cursed.'

Raphal fell to his knees, his head bowed. 'Larus protect us! The Prophecy is upon us! The Spear of Carris will rise again!'

'I don't give a jot for this talk of the Ward or the Spear,' said Skye. He took Ellen by the arm and met her eyes. 'Ellen. Can you find Cedrin? Can you lead us to him?'

Marken joined them. 'Can you do it, Ellen?'

For Ellen it was like a mist had cleared.

'Yes!' she said with sudden hope. She plucked feverishly at the bindings of her pouch, looking for the Seeker. It had been way too valuable to leave with her belongings. 'With this I can find him anywhere.'

'Let's go then,' said Skye. 'I have our amelak waiting outside.'

The companions made to leave. As they turned to go, Marken helped Raphal up from the floor.

'Are you coming with us, Raphal?' he asked.

'And miss the unfolding of the Prophecy?' said the old Druid with a glow in his eyes. 'Some things are even worse than the Hesguit's wrath.'

* * *

A dark figure slipped in front of Cedrin, blocking the way.

'No *Impersiolos*. The evil awaits.'

The bald, solid dome, the eyes that glowed faintly red in the darkness beneath bony brow ridges. Slowly Cedrin became aware of the dark figure of Bovosan. He had completely forgotten the squat, silent minitil. Of course. It had been him he had seen slipping back into the shadows. The minitil had followed him as he was drawn to the Iris.

'The Scion must stand in the Temple of the Iris,' declared Cedrin. Blue lights flickered at the corners of his vision. Nothing could stop him from reaching that tantalising place of promise.

He pushed past Bovosan, his eyes fixed on the space between the columns. The minitil seized him from behind, pinning his arms in a grip of tremendous strength. Cedrin struggled, slowly becoming enraged. He had never imagined the half-breed was so strong.

Golden lights appeared above the Iris, spinning rapidly around the great eye in the centre. In a heartbeat they accelerated into a whirlpool of shimmering streamers. Light flooded past the high columns, banishing the shadows. As the light increased, Cedrin could see at least a dozen black-clad warriors with greatscythes waiting close by, as if for the cue to attack. They meant nothing to him. The only thing that mattered was the Iris. It filled his vision, beckoning him like a lover.

'Let me go, you idiot!' snapped Cedrin.

He could see the minitil squinting against the light. Now was his chance. Cedrin swept his head back into Bovosan's face. The minitil saw the move at the last moment and ducked his head forward, protecting the bridge of his nose. Cedrin growled. He slammed his right foot down onto the minitil's right instep. He heard Bovosan hiss in pain, but the half-breed's grip did not

454

falter.

'Let me go.'

Cedrin kicked and struggled. If he could have reached his calvs he would have killed Bovosan without a second thought. Reaching the Iris was all that mattered. A rage built inside Cedrin. The Window appeared, a torrent of power pushing against it. This was the edge he needed.

He opened the Window and released the Fire.

Immediately a red nimbus flared up around Cedrin. Bovosan was thrown aside. The minitil landed heavily on the stone, and lay momentarily stunned.

At last he was free.

He stepped past the columns and into the Temple of the Iris. There was a flash of blue in his mind and Cedrin halted. The irresistible force that had driven him to enter the temple was gone. Even so, he was drawn to the centre, where the songs of the Iris were rising in a blaze of gold, building towards connection with the other Faces of the Iris.

'Stop!' called Bovosan.

Cedrin paused one step away from the spinning mural.

The minitil rose unsteadily to his feet. 'Fight it, *Impersiolos,*' said Bovosan in his heavy accent. 'Remember Kalyth warning!'

From a distant corner of Cedrin's mind, a small voice of reason began to assert itself. What had Kalyth said? *That the Iris was to be feared.* Slowly awareness returned. His vision expanded. He saw himself being led mindlessly towards the Iris under the influence of something alien, a power that had been hidden in his mind like an assassin, waiting for the moment to strike. Fighting to keep his concentration, he closed the Window. The red glow around him faded to nothing.

'The Beast is there. In the Iris,' said Bovosan.

Then in a rush, Cedrin knew.

The Behemoth.

The beast he had seen in his dreams. That was the great darkness that dwelt within the Iris. This was what Kalyth had tried to shield him from at Blackthorne when the Iris stirred.

Bovosan took his arm and dragged him out of the temple, away from the rising power. The light was brilliant now, bathing the courtyard that surrounded the temple. Cedrin's senses flared with alarm as he saw it was crowded with black-clad warriors. And standing there at their head — his silver hair shining in the lambent glow — was Raziin.

Cedrin shook off Bovosan's arm.

The Northmen had formed a cordon, blocking any escape.

Raziin advanced with casual ease, watching Cedrin with the cold eyes of a killer. At his left and right stood his lieutenants, Kyal and the giant Merceth.

Raziin's eyes narrowed as he saw Bovosan. 'You!' said Raziin. 'Marina's lackey. You are a long way from the court of Ciofran-Ac. It will be a pleasure watching *you* die.' Raziin's eyes darted between Cedrin and Bovosan. 'All the bastards and half-breeds together.'

Cedrin slipped the greatscythe off his back. The last time he saw Raziin was on the Spire – when he had frozen him and his friends with Sorcery.

Raziin looked at Cedrin and sneered. 'You will die soon enough. But not before you have won me my prize.'

Bovosan cursed Raziin in Cioan and spat at his feet, his mought hammer slipping easily from his belt into his grasp. Raziin waved his men forward with stabbing gestures. 'Merceth, maintain a defensive circle around the Iris. Kyal, pick four men and take down the minitil.'

Raziin turned to Cedrin. 'I will take care of the Athrian myself.'

Men surged at Bovosan, led by the thick-set Kyal. The attack drove them apart. Raziin's men would not let Cedrin near the minitil, but would not engage him directly either, merely blocking his attacks. Bovosan was set upon from all sides. He whirled about him with his mought hammer. One warrior drove in towards him, cutting deeply across his side, but in return had his skull crushed with a sudden blow of tremendous force. But the greatscythe had the superior reach, and for all Bovosan's skill, Cedrin knew it was only a matter of time before they found gaps in his guard.

Raziin leapt at Cedrin, driving in with swift, powerful attacks. Cedrin gave ground towards the temple entrance and extended his blades. He could not afford to take any risks until he got a feel for Raziin as an opponent. The golden light issuing from the temple was brighter than daylight. The Song of the Iris surrounded them.

Kyal and his men circled Bovosan warily.

'The Iris. Stay away from it!' called Bovosan as swayed back from a feint by one of Raziin's men.

Cedrin looked across his shoulder to see the entrance to the temple only feet away. Merceth stood before the column, flanked by black-clad warriors, watching implacably. Waiting. The light and sound filled the plaza to overflowing, obscuring everything in a landscape of discharging energy.

I am being pushed into a trap.

Chapter Twenty-Nine

Raziin's warriors were not in position to keep him out of the Iris, but to force him *into* it. Whatever the Behemoth wanted, Raziin wanted too. Cedrin had to start pushing back. He feinted at Raziin and side-stepped away from the temple. Raziin immediately cut in with his greatscythe. He was *fast*. Cedrin blocked instinctively and their blades met with a grinding squeal of lanedd, jarring Cedrin's arm to the elbow.

'Until I claim my prize, I need you alive,' said Raziin, his smile like a death's head grin. 'But there is nothing preventing me from cutting you first.'

Raziin drove forward, his blades flashing with the light of the Iris. Cedrin met each blow then counterattacked. Then he was forced to give ground as Raziin feinted in, then sent a reverse cut at his head. Cedrin blocked, following with a reverse sweep. His left blade sliced through the front of Raziin's leather armour – less than a thumb's width from disembowelling him. Raziin grunted in surprise and fell back.

'Stinking dock-scum,' growled Raziin. The Cioan attacked again, his face twisted in fury. Cedrin's concentration was total. He met every attack, then feinted in with a right cut. At the last moment he swung his weapon, forcing Raziin to leap back as his left blade shot past his face. This was the very first movement Kalyth had shown him, the drill he had practised until his arms ached.

'Is that the best you have?' said Cedrin, taunting Raziin. 'But that's right though, isn't it? You are more used to unarmed men.' Cedrin thought of his friend Jaso, cut into pieces by Raziin on the Spire.

Raziin said nothing. The Cioan shifted position, changing his attacks. He was still trying to force him into the Iris. Cedrin fended him off, then circled around him.

Raziin growled in frustration. Cedrin's head swam with the exhilaration of triumph and he fought to keep his mind clear, his spirit calm. He may be new to the greatscythe, but he was a veteran of single combat. Raziin attacked again, stabbing in. He blocked each strike, alert for the change to sweeping attacks. He owed a debt to Kalyth for preparing him for this. His heart soared. Since that ill-fated night in Athria, he had feared Raziin like a demon, or a creature of Uros. Now he knew he could best him. It was time Raziin paid for his ruthless murder.

Cedrin went on the attack, driven forward by the white-hot flame of revenge. His greatscythe moved like a deadly whirlwind, the blades striking in a blur. Raziin fell back, his weapon moving furiously to counter. The Northman's angry scowl was soon replaced by a tight grimace.

Then Raziin leapt back, out of range of Cedrin's weapon.

Something tugged at Cedrin's gut. Something familiar.

A bolt of Force hit Cedrin in the stomach and suddenly he was airborne. He landed hard, the breath driven out of his lungs. Another solid ball of silver Force hit him in the chest. He tumbled backwards, his greatscythe flying from his grasp. When he came to a stop, he scrambled to his feet. Raziin strode towards him, a sheen of sweat glistening on his pale skin as his brow creased in concentration.

The Song of the Iris was deafening, the light was everywhere, but Cedrin dared not take his eyes off Raziin.

'I'm done playing games. I want my prize,' said Raziin.

The Northman stretched out his arms. The bolt struck with stunning force, pushing him straight into the Temple of the Iris. Cedrin staggered back onto the mural. Although it felt solid beneath his feet, it confounded his eyes, rippling constantly through myriad images, each unique in its five-fold symmetry.

Merceth watched impassively as Raziin followed Cedrin into the vast, turning pool of light.

Cedrin had one last glimpse of Bovosan, holding four

warriors at bay. The minitil attacked and Kyal dodged away from his mought hammer, cursing fluently.

'We have your measure, minitil. We will soon bring you down,' said Kyal.

Within the Iris, the Song was silent, something felt but not heard. Threads of power rippled, forming a thick curtain that cut off all vision of the outside. Distantly, Cedrin heard Bovosan scream. Then there was nothing but that landscape of light, turning around the centre of the Iris. He caught glimpses of Raziin on the other side of the temple, his face alight with anticipation. The bright, heavy atmosphere pressed down on Cedrin like an anchor-stone.

Out of the centre of the Iris walked a thickset, silver-haired man in leather armour. His whole body was sheathed in Fire, flooding from the tip of the ancient spear he held in his hands. A fine web of blue lines snaked around the man's body, flickering across his skin. The blade of the spear was not of lanedd or darkglass, but of forged metal. Gold – pure gold – somehow divorced from its native light. It seemed so *unnatural*. All metal on Yos was glowmetal, each inextricably linked with its own web of light and locked into the form of its first creation – impossible to reshape or destroy. The youngest child knew it. The golden blade was almost too bright to look at as it pulsed with the Fire. The man turned to Cedrin, studying him carefully. Blue lights danced inside his eyes. Then he turned to Raziin.

'I am the Ward of Jykor. Set in place to protect the Spear. Which of you is the Scion?'

'I am!' called Raziin, stepping closer to the Ward.

'We shall see,' said the Ward.

Twin streamers of blue energy lashed out from behind the Ward's head like vipers, striking towards them. One of the blue tendrils sunk deep into Cedrin's mind, reaching into his memories. His life flashed past, racing to that night on the ridge when Kalyth told him the truth. The tendril withdrew.

The blue tendril that had latched onto Raziin had also recoiled, disappearing back into the mind of the Ward.

The Ward turned to Cedrin. The blue web writhed over the Ward's features, forming the image of another sharp-featured face in shades of blue.

'Greetings, grandson. I am the Emperor Jykor. You are the Scion of the Cinanac, and by providence both Old Blood and Adept. You are chosen to hold the Spear of Carris.'

The image of the face dissolved, once more giving way to the old man's.

Blue tendrils lashed out at Cedrin, this time wrapping themselves around his body, binding him tightly. The Ward turned back towards the Iris, walking slowly. Cedrin fought against them, but the tendrils flexed and tightened, drawing him forward.

The Iris drew closer, becoming insubstantial, translucent.

Through it, Cedrin could see another Temple of the Iris, set amid the ruins of a vast underground city. A massive cavern stretched overhead, every tumbled structure lit by the blaze of the Spear. Around the Iris lay hundreds of Eathal, cowering in fear, face down on the dusty floor. Near the edge of the circle was a bird-like being, feathered yet standing like a man, its big eyes looking back at him with awe and fear. Cedrin's stomach tightened as he saw a huge spider lurking behind the bird-being.

Cedrin turned and looked behind him. He could see the plaza of Cinanac through the blaze of energies and realised he stood at the threshold of two places.

Raziin was following them, forcing his way through the Iris, his face a mask of grim determination.

'Soon the Scion shall have the Spear,' said the Ward, holding up the ancient weapon.

Something dark began to rise from the Spear. At first it was nothing but a shimmering haze in the air, then it began to take shape. It looked like one of the keerhounds of Armon, bred for hunting, but it was massive, the size of a war-harena. Its single horn was cracked over part of its length, but still razor-sharp. It glared at Cedrin balefully, one eye grey-blue, the other glowing gold.

Cedrin's heart missed a beat, squeezed in a vice of fear.

The Behemoth.

Time slowed. The Ward, the Eathal around the circle, the

bird-man and the great spider, all stood frozen. He saw Raziin's eyes swivel towards him and the Northman's face darken. Like him Raziin was alert, but held immobile.

Only the Behemoth was free to move.

'Ward!' called Cedrin, seeking an ally against the Behemoth.

The Behemoth exhaled. Its rank breath washed over him.

The Ward has no dominion over Us. We are the true masters of the Spear. The Behemoth's voice filled his mind.

The beast stepped forward, its horn glinting.

We have need of a Spear-carrier. It is We who will choose.

Cedrin shivered. He felt a chill to the core of his being, as though all heat had been sucked away by its mere presence.

The Behemoth advanced.

Cedrin could feel the waves of lustful heat and darkness that was its essence, and smell the rotting corruption that riddled its body. The huge, razor-sharp horn was stained with death and old blood, the whites of its eyes yellowed with sickness.

The Behemoth drew a rattling breath. As it met Cedrin's gaze, it exhaled. A putrid stench flooded towards him, a hundred times worse than even the smell of the rotting fish-guts strewn across the Athrian harbour at low tide.

The dark core of the Behemoth reached out for Cedrin, touching not his mind, but his soul. He felt the acid of its substance as it explored the very depths of his being and knew a violation few spirits could survive. Somewhere in the inner chambers of his essence he found a seed of light, and he held to it as the darkness clutched and tore at him. Then suddenly, as though awakened by his touch, the seed blossomed into life. The Behemoth instantly recoiled, yet it recovered quickly.

The Behemoth roared in fury, then charged, the razor-sharp horn pointed at his heart. He was powerless to move. At the last moment it stopped, close enough so the foul stench of its breath made his eyes water. It growled deep in its throat. Fear squirmed inside him.

The beast turned from Cedrin to Raziin.

'Come, beast. Deliver it to me,' said Raziin.

The Behemoth padded up to the Northman, peering into him with its diseased eyes. It swayed back, then roared in triumph.

Yes. The Northman shall have the Spear. Cedrin heard the thoughts of the Behemoth clearly in his mind. *Be ready, Northman. At the moment the Spear is granted to the Scion, the Ward will cease to exist. At that moment – take it!*

'Ah – so this is what the Seer meant. What of Cedrin?' asked Raziin.

The Behemoth turned its gaze on Cedrin. *We need no rivals, Northman – kill him.*

* * *

Ellen squinted against the brilliant fountain of energies cascading from the Iris. She slipped the Seeker into the pouch at her side. The glowmetal had shown what she feared most. Cedrin – the Scion – was already inside the Iris. Beside her, Raphal's eyes were open in wonder.

The Temple of the Iris was ringed by Raziin's men and Bovosan lay besieged against a statue, his hammer lost, streamers of blood trailing across his dark skin. Only his shield remained to ward off the blows of Raziin's warriors. If not for the narrow alcove he had positioned himself in, he would have already fallen. A golden-skinned giant was in command; he watched them from across the plaza, his face cold and frightening.

Kalyth leapt from his amelak, unslinging his greatscythe as he did so. 'Where is he, Ellen?'

Ellen fought despair as the bright bands of energy that sealed the Iris filled her vision.

'He is within,' she said, her hoarse voice hardly above a whisper.

'You must destroy it, Ellen,' said Kalyth. 'Use everything Myan ever taught you. The Beast must not take Cedrin.'

With that, Kalyth ran forward to the Iris. To her left, Skye had climbed to the high pedestal of a monument. He fitted an arrow to his horn bow.

Marken hovered nearby.

'Help Kalyth,' said Ellen to Marken.

Marken's hand tensed on his scythe.

'No,' said Raphal. 'With both moons in the sky, you can be more help from here.'

'I'm not ready for that!' said Marken, watching the combat anxiously.

'Trust me, Marken. On the night of Asic's Blessing, even Templemen walk warily around Moon Druids.'

An arrow shot through the plaza and one of the warriors surrounding Bovosan fell, giving the minitil the respite he needed to regain his hammer. A thickset warrior near Bovosan spun towards Skye. A knife flashed through the air, but Skye was already moving, the knife tumbling through the space where Skye had been. On the other side of the statue, Skye shot again. Another warrior fell, a feathered shaft in his throat. The light was giving him easy targets.

The golden-skinned giant gave rapid orders in Cioan. The dark-clad warriors guarding the temple joined the others and moved into close-quarter fighting with Kalyth and Bovosan. The giant ducked behind a statue.

'Damn it. I can't get a clear shot!' said Skye, peering into the confused mass.

Four warriors pressed in at Kalyth. Three fell in the first moments, the last cut down as he turned to flee. Ellen was astounded at his speed and skill. Bovosan stood behind him, ready to protect his back.

The thickset warrior shouted orders in Cioan and more warriors charged at Kalyth.

'It's now or never,' said Marken.

Marken raised his arms. His face creased in concentration. A moment later, a jagged wall of Force, silver as moonlight, leapt forward from his fingertips. It hit the thickset warrior and the men on either side of him, throwing them back onto the cobbles in a tangle of limbs and weapons. Kalyth and Bovosan leapt into the breach. Raziin's men fell back to protect the other warriors as they scrambled to their feet.

His face livid with rage, the thickset warrior gave another order in Cioan, and the remaining warriors fled into the night.

Marken laughed in delight. 'Thank you for your power,' he

said, looking up at the moons above.

Raphal tapped Marken on the shoulder, pointing down at Bovosan. 'He needs healing.'

Marken hurried to Bovosan's side, as Skye emerged carefully from the shadows.

'I doubt if Raziin's men have ever been routed so quickly,' said Skye.

Raphal walked to the temple, drawn by the power of the Song. 'A complex weaving,' he said. 'Drawing six places into one, transcending time and space.'

And Cedrin was inside that maelstrom.

'Raphal. How can I destroy the Iris?' said Ellen.

The old Druid looked at Ellen as though she were mad. 'You cannot challenge that amount of Earth Essence. Not now. Tremendous energies are being focussed here.'

'I have to stop this, Raphal. Cedrin is in there!' said Ellen.

The old Druid looked grim. 'The Prophecies have spoken, Ellen. *The Scion and the Nemesis stand together in the Iris,*' he said. 'Let the gods decide.'

'No,' said Ellen, fury welling inside her. 'There must be a way!'

Raphal shook his head. 'The only way is to break the symmetry. To shatter the mural or break one of the columns. But Ellen, the energies are beyond mortal ken!'

Ellen walked to the Iris. The thought of Cedrin dead tore at her with a pain she had never experienced before. The facade of her life fell away like a collapsed cliff, leaving only her vulnerable heart behind. In that moment, she realised nothing else mattered. Not her position as Suul. Not the Empire. *Nothing.* With a shock, she recognised that desperate ache inside her. That willingness to do anything to save him. She loved him. She loved Cedrin.

The power of the Iris swirled around her.

A voice in the back of her mind warned of danger.

Ellen drew closer to the Iris. She squinted against the blazing light, examining the geometry of the Temple, determined to free the man she loved or die trying.

'Ellen!' pleaded Raphal, following her. 'For the love of Larus.

Don't tamper with this!'

Ellen was already concentrating, drawing on the Fire, filling herself with power until her body ached. She formed the Matrix of Force, using all her skill to make careful adjustments to the mental construct. *There.* She hurled a sleek, compact bolt of silver at one of the five columns of the Iris. It struck with a *crack*, and the column exploded into fragments. The tiled roof above it was blown into the sky along with its ancient timber supports. She could hear the distant crashes as the timber and tile fell to earth further back inside the temple district.

Her heart surged in triumph. She squinted into the light of the Iris, expecting the shattered stone of the column to tumble down into the square around the temple, then the Iris to falter; but it did not. The power of Iris had swelled outward from its core, and held each of the now motionless column fragments suspended in its grip. The ground shook. Around the temple, statues and idols fell from their pedestals, cracking into pieces as they hit the stone. Then the Iris drew the column fragments back together, forcing them back into the shape of the column. With a sound like a massive gong, the column fell back into place, whole.

The Temple of the Iris remained unbroken.

She hurled another bolt of Force. Once more the column shattered, but the fragments were held in place by great sheets of energy that spanned between the columns.

'No!' cried Ellen. She had to break him free. At any cost.

Ellen drew on the Realm of Fire, letting the energy fill her until she was lost within it. Soon the Window was swamped from view, and she knew she had gone past the point of no return. She would no longer be able to close the Window. She tried to channel the restless sea of Fire through the Matrix, but there was too much to contain. Instead she let it flow through her. She became nothing but a channel for the raw, hot force of it as it screamed through her. The Fire struck the Iris with a roar and her vision was lost in crimson. Ellen held on, directing that immense power at the Temple of the Iris.

She fell forward. Her knees stung as they cracked against the pavement. Then she could control the flow no more. Her head struck stone. The Window closed in automatic reflex. Ellen clung to consciousness. Her body was weak, trembling. Three of the columns had been turned to smoking heaps of melted rock. The energies of the Iris flickered wildly, then extinguished with a final flash, leaving only darkness and silence.

She had done it.

A figure ran from the Iris towards her, indistinct in the darkness. She pushed herself off the ground.

'Cedrin?'

The man's face was pale and cruel. It took her a moment to recognise him.

Raziin.

He advanced on her, his eyes gleaming with hatred. Ellen struggled to stand, but her body failed her. She reached for the Fire, but the Window slipped through her mental grasp. Raziin seized her by the hair and lifted her off the ground. She screamed in pain and lashed out with her fists, but the blows fell weakly.

'I was so close to holding it. *So close!*' said Raziin.

Behind Raziin, Ellen could hear people calling her name. The Northman looked around in fury and drew a calv from his harness.

'Here's my thanks!'

She gasped at a sudden, sharp pain in her chest. Ellen looked down. Raziin had driven the calv straight through her heart. She cried out in pain as he twisted the knife again and again. *No.* She heard running feet. Then she hit the stone as he cast her aside.

Her vision blurred. 'Father ...' She reached weakly across the stone. There was blood on her hand.

No. It was not her father, it was Raziin.

'I am the chosen one,' he said. 'The Spear and the power will be mine – as promised. I will have it, even if I have to go to Ranmyden to take it.'

Then she was alone in the gathering dark.

* * *

Cedrin made his way out of the darkened temple, careful to

avoid the red-hot piles of melted stone. When the light of the Iris flickered out, both the Behemoth and the Ward had vanished, leaving Raziin and himself in the ruins of the Olcis Iris. The Northman had fled immediately, with enough speed to make Cedrin think he had used magic to find his way through the smoking ruins. Cedrin did not know how he had been saved from the Behemoth, but he knew he did not want Raziin to escape.

Finally outside the temple, he paused to let his eyes adjust to the light of the two moons. He could see darkened figures around the courtyard, and a slight figure laying prostrate on the stone. A worm of fear ate into his heart, and before he knew it he was running, all thoughts of revenge forgotten. All at once he knew who had saved him from the Behemoth, thwarting both it and Raziin.

'Ellen.'

He knelt at her side and took her hand. Her eyes stared dully up towards the stars. Blood drenched the front of her shirt and spread in a dark pool beneath her. He leant down low across her, feeling the merest whisper of her breath on his cheek. He pressed his fingers against her throat. Her pulse fluttered weakly. She hovered on the edge of death.

'Raphal! *Marken!'* shouted Cedrin in desperate fear.

He drew a calv and cut away her blooded shirt, using the cloth to wipe away the blood. He froze as he saw the wound in light of the full moons. His throat constricted at the sight of the gaping hole, and the lifeblood pumping from it. His arms and legs trembled with sudden weakness.

'No,' he whispered. With a cold certainty, he knew she would die, her life forfeit because she had fought to save him.

Then Raphal and Marken were at his side.

'Save her,' he pleaded.

Raphal put his hands over the wound and closed his eyes. When he opened them, his eyes were haunted. 'The cut was savage. It has destroyed her heart completely. Even with the power of the Iris at my command … her wound is beyond me.' The old Druid touched her cheek. 'Oh, Ellen. I warned you not to challenge the Iris.'

Cedrin hovered over a deep pit. At that moment, his independent life meant nothing – not without Ellen.

He turned to Marken. 'Both moons are in the sky. Surely you can try?'

'I cannot rebuild a heart, Cedrin,' said Marken. 'It's beyond the powers of any Druid.'

Cedrin looked up to see that Kalyth, Skye and Bovosan had joined them. All stood motionless, shocked into silence by the sight of Ellen's bloodied body.

'No!' screamed Cedrin, his eyes filling with tears as his heart tore with grief. They had barely time to touch before fate ripped them apart.

Her eyes were pale and empty, far from the vivid green that had been so filled with intensity in life. Cedrin reached out with his mind and soul, seeking one last touch with her spirit, tears falling freely down his cheeks. Effortlessly, the Window flared open, creating a link between them.

He was immersed in her. Her spirit had not fled! It fought for life. She felt his presence and reached out with her whole being. Their spirits touched and merged, becoming one. They shared the pure joy of love. Communion.

The Bridge was formed.

Cedrin. This is my Matrix of Form.

Into the space around him came a complex shape, turning and rippling upon itself like a living nucleus. It held within it the characteristics of life.

Take it!

Cedrin could sense Ellen's desperation all too acutely. He took the Matrix, holding it in his mind's clumsy grip. As he held it, the shape grew less distinct, lopsided and somehow *wrong*. Cedrin knew he would have to change it, reforge it.

Suddenly he was back in Tarral's glassworks. He had passed his manhood ceremony and his father had accepted him as heir. But this day was a special day. It was the day he fired his masterpiece.

He withdrew the intricate shape of glass from the kiln and showed it to Tarral. It had collapsed on the firing bed and was askew. His father smiled in silent encouragement and seemed to say, 'Try again'.

Over and over Cedrin reworked the shape, starting with a fresh stock of glass rod each time.

His hands throbbed with burns as he drew the finished shape from the kiln one more time, sweat dripping freely from his brow.

This time it was perfect.

After it cooled, he held it up to the light. In an instant, it became a Matrix, reformed within his mind.

Now channel the Fire through it.

A breeze of power blew through him and into the Matrix of Form. A gust rose within the Realm and the power he channelled grew even greater as the Window widened.

His inner world fell away and once more he was kneeling in the square of the Cinanac.

Around Ellen's body a golden sheath of energy began to take shape, a spinning cocoon of arcane power. The grief-stricken onlookers stepped back in wonder, shielding their eyes as the golden cloud engulfed both Cedrin and Ellen.

At last the nimbus faded and Ellen stirred. She touched her chest, the wound now replaced by smooth, unbroken skin. She smiled in wonder. 'I am whole.'

Cedrin met Ellen's eyes. For an instant they were joined intimately, rejoicing in life and love as they touched across the Bridge. Then unconsciousness claimed her. Cedrin slid his arms beneath her and lifted her, cradling her protectively.

Bovosan had prostrated himself on the stone at Cedrin's feet. *'Makdiron Suphus! Makdiron Suphus!'* he chanted, his face aglow with adoration.

The others stood watching him strangely. It was only then that Cedrin realised how his Sorcery must have appeared to an onlooker.

Kalyth squeezed his shoulder. 'So this is the same Cedrin who travelled north with me?'

'Yes,' said Raphal. 'But a long way from a simple calvanni from Athria.'

'An Old Blood Sorcerer,' said Kalyth.

'And the Scion,' said Raphal, his voice trembling. 'We have

to leave Olcis quickly. The Hesguit's Templemen have glowmetals that can detect the use of the Fire.'

Cedrin tensed. A threat to him was a threat to Ellen. 'Someone will need to show me the way out. I can't even remember getting here.'

'This way,' said Raphal, leading them through the maze of temples and down into Olcis.

Cedrin's head swam at the thought of what he had done. The Sorcery had filled him, yet had seemed as natural as breathing. Ellen felt soft and alive against his chest, her breath warm on his tattooed skin.

And beyond the Iris, beneath a mountain in the distant north, the Ward and the Behemoth still lurked.

Chapter Thirty

Cedrin paced the room, the flickering lamplight chasing shadows through the pre-dawn darkness. Tasselled curtains of red velvet hung limp around Ellen's bed, while she herself had hardly moved since they laid her down hours ago. The maids had dressed her in a light shift of white silk. Marken and Skye were asleep in the next room, Kalyth and Bovosan standing a silent guard in the corridor. Since they reached the tavern on the outskirt of Olcis, there had been nothing but this agonised wait. It seemed impossible that it was the same night, but outside the streets of Olcis were still thronged with crowds celebrating Asic's Blessing.

'All that pacing will not make her wake any faster,' said Raphal.

Cedrin stopped. 'I know,' he said, stretching. He was too charged up with the energy that had come in the wake of the Fire to even think about sleeping.

Raphal sat on a chair against the wall, watching him calmly. Marken and he had examined Ellen thoroughly when they arrived and proclaimed her healthy. All she needed was sleep. Even so, he could not shake the image of her dull, sightless eyes as they stared up at the sky. He needed to see her awake and *alive*.

He himself was aching from a score of cuts and bruises, all earned during the fight with Raziin.

Ellen groaned, and Cedrin was across the room in a moment.

Her eyes flickered open and a rush of hopeful joy flooded through him.

Raphal came to her side and patted her hand. 'Welcome back to the land of the living, my child.'

Ellen pushed herself up into a sitting position and looked across at Cedrin. She smiled at first, then seemed less certain.

'How much to do you remember?' asked Raphal.

'I remember the Iris ... Raziin ... then...'

Raphal looked back and forward between them. 'I think I will leave you two alone,' he said, silently slipping out of the room.

'You... are the Scion,' she said, her voice hoarse.

'It changes nothing,' he said.

'It changes everything!' she said, throwing back the covers and closing the distance between them, her eyes alight.

Cedrin smiled at her.

'What?' she said.

'Nothing. It's good to see you alive, that's all.'

Her hair was loose, tumbled around her shoulders. Wisps of it curled around her cheek. He reached out and pushed a curl aside, his fingertips brushing across her bird totem. She tilted her head up towards him, her lips a deep red against her pale skin.

'Look at you. You are a mess,' she said.

Ellen reached out to touch a bruise flowering across his ribs. Her hand was warm and soft.

'You saved me from the Behemoth,' said Cedrin, his voice a low whisper.

'And you saved me from death. I had no Fire left to save myself,' said Ellen.

She looked up at him and smiled. 'But I do now.'

Cedrin sensed the Fire rise inside her. She paused to concentrate, then a moment later he found himself suspended in a nimbus of yellow. The pain in his limbs, in his side, vanished along with the bruises and cuts.

The Sorcery faded, but she was closer than ever. Her nipples were hard, pushing against the silk of her shift. Cedrin closed the gap. He moved his hands across the skin of her shoulders and neck, expecting her to push him back at any moment – but she did not. Her skin was smooth and fine, like a miracle beneath the calloused and scarred skin of his palms. He looked into her face. Her eyes were wide, her lips open. His whole body was responding to her, his leather trews uncomfortably tight with his awakened desire.

He slipped his hand behind her head and pulled her to him. She smelled of fine perfume and soap and he kissed her furiously. She pushed herself against him, her skin hot beneath her shift. Cedrin dropped his hands to her hips and crushed her against him. Her hands swept feverishly through his hair. Her lips parted, and he slipped his tongue into her mouth in a frenzy of passion, unable to get enough of her.

His whole body throbbed with need. All the withheld passion – the forbidden desire – finally broke through his control. He had to have her. The bed was right there, only paces away. He pushed her towards it. She gasped in shock as her back hit the polished bedstead, pausing to look up at him, her eyes wide, her breath coming faster. There was no stopping now. He took hold her thighs and lifted her up against the bedstead, forcing her legs open as he pushed himself against her. She responded, wrapping her legs around his hips and they kissed again. His heart hammered as he smelled her scent. Her shift rode up to her stomach, revealing the light silk of her laced undergarment. He lifted her shift over her head and tossed it to the floor, running his hands over her breasts.

He broke off another torrent of kisses to lift off his harness and throw it to the ground. The handles of his calvs thudded into the floor. Her hands moved over the rippling muscles of his stomach, moving over scar and tattoo up to his raised pectoral muscles. His own nipples grew taut as a ripple of pleasure swept through him, leaving the hairs on his skin standing on end.

His hands shook with desire as he untied his trousers. He pushed them to the floor and kicked them away. Fully naked now, he pressed into her. He crushed his mouth against hers, then reached down with thick fingers to tear away the soft silk of her undergarment.

She gave a sharp intake of breath. He dropped his hands to her hips and bottom, moving them hungrily over her skin as he lifted her up into position.

'We heard a noise. Everything all right?' It was Kalyth's voice, through the door.

'Yes. Everything's fine,' called Cedrin, his voice hoarse.

He looked down at her. Her whole face was alive, her lips wet from their kissing. He could wait no longer. He grabbed her hair and took her, right there against the bedstead, all the passion he felt for her driving him forward. He knew he should take it slow, should be gentle, but he could not. But she was ready for him.

A groan was torn out of him, and he was lifted on a wave of ecstasy. A bead of sweat trickled down his chest, over his toned muscles and down to his waist as he made love to her against the bed, kissing her neck, her face; her honey-blonde hair still gripped in this hand. Only in his wildest dreams had he imagined he would have her: Ellen Cintros, a Suul, a Sorcerer, a woman who had once sat on the throne of Athria. He never wanted it to end. The intensity built and built, until he feared he would let go early. *That* he did not want to happen. He lifted her up and carried her onto the wide bed, following her onto the covers and levering himself above her. She swept back her legs, eager for him. Her delicate pink nipples were hard. He lowered his head to her breasts, his tongue teasing across her left nipple before he slid into her once more. Then he was riding the crest of an unstoppable tide of pleasure. He pushed himself up on his arms to watch her. Her eyes were closed, her head tilted back. Her small breasts bobbed with the movement, and his eyes roamed over her slim hips and the smooth, toned muscles of her legs as they swept back on either side.

He dropped down, kissing her as he continued to ride, pushing down against her. She made a low noise, deep in her throat. She moved her hips, pushing herself against him. Suddenly she stiffened. She grabbed his hips with her hands, pulling him down, stopping his lunging movements and grinding herself against him. She cried out, a high pure scream of pleasure, then she squirmed her hips and relaxed again.

She opened her eyes. Her face was flushed with heat and life. He lifted himself up on his arms and rode on. Her hands played over the hard muscles of his stomach, slick now with sweat, then up to his pectorals, rigid as he supported his weight above her. He cried out, at last releasing himself.

Cedrin collapsed onto her, sucking in deep breaths. It took a moment before he realised she was tapping him on the shoulder.

'Move, you harena. I can't breathe,' she wheezed.

Cedrin rolled over to her side. She took a deep breath. 'That's better.'

They laughed together, then lay intertwined. At peace. It was a glorious moment, when they were neither Suul, nor commoner, just a man and woman sharing the languid sensuality that followed lovemaking.

'I never thought this would be possible,' said Cedrin at last, breaking the spell.

Ellen pulled the sheet up over her waist, covering the neat blonde hairs crowning her pubis. 'So much has happened,' she said, her bright green eyes studying him seriously. 'I have been blind. And Raziin, the Behemoth ... they are still out there.'

She shivered, and he pulled up the covers, sinking back into the warmth. Ellen melted into his side. It felt right, as though she was always meant to be there. How could he, someone with nothing except the ill-luck of being born the heir to a fallen empire, ever hope to keep Ellen Cintros?

'That's a problem for tomorrow,' he said, his voice already slurred by languor and exhaustion.

Then the warmth lulled him into the delicious embrace of sleep.

* * *

Ellen watched as Cedrin spun the Matrix before his mind's eye, turning it in space with a deft mental touch. Cedrin had a sharp mind, and she was impressed with how quickly he had mastered the form. They lay side-by-side in their wide bed. Outside, first light had begun to colour the pre-dawn sky.

This is the Barrier. Ellen sent her thoughts across the Bridge.

Cedrin watched the form rotate in the void that spanned the

gulf of soul and mind between them.

'It has nowhere near the complexity of the Matrix of Form,' he said. Cedrin had yet to master sending his thoughts across the Bridge in silence, and spoke aloud to focus them.

She sensed the Fire rise inside Cedrin as he opened the Window and carefully channelled its power through the Matrix. The Barrier sprung to life around him, severing the Bridge and leaving them both in the darkness of their own minds.

Cedrin gasped in shock, his eyes wide.

Ellen laughed.

'What's so funny?' he asked.

'The expression on your face,' she said. She swung onto her knees beside him, her breasts swaying with the movement. His eyes dropped down to watch them move and she felt a flutter of excitement low in her belly. She slid her arms around his neck, melting her body over the muscles of his chest and thigh and resting her head on his shoulder. The last few hours had been like a dream. A welcome respite from the fear and confusion of their first night in Olcis. The worst part had been the fear that she had not been living her own life – that the Compulsion that had possessed her had coloured her decisions. Thankfully she knew that was not true. She would have followed her father's will despite it. She did believe in the restoration of the Empire. And she had at last discharged her debt to Myan, by finding the Scion ... by finding Cedrin.

She lifted her head up, resting it on her hands as she watched him. He was a handsome man, though prone to serious thoughts that gave him a stern look. His grey-blue eyes were distant now, off in some other place, and he was frowning. She reached up and ran her hand down his rough, unshaven cheek.

'I know. I need to shave,' he said, with a wry smile.

'Maybe I like you rough,' she teased, although the reverse was true.

He leant down and gave her a long, lingering kiss. Warmth flooded between her legs as her desire re-ignited. She never wanted to let this feeling of closeness go. Soon the day would start, and everyone would want a piece of him. For now, he was hers.

She lay back on the bed and lifted one knee up against the rumpled covers in invitation. Her heart thudded. She did not want to think. Not about all that had happened, nor where things would lead them. She smiled and raised an eyebrow slightly, daring him.

Her heart surged in triumph as he took the bait. He ran his hand lightly over her breasts. The skin of his palms was rough and calloused. She shivered as her nipples grew taut, her belly flexing as her breathing came faster. His fingers traced the skin over heart.

'Not even a scar,' he said.

Ellen tensed as she remembered Raziin's vicious attack. The calv, stabbing deep, again and again.

'That's the Matrix of Form. It recreates the flesh,' she said, her mouth dry.

She saw his jaw clench, and his eyes grow distant once more. *No. Don't stop. Can't you see I need this more than anything?* But he had stopped.

'Are you all right?' she asked.

'Inside the Iris. The Behemoth had chosen Raziin to have the Spear of Carris. A moment longer and Raziin would have taken it.'

'But you said the Ward had chosen you,' said Ellen, struggling to suppress her frustration.

'Once the Ward gives me the Spear, the Ward itself will dissolve. The Behemoth has its own powers. It froze me in place with magic. It could do so again, then there would be nothing I could do to stop Raziin taking the Spear.'

'Then they planned to kill you … the Behemoth and Raziin?' asked Ellen.

'Yes. Can you imagine the Spear of Carris – that sort of power – in the hands of a madman like Raziin?'

Ellen rolled out of bed, covering herself with a simple robe of white silk. She poured some cold water into a bowl and splashed it on her face. Her body was still alive with desire, but it seemed she would have to wait.

'Raziin is heading north to Ranmyden. I heard him say it,' she said. The Ranmyden range was a remote, towering series of mountains in the far north of Kelas. Known to be impassable, they were believed by many to be at the edge of the world. Ellen knew they were merely the beginning of another realm – the Domains of the Verial.

'Why Ranmyden?' he asked.

'Because that is the northern Face of the Iris. That is where the Ward has chosen to bide its time with the Spear of Carris. Deep within a cavern, in a ruined city of the ancient Eathal. Belin is there – possessed by the Ward. So is my old teacher Erioth.'

'Teacher?'

'A Sorcerer. He was sent by his people to take the Spear to safety, but was taken prisoner by the Ward.' She hesitated to say more, wary of betraying her father's confidence. Erioth was a Verial, a winged being considered mythical in Kelas – and that would take some explaining.

She could hear birdsong starting outside and felt a sort of desperation. Soon, the others would all be awake, and this precious time would be gone. The first day of the new Scion would dawn – and with it the madness that would surround him from now on.

'We have to stop him,' he said, sitting up straighter in the bed. His face was so full of determination. It was this strength of will that she found so irresistible in him. Before she knew it, she was back on the bed, sitting astride his lap, her robe falling open as she straddled him.

'We do need to stop him,' she said, laying a finger on his lips, her breathing coming faster. 'But not today.' She slipped the robe off her shoulders and bent down to kiss him. Her groin ached. She had only had one lover before, the Suulqua Palsus, and she had never wanted him like *this*. She widened her legs and let herself press down into his stomach. It gave her a teasing touch of arousal. *But not enough.* She slid backwards until she felt him beneath her, quickly hardening with his own desire. She did not need the Bridge to know where his thoughts were now. She moved her hips back and forward. Her arms trembled with the desire to slip him inside her, but she held off, watching him as he watched her. Suddenly self-conscious, she stopped, moving to roll onto her back, but he stopped her.

'Stay there,' he said. His eyes flicked between her breasts, her stomach, and her face. She laughed lightly and relaxed. She knew how much he wanted her, how much he desired her. She had known it from the beginning. She lifted herself up, then down onto him. She gave a low moan and closed her eyes, losing herself in the pleasure. She rode faster and faster, sucking in quick breaths as a white-hot tide swept through her. Before she knew it, she was screaming. The wave came again, then again. She bit her lip, sagging forward against him. He gripped her hips, taking hold of her and lifting her in time with his own movements as he thrust up into her. The tide rose, crested once more, then slipped away as he came inside her. She could feel the hot warmth of him and let out a long sigh before rolling off.

They lay for a long moment together. Slowly the sounds of the day began to intrude. Ellen heard servants moving, and chairs scraping against floors. There was no stopping it.

She rolled out of bed and pulled the bell-rope for her servants. 'Do you want to share a bath?'

'How can I say no to an invitation like that?' he said.

* * *

Refreshed and dressed, they ate an early breakfast then sat by the window sharing steaming cups of tea as the suns rose over Olcis. They talked of Athria, swapping stories of their lives. She was exhausted, but would not have traded a moment for a week of sleep. Ellen listened in fascination to stories of his life in the Brotherhood, her hand lightly resting on his. Not once had they talked of the future.

'So how did Skye get that narsiit?' asked Ellen.

'Brought it from a Hendian Suul in Raynor ... or so he says,' said Cedrin.

'He's a strange one. What is his history?' asked Ellen.

Cedrin's face hardened. She instantly regretted the question. 'I'm sorry. I'm not asking you to break a confidence.'

'No. It's all right. Skye's father Astor was once weaponmaster to Myan. He was executed for killing a young

Suul lord in a duel.'

There was a moment of awkward silence between them. Ellen tried to think of some way to recapture the light-hearted mood.

There was a rapid knock at the door.

'Cedrin!' It was Marken. Cedrin snatched back his hand.

'What is it?' said Cedrin, automatically checking for the calv in his harness as he strode to the door. He opened it to admit his friend.

Ellen looked out across Olcis, her eyes aching with a sudden weight of tears. This was it.

'I think you both better come downstairs,' said Marken.

'Is it trouble?' asked Cedrin.

Marken laughed and raised his hands. 'No, nothing like that, but I ... I think you better come down.'

'Ellen?' asked Cedrin.

A single tear escaped. Ellen dabbed it away quickly before it smeared her makeup. She took a steadying breath and let the court mask slip down across her face. She could hear her old tutor. *The smile should give good grace, and yet not be too ingratiating. The rest of the countenance should form an alert and pleasant frame.* She had found the Scion, completed her quest. Wasn't this what she wanted?

'Yes?' she said. Her legs felt weak as she stood.

'We better go see what all the fuss is about,' he said.

'The sooner the better,' she said.

* * *

Cedrin and Marken descended the stairs to the common room, Ellen following behind at a measured pace. It seemed in one instant she had transformed herself into a Suul again. It unnerved him, though he tried not to show it. There was a tremendous din of voices. As they made their way down into the room they could see it was brimming with warriors, many of whom Cedrin knew. The phoenix standard stood out proudly above the crowd, woven in bright colours. It was the original from the throne room in Raynor, and standing before it was

Kranor himself, his stately wife Salis Cintor at his side. Cedrin could see Kalyth amidst the crowd, his armour at last removed to reveal a continuous web of tattoos across his chest, arms and back. They were all badges of distinction, given for skill and bravery, and amidst them was the phoenix, ripping a drakon asunder in its claws.

'By the Sisters ...,' said Cedrin, his face slack with astonishment at the gathering.

'Kalyth has told me the Truth,' said Kranor, striding forward. He looked across to Salis, who nodded slightly, as if in confirmation.

Kranor paused before Cedrin, his face stern and expressionless. Then he knelt. 'May I be the first to swear to the Scion of the Cinanac?'

Cedrin could only nod dumbly. Ever since he discovered his heritage, he knew this was inevitable. Still he was unprepared for it.

Cedrin looked across at Ellen. She watched him with a slight smile, her expression fixed and unreadable. Her hands were clasped together tightly in front of her. Marken had stepped back to give him room. Cedrin had a sudden sense of events tumbling out of his control. All he had ever wanted was to be master of his own destiny. Was that even possible now? The promise of power was dizzying. Because of one accident of birth, his own path was inextricably linked to the whole of Kelas.

'As I swore to Riin, so I swear to you,' said Kranor in a loud, ringing voice. Kranor drew an ornate ring from his pouch and presented it to Cedrin. 'Here is the ring of your father. Yours by right!'

Cedrin took the ring and stared at the finely cut ruby with awe, studying the delicately wrought phoenix crest. The ring of Emperor Riin Cinanac. His father's ring.

Kalyth pushed through the crowd to stand beside him. 'Put it on, fool,' said the old warrior. 'Index finger on the right hand. You'll have to move Belin's ring.'

Cedrin looked up. The room was deathly silent, the stunned bystanders as caught up in the excitement as the warriors. The crowd waited for him. He took the Kaidell ring off and slipped it onto the index finger of his left hand. As he put on the Cinanac ring, the crowd uttered a collective sigh. He held his hand out before him. The ring seemed heavy, and the red gemstone glittered with deep, unknowable highlights.

Kranor turned to face the crowd, raising his voice in a parade ground bellow.

'Behold! Cedrin Cinanac! Heir to the throne of Bulvuran!'

The men cheered again and again, and Cedrin was surprised to see Kanis in the crowd, joining in with fanatic fervour. Despite himself, Cedrin was caught up in the incredible enthusiasm of the crowd. Only one man did not cheer, secreting himself at the rear of the room, but Cedrin did not recognise him with his growth of short hair and the finely-crafted phoenix crest across his chest.

He felt a hand on his right shoulder and saw Skye standing there. 'There is no way you are keeping this quiet now.'

'No,' Cedrin shouted over the din.

'Typical, Skye. Always stating the obvious,' said Marken, with a grin.

'Him!' said Ellen. Cedrin could hardly hear her in the excited din. 'By the Sisters! That explains why he always stayed away from me and Raphal on the journey to Searn.' Her face was pale, and she was looking across the room at the tall warrior with the short hair, who was smiling and talking to those near him. Ellen pointed at him. 'He ... Sindar ... is Osterac the Pretender.'

'The false-Scion?' said Cedrin, hardly believing what he had just heard.

'Yes. The man who tore Raynor apart with his gambit for the throne of Bulvuran.'

'It was he who alerted Xyanthius to your identity,' said Kranor. 'The Warlord allowed him to escape Raynor in return for denouncing the Olcis Druids. The Warlord's agents came to me asking that he join Xyanthius' company. We were paid well – and our caravan was assured quick passage through the Warlord's domain with no questions asked.'

Ellen burst out laughing.

'What is it?' asked Cedrin.

'The whole trip north I was expecting the agents of the Warlord to find me, but I was travelling in the one caravan they had been ordered to ignore – by the Warlord himself.'

* * *

Cedrin slowed his amelak and turned it back towards Olcis. Ellen and his friends followed suit, their mounts kicking up a cloud of dust from the dry track. Skye's narsiit snorted in impatience and he patted its long neck, making soft, soothing noises. Both Skye and Marken had insisted on coming north, as had Raphal. Fleeing the Hesguit's displeasure in favour of witnessing the Spear's fate had been no contest for the old scholar, who had been in favour of travelling to Ranmyden from the start.

'Halt!' called Kalyth, stopping Cedrin's honour guard, who had been following close behind them. The guard consisted of thirty of Kranor's best warriors and Bovosan. The full complement of the One Hundred had yet to be assembled, as Kranor's warriors travelled to Olcis by fast mount from Raynor, Searn and many other garrisons. As a reward for identifying the Scion, Kranor had given Osterac the honour of a place in Cedrin's personal guard. Remembering the fearsome warrior Sindar who had travelled north with Kranor's company, it was hard to recognise him as the handsome, charming, young Suul noble who swapped jokes with the warriors, his short black hair glistening in the sun.

Kalyth urged his amelak up the road towards them. The old warrior rode bare-chested now, the stretched yet finely toned muscles on his lean frame hardly visible beneath the mass of inked honour marks. There was a zeal in Kalyth now – and a deference and distance towards him. Even so, as Cedrin's teacher in the art of the greatscythe, he was as uncompromising as ever.

'What is it, my Lord?' asked Kalyth. The honorific still made Cedrin wince, but he tried not to show it. In the frenzy of the ceremony yesterday, Kranor had even tried to get him to accept a Suul mark. *That* was too much. He was lord of nothing yet.

'I want one last look at Olcis,' said Cedrin. They had paused on one of the last hills within sight of the city. From here he could see a long dark line of men marching along the Olcis road into Tupur – the Hesguit's Legion, under the command of Lempar.

'Impressive,' said Cedrin.

'Yet not nearly enough,' said Kalyth. 'The Hesguit is a fool to send them into the field.'

Cedrin could see command officers moving ceaselessly along the lines on narsiit. One man moved with an entourage around him. *That must be Lempar himself.*

'Lempar has met the Eathal in the field before. At least he will know how to fight them,' said Ellen.

'Without Sorcerers to match the Eathal Sorcerer-Lords?' said Kalyth.

'The Hesguit would not send them against the Eathal without magical strength. They will have Templemen with them,' said Raphal.

'And what use will Uros Druids be when the Eathal attack at night?' said Kalyth.

'There will be others,' said Raphal, but his voice was sombre.

'And perhaps powerful glowmetals as well,' said Marken.

Raphal ran a hand across his bald dome and frowned. 'No. The Hesguit would not risk his prize glowmetals in the field.'

The column of marching soldiers seemed to go forever. Ten thousand men, and yet the Eathal had ten times this number. It was hard to conceive. Cedrin watched in grim silence. Where before he could consider the fate of Olcis as an abstract thing, he now felt a crushing weight of responsibility. The Cinanac had been the defenders of Kelas, and Olcis had been one of their cities. He had not been saved from death as a babe so he could sit by and watch the Eathal triumph.

'Well, I for one am glad we are leaving this war behind,' said Skye.

'I'd have to agree with that,' said Marken.

For now there was nothing Cedrin could do to aid the Warlord or the Hesguit in their struggle. Kranor had argued strongly that he should go to Raynor to meet with the Warlord, but Cedrin and Ellen had been adamant: they had to follow Raziin north to Ranmyden, if not to somehow defeat the Behemoth, then at least to prevent Raziin from taking the Spear of Carris for his own. If Raziin was not stopped, then the Eathal war, the restoration of the Cinanac – all would mean nothing. The megalomaniac would forge his own empire in innocent blood, and a dark age would dawn for not only Kelas, but the whole of Yos. Reluctantly, Kranor had agreed. The Suul and mercenary leader would soon return to Raynor, where he would present Cedrin's case to the court of the Warlord. Kranor's wife Salis Cintor remained with them.

News of the Scion had spread rapidly, causing a sudden hysteria as the still drunken crowds awakened to the news. An hour before they left the city, Kranor took the big phoenix banner and led a mounted procession of more than a hundred warriors in the direction of the Citadel, drawing the crowd behind him while one of his men played the part of the Scion. Shielded by the deception, Cedrin and his companions fled the city with the honour guard.

Kelas was soon to be at war, but their road lay north: through the wild foothills of the Mulisar range, the dark forests of Thilil and on to the haunted caverns of Ranmyden and the Temple of the Iris; where the Spear of Carris lay waiting for either the phoenix or the drakon to claim it.

Cedrin and Ellen exchanged a quick, private smile, then urged their amelak down the hill.

The long road lay ahead.

About the Author

Being able to escape into the realm of the imagination was handy growing up as the youngest in a family of eleven. Chris continues his fantasy and SF writing habit from his home town of Brisbane, where he lives with his lovely wife Sandra and three children, Aedan, Declan and Brigit. He has a third-dan black belt in Moon Lee Tae Kwon Do and also enjoys movies and exploring narrow alleyways. Chris is very passionate about music, if a little inconsistent, and loves singing and playing classical guitar.

Website: www.chrismcmahon.net.

Preview of Book Three – Sorcerer

Three days after Asic's Blessing and Cedrin Cinanac recognised as Scion by Kranor at Olcis

Faivel drew gently on the reins. He halted his jakkund on a low hill overlooking the Asgod River. The mount gave a low trumpet, dancing on its long, sleek legs. Its big ears swivelled as it scanned the ground ahead, alert for danger. Faivel squinted against the painful glare of Larus, adjusting the fall of the hooded scarf that blocked most of the yellow sun's savage light.

His detachment of fifty jakkund-mounted Eathal lancers formed a neat line behind him. His scouts were out of sight, ranging out almost a league.

'Warriors approach, my Lord,' said Huntmaster Arud.

'Ah, yes. I see them.' Faivel had yet to get the knack of coping with the light of the suns. Arud had more experience of the upper world than he did. As Hukum's second son, Faivel had escaped military duty – at least until his ferocious older brother had been slain by the human mercenary Raziin. The supreme leader of the Eathal had demanded justice for the death of his favourite. Faivel's comfortable life of scholarship had ended overnight. Whether he had desired it or not, he was now the Sundar's heir.

A line of dark-clad figures marched down by the river. Faivel channelled the Fire into the Lens Matrix. The view leapt into sharp relief. The marching lines resolved into ranks of Eathal clad in leather armour, with heavy hammers and shields slung across their backs. Like Faivel and his warriors, they were heavy-set and hairless, with heavy brows and thick, inflexible hips.

'Legion foot soldiers. Moving fast,' muttered Faivel. Arud remained silent, well used to his master's Sorcerous tricks. He scanned the lines, searching out the standard. A lean yellow teremb – the solitary hunter of the caverns – running on a dark background. 'Teremb legion. Lord Tynan. Why would Yeffrij order him north?'

'Shall we tell Sorcerer-Lord Tynan that Olcis is in the other direction?' asked Arud. Faivel smiled at his aide's wry humour, but rapidly sobered. He released his grip on the Fire.

They had pushed the swift jakkund mounts to their limits on their run south. Faivel's eyes flicked to the spare mount where the body of Raziin's warrior was ripening in the rising heat. The human's black leather armour was stained with old blood. Faivel wished he could have cut the foul thing free long ago, but he knew Yeffrij would need some tangible proof if he was to grant him the trackers and efreet messenger bats he needed to follow the renegade Raziin through the dense Thilil forest. He might be the Sundar's heir, but in the field Faivel ranked as Talonmaster, four levels of command below General Yeffrij. Hukum was determined that he would earn his place.

What he had learned from the dead warrior could change everything. He would need Yeffrij, his father's former apprentice, to reach Hukum across the Bridge of Minds and communicate the development directly to him.

'Let's find out what has drawn Lord Tynan so far north,' said Faivel.

The long-limbed jakkund flowed into eager motion, despite the sweat that lathered their dark fur. He felt the muscles in his mount's shoulders ripple beneath the saddle as he steered it down the hill to the river. The mouths of the jakkund worked like a bat's, uttering sounds pitched too high even for Eathal to hear. Their ears twitched as they sensed their path.

Faivel's men had picked up Raziin's trail outside Olcis and pursued him north into Tupur. They had clashed twice, but both times Raziin and his men had slipped his net. Their last battle had been on the edge of the Thilil forest. Four of Raziin's men had sacrificed themselves in a rearguard action, blocking a narrow defile against their pursuit. The last had survived — at least until Faivel's men had put him to the question.

The distance closed rapidly. Soon the outward elements of the Teremb legion met them, elite forward units equipped with stabbing spears and heavy shields.

They bowed to the Sundar's son as he passed, then continued north. Soon Faivel and his men had passed through the front lines of the advancing legion.

'There,' said Arud. The Huntmaster indicated with an outstretched arm.

Faivel pulled the light scarf from his face. He could see a small group of jakkund cavalry surrounding the Teremb standard. In a force comprised almost exclusively of footsoldiers, only a Sorcerer-Lord of the Eathal warranted the protection of the elite jakkund lancers.

Faivel held up his hand to halt his warriors and advanced on his own.

The Eathal warriors of Tynan's entourage eyed him without expression as their Lord turned to the newcomer. The Sorcerer-Lord wore the finest jakka-hide armour, inlaid with gems. His bald dome gleamed with fine oil.

'Lord Tynan,' said Faivel.

'Faivel,' said Tynan. As son of the Sundar, Faivel was entitled to being addressed as Lord. Tynan was taking the opportunity to enforce his senior rank as Sorcerer-Lord and General of the Teremb. The thal was a devoted follower of Hukum. Even so, it was no secret Faivel and his penchant for scholarship had always put him at odds with his father. He let the slight pass him by.

'Your forces are further north than I anticipated,' said Faivel.

Tynan's heavy brows creased in irritation.

'Since when does the strategy of Yeffrij's inner circle concern you?' snapped Tynan.

Faivel clenched his jaw in irritation. Tynan had always been an officious fool, but his connections were good. The command was a reward for his support of Hukum's faction in the Junta. Even so, his father had not included his legion in his crucial strike west to the human capital Raynor, sending him north with Yeffrij instead.

Faivel changed tack. 'My apologies, Lord. We have travelled from the north and scouted much of the way along the Asgod. Perhaps if I knew your purpose, I could given you information of value?' he said in a more conciliatory tone. He was used to appeasing witless fools.

Tynan glared at him for a moment more, then his pique was replaced by a smug excitement. 'We are in pursuit of the Olcis legion. The fools attacked our emplacement last night. We routed them easily and they fled north. No doubt in fear of our superior numbers.'

'They felt the wrath of Breathstealer,' said Tynan's aide with patriotic fervour. The Sorcerer-Lord's inner circle laughed in grim amusement.

Faivel's eyes flicked to the bulky shape of Breathstealer in the centre of the lines. The glowmetal was being drawn by jakka-drawn carriage. Each of the Eathal legions was proud of their offensive glowmetals. No two were alike, and they varied in power. Faivel had studied them all. In truth, Breathstealer was the merest of them, and the only glowmetal that Teremb boasted. The Sundar's Black Drakon legion carried nine glowmetals west to Raynor, including the Wallbreakers. All were formidable.

'Congratulations on the victory,' said Faivel smoothly. Their spies had reported that Lempar commanded the human legion of Olcis. He was an experienced general and would know better than to attack an Eathal legion at night.

'My Lord. I must report we have not seen any signs of a large group of human warriors,' said Faivel.

Tynan's face twisted in contempt. 'No? Why does that not surprise me?'

Faivel was speechless. His men were elite warriors. His scouts second to none. Before he could muster a response, Tynan had dismissed him and turned his entourage north to follow the main body of his troops.

Faivel sat motionless on his jakkund as the warriors of Teremb legion flowed around him. His anger quickly abated, replaced by uneasiness.

'My Lord?' Arud was at his side.

'South. Quickly.'

They moved out of the lines of the Teremb and raced south in its trampled wake. As the suns rose to the zenith, the heat became oppressive. The stench of the rotting corpse was a constant reminder of its presence. Faivel remained silent, alert for what lay ahead. Their scouts returned, and he sent them out again, more cautious than ever.

They turned west. When they reached the outskirts of Yeffrij's main camp, they came across the heaped bodies of human dead. Some one hundred warriors, their faces bluish-grey, eyes bloodshot and unseeing. The work of Breathstealer. Tynan's men were not simply boasting. Yet there were so few enemy dead. This hardly constituted a major attack.

They were challenged by a small squad of Eathal infantry. The Talonmaster bowed when Faivel identified himself.

'Where is General Yeffrij?' asked Faivel.

'The general is advancing to Rybol with the Red and Grey, my Lord. Hunter and Teremb defend the flanks.'

Faivel and Arud swapped a quick glance. The Teremb legion was far north of the flank. The idiot Tynan had broken formation in his eagerness to close with the humans.

'To the river,' Faivel ordered.

They passed through the deserted camp. Thousands of hide tents were set in neat rows. There was no faulting Yeffrij when it came to organisation.

They followed the main road towards the bridge of Rybol – a major artery connecting the province of Tupur to the vast human city of Olcis. As they neared the last rise, they saw a tall plume of smoke rising into the still air. He could hear the roars of Eathal in combat, mixed with human voices and the muted clash of arms.

Faivel crested the rise and drew up short.

The Red and Grey Drakon legions filled the plain to the river. The bridge at Rybol was in flames. As he watched, the main span collapsed, taking an advance detachment of Eathal with it. He winced. Eathal did not swim.

He saw shapes in the water and quickly enhanced his sight. Through the Lens, he saw they were rafts - running swiftly downstream. The saboteurs shot south, guiding the rafts with long poles. In a flash, he realised how the 'Olcis legion' that Tynan was chasing had escaped him.

It took him a moment to realise the sound of combat was coming not from the plain in front of him, but to the south. He turned his mount and raced along the ridge with his men.

It was to the south that the real attack was occurring.

Like the Teremb, the Hunter legion had been drawn away from the main force. Yet where Tynan was chasing ghosts, the Hunter legion had been drawn into an ambush among the maze of hills beside the river.

A full human legion — ten thousand men — engaged the Hunter legion. The Eathal force had been cut into three. The human phalanxes plunged deep into the disorganised Eathal ranks, while human javelin throwers, archers and slingers assaulted them from carefully concealed positions on the high ground. Faivel knew Kyan, the Hunter General, as a level-headed thinker. He could see the Eathal troops trying to draw back and re-form, but human cavalry thrust through the formations before they could coalesce. The Eathal, accustomed to fighting in darkness, had no missile weapons to speak of. What dart-throwers they did have were south with Hukum.

Even as his heart sank at Kyan's predicament, Faivel had to admire Lempar's masterful strategy. Without a doubt, the human general was the man behind this. He sought him out on the field, using the Lens, but all was confusion. He did find Kyan, standing with his banner-holders next to the Hunter legion glowmetal, Stomach Churner. Bolts of Force shot from the Eathal Sorcerer's hands, hammering into the human ranks, but the terrain gave him little scope. The whole combat had splintered into smaller engagements in the small valleys and defiles. The humans were fighting at the time of their strength - when the suns were at their brightest — while the Eathal were almost blinded.

Faivel felt a strange pressure sweep across him.

On the field, one of the detachments of human cavalry fell in confusion, men clasping their heads and stomachs. *Stomach Churner*. It was not enough though. The Hunter legion was taking heavy damage.

'Should we join them, my Lord?' asked Arud.

Faivel could hear the strain in his aide's voice. The warrior longed to join the combat, to take the fight to the humans. He himself could do much damage in the human ranks with his Sorcerous powers, but what he had learned from the dying human warrior stopped him. He would need Arud, and all his warriors, if he was to stop Raziin from reaching Ranmyden — and the prize he sought. 'We must hold here, Arud. Yeffrij will not desert them.'

'Yes, Lord,' answered his aide in a harsh whisper.

Time and again Kyan sought to reform, to manoeuvre, but Lempar always anticipated him. The human cavalry was unstoppable, sweeping through the valleys and down onto the Eathal. Like Teremb, the Hunter was one of the newly-formed legions. The elite Eathal legions were the Drakons, named for the fearsome hunters of the caverns. The inexperience of the Hunter warriors was showing.

After an agonising wait, Yeffrij's Red Drakon appeared on the horizon. With methodical slowness, the disciplined forward units swept south in a solid front of heavy shields, short spears stabbing forward with deadly precision. Yeffrij gave the human legions no room to manoeuvre. They overtook the beleaguered Hunter legion units, relieving them, and continued on, forcing Lempar's Olcis Legion into retreat. A dome of darkness formed across the front lines. Faivel smiled grimly as he imagined the panic in the human lines as they found themselves fighting blind. The Darkness was a potent glowmetal, and Yeffrij was using it with precision. Eathal could see heat. The shape of things was revealed to them, even where the light of the upper world never penetrated.

Faivel relaxed his grip on the reins of his jakkund, realising only now what sitting out of the fight had cost him.

A wedge of purple light rippled over a hill of human archers as the Door of Kallor was unleashed. A moment later half were down, others standing disoriented as the Red Drakon swept them to oblivion. The tide had turned on the humans.

A horn sounded across the battlefield. A human signal. Lempar's legion fled to the river.

'He is trapped,' said Arud.

'It cannot be that easy,' muttered Faivel under his breath. Lempar was too wiley to leave himself without a line of retreat.

Faivel channelled Fire into the Lens. *There.* The river bank was lined with rafts. Hundreds of them. The human cavalry reached the river first and crowded onto rafts. Even in retreat, Lempar was thinking clearly, preserving his most useful units. They pushed out into the Asgod and were quickly swept from sight. The rearward elements of human legion turned to form a shield-wall bristling with the long spears, giving the others room to organise their retreat. Behind them, warriors crowded onto the next wave of rafts. The crowd along the river bank thinned, but not before the Red Drakon reached the human rearguard. The fighting was fierce. Once more The Darkness was unleashed. Small whirlwinds buffeted those on the edge of the dome. *Secondary effects.*

When the dome of darkness faded, the human line was still standing. Behind them, the last of Lempar's fleeing legion escaped. Then the Door of Kallor was unleashed again. Its purple light swept across the human defenders. Faivel could hear men scream. Others dropped their weapons, staggering forward onto the spear-points of the Red Drakon, their eyes fixed on private visions of bliss or horror.

As the suns dropped in the west, the last defenders fell. Lempar's gambit was at an end. Perhaps half the Hunter legion had fallen – five thousand Eathal warriors against little more than six hundred of Lempar's men. Yet they had set back Yeffrij little more than a few days. His engineers would rebuild the Rybol bridge and the Eathal legions would roll inexorably towards Olcis. Lempar's single legion could do little but sting their flanks.

Without a word, Faivel led his mounted warriors down to the river. He steered his jakkund to the Red Drakon standard, knowing Yeffrij would be there. Now he had to convince Yeffrij to give him what he needed, persuade the Eathal General to contact Hukum and tell him the unthinkable. He swallowed, anticipating his father's reaction. Hukum was obsessed with the Destruction – the ancient cataclysm that destroyed the once widespread Eathal culture and drove the survivors into refuges like Maht. A destruction made possible by the Spear of Carris, a Sorcerous artefact of unparalleled power believed to have been lost long ago.

He looked back at Raziin's dead warrior. The man had endured much pain before he broke. He told them of Raziin's quest north, seeking to seize the Spear of Carris before the Cinanac heir, Cedrin, could claim it. If it was true – should either human take up the Spear — the Eathal would suffer a stunning defeat. Hukum's legions had left the refuge of Maht and its defensive glowmetals far behind them. They were stretched over hundreds of leagues now, vulnerable as never before in two thousand years.

Faivel shivered. He still could not believe it. Yet his men were experienced torturers and even to him the words of the human had the ring of truth. *Gentle Lidu, give me strength.* This was no longer about appeasing his father or vengeance for his brother Staraz. He had to destroy Raziin and this Cinanac heir, then seize the Spear for the Eathal. Anything less would spell disaster for all of them.